About th

Sophie Pembroke has been dreaming, reading and writing romance ever since she read her first Mills & Boon novel as a teen, so getting to write romance fiction for a living is a dream come true! Born in Abu Dhabi, Sophie grew up in Wales and now lives in Hertfordshire with her scientist husband, her incredibly imaginative daughter and her adventurous, adorable little boy. In Sophie's world, happy is for ever after, everything stops for tea and there's always time for one more page.

USA Today bestselling author, **Candace Shaw** writes romance novels because she believes that happily-ever-after isn't only found in fairy tales. When she's not writing or researching information for a book, you can find Candace in her gardens, shopping, reading or learning how to cook a new dish. She lives in Atlanta, Georgia with her loving husband and is currently working on her next fun, flirty and sexy romance. You can contact Candace on her website at CandaceShaw.net

Andrea Laurence is an award-winning contemporary author who has been a lover of books and writing stories since she learned to read. A dedicated West Coast girl transplanted into the Deep South, she's constantly trying to develop a taste for sweet tea and grits while caring for her husband and two spoiled golden retrievers. You can contact Andrea at her website: andrealaurence.com

Fake Dating

July 2023
A Business Deal

February 2024
Doctor's Orders

August 2023
Undercover

March 2024
Scandal in the Spotlight

September 2023
Family Feud

April 2024
Deceiving the Ex

January 2024
A Convenient Deal

May 2024
I Dare You

Fake Dating:

Deceiving the Ex

SOPHIE PEMBROKE

CANDACE SHAW

ANDREA LAURENCE

MILLS & BOON

First Published in Great Britain 2024
by Mills & Boon, an imprint of HarperCollins*Publishers* Ltd,
1 London Bridge Street, London, SE1 9GF

www.harpercollins.co.uk

HarperCollins*Publishers*
Macken House, 39/40 Mayor Street Upper,
Dublin 1, D01 C9W8, Ireland

ISBN: 978-0-263-32315-3

MIX
Paper | Supporting
responsible forestry
FSC™ C007454

This book contains FSC™ certified paper and other controlled sources to ensure responsible forest management.

For more information visit: www.harpercollins.co.uk/green

Printed and Bound in the UK using 100% Renewable Electricity
at CPI Group (UK) Ltd, Croydon, CR0 4YY

PROPOSAL FOR THE WEDDING PLANNER

SOPHIE PEMBROKE

For Ali, Ally and Ann Marie

CHAPTER ONE

LAUREL SOMMERS STEPPED back from the road as a London taxi sped past through the puddle at the edge of the kerb, splashing icy water over her feet, and decided this was all her father's fault, really.

Well, the fact that she was stuck in London, waiting in the freezing cold for a car to take her back to where she *should* be—Morwen Hall, the gothic stately home turned five-star hotel in the countryside an hour and a half's drive out of the city—was clearly Melissa's fault. But if their father hadn't wanted to have his cake and eat it for their entire childhoods then her half-sister probably wouldn't hate her enough to make her life this miserable.

Sighing, Laurel clasped the bag holding the last-minute replacement wedding favours that Melissa had insisted she collect that afternoon closer to her body as a stream of cars continued to rush past. It was three days after Christmas and the sales were in full swing. London was caught in that strange sense of anticipation that filled the space between December the twenty-fifth and New Year's Eve—full of possibilities for the year ahead and the lives that might be lived in it.

Any other year Laurel would be as caught up in that

sense of opportunity as anyone. She usually used these last few days of the year to reflect on the year just gone and plan her year ahead. Plan how to be better, to achieve more, how to succeed at last. To be *enough*.

Just last year she'd plotted out her schedule for starting her own business organising weddings. She'd been a wedding planner at a popular company for five years, and had felt with quiet optimism that it was time to go it alone—especially since she'd been expecting to be organising her *own* wedding, and Benjamin had always said he liked a woman with ambition.

So she'd planned, she'd organised, and she'd done it—she had the business cards to prove it. Laurel's Weddings was up and running. And, even if she wasn't planning her own wedding, she *did* have her first celebrity client on the books...which was why this year that optimism would have to wait until January the first.

All she had to do was make it through her half-sister's New Year's Eve wedding without anything going terribly wrong and she would be golden. Melissa was big news in Hollywood right now—presumably because she was a lot nicer to directors than she was to wedding planners—and her wedding was being covered in one of those glossy magazines Laurel only ever had time to read at the hairdresser's. If this went well her business would boom and she could stop worrying about exactly *how* she was going to earn enough to pay back the small business loan she'd only just qualified for.

She might not have the husband she'd planned on, and she might not be a Hollywood star like Melissa, but once her business went global no one would be able to say she wasn't good enough.

But of course that meant rushing around, catering

to Melissa's every whim—even when that whim meant a last-minute trip back to the capital to replace the favours they'd spent two weeks deciding on because they were 'an embarrassment' all of a sudden.

And, as much as she'd been avoiding thinking about it, a peaceful wedding also meant dealing with seeing Benjamin again. Which was just the cherry on top of the icing on top of the wedding cake—wasn't it?

Another car—big and black and shiny—slowed as it reached the kerb beside her. Lauren felt hope rising. She'd asked the last of the cars ferrying wedding guests from Heathrow to swing into the city and pick her up on its way to Morwen Hall, rather than going around the M25. It would mean the passenger inside would have a rather longer journey, but she was sort of hoping he wouldn't notice. Or mind having company for it.

Since the last guest was the groom Riley's brother—Dan Black, her soon to be half-brother-in-law, or something—she really hoped he didn't object. It would be nice at least to start out on good terms with her new family—especially since her existing family was generally on anything but. Her mother still hadn't forgiven her for agreeing to organise Melissa's wedding. Or, as she called her, 'That illegitimate trollop daughter of your father's mistress.'

Unsurprisingly, her mother wasn't on the guest list.

Dan Black wasn't a high-maintenance Hollywood star, at least—as far as Laurel could tell. In fact Melissa hadn't told her anything about him at all. Probably because if he couldn't further her career then Melissa wasn't interested. All Laurel had to go on was the brief couple of lines Melissa and Riley had scribbled next to every name on the guest list, so Laurel would understand why they were important and why they'd been invited, and the address she had sent the invitation to.

Black Ops Stunts. Even the follow-up emails she'd sent to Dan when arranging the journey and his accommodation had been answered by the minimum possible number of words and no extraneous detail.

The man was a mystery. But one Laurel really didn't have time to solve this week.

The car came to a smooth stop, and the driver hopped out before Laurel could even reach for the door handle.

'Miss,' he said with a brief nod, and opened the door to the back seat for her. She slid gratefully into her seat, smiling at the other occupant of the car as she did so.

'I *do* hope you don't mind sharing your car with me, Mr Black,' she said, trying to sound professional and grateful and like family all at the same time. She was pretty sure the combination didn't work, but until she had any better ideas she was sticking with it.

'Dan,' he said, holding out a hand.

Laurel reached out to take it, and as she looked up into his eyes the words she'd been about to speak caught in her throat.

She'd seen this man's brother Riley a hundred times—on the screen at the cinema, on movie posters, on her telly, in magazines, on the internet, and even over Skype when they'd been planning the wedding. Melissa hadn't *actually* brought him home to meet the family yet, but Laurel couldn't honestly blame her for that. Still, she knew his face, and his ridiculously handsome, all-American good looks.

Why hadn't it occurred to her that his older brother might be just as gorgeous?

Dan didn't have the same clean, wholesome appeal

that Riley did, Laurel would admit. But what he *did* have was a whole lot hotter.

His hair was closer cropped, with a touch of grey at the temples, and his jaw was covered in dark stubble, but his bright blue eyes were just like his brother's. No, she decided, looking more closely, they weren't. Riley's were kind and warm and affable. Dan's were sharp and piercing, and currently looking a bit amused...

Probably because she still hadn't said anything.

'I'm Laurel,' she said quickly as the driver started the engine again and pulled out. 'Your half-sister-in-law-to-be.'

'My...*what*, now?' His voice was deeper too, his words slower, more drawling.

'I'm Melissa's half-sister.'

'Ah,' Dan said, and from that one syllable Laurel was sure he already knew her whole story. Or at least her part in *Melissa's* story.

Most people did, she'd found.

Either they'd watched one of Melissa's many tearful interviews on the subject of her hardships growing up without a father at home, or they'd read the story online on one of her many fan sites. Everybody knew how Melissa had been brought up almost entirely by her single mother until the age of sixteen, while her father had spent most of his time with his other family in the next town over, only visiting when he could get away from his wife and daughter.

People rarely asked any questions about that other family, though. Or what had happened to them when her father had decided he'd had enough and walked out at last, to start his 'real' life with Melissa and her mother.

Laurel figured that at least that meant no one cared

about her—least of all Melissa—so there were no photos of *her* on the internet, and no one could pick her out of a line-up. It was bad enough that her friends knew she was related to the beautiful, famous, talented Melissa Sommers. She didn't think she could bear strangers stopping her in the street to ask about her sister. Wondering why Laurel, with all the family advantages she'd had, couldn't be as beautiful, successful or brilliant as Melissa.

'So you're also the wedding planner, right?' Dan asked, and Laurel gave him a grateful smile for the easy out.

'That's right. In fact, that's why I'm up in town today. Melissa…uh…changed her mind about the wedding favours she wanted.' That sounded better than her real suspicions—that Melissa was just coming up with new ways to torment her—right?

It wasn't just the table favours, of course. When Melissa had first asked her to organise her wedding Laurel had felt pride swelling in her chest. She'd truly believed—for about five minutes—that her sister not only trusted in her talent, but also wanted to use her wedding to reach out an olive branch between the two of them at last.

Obviously that had been wishful thinking. Or possibly a delusion worthy of those of Melissa's fans who wrote to her asking for her hand in marriage, never knowing that she tore up the letters and laughed.

'She's not making it easy, huh?' Dan asked.

Laurel pasted on a smile. 'You know brides! I wouldn't have gone into this business if I didn't know how to handle them.'

'Right.'

He looked her over again and she wondered what he saw. A competent wedding planner, she hoped. She hadn't had as much contact with Dan over the last few months as she had with the best man or the bridesmaids. But still, there'd been the invitation and the hotel bookings, and the flights and the car transfer—albeit she'd gatecrashed that. She'd been pleasant and efficient the whole way, even in the face of his one-word responses, and she really hoped he recognised that.

Because she knew what else he had to be thinking—what everyone thought when they looked at her through the lens of 'being Melissa Sommers's sister.' That Laurel had definitely got the short straw in the genetic lottery.

Melissa, as seen on billboards and movie screens across the world, was tall, willowy, blonde and beautiful. She'd even been called the twenty-first-century Grace Kelly.

Laurel, on the other hand—well, she wasn't.

Oh, she was cute enough, she knew—petite and curvy, with dark hair and dark eyes—but 'cute' wasn't beautiful. It wasn't striking. She had the kind of looks that just disappeared when she stood beside Melissa—not least because she was almost a whole head shorter.

No, Laurel had resigned herself to being the opposite of everything Melissa was. Which also made her a less awful person, she liked to hope.

Dan was still watching her in silence, and words bubbled up in her throat just to fill the empty air.

'But you know this isn't just *any* wedding. I mean, Melissa and Riley wanted a celebrity wedding extravaganza, so that's what I've tried to give them.'

'I see,' Dan replied, still watching.

Laurel babbled on. 'Obviously she wanted it at Morwen Hall—she has a strong connection to the place, you see. And Eloise—she's the manager there...well, the interim manager, I think... Anyway, you'll meet her soon... What was I saying?'

'I have no idea.'

'Sorry. I'm babbling.'

'That's okay.'

'Oh!' Laurel bounced in the car seat a little as she remembered where she'd been going with the conversation. 'Anyway. I was just about to say that there's lots planned for the next few days—with the welcome drinks tonight, the Frost Fair, and then the stag and hen dos tomorrow, local tours for the guests on Friday before the rehearsal dinner...'

'And the actual wedding at some point, I assume?' Dan added, eyebrows raised.

'Well, of course.' Laurel felt her skin flush hot for a moment. 'I was working chronologically. From my Action List.'

'I understand. Sounds like you have plenty to keep you busy this week.'

Laurel nodded, her head bobbing up and down at speed. 'Absolutely. But that's good! I mean, if this wedding goes well... It's the first one I've arranged since I started my own business, you see, so it's kind of a big deal. And it's not like I'm in the wedding party at all—'

Neither was he, she realised suddenly. Wasn't that a little odd? I mean, she knew why her sister wouldn't want *her* trailing down the aisle in front of her with a bouquet, but why didn't Riley want his brother standing up beside him for the ceremony?

Dan's face had darkened at her words, so she hurried

on, not really paying attention to what she was saying. 'Which is just as well, since there's so much to focus on! And besides, being behind the scenes means that it should be easier for me to avoid Benjamin—which is an advantage not to be overlooked.'

Oh. She hadn't meant to mention Benjamin.

Maybe he wouldn't notice.

'Benjamin?' Dan asked, and Laurel bit back a sigh.

Too much to hope for, clearly.

'My ex-fiancé,' she said succinctly, wondering if there was a way to tell this story that didn't make her sound like a miserable, weak, doormat of a person.

Probably not.

'He's attending the wedding?' Dan sounded surprised. She supposed that normal sisters wouldn't invite their sibling's ex-partner to their wedding. But the relationship between her and Melissa had never even pretended to be 'normal'.

'With his *new* fiancée,' she confirmed.

Because it wasn't humiliating enough *just* to have to face the man she'd thought was The One again, after he'd made it abundantly clear she wasn't his anything, in front of her family, celebrities and the world's media. She also had to do it with her replacement in attendance.

'His parents are old friends of my father's. We practically grew up together. Unlike me and my sister.' She was only making things worse. 'So, yeah, he'll be there—just to maximise the awkward. And I'm not exactly looking forward to it, I'll admit—especially since I haven't seen him since… Anyway, it'll all be fine, and I'll mostly be organising wedding things anyway, like I said, so…'

There had to be a way out of this conversation that

left her just a *little* dignity, surely? If she kept digging long enough maybe she'd find it—before her pride and self-confidence hitched a ride back to London in a passing cab.

'The Wedding March' rang out from the phone in her hand, and Laurel gave a silent prayer of thanks for the interruption—until she saw the name on the screen.

Melissa. Of course.

Sighing, she flashed a brief smile at Dan. 'If you'll excuse me?'

He leant back against the leather seats and nodded. 'Of course.'

Laurel pressed 'answer'. Time to see how her half-sister intended to make her day a little worse.

Considering that the hot little brunette who'd gate-crashed his ride to the hotel had done nothing but talk since they met, she was doing surprisingly little talking on her phone call.

'Yes, but—' Another sigh. 'Of course, Melissa. You're the bride, after all.'

Melissa. The blonde bombshell who'd exploded into his little brother's world a year ago and taken it over. Dan and Riley had never been exactly what he'd call close—the six-year age-gap meant that they'd done their growing up at different times, and their parents' blatant favouritism towards their younger son hadn't made bonding any easier.

But the distance between them didn't change the fact that Riley was his little brother and Dan loved him regardless. He'd loved him all through his Golden Boy childhood, through their parents cutting Dan off when he'd moved to LA and become a stuntman without their approval, and even through their outstanding hypocrisy when Riley had followed him nine years later.

Their parents were both world-renowned in their fields—cardiac surgery for their mother and orthopaedics for his father. That would have been enough to try and live up to under normal circumstances. But Dan had given up competing with anybody long before his younger brother had moved to Hollywood and become a star.

It wasn't as if he was doing so shabbily by anyone's terms—even his own. He owned his own business and his turnover doubled every year. He probably earned nearly as much as his hotshot brother, and even if the public would never know his name, the people who mattered in Hollywood did. He—or rather his company, Black Ops Stunts—was the first port of call for any major studio making an action movie these days. He'd made a success of the career his parents had been sure would kill him or ruin him.

Not that they cared all that much either way.

Dan shifted in his seat as he contemplated the week ahead of him. Five days in a luxury hotel—not so bad. Five days with the rich and obnoxious—less good. Five days dealing with his parents—nightmare.

When the invitation had first fallen onto his doormat he'd honestly considered skipping the whole thing. Formal events weren't really his style, and he spent enough time with Hollywood actors to know that some of them had surprisingly little respect for the people who saved them from risking their lives doing their own stunts. And from what he'd heard about Melissa Sommers she was definitely one of them.

In fact it was all the industry gossip about Melissa

that had persuaded him that he needed to be at Morwen Hall that week. Or rather the conflicting reports.

As far as Dan could tell every director and co-star who had ever worked with Melissa thought she was an angel. Anyone who ranked lower than a named credit in the titles, however, told a rather different story.

He sighed, running through his mind once more the series of off-the-record conversations he'd had recently. It wasn't an unfamiliar story—he'd met enough stars who played the part of benevolent, caring, charitable celebrity to the hilt when anyone who mattered was looking, then turned into a spoilt brat the moment the cameras switched off. He'd even been married to one of them. The only difference was that this time it was *Riley* marrying the witch—and he needed to be sure his baby brother knew exactly what he was getting in to.

Riley didn't *do* personas, Dan thought. In fact it was a mystery how he'd ever got into acting in the first place. It probably said something that he always got cast to play the nice guy, though. The 'aw, shucks, good old country boy' who found true love after ninety minutes, or the clean-cut superhero who could do no wrong.

That certainly fitted with the way their parents saw him, anyway.

But this week Dan was far more concerned with how *Melissa* saw him. Was it true love? Or was he her ticket to something bigger? Her career was doing well, as far as he could tell, but Riley was a step up. Stars had married for a lot less—and he didn't want to see his brother heartbroken and alone six months after he said, 'I do.'

'Melissa…'

Laurel sighed again, and Dan tuned back in to the phone conversation she was enduring. Seemed as if

Melissa didn't count her half-sister as someone who mattered. Hardly unexpected, given their history, he supposed. Everyone knew that story—inside and outside the industry.

He wondered why Melissa had hired her famously estranged half-sister to organise the celebrity wedding of the year. Was it an attempt at reconciliation? Or a way to make Laurel's life miserable? Judging by the phone call he was eavesdropping on, it definitely felt like the latter. Or maybe it was all about the way it would play in the media—that sounded like the Melissa he'd heard stories about from Jasmine, his best stunt woman, who'd doubled for Melissa once or twice.

This wedding would be his chance to find out for sure. Ideally *before* she and Riley walked down the aisle.

At least he had a plan. It was good to have something to focus on. Otherwise he might have found himself distracted—maybe even by the brunette on the phone...

'I'll be back at Morwen Hall in less than an hour,' Laurel said finally, after a long pause during which she'd nodded silently with her eyes closed, despite the fact her sister obviously couldn't see the gesture. 'We can talk about it some more then, if you like.'

She opened her mouth to speak again, then shut it, lowering the phone from her ear and flashing him a tight smile.

'She hung up,' she explained.

'Problems?' he asked, raising an eyebrow.

Laurel, he'd already learned, talked to fill the silence—something that seemed to be absent when she was speaking with her half-sister. If he let her ramble on maybe she'd be able to give him all the information about Melissa he needed to talk his brother out of this wedding. They could all be on their way home by dinner time, and he could get back to business as usual. Perfect.

'Oh, not really,' Laurel said lightly, waving a hand as if to brush away his concerns. 'Just the usual. Last-minute nerves about everything.'

Dan sat up a little straighter. 'About marrying Riley?'

'Goodness, no!'

Laurel's eyes widened to an unbelievable size—dark pools of chocolate-brown that a man could lose himself in, if he believed in that sort of thing.

'Sorry, that wasn't what I meant at all! I just meant… there are so many arrangements in place for this week and, even though I really *do* have them all in hand, Melissa just likes to…well, double check. And sometimes she has some new ideas that she'd like to fit in to the plans. Or changes she'd like to make.'

'Such as the wedding favours?' Dan said, nodding at the glossy bag by her feet.

'Exactly!' Laurel looked relieved at his understanding. 'I'm so sorry if I worried you. My mouth tends to run a little faster than my brain sometimes. And there's just so much to think about this week…'

'Like your ex-fiancé,' Dan guessed, leaning back against the seat as he studied her.

An informant who talked too much was exactly what he was looking for—even if he hadn't really thought about her as such until now. Fate had tossed him a bone on this one.

Laurel's face fell, her misery clear. Had the woman ever had a thought that wasn't instantly telegraphed through her expression? Not that he was complaining—anything that made reading women easier was a plus in his book. But after spending years learning to school his responses, to keep his expressions bland and boring, he found it interesting that Laurel gave so much away for free.

In Hollywood, he assumed people were acting all the time. In the case of people who had to deal with the over-expressive actors, directors and so on, they learned to lock down their response, to nod politely and move on without ever showing annoyance, disagreement or even disgust.

Laurel wasn't acting—he could tell. And she certainly wasn't locking anything down. Especially not her feelings about her ex-fiancé.

'Like Benjamin,' she agreed, wincing. 'Not that I'm planning on thinking about him much. Or that I've been pining away after him ever since...well, since everything happened.'

Yeah, that sounded like a lie. Maybe she hadn't been pining, but she'd certainly been thinking about him—that much was obvious.

'What *did* happen? If you don't mind me asking.'

Dan shifted in his seat to turn towards her. He was surprised to find himself honestly interested in the answer. Partly because he was sympathetic to her plight—it was never fun to run into an ex, which was one of the reasons he avoided celebrity parties these days unless he could be sure Cassie wouldn't be there—and partly because he couldn't understand why Melissa would invite her half-sister's ex-fiancé to her wedding. Old family friends or not, that was a level of harsh not usually seen in normal people.

Which only made him more concerned for Riley.

Laurel sighed, and there was a world of feeling in the sound as her shoulders slumped.

'Oh, the usual, I suppose. I thought everything was perfect. We were going to get married, live happily ever after—you know, get the fairytale ending and everything.' She looked up and met his gaze, as if checking that he did understand what a fairytale was.

'Oh, I understand,' he said, with feeling. Hadn't that been what he'd thought would be his by rights when he said 'I do' to Cassie? Look how wrong he'd been about that.

'But then it turned out that he wanted the fairytale with someone else instead.' She shrugged, her mouth twisting up into a half-smile. 'I guess sometimes these things just don't work out.'

'You seem surprisingly sanguine about it.'

'Well, it's been six months,' Laurel answered. 'Melissa says I should be well over it by now. I mean, *he* obviously is, right?'

Six months? Six months after Cassie had left him Dan had still been drinking his way through most of LA's less salubrious bars. He probably still would be if his business partner hadn't hauled him out and pointed out that revenge was sweeter than moping.

Making a huge financial and professional success of Black Ops Stunts wasn't just a personal win. It was revenge against the ex-wife who'd always said he'd never be worth anything.

'People get over things in their own way and their own time,' Dan said, trying to focus on the week in front of him, not the life he'd left behind.

'The hardest part was telling my family,' Laurel admitted, looking miserable all over again. 'I mean, getting engaged to Benjamin was the first thing I'd done right in my father's eyes since I was about fifteen. Even my step-mother was pleased. Benjamin was—*is*, I suppose—quite the catch in her book. Rich, well-known, charming...' She gave a self-deprecating smile. 'I suppose I should have known it was too good to be true.'

'So, what are you going to do now?' Dan asked.

Laurel took a deep breath and put on a brave smile that didn't convince him for a moment.

'I've sworn off men for the time being. I'm going to focus on my business and on myself for a while. And then, when I'm ready, maybe I'll consider dating again. But this time, I want to be a hundred per cent sure it's the real thing—the whole fairytale—before I let myself fall.'

Well, that was rather more information than he'd been looking for. Dan smiled back, awkwardly. 'Actually, I meant...how do you plan to get through spending a week in the same hotel as him?'

Laurel turned pale. 'Oh, I'm sorry. Of course you don't want to hear about that! Melissa always says I talk about myself *far* too much. Anyway... This week... Well, like I said, I've got a lot of work to do. I'm hoping that will keep me so busy I don't even have to think about him.'

If Melissa had her way Dan suspected Laurel would be plenty busy. And probably only talking about Melissa, too.

'What you really need is a new boyfriend to flaunt in his face,' he joked, and Laurel laughed.

'That would be good,' she agreed, grinning at him. 'But even if I hadn't sworn off men I've barely had time to sleep since I started organising this wedding, so I *definitely* haven't had time to date.'

That was a shame, Dan decided. Laurel, with her warm brown eyes and curvy figure, should definitely be dating. She shouldn't be locking herself away, even if it wasn't for ever. She should be out in the world, making it a brighter place. Less than an hour together and he already knew that Laurel was one of the good ones—and the complete opposite of everything he suspected about her half-sister. Laurel should be smiling up at a guy who treated her right for a change. A guy who wanted to spend the rest of his life making her smile that way. The prince she was waiting for.

Dan knew he was definitely *not* that guy. Treating women right wasn't the problem—he had utter respect for any woman who hadn't previously been married to him. But he didn't do 'for ever' any more. Not after Cassie.

Besides, he knew from experience that 'for ever' wasn't what women wanted from him, anyway. They wanted a stand-in—just like the directors did when they hired him or one of his people. Someone to come in, do good work, take the fall, and be ready to get out of the way when the real star of the show came along.

But maybe, he realised suddenly, that was exactly what Laurel needed this week.

A stand-in.

That, Dan knew, he could absolutely do. And it might just help him out in his mission to save his baby brother from a whole load of heartbreak, too, by getting him closer to the centre of the action.

'What if he just *thought* you had a boyfriend?' Dan asked, and Laurel's nose wrinkled in confusion.

'Like, lie to him?' She shook her head. 'I'm a terrible liar. He'd never believe me. Besides, if I had a boyfriend why wouldn't he be at the wedding?'

'He would be,' Dan said, and the confusion in Laurel's eyes grew.

He almost laughed—except that wouldn't get him any closer to what he wanted: a ringside seat to find out what the bride was *really* like.

'I don't understand,' Laurel said.

Dan smiled. Of course she didn't. That was one of the things he was growing to like about her, after their limited acquaintance—her lack of subterfuge.

'Me. Let me be your pretend boyfriend for the week.'

CHAPTER TWO

LAUREL BLINKED AT HIM. Then she blinked a few more times for good measure.

'Are you…?' *Pretend.* He'd said *pretend* boyfriend. 'Are you fake asking me out?'

Dan laughed. 'If you like.'

'Why?'

Because he felt sorry for her—that much was clear. How pathetic must she look to elicit the promise of a fake relationship? Really, there was pity dating and then there was *this.* How low had she sunk? Not this low, that was for sure.

'Because it feels wrong to let your ex wander around the wedding of the year like he won,' Dan replied with a shrug. 'Besides, I'm here on my own—and, to be honest, it would be nice to have a friend at my side when I have to deal with my family, too.'

His words were casual enough, but Laurel couldn't shake the feeling that there was something else under them. Something she was missing. But what?

'So it's not just a "Poor, sad Laurel, can't even get a date to the celebrity wedding of the year" thing?' she asked, cautiously.

Dan gave her a quick grin. 'I'm not even sure I know

what one of those would look like. No, I just figured...
we're both dateless, we both have to spend the week
with some of our less than favourite people, we're both
non-Hollywood stars in the middle of a celebrity extravaganza...why not team up?'

Who were his 'less than favourite' people? she wondered. Who was he avoiding, and why?

Suddenly the whole suggestion sounded a little bit
dodgy. Especially since...

'Aren't you a stuntman?' Laurel narrowed her eyes.
'Doesn't that count as a Hollywood star?'

'Definitely not,' Dan said firmly. 'In fact it probably
makes me the exact opposite. Put it this way: if I wasn't
related to the groom by blood there's not a chance I'd
have been invited to this wedding.'

'Same here,' Laurel admitted.

One thing they had in common. That, plus the whole
far-more-famous-sibling thing they both had going for
them. Maybe—just maybe—this was a genuine offer.

Leaning back against the car seat, she considered
his proposition. On the one hand, the idea of having
someone there to back her up, to be on *her* side for
once...well, that sounded pretty good. Especially when
she had to face down Benjamin for the first time since
that really awkward morning in the coffee shop, half
an hour after she'd walked in on him in bed with her
replacement.

*'You understand, don't you, Laurel? When it's true
love...you just can't deny that kind of feeling.'*

She hadn't thrown her coffee cup at his head. She
still felt vaguely proud of that level of restraint. And just
a little bit regretful... Breaking china on his skull would
have been a reassuring memory to get her through the

weeks that had followed—breaking the news to her family, cancelling the save-the-date card order, dealing with all the pitying looks from friends… And Melissa's amusement as she'd said, *'Really, Laurel, couldn't you even satisfy old Benjy? I thought he'd have done any-*thing *to marry into this family.'*

Her mouth tightened at the memory, and she fought to dispel it from her brain. Back to the problem at hand. A fake relationship? *Really?*

As nice as it would be not to have to face this week alone, who was she kidding? *She* wasn't the actress in the family. She couldn't pull this off. Even if Dan played the part to perfection she'd screw it up somehow—and that was only if they got past the initial hurdle. The one that she was almost certain she'd fall at.

They'd have to convince Melissa that they were in love.

Melissa and Laurel might not have spent much time together for half-sisters—they hadn't grown up in the same house, hadn't spent holidays together, celebrated Christmas together, fought over toys or any of that other stuff siblings were supposed to do. Laurel hadn't even known Melissa existed until she was sixteen. But none of that changed the fact that Melissa had known about Laurel's existence her whole life—and as far as she was concerned that meant she knew everything there was to know about her half-sister.

And Melissa would never believe a guy like Dan would fall for Laurel.

Fair enough—she was right. But it still didn't make Laurel feel any more kindly towards her sister.

Laurel shook her head. 'They'll never fall for it. Trust me—I'm an awful actress. They'll see right through it.'

'Why?' Dan asked, eyebrows raised. 'Do you only date A-List celebs like your sister?'

Laurel snorted. 'Hardly. It's the other way round. Melissa would never believe that you'd fall for me. Besides, when are we supposed to have got together? We've never even met before today!'

'They don't know that,' Dan pointed out. 'It's not like my family keeps a particularly tight check on my calendar, and Melissa and Riley have been in LA the whole time. I could have been over in London for work some time in the last six months. Obviously we'd been emailing about the wedding arrangements, so I suggested we meet up while I was in town. One thing led to another...' He shrugged. 'Easy.'

'Is that my virtue or the lie?' Laurel asked drily.

He made it sound so simple, so obvious. Did everyone else live their lives this way? Telling the story that made them look better or stopped them feeling guilty? Her dad certainly had. So had Benjamin. Could she do the same? Did she even want to?

'The story,' Dan answered. 'And as for no one believing it...'

He reached out and took her hand in his, the rough pad of his thumb rubbing across the back of her hand, making the skin there tingle. His gaze met hers and held it, blue eyes bright under his close-cropped hair.

'Trust me. No one is going to have *any* trouble at all believing that I want you.'

His words were low and rough, and her eyes widened as she saw the truth of them in his gaze. They might have only just met, but the pull of attraction she'd felt at the first sight of him apparently hadn't only been one-sided. But attraction…attraction was easy. A relationship—even a fake one—was not.

Laurel had far too much experience of her world being tipped upside down by men—from the day her father had declared that he'd been keeping another family across town for most of her life and was leaving to live with them to the most recent upheaval of finding Benjamin naked on top of Coral.

But maybe that was the advantage of a pretend boyfriend. She got to set the rules in advance and, because she had no expectations of for ever or fidelity, or anything at all beyond a kind of friendship, she couldn't be let down. Her world would remain resolutely the right way up.

Something that, after a week filled with Melissa's last-minute mind-changes and the vagaries of celebrities, sounded reassuringly certain. She eyed Dan's broad shoulders, strong stubbled jaw and wide chest. Solid, safe and secure. He looked like the human embodiment of his company brochure—which she'd studied when she'd been memorising the guest list. Black Ops Stunts promised safety, professionalism and reliability. Just what she needed to help her get through the week ahead.

Maybe—just maybe—this wasn't a completely crazy idea after all.

'Basically, it comes down to this,' Dan said, breaking eye contact at last as he let go of her hand. 'I have a feeling this is going to be the week from hell for both of us. Wedding of the year or not, I can think of a million places I'd rather be—and I'm sure you can too. But we're both stuck at Morwen Hall until New Year's Day, along with our families and all their friends.'

Laurel pulled a face. She'd been trying very hard not

to think too much about how much she wasn't looking forward to that. But when Dan laid it out flat like that she knew he was right. It really *was* going to be the week from hell.

'So I guess you need to decide something before we get there,' Dan went on. 'Do you want to go through that alone, or do you want a friend on your side? Someone you can rant to when people are awful and who understands *exactly* what you're going through?'

He was pushing it, she realised. This wasn't just for her, or just to make the week less awful. There was some other reason he wanted this—and it wasn't because he was attracted to her. The minute he'd dropped her hand she'd seen his control slide back into place, noted the way his expression settled into that same blankness she'd seen when she'd first got into the car.

Dan Black was after something, and Laurel wasn't sure she wanted to know what it was.

She shook her head. 'No. Sorry. It just won't work.'

'Your choice,' Dan said, with a no-skin-off-my-nose shrug.

Laurel frowned. Maybe she'd been wrong after all. It wasn't as if she was the best at reading people.

'I mean, we can still help each other through this week as friends,' she added quickly. 'Just… I'm no good at faking it—sorry. I'd mess it up.'

Not to mention the fact that Melissa would have an absolute fit if Laurel showed up with a new boyfriend at the last moment—especially Riley's brother. That was the sort of thing that might draw their father's attention away from Melissa, after all. And Melissa did *not* like people stealing her thunder.

Frankly, it wasn't worth the risk.

Besides, she could handle Benjamin. It had been six months. She was over it. Over men. And far too busy focussing on her career to let him get to her at all.

It would all be fine.

'Friends would be good,' Dan said with a small smile. 'And if you change your mind…'

'I'll know where to find you,' Laurel said, relieved. 'After all, I'm organising this party. Remember?'

Well, there went the easy option. Still, friends was good, Dan decided. He'd just have to make sure to stick close enough to Laurel to get the information he needed on her sister. Maybe he might even manage to get Melissa alone, for a little brotherly chat. The sort that started, *If you hurt my brother I'll destroy your career.*

See? He could do friendly.

Besides, Dan had been the rebound guy far too often to believe that it ever ended well. Laurel was looking for a prince, and he was anything but. A fake relationship was one thing, but a woman with a broken heart could be unpredictable—and Dan didn't have space in his life for that kind of drama.

One thing his marriage to Cassie had taught him was that giving up control was a bad idea. He'd never concede control of a stunt to anyone else, so why give up control of his heart, or his day-to-day life? Love was off the table, and so were complicated relationships. His was a simple, easy life. Complicated only by his family and by potential heart-breaking film stars who wanted to marry his brother.

'So, tell me more about this wedding, then,' he said, figuring he might as well ease Laurel into talking about her sister now, while he had her undivided attention.

'What's the plan? I mean, who takes a whole *week* to get married?'

'Celebrities, apparently,' Laurel said drily, and he knew without asking that she was quoting Melissa there.

'And you said something about a…?' He tried to remember the term she'd used. 'A Frost Fair? What on earth is one of those?'

Laurel grinned. 'Only my favourite part of the whole week! They used to hold them on the Thames when it froze over, back in the seventeenth and eighteenth centuries. It's like a country fair, I guess, with food stalls and entertainment and all sorts. It's going to be brilliant!'

'It sounds like a health and safety nightmare waiting to happen,' Dan replied, wondering when he'd become the sort of person who noticed those things. Probably when he starting risking life and limb for a living.

'We're not actually holding it *on* the river. It's probably not frozen over, for a start. We'll just be on the banks. But I've got an acting troupe lined up to perform, and a lute player, and a hog roast…'

Her enthusiasm was infectious, and Dan couldn't help but smile. 'It sounds great. I bet Melissa was really pleased when you came up with that one.'

Laurel's smile faltered, just a little. 'Well, I think she'll like it when she sees it,' she said diplomatically, but Dan got the subtext.

Melissa, he suspected, hadn't been actively *pleased* with anything Laurel had done.

He decided to play a hunch. 'Oh, well. A job's a job, right? And this one must be paying pretty well, at least?'

It was crass to talk about money, his mother had always told him that, but if her answer was the one he expected then it would be a clear indication that Melissa was the user he suspected her to be.

The answer was clear on Laurel's face as her smile disappeared altogether. 'It's great experience. And an opportunity to get my company name in the world's media.'

Translation: Melissa wasn't paying her anything, and Dan knew for sure that she and Riley could afford it.

'Right,' he said, ignoring the burning sense of unfairness in his chest. Laurel didn't deserve this—any of this. Not her ex at the wedding, not her sister taking advantage—not even him, using her to suss out the truth of his brother's relationship with Melissa.

It was a good job he'd decided that Laurel was off limits, because Dan had always had a soft spot for a damsel in distress, and a habit of rooting for the underdog. As a friend, he could help her out. But he couldn't let himself even consider anything more.

Which was where that iron-clad control he'd spent so long developing came in.

The car took a sharp turn and Dan turned away to peer out of the window. As they broke through the tree cover—when had they left the city? How had he missed that?—a large, Gothic-looking building loomed into sight, all high-peaked arches and cold, forbidding stone.

That just had to be Morwen Hall. It looked as if Dracula wouldn't feel out of place there, and as far as Dan could tell Melissa was the nearest thing the modern world had to a vampire, so that was about right.

'I think we're here,' he said.

Laurel leant across the empty seat between them, stretching her seatbelt tight as she tried to look out of his window. 'You're right. I'm sorry, I've spent the whole journey talking about me! We're supposed to be being friends, and I still don't know anything about you!'

Dan shrugged. 'I'm a simple guy. There's not much to know.'

She sighed. 'I was hoping I could pick your brains about your family. Get a feel for who everyone is before tonight's welcome drinks.'

Thinking back to all the highly detailed emails she'd sent him during the wedding planning process, Dan laughed. 'Come on—don't try and tell me you haven't got the guest list memorised, alphabetically and backwards probably, along with pertinent details on everyone attending. You probably know my family better than I do at this point.'

It wasn't even a lie. He hadn't stayed in close touch with any of them these last few years. When it came to their jobs, their hobbies, their movements, Laurel probably *did* know more than him.

She smiled down at her hands. 'Well, maybe. I like to do a thorough job.'

There was no hint of innuendo in the words, but something about them shot straight to Dan's libido as she looked up at him through her lashes. Laurel, with her attention to detail, her perfectionism…everything he'd seen through her emails as she'd been planning the wedding…maybe he knew her better than she thought, too. And he couldn't help but imagine what all that detail orientated focus would feel like when turned to their mutual pleasure.

Not that he would have a chance to find out. Seducing Laurel Sommers was not an option—not when she might still be harbouring feelings for her ex, and not when she was holding out for a prince. Which was a pity...

He shook the thought away as the car came to a stop directly outside the Gothic monstrosity that was Morwen Hall.

'We're here,' Laurel said, and bit her lip.

He flashed Laurel a smile. 'Time to face the mob.'

The mob. Her family, his family, her ex...most of the Hollywood elite and a delegation from *Star!* magazine.

All the people she'd least like to see. *Hooray.*

Laurel's knees wobbled as she stepped out of the car, but in an instant Dan was there, offering her his hand as she descended. A friendly hand, she reminded herself as he smiled at her. She wasn't going to waste time pretending that there could be anything more between them. Apart from anything else, if there was a chance of that he wouldn't have offered to be her *fake* boyfriend, would he?

Besides, she was waiting for the real thing—the right person, the right time, the right place. And Dan, at Melissa's wedding, surrounded by their families, while Laurel was working every second to make the week perfect and magazine-worthy, was definitely not any of those things.

She looked up to thank Dan for his assistance when something else caught her eye. A too-flashy car, pulling up beside theirs on the driveway. A shiny silver convertible, the sort that Benjamin had liked to drive...

Oh. Perfect. There he was, her cheating rat of an ex, all ready to make her miserable week just a little bit more unbearable.

Her feelings must have shown in her face, because as

Benjamin shut off the engine Dan bent his head so his mouth was by her ear and whispered, 'This is the ex?'

Laurel nodded, unable to keep her eyes off the car. She couldn't look at Benjamin, of course. And she couldn't look at Dan or he'd know how truly pathetic she was. And she *definitely* couldn't stare at the tall, leggy blonde that Benjamin was helping out of the car, even if she *did* look a bit like Melissa. The car seemed by far the safest bet.

Cars didn't betray a person, or break her heart. Cars were safe.

Far safer than love.

Love, in Laurel's experience, went hand in hand with trust and hope. None of which had ever worked out all that well for her.

Every time she'd had hope for the future that relied on another person, and every time she'd trusted a person she loved, she'd been let down. More than that—she'd been left abandoned, feeling worthless and hopeless.

Which was why, these days, she was putting all her faith, hope and trust in herself and in her business. That way at least if she got hurt it was her own stupid fault. One day her prince would come—and he'd be the kind of equal opportunities prince who loved it that she had a successful career, and thought she was brilliant just the way she was. In the meantime, she would never, *ever* feel that worthless again.

'Laurel!' Benjamin called out, a wide smile on his face as the blonde stepped out of the car, high heels sinking in the gravel of the driveway. 'How lovely to see you! Quite the venue you've picked here.' He shot a glance over at Morwen Hall and winced. 'It doesn't exactly scream romance, I have to say, but I'm sure you know what you're doing.'

Always that slight dig—that slight suggestion that she was doing something wrong. Never enough for her to call him on it—he'd just put his hands up and laugh, saying she was being over-sensitive. But just enough to leave her in no doubt that he knew better than she did. She wasn't *quite* good enough.

Well, the biggest advantage of not being in love with him any more was that she didn't have to care what he thought.

'Giving my sister the wedding of her dreams!' she said, smiling as sweetly as she could as she held a hand out to the blonde, for all the world as if she was meeting her for the first time and *hadn't* found her naked in her own bed six months previously. Because she was a professional, dammit, and she would prove it. 'Hi, I'm Laurel Sommers. The wedding planner.'

The blonde's smile barely reached her cheeks, let alone her eyes. 'Coral. Ben's fiancée,' she added, obviously wanting to make her status absolutely clear. As if Laurel didn't already know the whole sordid history of their relationship.

'Lovely to meet you, Coral,' Laurel lied. She glanced down at Coral's left hand, unable to help herself. There it was: a beautiful diamond, oversized and ostentatious and… *Hang on.*

That was *her* engagement ring. The one she'd given him back that morning in the coffee shop because she couldn't bear to look at the damn thing a moment longer and, besides, it was an expensive ring and she hadn't felt right keeping it.

She'd expected Benjamin to return it or sell it or something.

Not to give it to the woman he'd cheated on her with.

A strange, shaky feeling rose up in her—something between fury and confusion. How *could* he? Wasn't it humiliating enough that he was here at all? And now *this woman* was wearing *her* ring? How much embarrassment was she supposed to take? How little had she mattered—to Benjamin, to Melissa, to her own father—that she found herself in this position? Alone and humiliated and…

Wait. Not alone. Not quite.

Laurel took a deep breath. And then she made a decision.

Reaching behind her, she grabbed Dan's hand and pulled him forward, keeping a tight grip on his fingers as he stood beside her. 'Benjamin, this is Dan. My date for the wedding.'

Until that moment Dan had stayed quiet and still just behind her, not drawing any attention to himself, and it seemed that Benjamin and Coral had barely even registered his presence. Which, now she thought about it, was quite a trick. Maybe that was what you had to do as a stuntman—be mostly invisible or at least easily mistaken for the person you were standing in for. But since Dan had to be over six foot, and solid with it, disappearing in the pale sunlight of an English winter day was a real achievement.

Now he squeezed her fingers back, as if asking, *Are you sure?*

She wasn't. Not at all. But it seemed she was doing it anyway.

'Dan...' Benjamin echoed, holding out a hand, suspicion already in his gaze.

Laurel resisted the urge to roll her eyes as Dan dropped her fingers to grip Benjamin's hand hard enough that he winced slightly.

'That's right. I'm Laurel's *new* boyfriend,' Dan explained, with a sharp smile.

Laurel bit back her own grin as Benjamin's expression froze. Yeah, *that* was why she'd changed her mind about this crazy scheme. That look, right there. That look that said, *Really? Are you sure?*

Because of course Benjamin wouldn't expect her to have a new man already, given how crushed she'd been by their break-up. And even if she had he wouldn't expect it to be someone like Dan—someone big and muscly and gorgeous and just a little bit rough compared to Benjamin's urbane polish.

Sometimes it was nice to surprise a person. Besides, knowing that Dan was clearly not her type—and that she was almost certainly not his either—helped to keep it clear to both of them that this was just a game. A game that they'd need to discuss the rules of, she supposed, but how hard could that be? The charade would be over the minute the wedding guests departed anyway.

But until then...it would be kind of fun.

Coral was looking at Dan with far more interest than her fiancé, and Benjamin retrieved his hand and quickly took Coral's instead. Staking his claim, Laurel realised, just as he'd always done with her—holding her hand, or placing a proprietorial hand at her waist whenever she spoke to another man. Something else she really didn't miss.

Benjamin's gaze flipped from Dan back to Laurel,

and she stopped reflecting on the past in order to concentrate on fooling her ex in the present. Dan slipped a hand around her waist, which helped. Somehow it felt totally different from the way Benjamin had used to touch her there. Less possessive, more a gentle reminder that she wasn't alone.

She liked that, too.

'Actually, Laurel, it's handy we've bumped into you. Could you spare a moment? I have something I want to talk to you about...'

Laurel ran down her mental checklist of any outstanding Benjamin issues and came up with nothing. She'd already given back his ring—as evidenced by the fact that it was sparkling on Coral's left hand right now. He had no stuff left at her flat—mostly because he'd never left anything there longer than overnight if he could help it anyway. He'd kept all their mutual friends in the break-up, since they'd all been his to start with, and she was sort of relieved to have more time for her old uni friends instead of having to hang out with his society people.

What else could there possibly be for them to talk about?

'I should really get back to work,' she said, wishing she could sound more definite, more confident in her denial. Why couldn't she just say, *There is nothing left I want you to say to me*?

'It'll only take a moment,' Benjamin pressed, moving a step towards her.

Laurel stepped back and found herself pressed up against Dan's side. He really was very solid. Warm and solid and reassuring.

She could get used to having that sort of certainty at her back.

'Sorry, but the lady has a prior engagement,' Dan said.

Laurel knew she should be cross with him for speaking for her, but given that she couldn't say the words herself she was finding it hard to care. Besides, he *was* supposed to be her boyfriend. It was all just part of the act.

'I've had a very long journey, and Laurel promised to show me to my room the moment we arrived. Didn't you, honey?'

The warm look he gave her, the innuendo clear in his gaze, made her feel as if her blood was heating her up from the inside.

Just an act, she reminded herself. But, given the way Benjamin stepped back again, and Coral pulled him close, it was an act that was working.

'Sorry,' she lied, flashing the other couple a short, sharp smile. 'Maybe later.' Then she gave Dan a longer, warmer, more loving smile. 'Come on, then, you. I can't wait to give you a *thorough* tour of your room.'

Turning away, she led Dan up the stone steps and through the front door of Morwen Hall, victory humming through her body.

Maybe Melissa wasn't the only actress in the family after all.

'What an idiot,' Dan whispered as they moved out of earshot, leaving Benjamin supervising the retrieval of his bags and handing his keys over to the valet. 'What did you see in him?'

'I have no idea,' Laurel said, honestly.

'So—we're doing this, then? I thought it was a terrible idea.'

But he'd gone along with her lies the minute she'd told them, she realised. Even though she'd insisted not half an hour ago that they couldn't do it. A person who could keep up with her whims was a very useful friend to have, she decided.

'It probably still is.' Laurel flashed him a smile. 'But…it could be fun, don't you think?'

'Oh, definitely,' Dan replied, and the secret half-smile he gave her felt even warmer than the victory over Benjamin.

CHAPTER THREE

LAUREL LAUGHED SOFTLY as they entered Morwen Hall, and Dan congratulated himself on handling the situation with the ex well—*and* getting to play the game he'd wanted all along. It was hard enough judging how a woman wanted him to behave in such a situation when they really *were* dating, but trying to guess it on an hour or two's acquaintance with no notice... Well, he was just glad he hadn't got it wrong. If he had, he wouldn't have got to hear Laurel's giggle—and Laurel had a fantastic giggle. Low and dark and dirty, with just a hint of mischief. Totally at odds with her perfectionist organisational tendencies—and not what he'd expected.

If that giggle told the true story of who Laurel really was, underneath everything—well, then she was definitely someone he was looking forward to getting to know better.

She'd surprised him, though. When she'd dismissed his idea of a fake relationship in the car she'd seemed very certain. He hadn't expected her sudden change of heart—and he couldn't help but wonder what had caused it. Surely it couldn't just have been seeing Benjamin in the flesh again, since she'd been expecting that. Unless she really *was* still hung up on him, and this was all an act to make her ex jealous. Dan hoped not. Revenge games weren't the sort he liked to play at all.

He'd have to remember to ask her, later, he realised. Even if it was too late now to back out, having all the facts would make deciding how to play things a lot easier.

'Hey. You're back!'

A tall redhead strode towards them across the lobby, a clipboard in hand, looking every bit as professional and efficient as Laurel did when she wasn't giggling.

He glanced down at Laurel, keeping his hand at her waist as she gave a forced smile. Dan applied just a little pressure to let her know he was still there while he tried to read the situation. Was this one of the people destined to make his week miserable? Or might she be on their side?

'I am,' Laurel said, sounding uncomfortable.

Was she changing her mind again? Dan hadn't taken her for a fickle woman, but under the circumstances he might have to re-evaluate.

'And you brought company.'

The redhead's gaze flicked up to meet his, and Dan gave a non-committal half-smile. No point encouraging her until he knew which way Laurel was going to jump.

'Eloise, this is Dan. Riley's brother,' Laurel explained. The redhead didn't look particularly reassured by the information. 'Dan, this is Eloise. She's the manager of Morwen Hall.'

'Pleased to meet you,' Dan said, placing the shopping bag full of wedding favours that he'd lugged in from the car on the ground and holding out his hand.

'Acting Manager,' Eloise corrected, as if unable to stop herself, as she took it and shook. She had a good handshake, Dan decided. Firm and friendly. Much better than that idiot outside, who'd tried to crush the bones in his hands before realising, after a moment, that Dan hadn't even begun to squeeze.

'Not for long,' Laurel said, and this time when Dan glanced down her smile seemed real. Friend, then. *Good.* They needed some of those.

He upgraded his expression from noncommittal to cautiously friendly. 'So, what's been happening here?'

'Cassidy, the maid of honour, has taken a fall while skiing and broken her leg, so her husband is bringing his mistress to the wedding instead.'

Eloise's words came out in a rush, and Dan had to run them through his brain twice to process them. Maid of honour. Broken leg. Mistress. None of that sounded good.

Laurel's mouth fell open in an O shape, and her eyes were almost as wide. Apparently she'd reached the same conclusion. 'So Melissa doesn't have a maid of honour?'

Eloise winced. 'Not exactly. She's making me do it.'

Laurel's eyes widened even further, into dark pools of amazement. 'You poor, poor thing,' she said, sounding genuinely sympathetic.

Under other circumstances Dan might have been surprised that Laurel wasn't offended that she wasn't even her sister's *second* choice as maid of honour. But, given the phone call he'd heard in the car, he suspected she viewed it as a lucky escape.

'Yeah. I'm thrilled, as you can imagine. And it means I'll have to call in my deputy to cover for me at the hotel this week. He will *not* be thrilled. I can probably keep on top of the wedding events at least, so he only has to deal with the guests.' Eloise sighed. 'What about you? How did the favours go?'

She eyed Dan again, her gaze slipping down to where his hand rested at Laurel's waist. They might have passed the ex test, but now their unexpected fake relationship faced an even tougher challenge—convincing a friend. Still, it would be good practice for facing his family later, he supposed. *Oh, no, his family.* Maybe he hadn't thought this through properly either...

He reached down to pick up the bag of wedding favours again, just in case Laurel decided they should make a run for it.

'Fine, they're all sorted.' Laurel waved her hand towards the large glossy shopping bag in his hand. 'Then I got Dan's car to pick me up on the way back.'

'That was...convenient.' Eloise's stare intensified.

Dan glanced down at his fake girlfriend in time to watch her cheeks take on a rather rosy hue. Women didn't usually blush over him. It was kind of cute.

'Um, yes. Actually, I meant to tell you... Dan and I...'

Laurel stumbled over the lies and sympathy welled up inside him. She was right—she really wasn't good at this. Maybe he'd have to give her lying lessons. Except that sounded *really* wrong.

'So I see,' Eloise said, when Laurel's words trailed away.

Time for him to step in, Dan decided.

'We had sort of been keeping it under wraps,' he said, pulling Laurel closer against his side.

Laurel stiffened for a moment, then relaxed against him, warm and pliant. He could get used to that. Wait...

what had he been saying? Oh, yeah, making up an entire relationship history on the fly.

'What with the wedding and everything. Didn't want to steal Melissa's thunder, you know? But now the secret's out anyway...' Secret relationship...fake relationship. It was kind of the same thing. Right?

'This is brilliant!' Eloise burst out, and Dan blinked at her.

Either they'd been a lot more convincing than he'd thought, or there was something else going on here. Something that meant Eloise didn't want to examine their lies any more deeply than she had to.

'Melissa has insisted on Riley staying in a separate room until their wedding night, so I had to give him Dan's—sorry, Dan.' She gave him a quick smile. Dan didn't return it. 'But if you two are together, then that's fine because you'll be sharing anyway!'

There it was. That other shoe dropping.

He really, *really* hadn't thought this through. But, in fairness, he hadn't thought it would actually be happening. It had just been an idle suggestion—a possibility that Laurel had quashed almost instantly. If she'd said yes in the car, they'd probably have talked it through and realised how impossible it was. Instead here they were, stuck with a fake relationship Dan was rapidly realising was clearly destined for disaster.

'Sharing...right.'

Laurel's smile had frozen into that rictus grin again. He didn't blame her. How had things escalated this quickly?

Eloise frowned. 'As long as that's okay...?'

'Of course!' Laurel said, too brightly. 'I mean, why wouldn't we?'

'Exactly,' Dan said, trying not to imagine how his week had just got worse. 'Why wouldn't we?'

Because we're not a couple. Because it's all just an act. Because I was really looking forward to a quiet room and a mini-bar all to myself.

Because I'm not sure I can keep my hands off her for a full week.

No. *That* he could do. Laurel was cute—gorgeous, even. But Dan prided himself on his control—and this situation definitely required it. Especially considering all the people who would be watching.

He'd offered to be her fake boyfriend for the week, promised to be a friend—nothing more. And she needed that. This was going to be a hellish week for both of them, and they each needed someone to lean on—Laurel most of all. He couldn't take advantage of that just because she was hot and they only had one bed between them.

Besides, she was waiting for her prince, and he was all out of crowns and white chargers.

'Well, I'm glad that's all sorted,' Eloise said, clapping her hands together with glee. 'See you both later, then.'

And with that, the new maid of honour disappeared, leaving them to figure out how, exactly, they were supposed to share a room.

Dan looked down at Laurel. 'Honey, I think we need to talk.'

Laurel couldn't blame Eloise for this ridiculous situation, she realised as she led Dan towards the lifts. Melissa had obviously decided to be a cow—again—and who could blame Eloise for finding the best way out that she could? And, as an added bonus, Melissa would be really annoyed not to have caused Eloise trouble. So, really, this was all win-win for her.

Except for the part where Laurel now had to spend the next four nights sharing a room with the gorgeous guy who was pretending to be her boyfriend for the week.

Pretending. As in fake. As in a hilarious prank that had seemed a *lot* funnier before they'd realised they were sharing a room. A room with only one bed.

The worst part was she couldn't even blame *Melissa*. No, this was a full *mea culpa* Laurel mess. *She* was the one who had stupidly seized Dan's offer at the last minute and dragged him into this charade. He probably hadn't even been serious when he'd suggested it in the car. It had probably been a joke that she'd taken way too seriously and jumped on because she'd felt worthless in the face of Coral wearing *her* engagement ring.

One moment of ring-based madness, and now here they were.

'I'm really sorry about this,' she said as the lift doors shut and the lobby of Morwen Hall disappeared from view. At least here, in the privacy of the lift, they both knew the whole situation was a sham.

Dan stepped away from her, his hand dropping from her waist for almost the first time since they'd arrived. Her middle felt cold without it there.

'It's not your fault,' he said, not looking at her, obviously knowing that it totally was.

Instead, he seemed to be staring at their wobbly, muted reflections in the brushed steel of the doors. They looked hazy—indistinct blobs of colour on the metal. Which wasn't far off how she felt right now—as if she wasn't as sharp or as focused as the rest of the guests arriving for the wedding.

They all knew exactly who they were, what they were portraying. All Laurel knew was that she'd let herself get carried away with a pretence that was about to come back and bite her.

'Eloise means well,' she tried, not wanting Dan to spend the week blaming her friend, either. 'I suspect Melissa was just trying to make things difficult....'

'Seems to me that's what Melissa does best,' Dan said.

'Well, sometimes,' Laurel agreed. 'Most of the time. Possibly all of it.'

'And she's going to be my sister-in-law.' He sighed.

'You don't sound thrilled about that.'

Or was it just sharing a room with her he wasn't looking forward to? How was she supposed to know? She'd only known the man a couple of hours. Hardly enough to get a good mind-reading trick going.

'I just don't want Riley to make a big mistake.'

'Marrying Melissa, you mean?'

A cold feeling snaked down through Laurel's body. Was Dan planning on persuading Riley to call off the wedding? Because that kind of thing really *didn't* tend to get the wedding planner any repeat business, even if it wasn't her fault.

Dan flashed her a smile. 'Don't worry, I'm sure everything will be fine. I'm just...interested to meet her, that's all.'

'Right...' Laurel said, unconvinced.

Was this why he'd suggested the whole fake relationship thing in the first place? She'd *known* he had an ulterior motive—that was one of many reasons she'd turned him down. And then she'd panicked and forgotten all those reasons.

This was why she didn't do impulsive. It always ended badly.

Well, if Dan thought that Melissa was a bad choice for Riley, Laurel would just have to prove otherwise. Hard as it was to imagine trying to persuade someone that Melissa was a good person, apparently that was now the latest task on her wedding planner to-do list. Great—because that wasn't long enough already.

'So, tell me about your room.' Dan turned towards her, sharp blue eyes watching her face instead of their reflections now. 'For instance is it a suite, with multiple bedrooms and a stuffed mini-bar?'

'It has a mini-bar.'

'And bedrooms?'

'Bedroom. Singular.'

'Two beds?'

Laurel winced, and Dan turned away with a sigh just as the lift doors parted again, opening onto Laurel's floor.

'Sorry,' she said, leading him out into the corridor.

'I'll cope.'

'I'm sure you will.' Big, strong stuntman like him— he'd be fine anywhere. It wasn't him she was worried about.

What was the protocol for this? Laurel wondered as she slipped her key card into the door and pushed it open. He *was* the guest—did that mean she had to give him the bed? In fairness, she'd probably fit better on the tiny sofa than he would. But on the other hand it was *her* room… No. He was the one doing her a favour, pretending to find her attractive and worthwhile in front of her family. He probably deserved the bed.

It was just that it was a really *comfy* bed.

Dropping her key card on the tiny dressing table, Laurel moved across the room to the window, staring back at Dan, looming in the doorway. He was too big for her room—that was all there was to it. It had been the perfect room for just her—queen-sized bed with a soothing sage-coloured satin quilt, white dressing table with carved legs, a small but perfectly formed bathroom with rolltop bath…even the dove-grey wing-back chair by the window was perfect for one.

One her. Not her plus one oversized, muscular stunt-man.

Dan looked out of place in Morwen Hall to start with: his leather jacket was too rough, his boots too scuffed, his jeans…well, his jeans fitted *him* pretty much perfectly but, much as she liked them, they didn't exactly fit the refined Gothic elegance of the wedding venue. But if he was too…too much for Morwen Hall, he overwhelmed her little room entirely.

Who was she kidding? He overwhelmed *her*.

'So…um…how are we going to do this?' she asked, watching as he took in the room. *Their* bedroom. There was no end to the weirdness of that. 'The sharing a room thing, I mean. As opposed to the faking a relationship thing. Which, now that I come to mention it, is next on my how-to list, actually. But first… You know… We should probably figure out the room thing.'

'The room thing…' Dan echoed, still looking around him. 'Right.' Then, dropping the bag of wedding favours onto the dressing table, he moved through the bedroom, exploring the bathroom, pressing down on the bed to test the mattress, then yanking open the mini-bar door and pulling out a bottle of beer.

'So the plan is drink until we don't care which one of us sleeps on the sofa?' Laurel asked cautiously.

Maybe she should have found out a few more things about her supposed boyfriend before she'd started this charade. Like whether or not he tended to solve *all* his problems with alcohol. That would have been useful information about someone she now had to share a room with.

'We're sharing the bed,' Dan said, dropping to sit on the edge of the satin quilt.

Laurel's heart stuttered in her chest.

'Sharing. Like…both of us in it at the same time?'

Her horror must have shown on her face, because he rolled his eyes.

'Nothing to worry about, Princess. I'm not going to besmirch your honour, or whatever it is you're imagining right now.'

'I wasn't…' She tailed off before she had to explain that it wasn't his besmirching she was worried about. It was how she was going to keep her hands from exploring those muscles…

'We'll share the bed because it's big enough and it's stupid not to,' Dan went on, oblivious to her inner muscle dilemma. 'This week is going to be deadly enough without a chronic backache from sleeping on that thing.' He nodded towards the chaise longue, shoehorned in under the second window at the side of the bed. 'Apart from that…the bathroom has a door that locks, and we're going to be out doing wedding stuff most of the time we're here anyway. Especially you—you're organising the whole thing, remember? How much time did you really expect to spend in this room before I came along?'

'I figured if I was lucky I might get four or five hours here to sleep at night,' Laurel admitted.

He was right. They'd probably barely see each other all week, given how much she had to do. And the chances of her passing out from exhaustion the moment her head hit the pillow, regardless of who was snoring away beside her, were high. It would all be fine.

'There you go, then. Not a problem.'

'Exactly,' Laurel agreed, wondering why it still felt like one.

For a long moment they stared at each other, as if still figuring out what they'd let themselves in for. Then Laurel glimpsed the clock on the dressing table and gasped.

'The welcome drinks! I need to get ready.'

Dan waved a hand towards the bathroom. 'Be my guest. I'll just be out here.'

He leant back and stretched out on the bed, his black T-shirt riding up just enough to give her a glimpse of the tanned skin and a smattering of dark hair underneath. She swallowed, and looked away.

'Don't give me another thought,' he said.

'I won't.' She grabbed her dress from where it hung on the outside of the wardrobe, gathered up her make-up bag from the dressing table, and retreated to the relative calm and peace of the bathroom.

Where she promptly realised, upon stepping into the shower, that she still knew next to nothing about her pretend boyfriend and she had to go and meet his parents within the hour.

Clunking her head against the tiles of the shower

wall, Laurel wondered exactly how she'd managed to make this week even more unbearable than Melissa had managed.

Dan heard the click of the bathroom door opening and put down the magazine he'd found on the coffee table, which extolled the wonders of the British countryside. Laurel stepped through the door and he realised that the British countryside had nothing on the woman he was sharing a room and apparently a fake relationship with.

'Think I'll do?' Laurel asked, giving him a lopsided smile as she turned slowly in the doorway.

The movement revealed that the long, slim black dress she'd chosen—a dress that clung to her ample curves in a way that made his brain go a little mushy—draped down from her shoulders to leave her back almost entirely bare.

'I mean, we need this charade to be believable, right? Do you think your family will believe you'd date someone like me?'

'I think they'll wonder why you're slumming it with a guy like me,' he replied honestly, still staring at the honey-coloured skin of her back. Did she know what that sort of dress could do to a man? 'You look better than any of those actresses that'll be out there tonight.'

Laurel pulled a face. 'I appreciate the lie, but—'

'Who's lying?' Dan interrupted. 'Trust me, I've met most of them. And none of them could wear that dress like you do.'

She still looked unconvinced, so Dan got up from the bed and crossed over to her. 'This,' he said, laying a hand at the base of her back, 'is a very nice touch.'

'You don't think it's too much? Or…well, too little?'

She looked up at him with wide, dark eyes, all vulnerability and openness, and Dan thought, *Damn.*

This was where he got into trouble. Every time. A woman looked at him that way—as if he could answer all her questions, give her what she needed, make her world a better place—and he fell for it. He believed he *could* make a difference.

And then she walked off with the first *real* movie star to look at her twice. Every time.

Well, not this one. Laurel wasn't his girlfriend, his crush, or his lover. She was his partner in this little game they were playing. Maybe she'd even become a friend. But that was it. She was looking for a prince, not a stand-in.

Which meant he should probably stop staring into her eyes around now.

'It's perfect,' he said, stepping away. 'Come on. We'd better get down to the bar, right? I figure you probably have work to do tonight.'

Laurel nodded, and grabbed her clutch bag from the dressing table. Then she turned back to frown at him. 'Wait—you're going like that?'

Arms spread wide, Dan looked down at his dark jeans, the black shirt open at the collar, and his usual boots. Admittedly, they were somewhat more casual than the suits and ties he imagined the other guys in attendance would be wearing.

'You don't like it?'

'I love it.' A smile spread across her face as she opened the door for him. 'And not *just* because Melissa will hate it.'

Dan grinned back. 'All the more reason, then.'

* * *

The bar where they were holding the welcome drinks had been decked out with decorations in cool shades of icy blue and green. Not streamers and bunting and stuff—the sort of decorations Dan remembered from other kids' parties when he was younger. These decorations were…classy. Expensive. Yet somehow slightly over the top, as if they were trying too hard. But then, he was starting to get the feeling that that was just Melissa all over.

'It looks like the seaside threw up in here,' he said to a passing waiter as he grabbed a champagne flute from the tray he was carrying.

'Very good, sir,' the waiter said, as if his words had made sense.

Dan sighed. Laurel might have understood. Except Laurel had probably decorated the room herself, so maybe he wouldn't mention it. Just in case.

Besides, every time he caught a glimpse of Laurel through the crowd all he saw was that honey-gold back, taunting him. It was as if her very dress was screaming, *See this? You have to look at it, lie next to it all night, and never touch it. Ha!*

Perhaps the dress was punishment for something— except he hadn't even known Laurel long enough to do anything worth punishing. Unless it was more of an existential punishment. A general torture inflicted on him by the universe for past sins.

Even then, it seemed a little over the top. He hadn't been *that* bad. Had he?

As if to answer the question, he caught a glimpse of a balding head through the crowd, accompanied by a shrill voice, and realised that his parents had arrived. Apparently his day was about to get worse.

Steeling himself, Dan drained his champagne as his father spotted him and beckoned him over. Of course they couldn't *possibly* come to him. He had to go and report in with them. They'd travel all the way to England for Riley's wedding—just as they'd visited him on set across the States and the rest of the world. But they'd never once visited Dan's offices, or any film he was working on, even while they were staying with Riley in LA.

He supposed it was fair. He'd never visited their workplaces either—never made it to a lecture they'd given. Never even shown up and been the respectable son they wanted at any of their fancy events. In fact from the moment he'd realised that he'd always be second-best to Riley in their eyes he'd given up trying all together.

Why bother trying to live up to expectations he could never match, or trying to be good enough for people who not only expected more, but wanted someone completely different? He wasn't the son they wanted, so he didn't try to pretend otherwise. In fact, for most of his teenage years he'd gone out of his way to be the exact opposite. And during his twenties, actually.

Even marrying Cassie had been a big middle finger to his parents, who'd hated every inch of the trailer-trash-made-average actress. Of course that little act of rebellion had come back to bite him when he'd fallen in love with her, against his own better judgement. Love made you *want* to be good enough, something he'd spent his whole life avoiding.

When she'd left him he'd known he'd never try to be

good enough for anybody else again. He was his own man and that was enough.

Even if it meant dealing with his parents' disappointment every now and again.

He snagged another glass of champagne as he crossed the room towards them, but refrained from drinking it just yet. If the conversation went at all the way he expected he'd need it later.

'Quite the venue our Riley has managed to get for this shindig, huh, son?'

Wendell Black smacked Dan between the shoulder blades, too hard to be casual, not hard enough to actually hurt—even if Dan wasn't sure that hadn't been the intention.

'Oh, Wendell, I'm sure *Melissa* had the final say on the venue.' His mother's nose wrinkled ever so slightly. 'Didn't she work here once, or something?'

'Nothing wrong with working your way all the way up,' Wendell said. 'It's working your way down that's the problem!' He laughed—too loudly—and Dan clenched his jaw.

'Hello, Mother, Father,' he said, after the laughter had subsided. Just because *they'd* forgone basic greetings—as if it hadn't been two years since they'd last seen each other—it didn't mean he had to.

'Daniel.' His mother eyed him critically. 'Do you really think that's an appropriate outfit for tonight?'

'I'm hoping that Riley will be so pleased to see me he won't care what I'm wearing.' It was partly true; Riley generally cared far less than his parents about appropriate attire. Probably because he just let Melissa or his stylist dress him for all events.

Dan shuddered at the very idea. The last thing he

needed was someone telling him what to wear. In his experience next came what to say, then what to do, then who to be.

He was very happy being himself, thank you.

Letting his gaze roam around the room, he tried to pretend he was just taking in the occasion, even though he knew there was really only one person he was looking for. One long black dress, and dark brown hair pinned up at the nape of her neck above that bare back. How had she captivated him so quickly? Dan couldn't help but think he wouldn't mind taking directions from Laurel, under certain circumstances. Especially if she was telling him what clothing to take *off* rather than put on.

But that line of thinking was dangerous. If anyone had expectations it was Laurel. And he had no intention of trying to live up to them.

'So, I suppose I should ask how the business is doing,' his mother said, ignoring his comment about Riley, just as she always ignored anything she didn't agree with.

'It would be polite,' Dan agreed. He'd scanned the whole bar and not spotted her—and she was hard to miss in that dress. Where was she?

'Daniel,' his mother said, warning clear in her voice.

He shouldn't make her actually ask. That would be showing far too much interest in his disreputable industry.

How his parents managed to live with the hypocritical distinction they made between cheerleading Riley's A-List celebrity career and looking down on his own lucrative and respected film-related business, Dan had no idea. He suspected it had something to do with column inches in the celebrity magazines his mother pretended she didn't read.

There. There she was. Laurel stood at the bar, her posture stiff and awkward as she talked to an older couple. He squinted at them. Nobody he recognised, so probably family. In fact, probably *her* family. And she looked about as excited to be talking to them as he was to be stuck alone with his.

Well, now. Wasn't that just a win-win situation for everyone in the making? He could swoop in, save Laurel from her family, then drag her over to meet his and she could at least keep him company and give him something pretty to look at while his parents put him down.

'Sorry, Mother. If you'll excuse me a moment, there's someone I'd really like you to meet. I'll be right back.'

Not waiting for an answer, Dan pushed his way through the crowd towards the bar—and Laurel. Spotting Benjamin watching him as he crossed the room, he gave Laurel's ex a flash of smile and a small wave, just to remind him that *he* was Laurel's boyfriend now. Fake or otherwise.

Then he got back to the task in hand—rescuing Laurel. He paused just a metre or two away from where she stood, hands twisting round each other in front of her belly, and took stock of her companions.

The man who Dan assumed was her father was short and stocky, with a thatch of grey hair above deep-set eyes. His suit looked expensive, but he fiddled with the cufflinks as if they were still a little unfamiliar. Dan guessed that Melissa had dressed her parents up for the occasion, the way she wanted them to be seen. See? It wasn't even just wives who did that. Perhaps all women were just as culpable.

Except Laurel. She'd thought his outfit was perfect—if only because it would annoy her sister. Which was a good enough reason for him to keep wearing it.

Melissa's mother—Laurel's stepmother, he supposed—wore a peacock-bright gown that looked too flashy next to her faded blonde hair. Her make-up was heavy, as if trying to hide the lines of her age, but somehow making them all the more obvious.

Then Laurel turned slightly, glancing over her shoulder—maybe looking for him? Dan stepped forward, ready to play knight in shining armour for his pretend girlfriend even if he couldn't manage to be a real prince.

'Laurel.' He smiled, resting his fingertips against her shoulder as he moved behind her. 'There you are. Do you have a moment, honey? I know you're busy working, but there are some people I'd like you to meet.'

Or rescue him from. It was practically the same thing, right?

The relieved smile she sent up at him told him he'd done the right thing, even if her parents were looking rather less impressed at the interruption.

'Dad, Angela, this is Dan. He's my...' She faltered for a moment, then started again. 'We're together.'

'Dan?' Angela's eyes narrowed. 'You didn't say you were bringing a date to the wedding, Laurel. I know we talked about the exclusivity of the guest list, under the circumstances. It's not like this is any old wedding.'

'And I'm not any old date,' Dan said cheerfully as he held out his hand to Laurel's father. 'Dan Black, sir,' he said as they shook. Then he turned to offer his hand to Angela. 'Riley's older brother.'

Angela's face tightened as her handshake turned weak and she tugged her fingers from his. 'Riley's brother.' She turned to glare at Laurel. 'Well. This *is* unexpected. Does Melissa know that you two are...?' She waved a hand vaguely between them, as if articulating the relationship was too disgusting even to contemplate.

'Not yet.'

Laurel's words came out small, subdued, and Dan reached out to touch her again, to remind her that she wasn't alone. Wasn't that the whole point of this charade, anyway?

'We thought we'd share our good news with her this evening,' Dan said, trying to keep his tone bright and his expression oblivious to the glares Angela was spreading around their little group. 'I'm sure she and Riley will be very happy for us.'

'I'm sure they will,' Laurel's father said, apparently also immune to the glares. At least until Angela elbowed him in his soft middle. 'Oh, but...perhaps tonight isn't the night to tell them, darling,' he added, having finally got a clue. 'It's a very big night for Melissa.'

'It's a very big week all round,' Dan agreed. 'But, really, I do always think that keeping love a secret sends the wrong message, don't you? And I wouldn't ever want Laurel to doubt my feelings about her.'

Maybe that was going a little far, judging by the way Angela's face paled and Laurel's father's cheeks turned a rosy shade of red at the reminder of how she'd been his mistress for almost two decades. Dan tested his conscience and discovered he didn't care. If they couldn't take it, he decided, they really shouldn't spread such poisonous looks and comments around in the first place.

'Now, if you'll excuse us a moment?'

He reached an arm around Laurel's shoulders, trying hard only to touch the dress and not her bare skin—which, given the design, wasn't easy. But he knew that if he placed his hands on that long, lean back he'd be done for. And he needed all his wits about him if they both wanted to make it through the evening intact.

'You shouldn't have said that,' she whispered to him as they turned away.

'Probably not,' he agreed. 'But you have to admit it *was* fun.'

The secret smile she gave him was reward enough.

'Where are we going?' she asked as he steered her across the room.

'Ah.' As much as he wished he could just lead her out of the bar, back through the endless hotel corridors to their room, he had promised his parents he was coming back. With her. 'Well, if you consider your parents the frying pan…let's just say our next stop could be thought of as the fire.'

Laurel groaned. 'I'm going to need more champagne for this, aren't I?'

'Definitely,' Dan said, and flagged down a passing waiter.

CHAPTER FOUR

LAUREL'S MIND WAS still replaying the moment Dan had managed to insult and embarrass her father and step-mother all in the same moment, with just one passing comment, as he handed her a glass of champagne and they continued their journey across the huge hotel bar. She had a feeling she'd be reliving it all week, as an antidote to whatever repercussions Angela deemed appropriate for the injury. The thing was, of course, she couldn't *actually* disagree with anything Dan had said. Just the implications, and the suggestion that he had every intention of sharing the news of their relationship with the bride that evening.

Melissa, Laurel knew, would be livid. The thing she hated most in the world was people stealing her thunder. And while at her own wedding that might be moderately understandable, the fact was it wouldn't matter what the circumstances: Melissa hated anyone else getting any attention at all—especially if she felt it had been taken away from her.

Perhaps it was a hold-over from her childhood when, ignored by her own father for sixteen years, she'd had to try and win attention in other ways. Maybe that ex-plained why she'd become not just an actress, but a celebrity, whose every move and look was pored over by the press and the public.

As far as Laurel was concerned it certainly explained why she'd become a stone-cold witch.

'Brace yourself,' Dan muttered as they approached another older couple—far more polished and professional-looking than her own father and stepmother, despite Melissa's insistence on stylists for them both for the week.

'This is the worst Meet the Parents evening ever,' she murmured back, and Dan flashed her a quick smile.

'And we're only halfway there.'

Halfway. That was something. She'd survived her own parents—with Dan at her side had done more than just survive. She'd left on her own terms and with the upper hand—something she wasn't sure had ever happened before in the history of her relationship with them.

Now she owed Dan the same.

'Mother. Father.' Dan gave Laurel the slightest push so she stood half in front of him. 'I'd like you to meet my girlfriend—Laurel.'

There was no hesitation in his speech, no hitching of his voice over the lie. He seemed perfectly comfortable introducing an almost total stranger to his parents as his one and only love. Maybe she should be a little more concerned about sharing a bedroom—and a fake relationship—with such a consummate liar.

But Dan's parents' attention was entirely on her, and there was no more time to worry about it. It was time to put on the show.

'Laurel, these are my parents—Wendell and Linda Black.'

'It's a pleasure to meet you both at last,' Laurel said, pasting on her prettiest smile. 'Dan's told me so much about you, and of course we've been in touch over the wedding planning.' She just hoped they didn't ask exactly *what* he'd said about them, since the sum total of her knowledge of them was their names and what she'd scribbled down in her notebook when Melissa had been running through the guest list.

'You're the organiser woman,' Wendell said, clicking his fingers. 'Of course! All those detailed schedules and flight plan options. Well, Dan, I have to say, she's not your usual type!'

'Which can only be an advantage, I suppose,' Linda added drily.

She scrutinised Laurel so closely that she felt almost as if she were on a doctor's examination table.

'So. You're a wedding planner.'

'She owns the business organising Riley and Melissa's wedding,' Dan corrected her, before Laurel could answer. 'The biggest celebrity wedding of the year. Quite the coup, I'm sure you'll agree.'

'Unless your sister is the bride,' Linda said, and Laurel gritted her teeth.

Melissa being her sister had only made this job harder, not easier, and the truth was she'd done an amazing job in difficult circumstances. Somehow, she didn't think Dan's parents were the sort of people to appreciate that.

'So, you purposely set out to build a business that… organises people's weddings for them?' Wendell was frowning, as if he couldn't quite make sense of the idea. 'Why? I mean, you're obviously a bright young woman. You'd have to be good with details and planning to pull

off this sort of affair. Why not use your talents somewhere they could really matter?'

'Maybe you were wrong, Wendell,' Linda put it.
'Seems like she's just like Dan after all.'

Beside her Laurel felt Dan stiffen, and wondered how
many times they'd said the same thing to him. That he
was wasting his time doing what he loved, running the
company he'd built from the ground up all by himself.
That his success didn't matter because he wasn't doing
something they approved of. That he was wasting his
time on something unimportant.

Did they feel the same way about Riley? Or was
his celebrity status enough of an achievement to avoid
their censure?

Dan hadn't spoken, and when she glanced up at him
his expression was stone-like, flat and hard and unyield-
ing. She hoped the glass stem of his champagne flute
was strong, given the tight grip he seemed to have on it.

Time for her to return the parental put-down for him.

'You're both doctors, aren't you?' she asked, still
smiling sweetly. 'Very successful and famous ones,
by all accounts.'

'That's right,' Wendell said, puffed up with his own
pride.

Linda nodded a little more cautiously.

'I think that's marvellous,' Laurel said honestly. 'I
think it's wonderful that your natural talents have led
you to a field where you can make such a difference in
the world. I think it's so important for *everyone* to follow their natural talents, wherever they lead, don't you?'

'I suppose so,' Wendell agreed, but he was frowning as he spoke.

'Some talents are obviously more valuable than others, though,' Linda added.

Laurel tilted her head to the side. 'Do you really think so? I've always believed that *every* talent is equally valid and valuable. I mean, imagine if everyone in the world only possessed the same sort of talent! If we were all doctors there'd be no one left to do anything else. You'd suddenly find yourselves spending your whole days learning how to design a car, or having to clean your own home, or write your own books to read—and have no time left for medicine at all.'

'Well, I hardly think that's going to happen.'

Linda folded her arms over her chest, and for a moment Laurel wondered if she was simply going to walk away from her. But she didn't. Whether it was politeness or morbid curiosity, she was going to wait and see where Laurel was going with this.

Good.

'Of course not,' Laurel agreed. 'Not everyone is going to be a doctor. Or a wedding planner, for that matter. But the thing is, the people I organise weddings for…quite often they're not good at the same things as me. They're not good at the details, or the inspiration, or the planning. I can take that off their shoulders so they can get on with what they *are* good at—whether that's saving lives, educating children, or starring in movies. And at the same time I get to do what I love—and make a decent living out of it, thank you. So it works for everyone.'

'Not to mention the fact that a wedding can be the most important, memorable day in a person's life,' Dan put in. 'Laurel makes sure that it is perfect for them.

She literally makes their memories. I think that's pretty important, don't you?'

He reached out to rest a hand at the small of her back and Laurel froze at the contact, feeling the warmth of his touch snake all the way up her spine. Why on earth had she chosen this dress? Couldn't she have picked something with a little more fabric? Something that didn't make her feel as if she was naked in front of his parents?

Of course when she'd packed it she hadn't expected to be spending the evening as someone's girlfriend.

'And the same goes for Dan's business, of course,' Laurel added, smiling dotingly up at him. 'He's made a hugely successful career out of doing what other people can't—what they wouldn't dare to try. I imagine Riley's career in blockbuster action movies would have been a lot less successful without people like Dan stepping in to do the really wild stuff. Don't you agree?'

Even if they did, Laurel was sure Wendell and Linda wouldn't say so. But sometimes, as she'd found with her parents, just letting them know that their opinion wasn't the only one was enough. Enough to make her feel a little better about never being *quite* good enough for them.

And, from the way Dan's fingers caressed her spine, she suspected he felt the same.

Leaning in against his side, she let herself imagine for a moment that this wasn't an act. That he really was there to support her.

Wait. That part *was* true. They might not be a couple, might not be in love, but they were both there to help the other through the week from hell. And suddenly Laurel realised that that might be all she needed after all.

'Linda! Wendell!'

Laurel stiffened again at the sound of her stepmother's voice. Yes, that was what this situation needed—more awful parents.

'Angela.' Linda's voice was tight, her smile barely reaching her lips. 'And Duncan. So lovely to see you both again.'

'Well, we should probably—' Dan started, but Angela interrupted him.

'Oh, no, Dan, do stay. I mean, now we're all going to be family I'm sure we're all just *dying* to hear exactly how you met our Laurel and how you came to be together. *Such* a surprise—don't you agree, Linda?'

'A total shock,' Linda said flatly. 'But then, we're rather used to those from Dan.'

'So, how *did* you two meet?'

Laurel glanced up at Dan at her father's words, hoping he might have a suitable story prepared. Why had she wasted so much time hiding from him in the bathroom when they could have been preparing for this exact question?

'Well…' Dan said.

Laurel held her breath, waiting for the lie.

But before he could start to tell it the main door to the bar flew open and there stood Melissa, resplendent in the forest-green gown her stylist had finally got her to agree to, after twenty-two other dresses had been deemed unsuitable. Riley was half hidden behind her, his tux making far less of an impact even with his all-American good looks.

'Friends! My fiancé and I are just so delighted to welcome you all here to celebrate our wedding.' Melissa beamed around the room and Riley stepped out of her shadow, looking awkward in his dinner jacket, and gave

a little wave. 'I hope you all have just the best time—'
She cut off abruptly, her sideways smile replaced by a
sudden scowl as her gaze fell on Laurel and Dan.

Oh, dear.

Laurel made to move away from Dan's side—just
enough to give them plausible deniability until Melissa
had finished her public announcements. But Dan's arm
tightened around her waist, holding her close, and when
she looked up at him his eyes were locked with Melissa's.

He wanted this. Wanted the conflict and the decla-
ration and Melissa's wrath. But why? Just to see her
reaction?

Laurel couldn't help but feel she was missing half
the story, here, and she really didn't like it.

'What the *hell* is going on here?' Melissa demanded,
still staring at them, her hands on her hips.

'We…' Laurel started to speak, but her mouth was
too dry and the word came out as little more than a
whisper. Her whole body felt too hot, flushed with panic
and the sort of intense guilt and fear that only Melissa
could make her feel. Only the half-sister whose life
she'd stolen, whose happiness she'd lived, even when
she hadn't known Melissa even existed.

She could never make that up to Melissa, no matter
how hard she tried. But Laurel knew she had to keep
trying, regardless. That was only fair.

And now she was ruining Melissa's big night. She
was a horrible person.

From nowhere, Eloise appeared, looking slightly
flustered and flushed, her cheeks a shade of pink that
clashed horribly with her red hair. She swooped in and
put an arm around Melissa's shoulders, whispering fast

and low into the bride's ear. Slowly Melissa's thunderous expression retreated, to be replaced with the sweetness-and-light smile that she usually displayed for the crowds and her public.

'Anyway, I do hope you are all enjoying your evening,' she went on, as if her previous outburst had never happened.

Whatever Eloise had said, it seemed to have worked. The tightness in Laurel's chest started to ease just enough to let her breathe properly again. Dan stroked the base of her back once more, and she relaxed into his touch. She wasn't alone. She wasn't the only one Melissa was furious with right now. Whatever happened next, she had back-up.

And that meant a lot today.

'I'm looking forward to talking with every one of you, and welcoming you personally to Melissa and Riley's Wedding Extravaganza!' Melissa finished, with a flourish, holding out her skirt and giving a slight curtsey.

As sponsored by Star! *magazine*, Laurel added mentally. It was still all a show to Melissa. She wondered if the actual marriage part—the bit that came next and theoretically for the rest of their lives—had even really registered with her half-sister. She hoped so. Because otherwise she had a feeling that Dan would be having words with his brother, and she really didn't want this whole thing called off at the last moment.

The crowd applauded, as if on command, and then turned back to their own conversations. The moment the attention was off her Melissa's face dropped back into a disapproving scowl once more. She strode across to where Dan and Laurel were standing with their parents, Riley tailing behind.

'Something you'd like to tell me, *sister*?' Melissa asked, her voice dripping with sarcasm.

Laurel felt her chest start to tighten again. 'Um… Well…'

Dan's fingers splayed out across her bare back—a reassuring presence. 'Melissa. It's so lovely to finally meet you,' he said, all politeness. 'Obviously I've heard plenty about you already, but it's nice to actually meet my sister-in-law-to-be in the flesh, so to speak.'

Melissa blinked up at him, wrong-footed by the polite tone. 'Of course. It's lovely to meet you too. Dan. I just wasn't aware that you were so well acquainted with my sister.'

Half-sister, Laurel's brain filled in. Melissa always referred to her as her half-sister, unless there was something to gain by claiming the full connection. In this case, she guessed, that would be guilt. Laurel's guilt, particularly. She wanted Laurel thinking, *How could I possibly do this to my sister at her wedding?*

And, of course, that was exactly what she *was* thinking.

'Dan and Laurel were just about to tell us how they met, darling,' Angela said, leaning over to kiss her daughter on the cheek. 'You look stunning, by the way.'

'Thank you,' Melissa replied, accepting the compliment automatically, as her due. 'That's a story I'd be very interested to hear. It's really quite difficult to imagine *how* or *when* you two might have been able to meet and start a relationship. Or what on earth you've found in common.'

You mean, what on earth does he see in me? Laurel

translated. She'd been interpreting Melissa's put-downs and comments for enough years now to figure out exactly what their underlying message was. It helped to know that whenever Melissa next got her alone, Laurel could be sure to hear the unfiltered version—the cutting words she wouldn't say in front of other people. Laurel had taken to treating it as a game, a way to distract herself from the hurt Melissa's comments caused, scoring herself on how accurate her translations were rather than dwelling on what truth there might be in her half-sister's words.

'Oh, we got chatting over email to start with,' Dan said lightly, answering the question Melissa had actually asked rather than the implied one. 'All that wedding planning, organising flights and such. I had some scheduling issues, and Laurel helped me sort them out. Went above and beyond, really.'

All true, so far, Laurel observed. Obviously he was banking on the fact that the truth was easier to remember than a lie.

But next came the part where he started making things up.

'Then I got a call inviting me over to London for some meetings with a couple of people in the industry here,' Dan said, shrugging. 'At that point—well, it seemed natural that I suggest we meet up for a drink while I was over here. One thing led to another...'

'I don't think we need to hear about that, Daniel,' Linda said sharply, and Laurel hid her grin.

'You never said, man!' Riley beamed at his brother and held out both hands, clasping Dan's between them. 'This is so great! We'll be like, brothers, but we'll also be, like, brothers-in-law!'

'It's all still fairly new,' Laurel cautioned, sensing that Riley was about to get carried away.

The last thing she needed, after the humiliation of one broken engagement, was for her family to start believing she'd be the next one up the aisle, when in truth they hadn't even made it to a first date. Which was kind of a shame, really. Under normal circumstances maybe she and Dan *could* have gone out on a date like normal people. That was one thing this charade had taken firmly off the table, though.

Not the right place, not the right time, and not the right prince. She had to remember that.

'But it's serious,' Melissa said, looking at them both thoughtfully.

Apparently she'd bought the lie, Laurel realised. Which only made her more nervous about what Melissa planned to do with the knowledge.

'Very,' Dan lied, pulling Laurel closer.

Laurel tried to smile in agreement.

'Because obviously you wouldn't want to steal my thunder like this for a casual fling, would you?'

There it was.

'Of course not,' Laurel said, knowing that there was no way out now. This mock relationship had to make it all the way through to the wedding or all hell would break loose. The only thing Melissa would consider worse than Dan and Laurel getting together at her wedding, distracting attention from her, was them splitting up in any kind of public way between now and the wedding.

Which meant they were stuck with each other for good. Or at least for the next five days. Which kind of felt like the same thing. Laurel had found it impossible to see past New Year's Day for months now…the idea of a world in which she wasn't organising Melissa's wedding was just a strange, faraway dream.

'I'm afraid that true love just doesn't work to order, Melissa.'

Dan kissed the top of her head, and Laurel tried not to feel the walls closing in on her.

'Let's get some more champagne,' Eloise said, clapping her hands together and drawing the attention of a passing waiter.

'What a marvellous idea,' Laurel agreed.

It was a couple of hours before Dan finally managed to drag Laurel away from the welcome drinks. As the wedding planner, she'd insisted on staying until the bitter end, making sure that everything went according to her schedule. At least their parents had all toddled off to bed around midnight, shortly after Melissa's precisely timed and highly orchestrated departure. And, despite Dan's best efforts to get his brother alone for a chat—thwarted mostly by the endless stream of friends wanting to buy the groom a drink—Riley had sloped off shortly after Melissa, with far less fanfare, presumably to the room that was supposed to be Dan's.

So when all that was left was a few of the hardcore drinkers, doing shots at the bar, Dan steered Laurel towards the door.

'Come on. There's nothing left for you to do here. I'm shattered, and you must be too. Let's go get some sleep. It's going to be another long day tomorrow.'

Laurel smiled up at him wearily. 'You're right, I know. I just hate leaving before everything is finished and tidied away.'

Dan glanced back towards the bar. 'You could be here all night with this lot. Better save your energy for a more important battle.'

Which, in Dan's case, he suspected would be trying to sleep in the same bed as Laurel without touching her. It was one thing to decide that a woman was off-limits, employing that famous control he was so proud of. It was another thing entirely to *like* it. Resisting temptation was always harder when temptation was lying right next to him.

'Like managing Melissa,' Laurel said, and sighed. 'Yeah, okay.'

They made their way up to their room in companionable silence, but Dan couldn't help but wonder if she was doing the same thing he was—mentally reliving their evening together.

The strangest thing, he decided, was the difference in Laurel when she spoke to her sister. With her father and stepmother she'd been reticent, as if she was holding back from saying what she really felt. She'd had no such compunction with his parents, he realised. She'd been polite, charming, but forthright with it—and left them in no doubts about her views.

A warm feeling filled his chest when he remembered the things she'd said about him and the importance of living according to your *own* talents, dreams and values, not someone else's. For the first time in years he had honestly felt as if someone understood what he was doing, what he wanted. Understood *him*.

It was almost a shame it was all an act, really.

Besides, that confidence and conviction had disappeared the moment Melissa had entered the room. He'd watched it drain away from her, as if Melissa had sucked it out, leaving her half-sister empty.

He hadn't liked seeing Laurel like that. Since the moment they'd met she'd been so bright and vivacious—except when Melissa was there, in person or on the phone, commanding her complete attention and energy.

'Here we go,' Laurel said, rubbing her eye with one hand while the other fumbled with the key.

Dan took it from her and opened the door, letting her through first. As it swung shut behind him he headed straight to the mini-bar. 'Want anything?' he asked, staring at the contents as he tried to decide if one more drink would make things better or worse. Alcohol wasn't always the best thing for retaining his control.

Of course his control would be a lot easier to hold on to if he knew that Laurel wasn't at all interested. Maybe he should just ask her—get it out of the way. She'd tell him once again that she was holding out for a hero, or whatever, and that all they could ever have was a fake relationship. Then he could move on, safe in the knowledge that there was no risk of anything more at all.

Except...there were hints. Tiny ones. Hints Laurel might not even be aware of but he couldn't help but catalogue and add to his list of things he knew about Laurel.

The way she leant into his touch. The warmth in her eyes when she looked at him. The shiver he'd felt go through her when he'd first touched the base of her back...

Laurel had told him herself that she was a terrible actress. So why was she acting as if she was as attracted to him as he was to her?

Dan stared balefully at the tiny bottles of spirits

in front of him, knowing that the chances were they wouldn't help at all.

Laurel shook her head. 'I'm done.'

'Me too.' He let the fridge door close. 'Want to use the bathroom first?'

It was a gentlemanly offer, and had the added advantage that Laurel looked so exhausted that if she got into bed first Dan was pretty sure she'd be passed out before he even managed to slip between the covers.

At least that way she wouldn't notice if he couldn't sleep at all.

As she locked the bathroom door behind her Dan took the opportunity to strip down to his boxers and a T-shirt. That was acceptable nightwear, right? Usually he didn't bother, but he figured even sleepy Laurel would object to complete nudity when she woke up in the morning.

Sitting on the edge of the bed to wait his turn, Dan tried not to imagine what Laurel might be doing in there. Whether she was naked, most specifically. What she wore to bed. How she looked sleep-tousled, her hair loose around her shoulders...

It didn't matter. She was *off-limits*.

As much as he might fantasise otherwise.

Finally she was done. She waved a hand to motion him towards the bathroom as she passed him, and before he could stand she'd already slipped under the covers— on the side of the bed *he* usually slept on. Fantastic.

Still, she looked so tired he couldn't even object.

In the harsh light of the bathroom he stared into the mirror at his familiar old face and tried to convince himself that this wasn't a big deal. So he was sharing a bed with a beautiful woman? So what? It wasn't as if it hadn't happened before. And he sure hoped it would happen again. Often.

So why was his heart hammering just a little too fast in his chest? And why did his hands shake as he reached for his toothbrush?

Okay, fine. He knew exactly why, and he couldn't even claim it was all down to Laurel.

It was the Cassie thing.

But Laurel didn't know that he hadn't spent a full night in bed with another woman since his divorce—and she didn't need to know. Yeah, it might feel a bit strange, but so what? This wasn't romance, and it wasn't love—they'd been clear about that, if nothing else. He wasn't going to get his heart trampled on when Laurel looked around and found someone better.

This was platonic. All he had to do was keep his hands to himself for the night and it would all be fine.

Pep-talk over, he switched off the light and headed back into the bedroom, trying to be as silent as he could to avoid waking Laurel.

But to his surprise, when he settled under the covers, she murmured, 'Goodnight,' and he realised she wasn't asleep at all.

'Night, Laurel,' he whispered back.

And then he lay there, staring at the ceiling and listening to her breathe.

She wasn't a heavy breather, at least. Her shallow breaths were barely audible, even in the stillness of the night. He waited almost without realising he was doing so for them to deepen, for her breathing to grow slow and steady, the way it did when a woman was sleeping. Usually it would be a signal that it was time for him to leave. Tonight…tonight maybe it would mean that he could sleep.

Except her breathing *didn't* even out. It didn't grow deeper.

Because she wasn't sleeping.

Dan held in a sigh. One of them was going to have to cave and fall asleep first—and it wasn't going to be him.

In which case… Well, since they weren't sleeping anyway, they might as well get to know one another properly, at last.

CHAPTER FIVE

LAUREL STIFLED A sigh as Dan remained resolutely awake beside her in the darkness. He lay motionless under the covers, but even with her back turned to him she could tell that he hadn't relaxed a single muscle. How was she supposed to sleep with the world's tensest man in bed with her?

And why on earth was *he* so tense anyway? He was probably used to sharing a bed—a guy who looked as good as Dan did couldn't be short of partners when he wanted them. She, on the other hand, hadn't shared anything with anyone since she'd broken up with Benjamin—and even before that, he hadn't stayed over for months. Well, not with her, anyway.

She was used to her own space. Used to spreading out starfish-style, in the bed. Used to not having to worry if she snored, or if her hair looked like bats had been living in it, or if she'd missed a bit of last night's mascara which was now smeared across her cheek.

She was *not* used to having a big, gorgeous, untouchable man taking over her space.

'Why are you scared of Melissa?'

And asking her difficult questions in the middle of the night.

Laurel's body tensed at Dan's words, and she forced herself to try and relax. 'I'm not scared of her.'

'Really?'

The covers rustled as Dan turned on his side, and Laurel could feel the movement of the mattress, of his body, even if she couldn't see it. She stayed facing away from him, her eyes tightly closed, and hoped he'd give up. Quickly.

'Really,' she said firmly. 'Now, if you don't mind, I'm trying to get to sleep.'

'No, you're not. You're lying there wide awake, same as me.' Dan shifted again, and the warmth of his body radiated out towards her as he grew closer.

Her eyes flew open. 'What are you doing?' Dan's face loomed over her as she flipped onto her back.

'Proving my point.' He pulled back. 'I'm not asleep… you're not asleep. We should take advantage of this time to have that getting-to-know-you conversation we should have had before we decided to stage a fake relationship this week.'

'You mean the primer we needed *before* we had to meet each other's families?' Laurel asked, eyebrows raised. Talk about shutting the barn door once the horse had stood around, drunk too much champagne and been vaguely insulting to everyone. Wait…that probably hadn't been the horse…

'So it's a little late?' Dan shrugged, pulling himself up to a seated position, his back against the headboard. 'Doesn't mean it's not still worthwhile. I mean, we have to spend the whole week with these people.'

'Fooling them,' Laurel agreed reluctantly. They really did need to talk. And if they didn't do it now, goodness only knew when they'd get the time.

Dan obviously sensed her agreement. He patted the pillow beside him and she dragged herself up, tugging the slippery satin of her pyjama top with her to make sure she was still decently covered. The problem with curves like hers, she'd always found, was that they liked to try to escape, and normal clothes weren't always built to stop them.

'But you definitely get to start,' she said as she settled herself down. It felt oddly intimate, talking in the darkness with Dan. 'Everyone in the world already knows everything there is to know about my family and Melissa.'

'Not everything,' Dan said quietly.

His earlier question echoed through her brain again. *'Why are you scared of Melissa?'*

'Enough to be going on with,' she countered. 'So, your turn. What's the deal with your parents? Can't cope with their sons not going into the family medical business?'

Dan shook his head slowly. 'Not exactly, I don't think. Partly, I'm sure. As you probably noticed, they don't have all that much respect for what I do.'

'Or what *anyone* does if it isn't saving lives?' Laurel guessed. 'Except they're not like that with Riley. Or are they?'

'Riley's always been different.'

His voice sounded rough, as if it carried the weight of a thousand slights, of a hundred times he'd not been as good. Laurel wondered for a moment if that was how Melissa had felt those first sixteen years.

She waited, silent in the dark, until he was ready to fill the void with his story.

'Riley was always the golden boy, from the moment

he was born. I was…eight, I guess, so old enough to re-member life without him. Before him everything just seemed normal. Probably because I didn't know any-thing else. But when Riley was born…' He sighed. 'He was their miracle boy. The baby they never thought they'd be able to have. The doctors had warned them, after they had me, that my mother might struggle. But you've met my parents. They don't give up without a fight. And they love to celebrate their victories.'

'So Riley was a victory to them?' Laurel shifted a little closer, tugging the duvet up to her shoulders to keep warm.

'Riley was *everything* to them. It was like I ceased to exist.'

'I know that feeling,' Laurel said, and the image of her father's face when he'd seen her in Angela and Me-lissa's house for the first time filled her mind. That was the moment when she'd realised that her father had a new life, a new daughter. That he didn't need her any more.

Dan's arm snaked around her shoulder, pulling her against his side, and the warmth of his body took the chill from her thoughts.

'I suppose you do,' he said. 'I guess we're more alike than I would ever have thought.'

'Both older siblings of a more famous brother or sis-ter?' Laurel guessed. 'Or both the least favoured child?'

'Either or,' Dan said easily. 'You and me…we're the ones in the shadows, aren't we? The ones who just get on with the business of living.'

The business of living. She liked that. She liked the idea that her life could just carry on going, regardless of what Melissa chose to do. That she still had her own life, her own value, when the spotlight of Melissa's fame moved on again, as it always would.

'I guess we are,' she said. 'It's nice to have someone who understands for a change.'

And strange to think that if it hadn't been for Melissa's last-minute change of heart about the wedding favours they might never have been in a position to discover that about each other.

Suddenly the idea of making it through the week without Dan by her side felt…impossible.

'So, what did you do?' she asked. 'When you realised you could never live up to Riley in their eyes?'

It was something she often wondered about herself. Whether, if she'd known about Melissa earlier, if her father had left when she was a baby rather than a teenager, her life would have been different. Would she still have spent her whole adult life trying to be good enough? She certainly wouldn't have spent the last sixteen years trying to make amends to Melissa for something she knew in her heart wasn't even her fault.

Maybe Melissa would have tried to make amends to her, impossible as that sounded.

'Do? Nothing,' Dan said. 'Well. Not really. I mean, I knew I couldn't be what my parents, what everybody wanted me to be. I couldn't be Riley. So I decided to do the opposite. I rebelled in basically every possible direction for years. Then I joined the army straight out of school, more as a way to escape than anything else.'

'The army? How did that work out for you?'

Dan gave her a rueful smile. 'Turned out I didn't like them telling me what to do any more than I liked my parents doing it. I served my time, got out the minute I could and moved to LA.'

'And became a stuntman?'

Dan shrugged. 'It was a job, and I was good at it. I had the training, and the control, and I knew how to make sure people didn't get hurt. Soon enough I had more work than I could handle, which is why I set up Black Ops Stunts.'

'You'd think that would be enough to make your parents proud.'

'Any parents but mine,' Dan joked, but Laurel could hear the pain under the flippant words. 'At least in the army I was doing something of value, even if it wasn't what they wanted. But in LA no one even knows it's me. I think that's what drives them crazy. They're all about the recognition, the fame.'

'And you're not.'

'It's the ultimate rebellion, I guess.'

How crazy. And she'd thought *her* family were dysfunctional. At least no one expected her to be famous— that was Melissa's job. In fact she wasn't sure what they wanted from her at all.

And all she wanted was to be good enough for them at last. To earn her place back in her family.

Melissa's wedding was her chance to do that.

'So. Your turn,' Dan said. 'I've heard how Melissa tells your story. How do *you* tell it?'

'Pretty much the same, I guess,' Laurel said with a small shrug. The facts were the horrible, horrible facts, and nothing she said could change that.

'Tell me anyway,' he said.

Laurel shifted under the covers, sitting cross-legged as she twisted to face him. Her side of the story… She didn't think she'd ever told that before.

'Okay… Well, until I was sixteen everything was

perfectly normal. Normal parents, normal house, normal school, normal teenage angst. Then one day my dad came home from work and said he was leaving.'

She took a deep breath and for a horrible moment she could feel tears burning behind her eyes. She hoped Dan wouldn't be able to see in the darkness.

'My mum followed him upstairs, and I could hear her sobbing and shouting while he packed his bags. Then he came downstairs, kissed me on the forehead, said he'd see me very soon and left.'

The pain didn't fade. It stung all over again as she remembered it.

'And did you?' he asked. 'See him soon, I mean?'

Laurel nodded. 'I didn't figure out what was really going on until a few days later. I was busy taking care of Mum, so I didn't leave the house much. But eventually I had to go out for some shopping. I kept my head down at the supermarket, but it didn't take long for me to realise that people were whispering and pointing at me. I started listening to those whispers…and that's how I found out that my dad had another daughter. Another family—another wife, to all intents and purposes. And he'd chosen them over me.'

Okay, never mind the other stuff. *That*, right there, was the killer. That was the part that burned every day.

'Anyway, for a while I tried to ignore it. I had Mum to look after and she…she just fell apart when I told her I knew what had happened. Maybe she could deny it if no one else knew. But once I confirmed what Dad had told her…it was like she gave up completely.'

Laurel shuddered at the memory. All those horrible days coming home from school to find her mum in the exact same position she'd left her at eight-twenty that morning. She'd tried so hard to be enough for her mother, to be reason enough for her to come back to the land of the living, to give her the love she'd lost when her dad had left.

But she'd never been able to fill the hole in her mother's heart that her father's walking out had left. And her mother had never been able to forgive her for being her father's daughter.

It was horrible to think it, but Laurel couldn't help but believe that her mum moving away to Spain eight years ago to live with an old schoolfriend was the best thing that could have happened to their relationship. Postcards and the odd phone call were much easier than dealing with each other in person.

'Eventually, once it was really clear he wasn't ever coming back, I confronted him.' Laurel continued her story, twisting her hands around each other. 'It was easy enough to find out where he was living with...*them*. People were falling over themselves to tell me.'

'Probably wanted to follow and watch,' Dan muttered.

'Probably,' Laurel agreed. 'He looked shocked to see me. Like his two worlds were colliding and he didn't like it—even though it was all his fault. Eventually he invited me in...introduced me to Melissa and her mother. We had the world's most awkward cup of tea, and then... I left.'

'That was it?' Dan asked, sounding confused. 'You didn't yell, scream at him? Anything?'

Laurel shook her head, smiling faintly. 'Melissa's mother, Angela, explained it to me. I'd had my fair share—I'd had sixteen years of a loving, doting father that Melissa had missed out on. And now it was her turn.'

Dan frowned. 'And you bought that?'

'It was the truth,' Laurel said with a small shrug. 'What else was there to say? He didn't want us any more—he wanted them. And Melissa *had* missed out.'

And she'd been making Laurel pay for it ever since.

'But that can't be your whole life,' Dan said. 'Everything didn't stop when you turned sixteen.'

'Sometimes it feels like it did,' Laurel admitted. Then she sighed. 'What happened next? Um… I went away to university, studied subjects that were utterly useless in the real world. Got a job at a small events company and worked my way up. Met up with Benjamin again in London and started dating—you already know how that ended. Then last year I decided it was time to go out on my own and start my own wedding planning business.'

'And Melissa hired you for her wedding.'

Laurel nodded. 'See? It pretty much always comes back to her in the end.'

'I know the feeling,' Dan said wryly. 'Trust me, when you're Riley Black's brother you spend a lot of time in the shadows, too. It's like you said—we understand each other. Which is why I'm going to ask you again. Why are you scared of Melissa?'

Sighing, Laurel stretched out her legs in front of her, and on impulse rested her head against his shoulder. Why couldn't constant support and understanding somehow magically come without having to actually *talk* about things? She wasn't used to having to talk about herself instead of Melissa. She didn't like it.

'I'm not scared of her. Not exactly…' she began.

Dan snorted. 'That's not how it looked to me.'

'Oh, really? Perhaps that was because you were egging her on.' Laurel bristled. 'Don't think I didn't notice how you suddenly started playing up the close body contact and the kisses on the top of the head the moment she arrived.'

Dan's laugh was utterly unrepentant. 'Can you blame me? I mean, what's the point of doing this if we can't enjoy it.'

'And you enjoyed upsetting my sister?'

'No,' he said slowly. 'But I'm not going to deny that reminding her that she's not the only thing that exists in the universe—let alone the only thing that actually matters—felt kind of good.'

Laurel sighed. 'I know what you mean. Melissa…she gets a little self-focussed. I don't know if it's a celebrity thing, or a no-father-until-she-was-sixteen thing—'

'I think it's a Melissa thing,' Dan interrupted. 'Yeah, she had some issues growing up. And, yeah, now she's a big star. But that doesn't mean she should be able to get away with treating everyone else like they don't matter.'

Laurel looked at him, trying to make out his features in the darkness. The same fears she'd felt earlier rose up inside her and she knew she had to ask. 'Are you planning on trying to stop the wedding? I mean, if you think so little of Melissa…are you really going to let her marry your brother?'

Dan sighed. 'The thing is—and this is one of those things Melissa doesn't understand—it's not up to me. I don't get to say who my brother falls in love with, or when. Do I want to make sure that he understands who he's marrying, make sure she's not lying to him about anything? Sure. But stop the wedding…' He shook his head. 'Like I told Melissa. True love doesn't work to order.'

'You meant that? I figured you were just winding her up.'

She felt him shrug, his T-shirt rubbing against her bare arms under the blanket. 'In my experience love is the most unpredictable—and inconvenient—thing in the world.'

He sounded more resigned than bitter, which Laurel took as a good sign. But his comments still left her with more questions than answers.

'You've been in love before?'

The way he'd said it, she knew he meant real love. The for ever, all-encompassing kind. Not whatever she'd shared with Benjamin. She wondered what that felt like—and how it must tear a person apart once it was gone.

'Once,' he said shortly. 'I don't recommend it.'

They sat in silence again, until Laurel felt a yawn creeping up her throat and covered her mouth as it stretched wide.

'You need to get some sleep.' Dan slid down, back into a lying position, taking her and the covers with him. 'Big day tomorrow.'

'I know.'

But going to sleep would mean breaking this fragile connection between them—and moving away from the comfort of his embrace. His arm around her, his body at her side…they were physical reminders that she wasn't alone in this. And here in the darkness, with Melissa's barbs and meanings twisting in her brain, she needed that.

But needy was never a good look on a person. For

all she knew he was starting to regret ever suggesting this thing. Maybe if he'd known how damaged she really was he wouldn't have bothered.

She wouldn't have blamed him.

With a breath so deep it was nearly a sigh, she shuffled back down into the bed and rolled away from him, turning her back as she tried to get comfortable enough on her side to sleep.

'Goodnight, Dan,' she whispered.

In response a hand brushed over her side, finding her fingers under the duvet and holding on. She clung to them, relief flooding through her.

'Goodnight, Laurel.' He squeezed her hand, then let go again. 'I'm glad we have each other this week.'

He wouldn't have said it in the daylight, Laurel realised. Even though it was the premise of their whole agreement, he wouldn't have admitted that need when she could see him.

But in the darkness…there was no need for secrets.

Laurel smiled into the night. 'Me too.'

Laurel was already gone when Dan woke up the next morning, and for a brief, stupid moment he felt his heart clench at her absence. Another woman gone—except he wasn't trying to keep this one, was he?

Keep it together, Black.

Rolling over, he squinted at his watch on the bedside table. Eleven-thirty. No wonder he was waking alone. Laurel must have been up early and working, while he slept off his jet lag and too much champagne.

He'd feel guiltier if it hadn't been the best night's sleep he'd had in years.

Not that he was putting that down to Laurel being

in the bed with him. But maybe it was those shared confidences in the darkness, the reassurance that he wasn't alone in dealing with his family for once. Even the memory of his mother's face as Laurel went on about the importance of following a dream. All of it had added up to let him feel…what, exactly? Safe? Secure? He'd been those things for years, except when he was making a movie. Except it wasn't *physical* safety he'd felt. More a feeling of…*home*.

Which was crazy—and clearly the jet lag talking, because he was three thousand miles away from home, and stuck there all week.

But at least he was stuck there with Laurel.

And that really wasn't a thought he wanted to examine too closely.

He showered and dressed quickly, whistling as he ran a towel over his damp hair. It was bitterly cold outside, but his hair was short enough to dry fast, hopefully without freezing. Dan pulled his leather jacket on over his jeans and jumper and headed out to find his fake girlfriend.

'All the other guests are already down at the Frost Fair, sir.'

The man behind the reception desk eyed him with suspicion. Dan wasn't a hundred per cent sure if he was concerned about what Dan might have been up to all morning, or if he felt that he wasn't suitably attired or recognisable enough to be attending the wedding in the first place. Either way, Dan was satisfied with the outcome. He didn't *want* to look the same as all those overpaid mannequins, and making people worry about what he might have planned was always fun. So he flashed the receptionist a smile, and headed out in the direction of the river.

He heard the Frost Fair before he smelt it, and smelt it long before he saw it. The scent of cinnamon and apple and winter hung in the air, all the way up to Morwen Hall, and the sound of laughter, conversation and strange music hit him as he turned the corner down to the water.

Dan smiled at the sounds, grinning even more widely as a veritable village of wooden stalls and rustic huts came into view along the riverbank. It looked like fun—and utterly unlike the showbiz parties the women he dated from time to time were always trying to drag him along to or use him to get into.

This, he knew, had to be all Laurel—not Melissa. Yes, it was a spectacle, and impressive. But it was also something new, something different, and relaxed in a way Melissa wouldn't even have begun to imagine when she'd been planning her wedding. But more than anything it was *fun*. Not a statement, not the latest trend, just pure, wintry fun.

And fun this week was always down to Laurel, he was learning.

Dan made his way through the rows of stalls and entertainment booths, helping himself to some spiced apple cider and admiring the wood carvings and painted pottery on the way. Local craftspeople, apparently, showcasing their wares.

He nodded to himself. Yep, definitely all Laurel. Except his wedding planner was nowhere to be seen.

Sipping his cider, he continued his search, nodding at acquaintances as he passed and ducking behind a stall providing a hog roast for the guests when he spotted his parents across the way.

He finally found Laurel at the far end of the Frost Fair, looking completely out of place in her smart coat and holding her clipboard. The whole day felt so relaxed—like a holiday—but Laurel was still all work, keeping everything running smoothly for Melissa. Where *was* the bride, anyway? Had she even come down to see the festival Laurel had put on for her? Somehow Dan doubted it.

Seemed to him that Laurel spent far too much of her life trying to satisfy her half-sister, to make up for a past that wasn't even her fault. And in return Melissa spent *her* time making life even more difficult for Laurel.

And probably, in the future, for Riley. Dan's gaze darted around the crowd. He should find his brother—try to have that conversation they needed to have. Hopefully while Melissa was distracted with something—anything—else.

Except... Laurel looked harried. Not that she'd admit it, but there was a tiny line between her eyebrows that he only remembered seeing before when she was talking to Melissa.

Dan was learning that Melissa wasn't so hard to read, or to understand. Making sure Riley understood what he was getting into might be another matter, but it was one that could wait until the stag do tonight, he decided. Dan stopped looking for Riley and stepped forward to see what he could do to make Laurel's day better. After all, wasn't that what fake boyfriends were for?

'I'm sure that can be arranged,' she was saying to a discontented wedding guest, ignoring the phone buzzing in her hand.

She kept a permanent smile on her face, nodding

politely as the guest launched into another diatribe—
something about the brand of bottled water in the mini-
bar, from what Dan could overhear.

Definitely not something that mattered.

'You'll excuse me.' He flashed his most charming
smile at the complaining guest, then yanked Laurel towards him by her elbow. 'But I'm afraid I have to borrow my girlfriend for a moment. Wedding emergency.'

The guest looked displeased, but didn't argue, so
Dan took advantage and dragged Laurel out of view,
behind an apple cider stall.

'Was he seriously complaining about water?' he
asked as Laurel's phone started to ring again.

'Yes.' She lifted the phone, but paused before pressing answer. 'Wait—what's the emergency?'

Dan shrugged. 'I need a tour guide for this Frost
Fair of yours.'

Raising one eyebrow, Laurel pressed 'answer', but
the phone stopped ringing seconds before her finger
connected with the screen. 'Sorry. I'd better—'

Dan reached out and took the phone from her. 'What
about my emergency?'

'That's not an emergency. That was Eloise calling.
She might have an *actual* wedding emergency that really needs my help.'

'Like?'

'Like… I don't know. They were having final dress
fittings this morning. Maybe something went wrong.
Maybe the maid of honour's dress can't be refitted for
Eloise and she's going to make me do it. Maybe Melissa
now hates her dress. Maybe—'

Her face was turning red, and Dan wasn't sure they

could blame the cold for it. Plus, that line between her eyebrows had returned and brought a friend.

He handed her back the phone. 'Fine. Call. But only because I'm scared you might hyperventilate with all those "maybes" otherwise.'

Laurel redialled quickly, and Dan waited as the phone rang. And rang. And rang.

'Obviously not that much of an emergency, then,' he said as it clicked through to voicemail. 'Looks like you have time to show me around this place after all.'

Laurel glared at him, and he laughed. 'Oh, come on! Won't it be more fun than listening to people complain about water?'

'I suppose…'

'I'll buy you an apple cider,' he offered.

'All the drinks are free,' Laurel pointed out.

Dan shrugged. 'Then you can have two.'

She rolled her eyes, but put her phone away in her pocket, her forehead clear and uncreased again. He had her now—he knew it. 'Come on, then. Let's go.'

CHAPTER SIX

IT FELT STRANGE, wandering around the Frost Fair with
Dan, pointing out the different stalls, introducing him
to the various local craftspeople she'd researched and
persuaded to come along for the day and showcase their
work. Strange because it didn't feel like work, but also
because she wasn't used to having someone so interested in what she was doing. Even Melissa had rou-
tinely zoned out when it had come to talking about the
parts of the Wedding Extravaganza that didn't exclusively star the bride.

It should have felt odder still when, somewhere between the hog roast and the dreamcatcher stall, Dan
reached out and took her hand, holding it warm and
tight within his own. Benjamin had never really been
one for public displays of affection, unless he was trying to prove a point—usually to keep her in line.

Really, she should have got a clue that he didn't think
she was good enough for him long before she'd caught
him with Coral.

When she glanced up at Dan he shrugged. 'People
might be watching,' he said, his eyes already on the
next food stand.

But he didn't let go of her fingers.

The weird thing was, people really *weren't* watching. Nobody cared about them. She'd expected this week to be five days of people staring and pointing, knowing that she was Melissa's half-sister and the reason the bride hadn't had a father for her whole childhood. But as it turned out no one much cared about the wedding planner—the sister who wasn't even a bridesmaid. Not even when she was supposedly dating the groom's brother.

Nobody cared. Nobody expected anything from her. Not even that she try and live up to Melissa. It was amazingly freeing.

For about thirty seconds, until Dan said, 'So, I hear people have been talking about us. After last night.'

'What?' Laurel looked up, startled, from the dream-catcher in her hand. 'When? I haven't heard anything.'

Dan shrugged. 'I caught a few whispers on the wind today, that's all. Let's just say Melissa's outburst at the drinks thing last night didn't go unnoticed.'

Oh, well that made more sense. It wasn't her and Dan they were interested in. It was only the reaction they'd provoked in Melissa.

It was all always about Melissa in the end. And Laurel found she preferred it that way.

'Do you mind?' Dan asked.

'That they're talking about us?' Laurel shook her head. 'They're not really. They're talking about Melissa, and we just happen to be nearby. That's all.'

'What about Eloise? Do you mind that Melissa made her maid of honour instead of you?'

For a man who looked the stoic and silent type, he certainly asked a lot of questions. And, while she expected him to ask them about Melissa, she couldn't quite get used to him asking about *her*. About her feelings, her thoughts—not just how she related to her sister.

Maybe it was because he was in the same situation as her in lots of ways. How had he put it? They were the ones in the shadows. And Melissa and Riley cast very long ones.

'What about you?' she returned, twisting the question back on him. 'Are you bitter that Riley chose Noah as best man rather than you?'

Dan laughed, shaking his head. Under the bright and icy winter sky his eyes looked bluer than ever. She almost wished she'd been able to see him like this when they'd talked the night before—except then maybe neither one of them would have said so much.

'I've never been the best man—or even the better man—before,' he said, but despite his denial there was just a hint of bitterness behind his words. 'Why would I want to start now?'

She wanted to ask him what he meant, but before she could find the words a cheer went up from where a crowd was forming, just around the bend in the river.

'Come on,' Dan said, tugging her along behind him. 'I want to see what's going on over there.'

'It'll be the troupe of actors I hired,' she explained as they wove their way through the crowd. 'They're performing some Shakespeare scenes and such.'

'No one cheers like that for Shakespeare.'

Laurel was about to argue the point when they finally reached the front of the crowd. She blinked up at the small wooden stage she'd seen being assembled that morning. On it stood a beautiful redhead in a gorgeous green and gold gown, and a man she was more used to seeing on the movie screen than wearing a doublet and hose a mere metre or two away.

'Is that—?'

'Eloise and Noah,' Dan confirmed. 'Guess we know what she was calling about before.'

'And why she didn't answer.'

As they watched, Noah and Eloise launched into a segment from *Much Ado About Nothing*, bickering as only Benedick and Beatrice could.

'They're good,' Dan observed, clapping as the section came to an end. 'Some of these Hollywood actors can't act to save their lives. Would have figured Noah for one of them, but actually...he's not half bad.'

He said it easily, as if it didn't hurt him at all to compliment the guy his brother had chosen to be his best man over him. But his earlier words still rang in Laurel's brain, and as Noah and Eloise started in on their next scene she couldn't help but ask the question she'd been thinking about ever since.

'What did you mean? When you said you weren't ever the best man before?' Because to her mind he'd been pretty perfect since the moment his car had picked her up in London the day before.

'It doesn't matter.' Dan didn't look down at her as he spoke, keeping his eyes focussed on the stage.

Laurel scowled with frustration. 'It matters to me. Is it because of your parents?'

'No.' Dan sighed, and scrubbed a hand over his hair. 'You're not going to give this up, are you?'

He sounded resigned. *Good.*

'Unlikely.' She gave him an encouraging smile.

'Fine. I wasn't talking about my parents. I could have

been, I suppose. But, no. I was thinking about my wife, actually.'

The cold winter air chilled her blood as his words sank in. 'Your wife? You're married?'

Of all the possibilities that had floated through her mind since they'd started their fake relationship that really hadn't been one of them. How could he pretend to be dating her if he already had a wife back in California? No wonder his parents had been so disapproving.

'Ex-wife,' Dan clarified, and the world shifted back to something approaching normality. 'Sorry. It's been... two years now, since she left.'

Well, that made more sense, at least. Apart from the bit where she'd apparently left him. Who would leave Dan? From what Laurel knew of him, on one day's acquaintance, tying a man like Dan down to marriage must have been a feat and a half in the first place. What sort of idiot would go through all that and then just *leave*?

It didn't make sense.

'She left? Why?'

Dan's smirk was lopsided, almost sad. 'She found someone better. Why else? I was just a stuntman, remember. Even if I *did* own my own company, even if I *was* on my way to being a success. She was an actress—and an ambitious one, too. I couldn't match up to a Hollywood star, now, could I? I was just the stand-in, same as always, until something better came along.'

The sad part was that it made sense, in a twisted sort of way. As much as Laurel hoped that Riley and Melissa truly were in love, she knew that part of the attraction for her sister was Riley's A-List status. Even Benjamin... If she was honest with herself, Laurel had to admit that a small part of the attraction she'd felt for him came from knowing that he'd be seen as a good match for her. Why should Dan's ex-wife be any different? But for someone like Dan, who'd already spent his life since the age of eight knowing he'd been replaced in his parents' affections by his brother, knowing that he could never match up...

'Ouch, that must have hurt. I'm so sorry.'

He shrugged. 'Don't know why I was surprised, really. It wasn't like Cassie was the first woman to want me just until she got a shot at the real thing—a proper star. She was just the only one I was stupid enough to marry.'

The way he said it—without emotion, calm and even—made her heart ache. She knew how it felt to be cast aside for a better option—first by her father, then by Benjamin. But Dan... He seemed to have made a profession out of it. Of being the one they called on set only to do the dangerous work, never to get the credit. To be replaced by the actor with top billing. And it wasn't only his work. Apparently his relationships had followed the exact same pattern.

And that was just crazy.

'Why?' she asked. 'Why just...accept that? Why always be the stand-in?'

'What else is there?'

He hadn't known anything else, she realised. Not since he was eight and his brother came along and usurped him. It had been bad enough for her at sixteen, but at least she'd still had her mum...in a way. Dan hadn't had anyone left at all.

Were they both just doomed to repeat the same old patterns? Not if she could help it.

'You know, Melissa might be the big star in our family, but I like to think I can at least be the heroine of my *own* story,' Laurel said. 'You don't even seem to believe you can be that.'

'The heroine of your own story?'

Dan raised his eyebrows, and Laurel felt the heat rising to her cheeks.

'What kind of heroine scampers around after her half-sister, giving up everything to make her day perfect?'

'Cinderella,' Laurel snapped back, without thinking, and Dan tipped his head back as he laughed, long and loud.

'Waiting for your prince. Of course. I'm sure he'll be along soon enough.' Dan flashed her a sharp smile. 'And until then maybe I'll do.'

'Maybe you will.'

They were standing too close, Laurel realised suddenly. As the conversation had turned more private, more intimate, they'd each leaned in. Talking quietly under the laughter and cheers of the crowd, they'd needed to be close to hear one other. Dan had moved his hand from hers and rested it at her waist instead. His arm was around her back, holding her close to him as they spoke.

Laurel stared up into his bright blue eyes and swallowed hard at what she saw there.

'Kiss her again!'

The cry went up through the crowd and broke the spell between them. Laurel jerked her gaze away, turning her attention back to the stage, where Noah was kissing Eloise very enthusiastically.

'That looks like fun,' Dan commented, and Laurel's face turned warm. Too warm.

Because it *did* look like fun. But she didn't want to be kissing Noah Cross, film star extraordinaire, no matter how good-looking he was.

She wanted to be kissing Dan.

Wrong place, wrong time, and categorically not her prince.

'It really does,' she breathed, and grabbed Dan's hand as he started to pull away.

She knew what he was thinking now. And she couldn't let him think it a moment longer. Turning her body towards his, until she was practically pressed up against him, she decided to take a chance.

If she was the heroine of her own story, then it was high time she got kissed. Even if it *was* only pretend. She might have given up on relationships until she found the right one, but that didn't mean she couldn't keep in practice in the meantime. And what better way than with a fake boyfriend? In a relationship that couldn't go anywhere because it had never existed to start with?

'You know, if we really want this charade of ours to be believable it's not just our backstories we need to get right.'

'No?' Dan asked, eyebrows raised. 'What else were you thinking?'

'It needs to *look* real, too,' Laurel said, her mouth dry. 'It needs to look every bit as real as Noah and Eloise do up there.'

'You're right.' Dan tilted his head, ducking it slightly until his lips were only a couple of centimetres from hers. 'So...what? Are you asking me to kiss you?'

'Well, if you want to be convincing...'

'I'd hate to fall down on the fake boyfriend job,' Dan murmured.

And then his lips were against hers, strong and sure, and Laurel's whole body woke up at last.

The only problem was it didn't feel fake at all.

The crowd cheered, and just for a moment Dan thought they might actually be cheering for him. For him and Laurel and a kiss that would have broken records, if such things existed.

If their relationship was fake—and it was, he mustn't forget that—they were both rather good actors. *They* should be the ones up there on the silver screen, convincing the audience they were in love. Heaven knew, if he hadn't known better, that kiss might even have convinced him.

But he always knew better. He knew exactly who he was, and how much he could expect. And it was never everything.

Except for one moment…with Laurel in his arms… he'd wanted to believe there was a chance. A possibility of something more.

And then, of course, she'd pulled away.

Her cheeks were pink, her eyes bright, and the smile on her lips couldn't all be pretend. But he'd kissed enough women to know it wasn't sufficient for him to be a great kisser. They wanted something more—something he didn't have. A kiss was only a kiss.

'I need to get back to the hall,' Laurel said.

On stage, Noah and Eloise took their bows and the crowd began to disperse.

'I need to get things ready for the hen night.'

'Sure,' Dan said, letting her go easily. At least he

hoped it looked easy. It didn't feel it. 'Don't let me keep you from your work.'

She hesitated before leaving, though. 'I'll see you later?'

'We're sharing a room, remember.'

Not just a room. A bed.

If last night had been difficult…trying to sleep beside her, knowing he couldn't touch her…how much more impossible would it be tonight, now he knew how it felt to have her in his arms, to kiss her like that?

He was doomed.

'Better make sure you don't drink so much at the stag night that you don't make it back there, then.'

'The stag night. Right.'

Where he would try to corner his brother alone, make sure he really knew what he was letting himself in for with this marriage. He mustn't forget that. *That* was why he was here, after all. Not to play make-believe love affairs with Laurel.

Except after he spoke to Riley he'd have to go back to his room and sleep with Laurel. No, *next* to Laurel. An important distinction. Unless…

'I'll see you later, then. Although I might be in bed by the time you get there.'

And with that Laurel stretched up onto her tiptoes and pressed another kiss against his mouth. Almost swift enough to be a goodbye, but just long enough to hint at a possibility. A promise, maybe, for later.

Suddenly Dan knew that, no matter how badly his conversation with his brother went, he would *not* be getting drunk with Riley and his friends that night.

Just in case.

* * *

Up in the hotel bar, Laurel tied pink and purple balloons to ribbons and hung them from the wooden beams that rose from the bar and along the ceiling. Each balloon had a piece of paper in it—a question for the bride, the maid of honour, or one of the bridesmaids. Laurel had tried to get a look at them, but Melissa had written them herself, then folded them up tight and watched as Laurel blew up the balloons and put the notes inside. Once she was satisfied that Laurel hadn't read them, she'd departed, leaving Laurel to finish organising the rest of the hen party.

The balloon game was only one of many Laurel had planned. The way she figured it, the busier she kept all the guests with silly party games, the less time there was for anything to go desperately wrong. There were a lot of famous people in attendance, and a lot of egos. The last thing Laurel wanted was a row at the hen night.

All she wanted was for everything to go smoothly, no one to get too drunk, and for everyone to go to bed nice and early so she could go back to her room and...

Well...

What exactly was she going to do? Wasn't that the question of the day?

In the moments after that kiss she'd known exactly what she wanted to do that night—seduce Dan. But after twenty minutes of Melissa and balloons, and then another twenty of checklists and setting up, and worrying about everything that still needed to be done, her resolve was failing.

Maybe she was the heroine of her own life, but this week she was also a wedding planner—and that had to come first. Once she'd done her job—and done it well—she could get back to thinking about her own love life. That was the plan. Wait for the right time, the right place, then let herself think about finding the right man.

Except by then Dan would be on his way back to LA and she'd have missed her chance. He might not be her prince, but he was an excellent fake boyfriend, and it seemed silly not to take advantage of that. After all, heaven only knew how long it would take her prince to come riding up. And a girl had needs.

Which led her back to the seduction idea.

Laurel sighed, and decided just to get on with work for now. Maybe the 'Make a Male Body Part out of modelling clay' game would inspire her. Or put her off for life. It really could go either way.

She'd just finished setting up the tequila shots on the bar when the door opened. She turned, smiling, expecting it to be Melissa, or maybe even Dan…

'Oh. It's you.' Smile fading, Laurel glared at her ex-boyfriend. 'What do you want?'

Benjamin put up his hands in a sign of surrender. 'I come in peace. No need for the death glare. I thought we decided we could still be friends?'

'*You* decided,' Laurel replied.

She hadn't had a say in the matter. Benjamin had said, 'We'll still be friends, of course,' and that had been the end of the discussion.

'I thought about it some more, and decided that my friends wouldn't treat me the way you did.'

Funny how once you decided you were the heroine in your own story it became a lot easier to speak the truth to people who didn't respect that. Just yesterday, when she'd seen him again for the first time, she'd dived for cover behind a pretend relationship. Today, after talking with Dan, she'd realised a few things. And one of those was that she had no place in her life for people like Benjamin.

'Oh, Laurel.' Benjamin shook his head sadly. 'You always were so naive. You really are going to need to toughen up if you want to survive in this world, you know.'

Was that really what she needed to do? Develop a tough outer shell that would help her ignore all the awful things that people did? It might at least help her to deal with Melissa. But on the other hand…

'Is that why you love Coral? Because she's tough?'

'I love Coral because she's driven. Ambitious.'

I'm ambitious. Just not the way you wanted.

Gratitude flooded her as she realised how lucky she was to have escaped her romance with Benjamin when she had. She might not have enjoyed the circumstances at the time, but with some distance between them she now knew it was the best thing that could have happened to her. Imagine if she'd gone on believing that he truly was her prince… She might not even have recognised the real thing when it *did* come along. And that would have been a very sorry state of affairs.

'She's a journalist—did you know?' Benjamin went on, looking stupidly proud of his new fiancée.

'Really? I thought she was a gossip columnist.'

It was petty, perhaps, but since Laurel had been responsible for getting every guest to sign a non-disclosure agreement about the wedding, banning them from speaking to the media, publishing photos online, or doing anything else that would jeopardise the exclusive agreement Melissa and Riley had signed with *Star!* magazine, she felt it was relevant.

She'd actually argued against her being invited to the wedding at all—something that Melissa had decided was sour grapes.

'Really, Laurel, you have to grow up. We're all adults and professionals here. We know how the industry works—well, everyone except you, anyway. Just because she won Benjamin, you can't be petty about it.'

Petty. If Benjamin and Coral had betrayed Melissa the way they had Laurel, she was sure they'd have been blacklisted from every celebrity event involving Melissa for all time. But Laurel was being petty for being concerned that a gossip columnist might take a chance and ruin the exclusive with *Star!* magazine, so that Melissa and Riley would have to forfeit the obscenely large fee they were being paid.

Benjamin scowled. 'She's very talented.'

'I'm sure she is.' Suspicion prickled at the back of her neck. This wasn't about being friends—that was rapidly becoming obvious. So what *was* it about?

'What exactly do you want from me, Benjamin? Because, in case you hadn't noticed, I have got a wedding to organise here.'

'Of course. For your sister—sorry, half-sister.'

Benjamin's expression formed into a perfect facsimile of concern, but somehow Laurel was sure it was fake.

'How *are* things between the two of you? I know your relationship has always been difficult, and I can't imagine that the stresses of organising her wedding have helped.'

Laurel's eyes narrowed. 'What do you want, Benjamin?'

'I'm sure you weren't always this blunt.' He sighed, and dropped the fake concern. 'The magazine Coral works for—they've ordered her to get details of the wedding, and the dress, so that they can get them up on the website *before* the *Star!* exclusive goes to print.'

'She can't.' Laurel shook her head. 'She's signed a non-disclosure agreement. If she gives them *anything* she'll be sued.'

'I know. But someone else could.'

'Everyone attending the wedding signed the agreement. It was to be sent back with the RSVPs.' Which made it one of the more absurd aspects of her job, Laurel conceded, but she'd done it.

'What about you?' Benjamin asked.

Laurel froze. She hadn't RSVP'd because she hadn't needed an invitation. She'd signed a contract for the job, sure, but that had been *her* newly developed standard contract, and Melissa had barely looked at it.

She hadn't signed a non-disclosure agreement. She could tell anyone she liked about the details of this wedding and there was nothing Melissa could do about it.

'You didn't sign one, did you?' A Cheshire cat-like grin spread across Benjamin's face. 'I told Coral you wouldn't have. Melissa is too sure of you—too certain that you're under her thumb—to even think that she needed to get you to sign. This is perfect!'

'No. No, it's not.' Laurel gripped the back of the chair in front of her, knuckles whitening. 'I'm a professional. I still have an obligation to my client.'

'Really?' Benjamin raised his eyebrows. 'After the way she's always treated you? Just imagine her face when her *Star!* deal goes down the pan. Wouldn't that be glorious? And…if revenge isn't enough for you… Coral's employers are willing to pay good money for the information. Especially if you can get a snap of the wedding dress before the big day. Serious money, Laurel. The sort of money any new business needs.'

'My business is fine.'

'Sure—for now. But be honest. How much is Melissa paying you? Is it a fair rate? Or did she insist on a family discount?'

Her face was too hot, her mind reeling as she remembered Dan asking almost the same question, and the pitying look in his eye when he realised she wasn't being paid at all.

'The exposure of such a big wedding is great for my business.'

Benjamin barked out a laugh. 'Good grief. Is she paying you at *all*? Beyond expenses, I mean? This wedding must have been all of your billable hours for months now. Whatever she's paying you, I can tell it isn't enough.'

He leant forward, into her personal space, and Laurel recoiled.

'She *owes* you, Laurel. And we'd like to help make her pay up—one way or another. Help us out and Melissa gets everything she deserves. So do you. It's win-win.'

'She's my sister,' Laurel whispered.

Benjamin shook his head. 'She really isn't.' Straightening up, he turned and headed for the door. 'Just think about it, Laurel. But remember—you haven't got long to decide. We need whatever you can get *before* she walks down the aisle on Saturday.'

And then he was gone, leaving Laurel with a lot of very uncomfortable thoughts.

CHAPTER SEVEN

WHERE ON EARTH was the best man? Dan scanned the room, trying to find Noah, but he was nowhere to be seen. Not that Dan could blame him; if he'd been able to find an excuse to get out of the stupid stag night he'd have left hours ago. Noah was probably cosied up in bed with the maid of honour—and more power to him.

If Laurel hadn't been stuck throwing the hen do Dan might well have dragged her off to bed himself.

It was all he'd been able to think about ever since that kiss. That knockout, blindsiding kiss.

Or at least it had been until the stag party had got out of hand.

Riley had insisted on throwing the stag party himself, with no help from Laurel. Dan assumed that Noah and his other mates had had a hand in it, though, because everyone knew Riley couldn't organise his way out of a paper bag.

The groom, in his infinite wisdom, had decided that his stag party would be an homage to frat movies past—complete with beer keg, red cups and some dubious-looking cigarettes over on the other side of the room that Dan wasn't investigating too closely.

Of course frat parties only ever ended one way—

with the good old frat boys drunk out of their minds and often getting into a brawl.

Riley had always liked his roles to look authentic, and by the time Dan had arrived—not late, but not exactly early either—it had been clear from his brother's slurred greeting that the conversation he'd hoped to have about Melissa, and love, and marriage, was firmly off the cards. So he'd settled down with a bottle of proper beer from the bar, and winced as he watched Riley tackling a yard of beer.

And things had only got worse from there.

Dan yanked his brother out of the way of his mate's flying fists and tossed him back into the chair behind him. Then he turned to the fighter, sighing when he saw that the drunken idiot intended to try and take *him* on next.

'No,' Dan said, with finality in his voice. 'We are *not* doing this.'

'Scared to fight me?'

The man could barely look in one direction, he was so out of it, but Dan couldn't fault his courage.

'Yeah, sure. That's exactly it.'

In one swift movement he'd caught the guy's fists, wrapping his hands behind his back and holding them there. Then he marched him across to the other side of the room, deposited him in the corner behind the pool table Riley had had brought in, and placed one foot lightly on his chest to hold him in place. Then he turned to address the room.

'Okay—here's what is going to happen next. I'm going to go take my brother back to his room and put him to bed. I'm also going to send some hotel staff up here to finish this party. I suggest that all of you go drink about a gallon of water, take a couple of aspirin, and get some sleep—so you can function well enough for whatever our beautiful bride has planned for you tomorrow.'

'Hey, why do *you* get to call time? We're having fun! It's a stag party, man.'

Dan rolled his eyes at the man who'd spoken. 'Yes, it is. But the stag has practically passed out already, there's no stripper coming, and honestly…? We're all a little old to be playing at frat boys.'

And he'd never felt quite as old as he did tonight. He was almost a decade older than a lot of these guys, but not all of them. And even they should be old enough to know better.

'Feel free to ignore my advice, boys. But I wouldn't want to be in your shoes tomorrow.'

With that, and feeling about a hundred years old, he went and retrieved Riley from where he was still slumped in his chair. Wrapping his brother's arm around his shoulders and hoisting him up onto his feet with an arm around his waist, he half led, half carried him out towards the elevators.

Fate, or just blind luck, meant he had to walk past the bar where the hen party was happening to get there. And just as they approached he saw Laurel step out into the corridor and stand there, her head tipped back to rest against the wall, her palms flat against it at her side, eyes closed.

'Long night?' he called out, and she turned her head, smiling as she opened her eyes to look at him.

'No longer than yours, by the look of things.'

Riley gave an incoherent mumble, and Dan rolled his eyes.

'I can't believe you let him organise his own frat-movie-themed stag do.'

Laurel shrugged. 'Melissa said as long as there weren't any strippers she didn't care what they got up to. And, quite frankly, I'm not being paid enough to worry about idiot boys.'

'Join the club.' He hefted Riley up again, to keep him from sliding out of his grasp and onto the carpet.

'Want a hand?' Laurel offered.

'I thought you weren't being paid enough?'

'This one's a freebie.' She met his eyes. 'Or you can pay me back later. Personally.'

Heat flared between them again, just as it had when they'd kissed that afternoon, and Dan mentally cursed his brother for being a lightweight.

'Help me get him to his room?' he asked, flashing her a grin. 'I promise I'll make it worth your while later.'

Laurel slipped under Riley's other arm, helping bear his weight as they lugged him towards the elevators. 'I'll hold you to that.'

'Please do.'

It took longer than Dan would have liked to get Riley settled. He was all for tossing him onto the bed and leaving him there, but Laurel insisted on removing his shoes and belt at least, and trying to get him to swallow some water before they lay him down in the recovery position.

Laurel left painkillers and a large glass of water on his bedside table, dimmed the lights, and placed a call down to Reception for someone to sneak in and check on him throughout the night.

'Well, it's not like Melissa's going to do it,' she

pointed out. 'I doubt he'll be with it enough to even notice, but I won't sleep if I'm worrying about him.'

If Dan had his way she might not be sleeping anyway, but he didn't mention that.

Laurel shut the door behind them, and suddenly it was just them again, heading back to their room like an old married couple at the end of the night.

'Are you...?' Laurel started, then trailed off. 'Did you enjoy the stag party? I mean, apart from the last part.'

'Not really.' Dan gave her a one-shoulder shrug. 'Not my kind of thing any more.'

'Frat parties? No, I guess not. So, what is?'

His kind of thing? *You. Naked. With me.* Yeah, that probably wasn't what she meant.

Laurel punched the button to call the elevator, and Dan felt his body tensing, getting warmer the closer they got to being alone with a bed. How had he ever imagined he'd be able to survive another celibate night after that kiss? He really hoped he didn't have to...

'My kind of thing?' he echoed as the elevator arrived and they both stepped in. The enclosed space felt airless, and Dan struggled to concentrate on the conversation. 'Uh... I don't know. Not Hollywood parties either, I guess. I just like...quiet nights. A few good friends, good food, quality drinks. Conversation.'

The sort of night he found almost impossible to have in Hollywood, even with his oldest friends. There was always someone new tagging along. Dan wasn't against new people in principle, but when they were only there to get a foot in the door of the industry...it got old pretty fast.

Laurel smiled up at him, her eyes warm and her lips

inviting. 'Same here. In fact...' She bit her lip. 'It kind of felt like that last night. With us.'

'Once we got rid of our families...yeah. It did.' Amazement flowed through him at the realisation. He'd known that last night had been something new, something meaningful. He just hadn't realised how close it had been to everything he wanted.

Except it was only pretend. And he wasn't anything close to what *she* wanted.

Laurel wanted everything—but all they could have was tonight.

He'd just have to hope it would be enough.

But he couldn't assume. Couldn't be sure that it was what she wanted unless he asked.

The doors opened and Laurel stepped out first, leading him towards their room. Dan paused at the door as she slid the key home.

'Wait.' He grabbed the door handle to hold it closed.

Laurel looked up at him in confusion. 'What's the matter?'

'Nothing. Just...' Dan shook his head, trying to rid himself of the confusion that came more from her presence—the scent of her, the feel of her—than the couple of beers he'd had at the stag party. He took a breath and tried again. 'Once we go in there... I liked last night. I liked spending it with you. And if that's what you want again I'm fine with that. But...'

'But...?'

Was that hope in her eyes? He couldn't be sure. But he had to take a chance that it was.

'When you kissed me today I realised...it could be more. *We* could be more. I know this isn't real—that this whole wedding is like a week out of time. But while we're here, pretending to be together…'

'Why not *really* pretend?'

She was closer now, suddenly, her curves pressing against his chest, one hand on his arm. And he knew from her smile, from her eyes, that she wanted this every bit as much as him.

Oh, thank goodness for that.

'Exactly.' He lowered his lips to hers, sinking into her embrace, letting her kiss overwhelm every one of his senses.

This. This was exactly where he was meant to be.

He wrapped his arms around her waist, pressing her up against the door, moaning against her mouth as she responded by twining her arms around his neck and holding him closer. He reached lower, boosting her up until her legs were around his middle and he could feel every inch of her against him…

'Inside,' she murmured against his mouth. 'Oh. The…the room. Not me. Yet.'

The room. The bedroom.

Geez, they were still in the hallway. What was she doing to him that he'd lost all track of space and time?

'Inside,' he agreed, reaching for the door handle behind her. 'One and then the other.'

It looked as if it was going to be a good night after all.

Later—much later, Laurel suspected, although she was too boneless with pleasure to check the time—they lay together in the darkness of the room, much as they had the night before, except with fewer clothes.

'You know, this fake relationship plan was a really good idea,' she said, her words coming out breathless.

Dan laughed. 'I do have them. Sometimes.'

'You do.' Even this—even knowing it was just for the week, just pretend—Laurel couldn't see it as a mistake. Even if the relationship was fake, the passion between them was real. So why shouldn't they indulge it...make the most of their time together? Everyone thought they were together anyway. This could only make the charade more realistic.

And a hell of a lot more fun.

There was time for 'perfect' later. Her prince would show up eventually. And in the meantime... She pressed a kiss against Dan's bare shoulder and his arm tightened around her.

'So,' he asked after a moment. 'How was your night?'

'Are you fishing for compliments? I'd have thought my enjoyment of the night was pretty obvious.'

She hadn't held anything back with him, she realised. With Benjamin, and the one serious boyfriend she'd had before him, she'd always been too concerned about how she looked or sounded, or what they were thinking about her, to really let go. To let herself fall into the pleasure.

With Dan, it hadn't mattered. He wasn't staying, so he couldn't leave her—not really. Leaving and leaving *her* were very different things, and Dan was already committed to the first. So what did it matter how she looked or sounded? As far as she could tell he was enjoying himself too much to notice anyway.

'I meant before we met up again,' he said, chuckling. 'But it's good to have confirmation all the same.'

The hen party. She'd almost forgotten about it—and

the conversation with Benjamin that had taken place before.

Laurel shifted, resting her head on Dan's chest as she spoke. His fingers tangled in her hair, teasing out strands as he smoothed it down. It felt strangely comforting...as if it might lull her into sleep if she stopped talking.

'The hen party was fine, I guess. By the time I left we'd done all the games—stupid party games Melissa found on the internet, mostly. Eloise disappeared ages ago, and the rest of them were settling in for tequila shots, so I figured no one would miss me.'

'Noah left early on, too. Reckon they're together.'

'Probably,' Laurel said. 'Although they'd almost certainly deny it if you asked them.'

'How was Melissa?' Dan asked.

'Oh, you know. Melissa-ish.'

In truth, she'd ordered everyone around, tried to humiliate Eloise, and made pointed comments about each of her bridesmaids. Laurel had been glad to escape when she had. She was under no illusions that she wouldn't have been the bride's next target.

'Fun.'

'Yeah.'

Benjamin's words from earlier came back to her, unbidden. *She owes you, Laurel. Help us out and Melissa gets everything she deserves.*

She tensed at the memory, and Dan's hand stopped moving through her hair in response.

'What? What did she do?'

'It wasn't her, for once.'

Sighing, Laurel sat up, tugging the duvet over her as she crossed her legs and looked down at him. She needed someone to talk to about Benjamin's offer, and who better than her fake boyfriend?

'I had a conversation with Benjamin. Before the party.'

This time it was Dan who tensed, his muscles suddenly hard and his jaw set. 'What did he say?'

Laurel took a breath. There was no way to make Benjamin's offer sound good. 'His fiancée, Coral, is a gossip columnist. Her magazine is offering big money to anyone who can get them a photo of Melissa's dress, or any details of the wedding ceremony, before the big day—before the *Star!* exclusive goes to print.'

'Except all the guests have had to sign a non-disclosure agreement, right? No exceptions.'

'No exceptions,' Laurel agreed. 'Except…one.'

'You,' Dan guessed. 'Melissa didn't make you sign one?'

'I guess she thought she didn't need to.' Laurel sighed. 'Benjamin said I was so under her thumb she knew I'd never do anything to betray her like that.'

'Is he right?' Dan looked up at her, his gaze steady but with no judgement. 'Or rather, is Melissa?'

She looked away. 'Probably. She's still my client. My sister.'

'Yeah, she is.'

'Even if she isn't paying me properly or treating me like one.'

'He knew just what buttons to press, huh?' Dan shifted to rest against the headboard, pulling her against his bare chest.

'He really, really did.' She sighed. 'I can't do it. I mean, I *could*—but I won't. But the way he said it… the way he knew that I'd be tempted…'

'Who wouldn't? The way she treats you…her over-whelming sense of entitlement…it's natural to want to bring her down a peg or two. It's what you decide to do next that matters.'

'Yeah. I guess.'

He gave a low chuckle. 'Funny to think you're the only person in the whole hotel who couldn't be sued for leaking those details and she put you in charge of planning the whole thing. She must really trust you.'

'I don't think it's trust,' Laurel said thoughtfully. 'I just don't think she sees me as a real person at all—a person with her own thoughts and feelings beyond the ones that matter to her. Do you know what I mean? Maybe that's why she was so angry about us being to-gether.'

Dan nodded and held her closer. 'You're real to me,' he said. 'I don't know if that helps, but you are.'

Real. Despite everything that was between them being fake, right then—in the moment—Laurel felt more real than she ever had before. More herself.

And it was all thanks to Dan.

'It does.' Laurel stretched up to kiss him again. 'It really, really does.'

This time when Dan woke up Laurel was still in bed be-side him, her legs tangled with his and her hair stream-ing out across the pillow. He breathed in the scent of her shampoo and marvelled at how right it felt, being there with her.

He hadn't expected this. Hadn't thought anything like this was even remotely possible for him any more.

How could it only have been two days? Two days since he'd been suggesting a stupid prank to the hot brunette in his car. Two days since he'd stepped up, taken her hand and shouldered the role of Laurel's fake boyfriend.

Two days since he'd started something he suddenly didn't want to finish.

But he would—he knew that. It was Friday morning. In another two days the wedding from hell would be over and he'd be on the flight Laurel had booked him back to LA. Back to his real life.

And that was exactly how he wanted it. And how Laurel wanted it too—she'd made that clear. He wasn't the prince she was waiting for, and she wasn't miraculously going to be the first woman who thought he was enough. Life didn't work that way.

This week was a space out of time, and it was wonderful. But it couldn't last. It never did—not for him.

He'd rather take these five days and enjoy every moment of them without worrying about when things would change. When Laurel would realise she needed something more. Something else. Some*body* else.

Laurel wanted to be the heroine of her own story. She needed a leading man for that—not a stand-in. And that was all he could ever be.

No, he'd have his five days and be grateful for them. And then he'd get back to reality.

Laurel stirred in his arms, and he kissed the top of her head. 'Morning. I thought you were channelling Cinderella, not Sleeping Beauty.'

Even the joke stung—just a little. After this week she would always be a princess, just out of reach. And the chances were he'd never even see her again.

'Someone wore me out.'

She stretched up and kissed him, long and easy and

sweet. But before he could deepen it, roll her over on top of him and relive some of the highlights from the night before, she slipped out of his arms and padded naked across the room to the bathroom.

'Come on. I've got work to do, and you've got a tour of the local sights to go on with the other guests. Might as well save time and shower together...'

She looked back over her shoulder from the doorway and Dan grinned, throwing off his doubts with the covers and hurrying to follow her.

He was *definitely* making the most of the time he had left with Laurel.

Which was why, once they were showered and dressed and heading down to the lobby, he set about convincing her to come on the tour instead of staying at Morwen Hall with the wedding party.

'They're doing the wedding party photo shoots and the interviews for *Star!* magazine,' Laurel said, shaking her head. 'I need to be here for that.'

'Why?' Dan asked. 'It's for the wedding party, right? And you're not in that.'

'No, but—'

'And in fact your job is organising the entertainment for the guests. Which, today, is this stupid tour of the local area.'

'You don't have to go if you don't want to,' Laurel said, rolling her eyes as they reached the lobby.

Dan caught her waist and spun her up against the wall, pressing a light kiss to her lips. 'Maybe I *do* want to go. But only if you're there with me.'

He saw the hesitation in her eyes and kissed her again, hoping to convince her.

'Let me talk to Eloise,' she said, coming up for air. 'As long as she's okay with it…'

Dan grinned at the victory and kissed her a third time—just because he could.

Eloise raised no objections, so Laurel and Dan boarded the coach, together with all the other guests, and headed out into the surrounding countryside.

Dan was only slightly disappointed to see that the parents of the bride and groom had also been deemed surplus to requirements for the photoshoot—presumably because they weren't famous enough. He resolved to try and avoid all four of them. He had a feeling that family bonding wouldn't help him enjoy his last couple of days with Laurel.

'So, where are we going?' he asked as he settled into the luxurious coach seat beside her. Where Laurel had found a coach fancy enough to make it suitable for Hollywood royalty he had no idea, but he was starting to believe that Laurel could do anything she set her mind to. It even had a mini-bar and a top-end coffee machine, with its own barista to operate it.

'The seaside,' Laurel replied, grinning like a small child on her way to see the ocean for the first time. 'It's going to be brilliant!'

'Not exactly beach weather,' Dan pointed out, looking out of the coach window at the frost still lingering on the trees.

'We're not going to sunbathe.' Laurel rolled her eyes. 'Have you ever been to the British seaside before?'

He shook his head.

'It's the best. There'll be tea shops and amusement

arcades—oh, and there's a castle up on the cliff above the beach that we can walk to, if you like?'

Dan didn't care what they did, as long as it kept that smile on Laurel's face. But he said, 'That sounds great,' anyway, and it was worth it when she kissed him.

'Okay, so this isn't exactly what I was imagining when you said the beach,' Dan said, looking down at the pebbles under his feet. 'Don't beaches normally involve sand?'

'Not this one.' Laurel skipped ahead, following the water line along the beach as the waves lapped against the stones.

The crisp winter air whooshed through her chest, making her whole body feel fresh and new. She was miles away from Morwen Hall, and the stone walls and Gothic architecture were fading away, freeing her from the wedding, from Melissa, from all that responsibility. Today it was just her and Dan.

'Come on! I want to climb up to the castle.'

Probably she should be supervising the other guests, or at least making herself available for questions. But since they'd mostly scattered, to explore the little shops that peppered the side streets of the seaside town, or to indulge in cream teas in the cafés, Laurel figured she was allowed some fun too. If it hadn't been for Dan she wouldn't even be there—she'd be back at Morwen Hall, watching Melissa play sweetness and light for the cameras.

She was really glad she was at the seaside instead.

'So, tell me about this castle,' Dan said, catching her up. He had a smooth round pebble in one hand, and was turning it over and over between his fingers. 'Is it a real one? Any princesses living there I should know about? Are we visiting your royal brethren?'

Laurel laughed. 'Yes, it's a real castle. But, no—no one has lived there for hundreds of years. It's probably missing half its walls, and definitely its roof, for a start.'

'Probably no princesses, then,' he said seriously. 'The way I hear it, those royal women are kind of demanding. They like walls, and real beds, and walk-in showers for two...'

Laurel blushed at the reminder of their early-morning activities. Yes, if she were a princess she would be a big fan of showers for two.

'No princesses,' she agreed, smiling up at him. 'Now, come on.'

The cliff path was a steep one, but Laurel scampered up it easily, knowing Dan was right behind her. The icy winter air had moved from bracing to become stinging, filling her lungs as she breathed it in, deep and invigorating. Her face felt wind-burned and scratchy, and her hair whipped around in her eyes. She didn't care. She was free and happy and *alive*.

'You look beautiful,' Dan said as they reached the top at last, and she turned to him, trying to catch her breath.

She gave up at the sight of him—his short hair tousled beyond repair, his blue eyes as bright as the winter sky. He looked every inch a film star—only *better*. He looked real in a way none of them ever seemed to.

And he looked at her as if she mattered. As if she was real too.

'I wish you didn't have to leave so soon,' she said without thinking—and he turned away, a rueful smile on his face.

'Yeah, well… Don't want the novelty to wear off, now, do we?'

But it wouldn't, Laurel knew suddenly. It couldn't. Not for her, anyway. But for him… He had to be used to a new woman every week, didn't he? The way he told it they all moved on quickly enough, but she wondered suddenly if that was the whole story. If they left him or if he kept them at such a distance that there was nothing for them to stay for.

He'd given up trying to be good enough for anyone the minute his brother had come along, while she'd kept on striving to prove her worth to a family that she was starting to realise might never see it. But if he rebelled against being what others wanted how would he ever know what it was like to be someone's everything?

Laurel wanted to find her prince. But part of her heart ached for Dan, who might never find his princess.

'Come on,' he said, striding ahead. 'I want to see this castle.'

Frowning, and still lost in her thoughts, Laurel followed.

She caught up to him as he crossed the moat into the keep, standing in the centre of the square of grass inside the walls. Hands on his hips, he turned around, taking in the crumbling stone of the battlements and the sky stretching out beyond it.

'It's pretty impressive, huh?' Laurel asked, leaning against the stone of the gatehouse.

'It is,' Dan said. 'It's strange. I thought it would feel like a movie set. Or something of another time. But it doesn't. It's here—now. It's survived.'

'Well, some of it has.' She pushed off the wall and crossed the grass towards him, leaning her back against his chest as she tried to see what he saw. He wrapped his arms around her waist and kissed the top of her head. 'I love it here,' she said.

'I can tell.'

'I'm glad I got to bring you.' Glad they could have this moment, this perfect time together. Even if they both knew it could never last.

'Me too,' Dan said, and spun her round to kiss her again.

After the castle, Laurel took him down into the small seaside town and introduced him to the wonders of gift shops that sold small boxes covered in shells, and pebbles with googly eyes stuck on them. Dan smiled as she darted from shelf to shelf, fascinated by all the wonders, like a child looking to spend her first allowance.

'What's that?' he asked, pointing to the flashing bright lights of a storefront across the way. It looked like a mini-casino, but there were kids walking in so he figured it couldn't be.

'The amusement arcade!' Laurel's eyes lit up as she grabbed his hand and dragged him across the road towards the lights.

Inside, the darkness of the room was punctuated by the glow of slot machines, and the air was filled with beeps and tinny music and the sound of coins falling.

'Feeling rich?' he asked as she stepped towards a change machine.

She shook her head as she popped a single pound coin into the slot and a cascade of coppers tumbled into the pot she was holding. 'I'm not a gambler,' she said, turning back to him. 'I don't risk more than I can afford. So...' She held up the pot. 'Tuppenny Falls!'

Feeding the machine full of two-pence pieces, being pushed by moving bars with coins kept them entertained for a full fifteen minutes, as coins dropped off the edge of the ledge and into their pot every time they thought they were about to run out. Dan spent more time enjoying the childlike glee on Laurel's face than he did watching the coins, loving the way she brought so much life and appreciation to everything she did.

He knew she felt she could never live up to her sister, or be good enough to win back her father's affection—knew it deep down in the same place *he* knew that he could never be Riley for his parents. He didn't need her to say it.

But he also knew that she was wrong. She was worth a million Melissas, and her family were fools if they couldn't see it. He just wished that before he left he could make Laurel see that the only person she needed to be good enough for was herself.

Eventually their coins ran out, and Laurel shook her head when he offered to fetch more change. They headed for the exit, with the lights and sounds of the amusement arcade still buzzing in Dan's brain.

'So, what's next?' he asked as they stepped back into the brisk winter air. 'We have—what? Another hour before the coach comes back?'

An hour didn't seem long enough. Already it felt as if his time with her was ebbing away, like the tide going out on the pebble beach.

'Something like that,' Laurel agreed. 'Ready for tea and cake?'

'Definitely.'

The café she chose had tiny delicate tables in the window, draped with lace. Dan took a seat on a slender-legged white chair and hoped it wouldn't collapse under him. He was under no illusion as to how out of place he looked here, even without the old women at the next table glaring at him.

Laurel sat down opposite him, her cheeks still flushed. 'I've ordered us two cream teas.'

'Sounds great.'

They sat in silence for a moment, while a million questions flooded Dan's brain. Everything he wanted to ask her if only they had time. He wanted to know everything, but what was the point when he was leaving so soon?

In the end he settled for the questions he might get to see the outcome of.

'So, did you decide what to tell Benjamin?'

Laurel pulled a face. 'I'm hoping he won't ask again. But if he does... I can't do it. Not even to Melissa.'

Dan smiled faintly. 'I never thought you would. Not for a moment.'

'Because I'm too scared of Melissa?' Laurel asked, eyebrows raised.

'Because you're the heroine in your own story,' he corrected her. 'And *she* wouldn't do that. Would she?'

'No,' Laurel admitted. 'She wouldn't.'

Dan leant back in his chair gingerly, trying not to put too much pressure on the flimsy wood. 'So, what would she do?'

'Hmm?' Laurel asked, distracted as the waitress, dressed all in black with a frilly white apron and mob cap, brought pots of tea and two giant scones with jam and cream on the side. 'Look at the size of those things! We'll never eat at the rehearsal dinner tonight.'

'No offence to the chef, but I doubt whatever Melissa

has ordered could live up to these,' Dan said, smearing jam over half a scone. 'What is for dinner, anyway?'

'Seven-course tasting menu.'

'Of course.' Pretentious, and not enough of anything to really enjoy it. Just like Melissa's latest movie.

Laurel took a bite of her scone and a blissful smile broke out across her face as she chewed. 'Mmm...that's good.' She swallowed. 'Sorry, you asked me something. Before I got distracted by food.'

'I was asking what she would do next. After the wedding. Your heroine, I mean.'

Laurel gave a low laugh and looked down at her plate, tearing a bit of scone off and crumbling it between her fingers.

'Do you know, I have no idea?' she said after a moment. 'For months, whenever I've tried to think beyond this wedding, it's like the whole world has gone blank. Like everything ends the moment Melissa and Riley say, "I do".'

'The end of the movie,' Dan said. 'Credits roll.'

'Exactly. They get their happily-ever-after, and I... cease to matter.'

'Except you're not living in Melissa's movie, remember? You're living in your own.'

'I know.'

However much she said it, Dan couldn't help but think she didn't believe it yet. Maybe it wouldn't be real to her until after the wedding, when the credits *didn't* roll. When life went on, away from Melissa's influence.

He almost wished he'd still be around to see it.

'So, if you could do anything what would it be?' he asked. 'Would you be a film star, like Melissa? Own a castle? Marry actual royalty? Take over the world?'

Laurel laughed. 'None of those things. I think…' She crumbled another piece of scone, chewing on her lip as she did so. 'I think I'd like to make my business a success. I'd like to make people's dream weddings come true. And I'd like… I'd like my own, one day. Maybe a family. Like I said before, I want my prince—the man who is perfect for me, who comes riding up just when I need him.'

'The right guy, right place, right time. Right?' His chest ached. He knew that he could never be that for Laurel, even if he wanted to. He wasn't anyone's prince, but more than that he couldn't even risk trying to be. Laurel deserved every happy ending she dreamt of, and he knew from past experience that he couldn't live up to that sort of expectation.

'Yeah. But really all I want is… I guess mostly I'd just like to be happy. Fulfilled and content and *happy*.'

Dan smiled, even though it hurt, and raised his tea cup to her. 'That sounds like a pretty damn fine ambition to me.'

And she'd fulfil it—he had no doubt. That, right there, was the future he wanted for Laurel…even if it was a future he couldn't be part of.

She clinked her china cup against his. 'So, what about you? You already have the successful business, by all accounts. What's next for you? True love?'

Love. Thoughts of Cassie and the day she'd left rolled through him again, turning his tea bitter in his mouth.

'I already tried that, remember? It's not for me.'

Something to be grateful for, he supposed—whatever was between him and Laurel, it wasn't love. Couldn't be after just a few days of knowing each other. No, their pretend relationship had grown into something less fake, he'd admit. But that didn't make it *real*. Not in the way that hurt.

'Then what?'

Laurel's eyes were sad as she asked, and he realised he had no answer for her. She had all her dreams laid out before her, and he had...

'Maybe I'm happy just as I am,' he said.

'Maybe...' Laurel echoed. But she didn't look as if she believed him.

And Dan wasn't even sure he blamed her.

CHAPTER EIGHT

BY THE TIME they made it back to Morwen Hall Laurel
was ready for a nap. But instead she had to prepare for
the rehearsal dinner.

The staff at the hall had been busy setting up most
of the decorations, table settings and so on, but Laurel
knew she wouldn't be able to relax if she didn't check
on them. Leaving Dan to find his own way to their
room to prepare, she headed to the restaurant—only
to find she wasn't the only person checking up on the
arrangements.

'Hey!' Laurel called as she crossed the restaurant
to where Eloise was slumped at a table. 'Everything
ready here? We just got back. Everyone's gone to get
changed for the rehearsal dinner. Which I'm guessing
you will be too...?'

She left it hanging, not entirely sure Eloise didn't
plan on attending in her suit. Eloise didn't like dressing up, she'd learned, and after a day of being poked
and prodded by stylists for the photoshoot she wouldn't
blame her for being done.

'Yeah.' Eloise glanced at her watch. 'Oh, yes, I'd better get moving. Did the tour go okay? Nice romantic
day out with Dan?'

'Yes, thank you,' Laurel said simply.

There weren't words to explain how perfect her day had been—or how bittersweet. Not without explaining the whole fake relationship and her feelings about the fact he was leaving in two days. And nobody had time for that this week.

'What about you? How were the interviews?'

'All fine,' Eloise said, and Laurel relaxed a little.

She was incredibly grateful she hadn't been thrust into the role of maid of honour, and so didn't have to deal with photoshoots and interviews, but she had been a little nervous about how Eloise would cope with it. She wasn't used to the spotlight any more than Laurel was. She was glad it seemed to have gone off without incident.

'And how is the very gorgeous Noah?'

Laurel raised her eyebrows expectantly. Because, really, wasn't that what everyone in the hotel wanted to know? After their kiss at the Frost Fair the day before *everyone* had an opinion on the possible relationship between the best man and the maid of honour. She'd heard at least three theories on the bus back from the seaside, but there was definitely a prevailing one.

Eloise groaned. 'Don't ask.'

'So there *is* something going on with you two!' Laurel cried triumphantly. 'I knew the gossip was wrong.'

'Gossip?' Eloise jerked her head up. 'What gossip? What are they saying?'

'Nothing bad, I promise.' Laurel pulled out the chair next to Eloise and sat down. 'Nobody's laughing or anything. In fact everyone seems to think that you're keeping Noah at arm's length. I take it that's not entirely the case?'

'It's a secret,' Eloise blurted out. 'I don't want anyone to know.'

'Well, so far, they don't. In fact, from what I heard people are pretty amazed. They've seen him hanging around, chasing after you—apparently that's not his usual *modus operandi*.' She didn't mention the more outlandish theories—that Eloise was actually his estranged wife and he was trying to win her back, or that everything that seemed to be going on was actually an audition for a new film, or something.

Eloise sat back in her chair and stared at her. 'Really? How do you mean?'

Laurel shrugged. 'Seems he usually lets people come to him. He's the chase-ee, not the chaser, if you see what I mean.'

When it came to her and Dan, which one of them had chased the other? Laurel wondered. Dan had suggested the fake relationship plan, but *she'd* put it into action. And she would be hard pressed to say exactly which of them had kissed the other first. And as for last night... There hadn't been any chasing at all, she realised. Just two people coming together as if it were simply too much effort to stay apart. As if gravity had been dragging them in.

Until Sunday—when all forces would be reversed and they'd be thrown apart again.

She shook her head, hoping to dispel the depressing thought. But when she turned her attention to Eloise she realised that her friend's expression echoed exactly the way she was feeling. She hadn't been able to put a name to it herself, but seeing it on Eloise's face it was suddenly so, so obvious.

'Are you okay?' Laurel asked, trying to ignore the lump in her throat. 'You look…scared.'

As terrified as I feel. Like you don't know what happens next, and you can't see your way clear to the happy-ever-after.

There *had* to be a happy-ever-after. That was the only thing keeping her going through all the wedding prep—knowing that once it was over she got to chase her own dream.

So why was she suddenly so reluctant for Sunday to come?

Laurel's heart tightened. *I don't want him to go. Not even if it means I don't get to go searching for my happy ending.*

'I'll be fine.'

Eloise pasted on a smile that Laurel was sure was only for her benefit. Underneath it, she looked utterly miserable.

'I need to go get ready for tonight.'

With a groan, she pushed her chair away from the table and stood, walking away without a goodbye, leaving Laurel alone at the table, wondering how the two of them had ended up in such a mess. And whether they could legitimately blame Melissa for the whole thing.

Dan had showered, changed and headed down to the bar before Laurel came back to the room. He figured he might as well give her the time and space to get ready for the rehearsal dinner in peace.

He wasn't avoiding her. Really he wasn't.

Well, maybe a bit. But only because if he was there and he knew she was in the shower…naked…there wasn't a chance of them making it to the rehearsal dinner on time. Or at all.

Besides, he still needed to find his brother. Theirs was a long overdue conversation that couldn't wait much longer.

He knocked on Riley's door on his way down, but there was no answer. Still, when he saw how many guests were already congregating in the bar he figured it was only a matter of time before Riley appeared too, so he might as well have a drink while he waited.

He signalled the barman over and ordered a beer, trying not to think how much more fun he'd be having if he'd stayed in the room and waited for Laurel.

Despite his decision to enjoy every second of the time he had left with her, somehow that seemed to be getting harder as the hours ticked by. Already he was counting down to Sunday, and he couldn't shake the feeling that everything would change then.

Laurel had said she couldn't see beyond the wedding itself, except for some fantasy happy-ever-after. He'd never had that problem—he'd known exactly what he was going back to, what was waiting for him, what his life would be.

The only problem was for the first time in a long time his life didn't seem like enough.

It was crazy—he knew that. He'd known Laurel all of sixty hours. That wasn't enough time to make any sort of decision on their acquaintance. And even if he wanted to, he couldn't.

Because however good it felt, being with her, he knew the truth: that it was all an act. He wasn't her prince, her happy-ever-after, or anything except her fake boyfriend. Yes, they had chemistry. Yes, they had fun.

But he'd had that before, with plenty of women who'd seemed perfect—and they'd all left him when something better came along. Someone more famous, someone who could help their career more. Or just someone who was willing to marry them.

He couldn't do that again. Not after Cassie. And Laurel deserved that fairy tale she wanted—which meant she couldn't have it with him.

End of story. Credits roll.

'Starting early, are we, son?' His dad's voice echoed across the mostly empty bar. 'Your brother seems rather less inclined to indulge after last night.'

'Have you seen him?' Dan asked quickly. With the wedding less than twenty-four hours away his time to talk to his brother about Melissa was running out. He should have done it sooner, he knew, but he'd been... distracted.

Wendell nodded. 'He was just heading to Melissa's rooms—that honeymoon suite out in the gatehouse.'

Dan cursed silently. If Riley was with his fiancée, then he had no hope of getting him alone. Why had he waited so long to do this?

Because I didn't want to, he realised. It wasn't just that he'd been busy with Laurel. He hadn't wanted to potentially ruin all Riley's hopes and dreams for the future.

Happy-ever-after might not be waiting for Dan, but that didn't stop him hoping that others might find it.

'I did invite him to join me for a drink, but he turned green around the edges at the very suggestion,' Wendell went on. 'What on earth did you do to him?'

Put him to bed and saved him from his friends, Dan thought. But there was no point saying it. His father expected *him* to be the bad influence, and no amount of facts or logic would change that.

'It was his stag night,' Dan said, shrugging. 'You were invited. You didn't want to come.'

'It was. And I didn't. But when I stopped by to see how it was going around midnight—your mother was still up reading and I couldn't sleep, so I thought I might as well—Riley wasn't there. And neither were you or his best man.'

'It had been a long day.'

'One of Riley's friends told me you'd taken Riley off to put him to bed. Is that right?' Wendell asked, one eyebrow raised.

'He'd had enough.' Where was his father going with this?

Wendell nodded. 'Probably for the best, then. So, where's that girlfriend of yours this evening? Working?'

'Getting ready, I think,' Dan said, frowning at the sudden change of subject. 'But she will be working, yes. It takes a lot of hard work to put on an event like this.'

'I'm sure it does,' his dad said, without even a glimmer of understanding. 'So, is this one serious? Are you considering settling down again? Your mother wants to know if she needs to clear some time in her schedule next summer.'

Dan blinked. His parents hadn't asked about a girlfriend since Cassie had left. And they hadn't even made it to that wedding—mostly because he and Cassie hadn't planned on getting married until they'd arrived in Vegas and suddenly it had seemed like the obvious idea.

Wendell rolled his eyes. 'Come on, Daniel. She might not be changing the world with her career, but it's obvious to anyone with eyes that she's changing *your* world.

I wasn't sure when we met her that first night—she seemed a little mouthy, I thought. But then I watched you today, walking with her on the beach, and later I spotted you in that café. And I saw that this is real for you.'

'It's not…' *Real.* The one thing his relationship with Laurel couldn't be. Even if it felt like it—felt more real than his *actual* life, in fact. 'It's still quite new,' he said in the end, knowing that at least it wasn't a lie. 'I don't know where it's going to go.'

That part was a lie, of course. He knew exactly what happened next for them.

His dad clapped a hand on his shoulder and Dan tried to remember the last time he'd done that. If ever. 'When it's love you know, son.'

Love. Was that really what this was? It hadn't felt this way with Cassie—that much was for sure. Cassie had been all high adrenaline and passion and never knowing what happened next—and then later their marriage had been bitter arguments and fear and pain. None of which he wanted to relive.

But with Laurel it was…peaceful. There was still passion, of course, but knowing he had nothing to lose—that he couldn't let her down because he'd never promised her anything beyond the weekend, that she couldn't leave him and break him because he'd be leaving first—had taken the fear out of it. He'd been able to relax, enjoy her company, to feel…at home, somehow.

Until now. Until his father had said 'love' and he'd realised that it didn't matter that he'd only met her three days ago, or that their whole relationship was fake.

Laurel *mattered* to him. And that changed everything.

'But what if you're wrong? What if you don't know?'

He didn't know what had made him ask the question, or where the desperate tone in his voice had come from. His dad looked at him in surprise, but he didn't seem to have an answer. His hand fell away from Dan's shoulder and they stood in awkward silence for a moment—until the best man, Noah Cross, came barrelling across the room looking for a drink and Dan was able to put down his glass and slip out unnoticed.

He stood in the hallway, resting his head against the wall, and tried to get a grip. He had to, he knew. He had to get control of his body, of his mind, of his emotions, before he saw Laurel again.

Usually he was good at this. Control was what he was famous for. The ability to control a fall or a dive or a stunt so perfectly that no one got hurt every time. The control to keep his face expressionless as directors waxed lyrical about the risks their stars took without even mentioning him or his team, and the fact that *they* did all the stuff the more famous actors couldn't. The control to keep his heart safe as another person walked away from him.

His mind drifted back to the strange conversation with his father. What had that been, exactly? An attempt to find a way back? To give some fatherly advice twenty years too late? Dan didn't know. But whatever it was…it had felt like the start of something. He just wasn't sure he was willing to risk it ending as abruptly as it had begun.

Just like him and Laurel.

As her name floated across his mind he heard her voice, not far away, and focussed in on it.

'Benjamin, I don't want to talk about this again.'

Benjamin. Her good-for-nothing ex. Well, Dan might not be her prince in shining armour, but he could save her from that idiot, at least.

He followed the sound of their voices around the corner in the corridor, finding them just outside the restaurant where the rehearsal dinner was being held. He hung back for a second, taking in the annoyance on Laurel's face—and the stunning dark red dress she was wearing.

'All I'm saying is you're running out of time to take advantage of this offer, Laurel.'

Even his voice sounded smarmy and weaselly.

'The wedding is tomorrow.'

'I had noticed, thanks. And I have quite a lot of work to do before then. So, if you'll excuse me…' She made to brush past him, but Benjamin reached out and grabbed her arm, holding her in place.

And that was it for Dan.

Striding forward, he wrapped strong fingers around Benjamin's forearm and levered it away from Laurel.

'The lady said she was leaving.'

'I haven't finished talking.' Benjamin looked up, annoyance in his face as he shook his arm out. He turned back to Laurel. 'I don't think you realise how important this is. Coral's job is depending on it.'

'And what about mine?' Laurel asked. 'If word gets around that I leaked confidential details of a client's wedding, who will hire me after that?'

'We can help with that!' Benjamin sounded excited, as if he thought he had her now.

Dan knew better.

Laurel sighed. 'Benjamin, no. I won't do it. Please stop asking me.'

'That sounds pretty clear to me.' Dan yanked Benjamin back a few feet and stood between him and Laurel, arms folded across his chest. 'I think we're done here. Don't you?'

Benjamin glared at him, then peered around to try and catch Laurel's eye again. 'It's not too late, Laurel. Even tomorrow morning a sneak preview of the dress could be worth serious money. Don't forget—she deserves it. Right?'

Dan took a step closer and Benjamin finally backed away. 'Fine, fine. I'm going.'

He waited until Benjamin had disappeared around the corner, presumably back to the bar, before he turned to check on Laurel. 'You okay?'

'Fine,' she said, nodding. 'I just… I really didn't need him tonight, you know? And he wouldn't listen. So, thank you.'

'You'd have got through to him eventually,' Dan said. He reached out to take her hand. 'I just speeded things up a little.'

'Well, I appreciate it.' She smiled up at him then, raising herself onto her tiptoes and pressing a kiss to the corner of his mouth. 'Thank you.'

'Any time,' he said, without thinking.

Because he wouldn't be there any time. He only had until Sunday morning. He had to remember that.

'I might take you up on that. Now, come on—we've got a rehearsal dinner to attend.'

She sashayed off down the corridor, her curves looking so irresistibly tempting in that dress that Dan couldn't help but follow.

Even if he *was* starting to fear exactly what he was following her into and how far he'd go.

CHAPTER NINE

SATURDAY MORNING—New Year's Eve—Laurel woke early, kissed Dan's cheek while he slept, then slipped out from between the sheets and into the shower. As much as she'd have liked to stay in bed with him it was Melissa's wedding day, and she had far too much to be getting on with.

The rehearsal dinner had gone off without a hitch—well, the dinner part anyway. Laurel closed her eyes as the water sluiced over her and tried to forget the way that Noah and Eloise had disappeared halfway through, only for a furious-looking Noah to return alone, behind a triumphant Melissa. Laurel didn't know what had happened, but she could only imagine that whatever it was would be back to cause trouble for her today.

As she rubbed shampoo into her hair she mentally ran through her list of things to do that morning. As she smoothed on conditioner she ticked off everything she needed to double-check on. When she switched off the water she was ready to start her day.

She grabbed her notebook and pen at the same time as her wedding outfit, making notes as she slipped into her dress and hoping the hairdryer in the bathroom wouldn't wake Dan. She smiled to herself. After last night she figured he probably needed the sleep to re-cuperate.

She didn't know what had changed, but he'd been frantic the night before—desperate to touch every inch of her, to make love to her for hours. Even as they'd slept he'd kept his arms wrapped tight around her.

Maybe he was feeling the pressure of their time limit as much as she was. Sunday was creeping ever closer—but first they had to make it through the wedding.

By the time she'd finished dressing, and her hair was pinned back neatly from her face, Laurel's checklist was complete—along with some extra notes for things she'd thought of in the shower. With one last glance back at the man sleeping in her bed she let herself out of the bedroom and headed down, out through the front door of the hotel to the honeymoon suite to wake Melissa.

The honeymoon suite was housed in the old gate-house, just a short walk away from the hotel proper, and the crisp winter air blew away the last of the cobwebs from not enough sleep and one more glass of wine than she'd normally allow herself at the rehearsal dinner.

It was still early, and when she'd left her room the hotel had seemed asleep. But as she approached the bridal suite she heard laughter—Melissa's laughter—echoed by two more voices that Laurel assumed be-longed to her bridesmaids. For a moment she was just grateful she didn't have to wake her up—her half-sister was notoriously grumpy first thing. But then her phone pinged in her pocket, and when Laurel checked it she knew exactly what Melissa must be laughing about.

She scanned the text as she waited for Melissa to open the door. It was one of the alerts she'd set up to notify her whenever a new article was posted about Melissa, Riley, or one of the wedding party. In this case she had a whole page of articles about Noah scrolling over her screen.

But not just Noah. Front and centre was a photo of Eloise, holding her dress up to her chest as she and Noah stumbled out of a closet she recognised from the same floor as the restaurant, obviously caught in the act.

Noah Cross says, 'A fling always makes a wedding more fun, right?'

Laurel closed down the image, but the horror and shame on Eloise's face stayed with her. *Poor Eloise.* Laurel wanted to run back up to the hotel and check on her friend, to try and find the words to make everything less awful.

But as she turned to go Melissa opened the door, beaming, and Laurel knew that somehow her half-sister was behind this.

'Did you hear?' Melissa asked, gleefully chivvying Laurel into the gatehouse. 'Noah and Eloise—who would have thought it? I mean, obviously he was just fooling around with her—but the poor girl looked thoroughly besotted with him. I imagine he must have broken her heart completely, saying what he did.'

'I saw,' Laurel said, trying to keep all emotion out of her voice. 'I do wonder how the photographer found them, though.'

A flash of something spread across Melissa's face. Not guilt. Laurel was sure of that. But perhaps…fear? Of being found out? Laurel couldn't tell.

'Well, they did go missing from the rehearsal dinner at the same time,' Melissa said, busying herself

with straightening the perfectly hung wedding dress
that was suspended from the spiral staircase leading
to the upper floor.

That was the only place with the height to hang the
dress without risking wrinkles to the train, Laurel remembered.

'I mean, it was only natural that someone would go
to find them.'

'That someone being you?' Laurel guessed. 'And
you just happened to take a reporter and a photographer with you?'

Because of course Melissa wouldn't be able to stand
that people were talking about Noah and Eloise instead
of *her*. That Eloise, whom she'd tormented through all
their teenage years by all accounts, might end up with
a bigger Hollywood star on her arm than Melissa had.

Laurel could almost see Melissa's thought processes
working. This was her wedding, and no one should be
talking about anyone except her. Not Laurel and Dan,
not Eloise and Noah. And God forbid any of them try
to step out of the roles Melissa had assigned them in
the movie of her life.

They were all there as bit players—extras to her
leading lady. And, as such, they didn't really matter to
Melissa at all. Not even if she destroyed them.

Laurel felt the heat of anger flooding through her,
and tried to keep it down. Anger wouldn't help her
today. What she needed was cold, dispassionate ratio-
nal thinking. She needed to get through this wedding
and get on with her own life—not Melissa's. That was
what Dan had been trying to tell her all week.

Just saying that she was the heroine in her own story

wasn't enough. She needed to live it. She needed to *believe* it.

Starting the moment this stupid wedding was over and done with.

Or maybe even sooner.

'It's funny how these things work out sometimes, isn't it?' Melissa said airily, dropping her hand from the wedding dress.

But she didn't turn to meet Laurel's eyes. And Laurel couldn't look away from the dress. Couldn't forget Benjamin's words. *She deserves it.*

'Anyway, Caitlin and Iona are already upstairs, checking through their responsibilities lists. I'm going to go and get showered, and then we can all run through the details for the day. Yes?'

Melissa didn't wait for Laurel's agreement. Instead she disappeared up the stairs to the bathroom, leaving Laurel alone in the main room.

With the wedding dress.

Biting her lip, Laurel raised her phone and snapped a quick photo of the dress.

Just in case.

Dan woke alone again, and felt that same sudden spike of panic before he remembered what day it was. New Year's Eve. Melissa and Riley's wedding day. Laurel would be rushing around the hotel somewhere, getting everything ready for the wedding, or out at the gatehouse with Melissa.

But tonight, once it was all over, she'd be done—and they could just enjoy their last night together.

Maybe not even their last night. Maybe he could change his flight—stay an extra day or two. A week at the most. By then surely they'd both be ready to move on. Really, they hadn't had enough time for this fling to run its course—not with all the wedding stuff Laurel had had to do. It only made sense to make the most of their passion before it ran cold.

But, no. He couldn't risk it. Dan knew that. One day would stretch to two. Which would become a week. Or a month. And before he knew it he'd be trapped. Drawn in. Attached.

He wouldn't be able to leave until he'd stayed long enough for Laurel to leave him.

And *he* had to be the one to leave this time. Whatever the truth about his feelings—and, really, what good would it do to examine them too closely at this point?—Dan knew he couldn't give Laurel the happy-ever-after she wanted. Couldn't live up to her fairy tale expectations.

And so tonight would be their last night. However much that hurt. Better to take the sharp sting of the controlled fall now than risk the much greater injuries that came from being unprepared for the blow when it came. Because that blow always came eventually.

Decision made, he rolled out of bed and went to get ready for the wedding of the year.

Half an hour later, dressed in his tux and as prepared as he could be for the day ahead, Dan headed down to the large hall where the ceremony would be held, looking for Laurel.

He spotted her adjusting the flowers at the ends of the rows of chairs either side of the aisle, and found himself grinning just at the sight of her. She was wearing a dark blue dress, cut low in a cowl at the back, but higher in the front, and falling just past her knees. Her shoes were high and strappy—far higher than he'd seen her wear before—and he wondered if it would change how they kissed if she was so much taller.

Maybe it was time to find out.

'I think that flower arrangement is lopsided,' he called—unhelpfully—then laughed when she looked up and glared at him. 'Kidding. Everything looks perfect.'

'It should. I've been up for hours getting everything just right. Including the bride.' She crossed the aisle towards him, slotting so easily into his arms he might almost believe she was meant to be there.

'How is she?'

'Gloating,' Laurel said, with bitterness in the word. 'Did you hear about Noah and Eloise?'

Dan nodded. 'It was all everyone was talking about at breakfast.'

'Poor Eloise.' She shook her head. 'I'm going back out to the gatehouse now, to try to protect her from Melissa's gleeful barbs.'

'I can't believe she's going through with being maid of honour. I'm assuming the whole photo thing was a Melissa set-up?'

'Of course.' She looked up at him, her expression serious. 'Are you *sure* you don't want to try to talk your brother out of marrying her?'

Dan pulled a face. 'I've been trying to get him alone all week, but somehow I keep getting distracted... Not to talk him out of it, exactly, but to check he's sure about this. That he knows what he's letting himself in for.'

'If he knew that I can't believe he'd really marry her,' Laurel said bluntly. 'I always thought... I knew she wasn't always a nice person to *me*, but I always figured that she had her reasons. That our relationship would always have to bear that strain. But to do this to Eloise…' She shook her head, as if the magnitude of Melissa's cruelty rendered her speechless.

'I might be able to manage a quiet word with Riley this morning,' he said. 'Won't that ruin all your hard work, though? If he decides not to go through with it?'

'At this point I'm not sure I even care.' She checked her watch and gave him an apologetic smile. 'I've got to get back out there. Sorry.'

'I'll walk you,' Dan said easily.

They were into their last hours now. He couldn't waste a moment of them.

'Great.' Her phone started to ring. 'Sorry—I just need to take this…'

Her call—something to do with the exact placement of various table centrepieces, as far as he could tell—lasted long enough for them to leave the hotel and walk across the gravel drive to the honeymoon suite in the former gatehouse. They were almost at the front door of the suite before Dan had a chance to talk to Laurel alone again. But somehow, he found himself just enjoying the sensation of being near her.

'I'm sorry,' she said, one hand on the door handle as the winter wind ruffled her hair. 'I wasn't much company for that walk, was I?'

'Never mind. We'll still have tonight. Once this is all over.'

'Before your flight tomorrow.' Laurel's smile faded as she spoke. 'Unless… I could always look at changing your flight. Put it back a couple of days. If you don't have anything to rush back for…? We could maybe enjoy ourselves a little longer—without the whole wedding party thing going on.'

He could hear the nerves in her voice as she suggested it, and he wanted nothing more than to pull her into his arms and tell her it was a great idea.

Except it wasn't. He'd already made his decision. He couldn't go back on that now. Couldn't give her expectations that he couldn't live up to.

His silence made her smile wobble even more as she chatted on, obviously trying to fill the gap where he hadn't responded.

'I know we said that this was just for the week. But I wondered if maybe that might change? I mean, it's been kind of wonderful, these last couple of days. It seems a shame to limit it, don't you think? Perhaps we could just…see where things go?'

She was trying to keep it casual, he could tell. Trying not to spook him. But she didn't get it—how could she? He'd thought she might understand—she of all people. But apparently even Laurel couldn't see that it was always better to get out before things went bad.

'That's not…' Letting his arms drop, he stepped back from her, trying to harden himself against the disappointment in her eyes. 'I don't think it would be a good idea.'

'But *why*?' Frustration leaked out of Laurel's voice. 'Why not try? We've got a good thing going on here.'

The worst thing was, she was *right*. And it still didn't change anything.

Because a good thing could go bad in a heartbeat, the moment her prince came riding by. He couldn't take that. Not from her.

'We have a *fake* thing going on here. A pretend relationship, Laurel—that was the deal. And, yes, it's been fun. And, sure, I'd like a couple more nights in your bed before I go. But that's all. This isn't love, it isn't for ever, and it isn't happy-ever-after. That's not what we agreed. You're waiting for your prince, remember? All I said was that I'd pretend to be your boyfriend for the week to give you some sort of moral support against your ex. That's it. The rest was just…fringe benefits.'

It was all the truth—every word of it. They'd never promised anything more—never expected it either.

So why did it hurt so much to say it out loud? Why did the pain in Laurel's eyes burn through him?

'I know what we agreed,' Laurel said slowly, her face pale and determined. 'But I thought… I hoped that things might have changed.'

Dan shook his head sadly. 'I'm not your leading man, Laurel. And I definitely can't be the prince you're waiting for. I'm only here until your ex isn't. I'm just a stand-in. The pretend boyfriend. That's it.'

He was so focussed on her face, on making her understand why he *couldn't* risk this, that he barely noticed the door behind her opening.

Until Melissa's incredulous laugh echoed through the air.

'Oh, my God! I was just coming to find out what all the shouting was about, but *really*! This is like the best wedding present ever!'

Laurel spun round to face her, and Dan took a step closer before he realised he shouldn't. Melissa stood there, dressed from head to toe in white lace, her silk gloved hands on her hips.

'This is none of your business, Melissa,' Laurel said, more calmly than Dan though he could have managed. 'Now, if you'll just give me a moment—'

But Melissa shook her head. 'Oh, no. This is far too

good. So let me get this straight. You were so scared about being at this wedding dateless—especially since your ex was bringing the new fiancée he cheated on you with, right?—that you persuaded poor Dan, here, to pretend to be your boyfriend!'

She laughed again.

'Well, that is just *precious*, honey. I mean, I can see why you'd be a tiny little bit intimidated, surrounded by all these wildly successful people, when all you've ever really done is arrange a few flowers and some cake. But, really, Laurel—*lying* to everybody? Trying to steal my thunder?'

'That's not what this is—' Dan started to say, but Melissa just gave a low chuckle.

'Oh, but it is. I heard the truth from your own mouth, Dan. There's no point trying to protect her any more, you know.'

Melissa turned her attention back to her half-sister, and Dan braced himself for whatever vitriol she came out with next.

'I should have known you couldn't score a *real* date for the wedding. I mean, even for a fake boyfriend you could only manage to snare the lesser brother—the stand-in stunt man. Really, Laurel. You're an embarrassment.'

Fury flooded through him at Melissa's words, hot and all-encompassing, burning through his self-control. 'You don't speak to her like that—'

'Dan.' Laurel's sharp tone pulled him up short. 'This has nothing to do with you any more—you've made that perfectly clear. I'll arrange for you to have Riley's room tonight, once he moves down here to the honeymoon suite, and the hotel staff will move your stuff. Now, if you'll excuse us, we have a wedding to prepare for.'

With that she walked past Melissa, into the honeymoon suite, not looking back at him for a moment.

Melissa flashed him a satisfied grin and slammed the door in his face.

And Dan felt his whole world crumbling around him as he tried to tell himself it was for the best…tried to find his famous control again.

'Honestly, Laurel, I can't *believe* you!'

Melissa gave Laurel what she imagined was supposed to look like a friendly pat on the back, but actually made her shoulder blade ache.

'You lot won't believe what this one has been up to! It's almost as outrageous as Eloise's fling with Noah!'

Laurel glanced around the room, looking for Eloise, but her friend seemed to have escaped the wedding prep somehow. Laurel was almost grateful; Eloise was having a bad enough day without having to deal with Laurel's disastrous love-life.

Given the choice, even *Laurel* would opt out of this one, thanks.

Iona and Caitlin, however—the other two bridesmaids—were listening to Melissa with rapt attention.

'Ooh, tell us!' Iona cried. 'You know how we love a bit of wedding gossip!'

'Can you believe Laurel actually guilt-tripped Dan into pretending to be her boyfriend for the week? I mean, how *funny*!'

'How desperate,' Caitlin said, giving Laurel a look.

Melissa tutted, and wrapped an arm around Laurel's shoulder. 'Now, Caitlin, don't be catty. Not everyone is as lucky as me, you know, to find such a perfect true love so easily.'

Laurel's shoulders stiffened under her half-sister's touch. Why was she doing this? Why bother pretending she was still sweetness and light? Surely everyone had to have at least glimpsed the real Melissa by now.

But from the way Iona was smiling at Melissa she knew they hadn't. They still believed that Melissa was on everyone else's side. That she wasn't a stone-cold witch who'd do whatever it took to take down anyone she perceived as a rival for her attention.

Of course, they were very, *very* wrong.

'Really, Laurel, what *were* you thinking?' Iona asked. 'Everyone knows that fake relationship plot device never works out well in the movies.'

Except it hadn't been a plot device, or a movie. It had been her life. Her heart on the line in the end.

She'd offered him a chance at a future, a shot at a happy-ever-after when the credits had rolled on Melissa's wedding. Their own story—together—without worrying about anyone else.

And he'd turned her down. He'd made it abundantly clear that all he was interested in was a few days of fun before he got back to his real life.

Which either meant he was an idiot, or he really didn't feel the same connection she did. Or possibly both.

Melissa and Caitlin had turned to look at her now, waiting for her to answer Iona's question.

Laurel took a breath and realised that her next words were in some way her first line. The first sentence of her new story—after Melissa, after Dan, after everything. Just her.

'Honestly?' she said. 'I was thinking that this was going to be the week from hell, and it would be nice to have some friendly company while I endured it. Now, if you two don't mind, I need to speak to my sister. In private.'

Iona and Caitlin both looked to Melissa, whose expression had turned flinty.

'Why don't you two head up to the hotel and wait for us in the lobby with the ushers? See if you can find my maid of honour, too,' she said. 'Dad will be here to walk me down the aisle at any moment, anyway.'

The bridesmaids didn't look happy about it, but they gathered up their bouquets and headed out to find their opposite numbers amongst the groomsmen. As the door shut behind them Melissa smoothed down her wedding dress once more and turned to Laurel.

'Well? What on earth do you have to say to me?'

'First off, you made a mistake inviting my ex-boy-friend to your wedding.'

Melissa rolled her eyes. '*That's* what all this is about? Really, Laurel, when are you going to grow up and understand that it can't be all about you all the time?'

The hypocrisy was almost enough to make her choke, but Laurel managed to go on. 'Not because of me—although, actually, any sister with a hint of empathy wouldn't do that to a person—but because he's engaged to a gossip columnist. One whose magazine has offered anyone who can get a shot of your wedding dress in advance a really hefty fee.'

Melissa sniffed. 'No one here would do that to me. They love me too much. Besides, they've all signed non-disclosure agreements. I'd sue them.'

Laurel restrained herself from pointing out that if she

was so sure they all loved her that much then surely they wouldn't have *needed* the non-disclosure agreements.

'Not everyone signed one.'

'Well, they should have done!' Melissa sprang to her feet. 'That was your job. If you let a guest RSVP without signing, or a member of the hotel staff—'

'Not a guest,' Laurel said calmly. 'And not the hotel staff. Me. You never asked *me* to sign a non-disclosure agreement.'

'Well, of course not! You're my *sister*. You wouldn't…' Uncertainty blossomed in Melissa's eyes. 'What have you done?'

'Nothing. Yet.'

Laurel moved to sit in the armchair at the centre of the room and motioned for Melissa to take the sofa opposite.

'Sit. I have a number of things I want to say to you.'

Frowning, Melissa did as she was told, and a brief surge of satisfaction bloomed in Laurel's chest.

'I *am* getting married in ten minutes. In case you've forgotten.'

'This won't take long,' Laurel promised. 'Besides, it's the bride's prerogative to be late.'

'So? What do you need to say to me so desperately?'

Laurel thought about it for a moment. She'd never expected even to get this far. Now that she had Melissa there…listening to her…she didn't think there was enough time in the world to make her understand everything she needed to.

So she decided to focus on what mattered most.

'I want you to know that I could have sent this photo to Coral's magazine and made a fortune—but I didn't.' She flashed the screen of her phone at her, showing the shot of the wedding dress hanging from the staircase. 'Not because you're my sister, or because you'd sue me, or anything like that. But because that's not the sort of person I want to be. Okay? But there was a part of me...not a small part of me, either...that thought you'd deserve it. For not paying me a decent wage for organising this wedding. For being so awful to people when the people who matter to you aren't looking. For what you did to Eloise. And for what you just did to me.'

'What did I do to you?' Melissa cried, indignant. 'You're the one who lied to us all.'

'I did—to start with,' Laurel admitted. 'But after that it was more than the lie, even if Dan can't admit that. But you know what? I was putting my heart out there. I was having a moment with the man I...'

Laurel swallowed, feeling as if there was a Christmas tree bauble stuck in her throat. But it wasn't a decoration—it was the truth, bubbling up inconveniently when she couldn't do a thing about it.

'The man I love. And you made it all about you. About your wedding, and your thunder.'

'You're in love with him?' Melissa looked incredulous. 'Why? He's just a stand-in. A stuntman.'

'He's more than you'll ever see,' Laurel said. 'He's real in a way you'll never be. In a way that I want to be.'

Dan wasn't a prince, wasn't a fairy tale. This wasn't the right time, or the right place. But he was the right man. And she knew in an instant, even after he'd turned her down, that she'd rather have him here, now, always, than some mythical prince who might never arrive.

It was just a shame she wasn't enough for him to take the chance.

She got to her feet, almost done. It was time to walk

out there, watch Melissa get married, and get on with her life—with or without Dan. And apparently it was to be without.

'So, here's what I want you to know most of all,' she said. 'It's not all about you. Life isn't the Melissa Sommers show. We all get our own starring roles, and we don't just have to play supporting actress to you. You can't treat people like they don't matter just because they can't give you something, or do something for you. And that means that I don't have to pay for your childhood any longer. I'm not responsible for what our father did, and it's not up to me to make you feel better about that. From now on I'm only taking responsibility for my own actions. And the only things I've done this week are try to give you a perfect wedding and fall in love. Okay?'

Melissa's eyes were wide, astonishment clear in them. But she nodded.

'Great. Then let's go get you married.' She held out a hand to her sister and helped her up.

At least then she'd be officially Riley's problem and not Laurel's.

CHAPTER TEN

DAN MADE HIS way along the frosted drive, back to the main hotel. His head was still spinning from everything Laurel had said, and that was all tied up with Melissa's laughter, echoing through his brain. *A chance. A future.* Everything she'd offered him he'd wanted to take. But he'd known he couldn't.

He wasn't good enough. He couldn't live up to the sort of expectations Laurel had for her future. She wanted everything—love, forever, happiness. And for the first time since Cassie had left he wanted to give that to someone. He *wanted* to be what someone else needed him to be.

But he couldn't. How could he promise Laurel everything she wanted when he already knew he wouldn't be able to deliver? He'd never been enough for anyone before—and he had no faith that he'd suddenly be able to be now.

Dan fought the urge to go and get lost in the woods—to escape, to run. His little brother was getting married. So he couldn't.

He couldn't do anything, it seemed, except what he'd always done. Rebel against expectations. Go the opposite way to the one people wanted him to. Carry on being who he was, with the little he knew he was allowed. Financial success, business success, friends, an estranged family and a series of women for whom he would never be 'the one'.

If he could have been anyone's 'the one' it would have been Laurel's, he realised. But he didn't have that kind of faith in himself.

His father was waiting at the door, and he frowned at Dan as he climbed the steps to Morwen Hall. Suddenly, the Gothic exterior seemed all the more appropriate for the week Dan was having, and he spared a glance up at the architecture rather than meeting his father's gaze.

'Where have you been? Melissa will be here any second and Riley has been asking for you.' Wendell grabbed him by the shoulder and led him off to a side room, near the hall where the ceremony was taking place.

'Asking for me?' Dan frowned. 'For *me*? Why?'

He'd been trying to get his brother alone all week, and now he had him he didn't have a clue what to say.

Don't marry her...she's the devil incarnate. But if you love her...if you think you can be what she needs and that she can be who you need...then take that chance. Jump and forget the safety net. Be a braver man than I am.

'Damned if I know. He's in here.'

And with that, Dan was cast into the side room, where his brother stood by a window, looking very much as if he'd like to climb through it and make a run for it.

'Riley?' Dan said, closing the door quietly behind him. He had a feeling this conversation would be best unobserved. 'Everything okay?'

Riley spun to stare at him, eyes wide with panic. 'Am I doing the right thing? Marrying Melissa?'

Dan closed his eyes. Everything he'd wanted to say to Riley had flown out of his head, pushed aside by the memory of Laurel's face when he told her no.

'How should I know?' he said eventually.

It wasn't as if he was the expert on all things romantic. Look at the mess he'd made with Laurel.

'Because you're my big brother!' Riley ran a hand through his hair in despair. 'Look, I've never asked you for anything before. I know you resented me coming along and ruining your only child status—'

'I didn't—' Dan cut himself off. *Had* he? He'd always thought it was the other way—that Riley had stolen everything from him. But what if that wasn't the whole story?

'Yes, you did. But that doesn't matter now. Because you're my brother, and I need you, so you have to help me. Okay?'

'Okay,' Dan said, settling down into an armchair in the corner of the room. 'What do you need?'

'Thank you.' Riley sank into the chair opposite him. 'So, how do I know if I'm doing the right thing? Marrying Melissa?'

'You remember that my only experience of marriage ended in divorce, right?' *Bitter, painful divorce.*

'Then I'll learn from your mistakes,' Riley said desperately. 'Why was it a mistake to marry Cassie?'

'Because I wasn't enough for her.' The words were automatic, the feeling ingrained. 'She wanted more than just a stuntman. She wanted a star.'

Riley frowned. 'That can't be all of it. She wouldn't have married you in the first place if that was all there was.'

'I…' Dan stalled. Was he right? What else had there been? He'd spent so long not thinking about Cassie, not wanting to examine what he'd lost. Had he missed something?

'She said… Right before she left she said that I wouldn't let her in. Wouldn't let her be what I needed.'

He hadn't known what she meant then, and he wasn't sure he did now. But he knew what he needed, at last. He needed Laurel. And yet he couldn't risk having her.

'Well, that's no help at all.' Riley sighed. 'Okay, well, what about Laurel? You two seem pretty close. How did you know that she was the one?'

'Riley, you and Melissa were engaged before I even *met* Laurel. Besides…it's not what it seems.'

'What it seems?' Riley raised his eyebrows. 'What is it, then?'

'We were…' Now Melissa knew it meant Riley would also know soon enough—along with the rest of the world. He might as well tell his brother himself. 'It was a prank, I guess. We're not really together. We just thought we'd pretend this week, so neither of us had to come to the wedding alone.'

It sounded pathetic, put like that. And more like a lie than telling everyone they were together had, somehow.

Riley's eyebrows were higher than ever now. 'A fake relationship? Really?' He shook his head. 'Man, you're a better actor than I gave you credit for. Because you two sure looked like the real thing to me.'

The real thing. Not an act…not a stand-in.

Could he have that? For real? He'd run when she'd suggested it, knowing he couldn't live up to expectations and not wanting to disappoint her—or risk the pain when she realised the universal truth that Dan Black was Not Enough.

But what if he *could* be? What if he could have been for Cassie? For Riley? For his parents, even?

What if he could change his story? What if it wasn't too late?

He shook his head. One epiphany at a time.

'Yeah, well. Today's not about me and Laurel. It's about you and Melissa,' Dan said, bringing the conversation back to the more urgent matter at hand.

The wedding was supposed to start... He checked his watch. Now. The wedding was supposed to be happening right now. He needed to sort out Riley's head—and then maybe he could start on his own heart.

'So...why did you ask her to marry you in the first place?' he asked.

'I didn't really, I don't think.' Riley's forehead was scrunched up a little, as if he was trying to remember. 'It was more like we'd been dating for a while, you know, and it seemed like the logical next step. Well, that's what Melissa said in her interview afterwards, anyway.'

'Of course.' Dan rubbed a hand over his forehead. 'Okay, tell me this. What's got you thinking all these second thoughts anyway?'

Riley sighed. 'It's this thing with Noah and Eloise. Melissa seems kind of...worked up about it. I think she might even have had something to do with it hitting the internet.'

'I'm certain she did,' Dan said evenly. 'So? How does that make you feel?'

He was starting to sound like that therapist Cassie had wanted him to see. He'd gone once and refused ever to go back. Even in LA, not *everyone* needed to see a therapist.

'A little uncomfortable, I guess. But…it's kind of part of the job, right? The publicity and everything. I mean, we take it when we want it, so we have to put up with it when we don't too.'

'I suppose so.' Another reason to be glad he was merely a very successful businessman and stuntman, rather than a star. He didn't want anyone prying into his private business, thanks. 'Okay, so, next question. Why do you want to marry Melissa?'

'Have you *seen* her? She's gorgeous. And she's a rising star. Together, we can be a proper Hollywood power couple.'

'And do you *like* her?'

Never mind love, Dan decided. That could be fickle as anything. But liking was important. Liking was what got you through the long days and the bad times. Having a friend at your side.

As he'd had Laurel this week.

Not thinking about Laurel.

'You know, I really do,' Riley said, smiling soppily. 'I mean, I know she can be a bit of a pain sometimes, but when it's just us…she's funny, you know? Like, when she's not being "Melissa Sommers, film goddess" she can just be Mel. And that's nice.'

'Sounds like you have your answer right there, then,' Dan said.

'Yeah. I guess I do.' Riley looked over at him and frowned. 'But what about you? There's seriously nothing going on between you and Laurel? Because, honestly, I thought the two of you might spontaneously combust, the looks you were giving each other at the dinner table last night were so hot. I reckon you could be in there if you wanted. You should give it a go, man.' He clapped a hand on Dan's shoulder and grinned. 'Love's great, you know?'

'If you say so,' Dan said, non-committal.

He knew how great it could be. Could sense even now how phenomenal he and Laurel could be together. But that only told him how much more it would hurt to lose it.

'Come on. We need to get you married.'

Then he could get back to his regularly scheduled life. Without love, without Laurel, and without all these feelings that made his chest too tight.

The wedding was perfect.

Laurel strode into Morwen Hall ahead of Melissa and their father, ready to stage-manage the wedding of the year and make sure absolutely nothing stopped Melissa and Riley from getting married—as long as they both still wanted to.

With all that determination she'd built up, it was actually kind of an anti-climax when nothing went wrong.

Riley was waiting at the front of the aisle when she checked, and even Eloise was waiting with the other two bridesmaids. She looked kind of detached—as if she wasn't going to let anything about the day affect her.

Laurel couldn't blame her for that.

She sidled up to Eloise as they stood outside the ceremony room, waiting for the signal to start the procession. Caitlin and Iona were fussing with Melissa's train, while the bride checked her reflection one last time and straightened the tiara on her veil-less head.

'Told you she wouldn't wear the veil.'

'You were right,' Eloise said, with no emotion in her voice.

'You okay?' Laurel asked, lowering her clipboard and looking up at her, concerned. 'I heard… Well, there's been a lot of talk this morning.'

'I'm sure there has,' Eloise replied serenely.

'You seem very…calm,' Laurel said. 'Serene, even.'

Eloise gave her a small smile and raised one shoulder in a half-shrug. 'What else is there to do?'

'I suppose…'

She could be calm too, Laurel realised. She could ignore everything Dan had said, go on about her life without him and pretend the whole thing had never happened. She could act as if it didn't hurt until the pain faded away for real.

Or she could get fired up, say what she really thought, and go after everything she wanted. Even if he said no, even if he didn't listen. Even if he could never love her… Wouldn't it be best to know for sure? To face him down and tell him everything he needed to hear before he made that decision?

To take a chance at being the princess who rescued the prince from a life of never being good enough for love.

That was a starring role Laurel could really get behind.

Never mind serenity. She had something much more important to fight for.

True love.

After so many years believing she wasn't good enough, and trying so hard to be anyway, she'd broken free. She was done with trying to earn love. She was going to *demand* it instead.

The string quartet at the front of the ceremony room started a new piece and Melissa gave a little squeal. 'It's time!'

'Good luck,' Laurel whispered as they lined up in their assigned order. 'I'm going to head in and watch from the front.'

Where she could keep an eye on everything. And grab Dan the moment this was over and give him a piece of her mind.

From his seat in the front row Dan watched Riley's face light up as he saw Melissa walking down the aisle towards him and hoped that his brother had made the right decision. As much as being married to Melissa would drive *him* insane, for Riley it was a different story. Anyone who made his face light up like that, as if his heart was beaming out happiness from within...well, he had to give his brother kudos for taking a chance on that, right?

Then he glanced across the hall and spotted dark brown hair above a blue dress and felt his own heart start to contract.

Laurel.

She'd slipped in to take a seat in the front row on the other side of the aisle, a few chairs down from her stepmother. Her cheeks were flushed, and even at a distance he could see the brightness in her eyes.

That was not a broken woman. Whatever she might have hoped for, his turning her down hadn't caused her any pause at all. She'd stormed inside, dealt with Melissa, put on the wedding of the year—and kept every ounce of her composure while doing it.

He was so proud of her he could barely breathe.

It was good that he was leaving, he reminded himself as Melissa and Riley took their vows. Good that she'd be free to seek out all the things she wanted from life, away from Melissa's shadow. Away from the distraction of their affair.

Laurel had the strength now to go out and find her prince, her happy-ever-after—he could feel it and he was *glad* about that. Really he was.

So...why did it feel so wrong?

Almost before he knew it the ceremony was over, and Riley and Melissa were walking back up the aisle, arm in arm, ready for what was sure to be the longest wedding photography session in history. Sighing, Dan got to his feet, hoping he could grab a drink at least before he had to loiter around waiting to see if they actually wanted the non-famous brother of the groom in any of the shots.

But before he could start to follow them out of the hall he felt a small hand on his arm and looked down into Laurel's blazing brown eyes.

'Don't *you* say a word,' she snapped, with all the fire and determination he'd seen in her earlier barely contained. 'Because I have a lot of things to say to you. And you are going to listen, and then I am going to go and organise the wedding breakfast. Okay?'

'Okay.' Dan blinked. 'Wait, I mean—'

'Too late. Now listen.'

She took a deep breath, and Dan braced himself for a list of all his faults—probably organised alphabetically, knowing Laurel.

'I know you think you can't have this. That love isn't something that stays for you. But you're wrong. Maybe you haven't found the right woman yet, or maybe you don't let any of them in enough to love you in the first place. But whatever it is you have to give it a chance, Dan. You have to be the hero of *your* story too, you know. You can't always be the stand-in, the fall guy, the one who gets beaten up and edited out. You don't have to be a star to chase your own happy-ever-after, okay? And this week…this week you showed me all that about myself. You gave me the confidence to stand up to Melissa—not to go behind her back and ruin her day, but to tell her the truth, to explain how I feel and to move on. To stop trying to earn her love because I thought I wasn't good enough. I *am* good enough—for me. And that's all that matters. You showed me that there's life beyond Melissa's shadow—and, trust me, I'm going out there looking for it. And I think it'll be a crying shame if you don't do the same.'

She let go of his sleeve and took a step back, staring up into his face as he tried to get his scrambled thoughts in order.

'I get it if you don't want to look for that happy-ever-after with me. You're right—we only agreed to a fake relationship and I'm not going to try and hold you to anything more. But if you don't want to try because you're too scared—because you think you can't be good enough, that you can't live up to expectations—you're an idiot. Because I'd rather have the real you than some mythical prince any day.'

He opened his mouth to respond, still unsure of the words he was looking for, but she reached up and put a finger to his lips.

'One more thing,' she said. 'You also taught me that we each need to be true to ourselves and our own dreams—not try to be the people our families or friends think we are. We have to be our own people. And I wouldn't be doing that if I didn't tell you that my own person is in love with yours.'

Love. *Love?* Dan started to shake his head, but Laurel was already walking away.

'Can't stop. I've got a wedding reception to pull off, before I can go and start my own life. Goodbye, Dan.'

No. Not goodbye.

She was leaving him...walking away...and it was all his own fault.

The reality of his own culpability came crashing down so hard that he practically fell into the seat next to him. It was Cassie all over again—a woman he cared for walking away, seeking her own happiness because he couldn't share it with her. No, not couldn't—*wouldn't*. He wouldn't take that chance, that risk of not being enough for her. And that meant he'd always be alone. Always be left behind and put aside—not because there was someone better, but because he wouldn't give enough of himself to find a true partnership.

He'd spent so long expecting people to leave, to be disappointed in him, he'd built up walls to stop them even coming in in the first place.

The question was, did he even know how to knock them down again? And if he did...could he risk it?

Laurel leant back against a pillar in the ballroom, wishing she could take off her stupid shoes, and watched Melissa and Riley take their first dance together as husband and wife.

She'd done it. She'd got through Melissa's wedding without any major disasters—if you didn't count the state of her heart. But even taking that into account she felt stronger, more certain about the future than she had in years.

The credits were about to roll on Melissa's big day, and Laurel was still standing.

She raised her champagne flute just a little, toasting herself, and took a sip as Noah and Eloise took to the dance floor too, for the planned 'best man and maid of honour' dance. Laurel winced at the distant look on her friend's face and hoped that the desperate way Noah was talking to her meant that he was apologising.

Somebody should, she felt. And, as she'd said to Eloise earlier, they couldn't let the men they loved break them.

She wanted Eloise and Noah to work things out—find their happy ending. Even if she couldn't just yet.

She would one day—that she was certain of. She had the tools and the knowledge she needed to be happy now. She knew she was enough just as she was—and she knew she needed a man who believed that too.

After that everything would be easy. She hoped.

'Laurel.'

She spun on her heel at the sound of Dan's voice, almost overbalancing until he caught her by the elbow.

'I've said everything I need to say to you.' She looked up into his eyes and swallowed, trying to keep any fledgling hope buried deep, where it couldn't disappoint her again.

'Then maybe it's my turn to talk,' Dan replied.

Laurel waited.

And waited.

'Well?' she said impatiently. 'Are you going to? Because if not I really do have some more work I should be getting on with.'

'I… This is hard for me, okay?' Dan said. 'I'm trying to find the right words.'

Laurel blew out a long breath. 'Maybe they don't have to be the *right* words. Maybe you just have to talk to me.'

'I love you,' Dan said suddenly, and all that hope in her belly bloomed bright and strong.

'That's… What?'

'I love you. And it's crazy because I've only known you four days. And it's stupid because I've given you no reason to believe me. And it's terrifying because you could walk away right now and I wouldn't even blame you. But I love you. And the thing is, I'm starting to think that I always will.'

'I don't… What changed?' Laurel asked, shaking her head in confusion. 'You said it was just an act. A game. You said it wasn't real.'

'I lied.' He sighed and took her champagne flute from her. After taking a long gulp, he placed it on the table behind them and wrapped his hands around her waist, pulling her closer. 'I was scared. Scared of what I felt and how I knew it would end. I… I always disappoint, Laurel. I've never once been enough for someone. And I couldn't bear for that to happen with you. You deserve everything—every happiness you ever dream of. And I wanted to be the man to give that to you… I just didn't believe I could.'

'And now?'

'Now… I'm willing to try.'

He swallowed so hard she could see his throat move, and she knew how difficult this must be for him, and loved him more for it.

'Because you were right—I was so certain that everyone would leave me, choose someone else over me, that I never gave anyone the chance to stay. I never let anyone choose *me*.'

'I would,' Laurel whispered. 'I'd choose you every time.'

His eyes fluttered shut and he kissed her forehead. 'I hope so. Because I realised today...when I saw you across the aisle... I've already chosen. It's you for me, Laurel. Whether you stay or go—whether it lasts or it doesn't. It's not even a choice. You're the one I love—the one I'll always love. The one I'm meant to be with.'

'So what is there to be scared about?'

He gave a shaky laugh. 'Are you kidding? *Everything*.' He gazed down into her eyes. 'But if you're with me...it's worth being scared.'

Stretching up, Laurel kissed him, long and deep and with every bit of the love she felt for him. Smiling against her lips, Dan pulled her behind the column, away from the watching eyes of the wedding guests. She liked that. This wasn't for them. They didn't matter to her at all.

All that mattered was that Dan was here and he was hers.

'So, what happens now?' she asked when they finally broke apart.

Dan shrugged. 'We start our own story. Here... there...wherever you want. I have faith that we can make it work.'

'We can,' Laurel agreed, nodding. '*Our* story. You know, I like that even better than *my* story.'

'Good. Because I've heard it's going to be an epic. One of those that just goes on and on and on...'

'And does it have a happy ending?' Laurel asked, smiling up at him.

Dan smiled back and kissed her lightly once more. 'The happiest,' he promised. 'For ever and after.'

New Year's Day dawned bright and blue and breezy. Most of the wedding guests were still in bed—probably sleeping off the prodigious bar bill, Dan assumed. But not him. With one arm around Laurel's waist he stood beside Eloise and Noah on the front steps of Morwen Hall and watched as Melissa and Riley climbed into the car that would take them to the airport and their honeymoon.

'We're really just here to make sure they're actually going, aren't we?' Eloise said, raising her hand to wave.

'Basically,' Laurel agreed. 'Are you looking forward to getting your hotel back?'

'I don't know,' Eloise said. 'I'm starting to think I might have other ambitions beyond Morwen Hall.'

'What about you, Laurel?' Noah asked. 'Are you looking forward to getting your life back?'

Laurel grinned, and Dan couldn't help but smile with her. 'Actually, I'm looking forward to starting a whole new one.'

'I know how that feels,' Noah murmured, kissing Eloise's cheek.

'So, what are you going to do first?' Dan asked. 'With this brand-new life of yours.'

'Honestly? I feel like I could sleep for a week,' Laurel said, making them laugh.

'A-List celebrity weddings are hard work, I guess?' Noah said.

'Very.'

'I suppose that means you don't fancy organising another one some time?'

Eloise elbowed Noah as he spoke, and he put up his hands in self-defence.

'What? Just asking. I mean, it never hurts to have the best in the business on your side, now, does it?'

'Best in the business, huh?' Laurel echoed. 'I like the sound of that.'

'And I'm not just saying that so you'll take the job. When the time comes,' he added quickly as Eloise glared at him.

'You might have to get in line, you realise?' Dan said, staring out at the beautiful blue sky as Riley and Melissa's car disappeared around the corner into the trees. 'I might have a wedding for her to arrange first.'

'Might you, indeed?' Laurel said. 'And whose would that be?'

'Ours,' Dan said, hardly believing the word as he spoke it.

But then he kissed her, and suddenly everything felt very real.

'Was that a proposal?' Laurel asked as they broke apart. 'For real?'

Dan smiled, as his future fell into place.

'For real,' he promised.

Because reality with Laurel beat every story he'd ever heard hands-down.

* * * * *

HER PERFECT
CANDIDATE

CANDACE SHAW

For my girlfriends Brenda, Kenyatta, Lisa, Mary and Tonya for their love and support as I embark on this new chapter in my life.

For my husband, Bobby. Where would I be without you? Love you!

A big thank you to my girls, authors Sharon C. Cooper and Delaney Diamond. I'm so happy we are on this journey together. Charlie's Angels for life!

Chapter 1

"Great!"

Megan Chase plopped her forehead on the steering wheel. It was early evening in rush hour traffic, and her SUV had just gotten a flat tire on Interstate 85 in Atlanta. Luckily, she was in the far right lane and was able to inch the vehicle over to the shoulder. She lifted her head, breathed deeply and eased open the door to survey the damage. But before her 4-inch heel could hit the pavement, she quickly drew it back in observing the cars zooming by at high speeds.

Shutting the door, she moved her laptop bag and purse from the passenger seat into the back, before climbing over the gearshift. The flat was on the back passenger side. She figured she could change it and then be on her way to meet her twin sister and her best friend at a scholarship fund-raiser event one of her clients had invited them to.

She hopped out of the SUV and walked carefully along the rocky pavement.

"Of all the days to dress up," she said, pulling her short black dress down to barely touch her knees. She stooped down to look at the damaged tire. The tires were new, so she wasn't quite sure why she had a flat. A nail, probably, she thought.

Earlier that day, she'd put the finishing touches on decorating a model home in a new subdivision outside of Atlanta. Houses were in the process of being built, and Megan had toured the subdivision to see the homes. She figured she'd run over a nail in the process.

As she popped the trunk to retrieve the tire, she heard her cell phone blaring from her purse in the backseat. Climbing through the trunk of her SUV to reach the phone, she knew who was calling before she even looked at the display. Now, glancing down at the caller ID to confirm her suspicion, she saw Sydney Chase's name flash on the screen. Megan knew if she didn't answer the phone, Sydney the worrier, would probably have the FBI, CIA and the SWAT team scouring the city for her within the hour.

The sound of a horn and tires on the gravel behind Megan stopped her from answering the call. She grabbed the mace she always carried in her purse and began to climb backward out of the SUV. Her finger placed firmly on the spray button.

As she turned around to step down, a fine-looking

tall man was standing in front of her opened trunk, with his hand out to assist her. She blinked twice and stifled a "Goodness he's gorgeous" with a slight gulp. The sun was going down behind him radiating an aura of bright yellow and orange.

"Need some assistance, pretty lady?" the sexy, baritone voice offered.

Megan tossed the mace spray over the backseat and placed her empty hand in his. His touch on her skin, although brief, sent a warm shiver through her veins. Once settled onto the pavement, she squinted her eyes and placed her right hand straight across her forehead to see him better without being blinded by what was left of the sun.

She looked up in amazement at the most handsome man she had ever laid her eyes upon. He was quite tall, at least a few inches over six feet. His hair was neatly trimmed with black wavy ripples. The evening sun was bringing out the color of his smooth, milk chocolate skin, and she fought back the urge to run a hand over his hairless, chiseled face. He had thick eyelashes that supermodels would give up purging their dinner for. His charming smile displayed pearl-colored teeth between his inviting lips. While he had let go of her hand, she could still feel the warmth of it on her skin. She wondered how his strong hands would feel on the rest of her body.

For a moment time stood still. She didn't notice the cars zooming by them or the April sun bearing down on her. Instead, she thought about how he reminded her of the man she always dreamed about.

The man who would one day rescue her on his white horse and love her forever.

Suddenly remembering that he'd asked her a question, she blinked several times before coming down from cloud nine.

"Do I know you?" she asked, studying his captivating face.

A delicious grin crossed his mouth causing her to almost sigh out loud. *Stay composed, girl. You see handsome men all the time.*

"I don't think so. I would definitely remember you if we knew each other," the sinfully sexy gentleman stated in a tone that caused another wave of heat to rage through her.

What the heck is wrong with me?

"Oh, sorry for staring so hard, but you look familiar," Megan replied, studying his face carefully. Megan wasn't good with names, but she never forgot a face, especially one as intriguing as his. She couldn't help but stare at the yummy dimple on his right cheek that appeared every time he smiled.

"What's your name?" Megan asked.

"Steven."

"Nice to meet you. I'm Megan."

"Do you need some help changing that tire?" he asked, nodding his head in the direction of the flat. "It's too dangerous for you to be out here alone."

"Oh, yes. I..." she stuttered, glancing toward the tire. *This man is making me forget why I'm standing out here in the hot sun in the first place.* "I was just about to change it."

His left eyebrow rose. "Really?" His gaze traveled the length of her body. "Wearing Louboutins and a very…um…sexy little freak'um dress. Are you trying to cause accidents? Seeing you bent over trying to change a flat tire will cause a ten car pileup," he teased, taking off his blue suit jacket along with a red tie and handing them to her. "I'll take care of it, while you call back whoever keeps calling you." He nodded down to the cell phone in her hand that kept vibrating. "Your man is probably worried."

She shook her head and glanced at the caller ID. "It's my sister. We're supposed to meet for an event…" She stopped to glance at her watch. "I'm thirty minutes late and big sis is concerned," she said, watching Steven take the spare tire and jack out of her trunk. He then slammed it shut and turned to look at her.

"I completely understand. My brother is always checking on me and he's younger. How many years apart are you?"

"Two minutes," she answered. "We're twins."

"So there are two of you?" A cocky grin formed on his lips. "Nice," he commented, barely loud enough for her to hear as he rolled the spare tire over to the flat one. "You're more than welcome to sit in my SUV and wait. The sun is going down, but it's still hot. Crank the ignition and turn up the air conditioner if you'd like."

Megan looked past him at the white Range Rover. *He seems like the type to own such an elite SUV. Tai-*

lored business suit, expensive watch and a powerful, masculine presence.

"Thank you. I'll call my sister and let her know I'm fine." She walked steadily on the gravel toward the passenger side of his Range Rover. Once settled in the plush leather seat, she cranked the car as he suggested and was pleasantly surprised to hear Sade singing "Smooth Operator" through the speakers. She turned the volume down when she saw the light flash on her cell phone again.

"Hello?"

"Megan, where are you? I've called you like five times!" Sydney exclaimed.

"Syd, I'm sorry. I had a flat tire, but I'll be along soon," Megan answered quickly. She was too busy gazing at the jaw-dropping man who was now peeling off his dress shirt to reveal a white undershirt. The shirt did little to hide the gorgeous muscles of his arms, chest and back. A thin sheen of sweat glistened on his forehead. *He looks so damn hot and fine.* Megan reached over and turned the air conditioner to full blast.

"Are you listening?" Sydney asked in an impatient manner.

Who could listen at a time like this?

"Huh? What did you say?"

"I said do you need any help? Or are you changing it yourself?"

"No, this kind man is changing it for me." Megan continued to watch as Steven lifted the flat tire off, showcasing the toned muscles of his arms. *Oh, my goodness!*

"Kind man? You mean strange man! Where are you?"

"Calm down, Agent Chase. I'm sitting in his Range Rover watching him change my tire. He's almost done," Megan said, a little disappointed. "Poor thing, he's sweating. I think I have some bottled water still left in my lunch cooler. Syd, this man is so gorgeous!"

"Um…is this the same Megan that swore off *all* men almost two years ago when her ex-boyfriend cheated?"

"I didn't swear off all men, I just said I needed a break from dating and that mostly included all of the blind dates you, Jade and Tiffani had been arranging for me. I don't have a problem being single." She frowned as Steven replaced the last lug nut. He looked up and flashed a million-dollar smile, causing her to suck in her breath and become slightly turned on.

"He's done. I'll see you in a few." Megan abruptly hung up the phone to avoid any lectures from her sister about being safe. Sydney was a criminal profiler with the Georgia Bureau of Investigations, and in her book, everyone was a suspect.

Megan hopped out of the passenger seat and walked over to Steven who was wiping the sweat off of his forehead with his dress shirt.

"You're going to ruin that shirt," she said, opening the back door of her SUV and reaching over to pull out a small, unopened bottle of water from a small ice cooler. She opened the cap and handed him the water.

"Thank you, pretty lady." He gulped down half of the bottle before taking a breathing break and then downed the rest of the water. "The shirt will be fine. I'm headed home to change clothes anyway."

Megan watched him intently as she thought of something else to say. She knew in a minute they'd be back in their own vehicles, going back to their already scheduled day. She didn't notice a wedding ring—just a college ring. But that didn't mean he wasn't seeing someone.

"Thank you so much for changing my tire for me. I must've run over a nail today while driving around a subdivision's construction site."

"Having a home built?"

"No. I'm an interior decorator. I just finished a project in one of the model homes and decided to drive around the subdivision." She hoped to find some way to keep the conversation going, but he was already buttoning his shirt and checking his Rolex. She decided not to delay him any longer. He needed to go, and she needed to leave as well before Syd assumed she'd been kidnapped.

He stepped toward her as she closed the back door. She leaned against the SUV as he stood directly in front of her, literally in her personal space. The woodsy scent of his cologne swirled in her nose, sending tingles through her body. *I wonder what his scent would smell like intertwined with mine?*

Her lips parted slightly as he stared down at her, she thought surely he was undressing her with his eyes as they raked over her.

"Thank you again. I hope I didn't inconvenience you, Steven."

"No, not at all. I'm very glad I pulled over to help you," he stated in a sincere tone, running his eyes over her body one more time before they settled back on her face.

She smiled up at him before stepping over to the passenger door. He opened it for her and she slid in, crossing her legs and turning her body to face him.

"Bye, Megan," he said hesitantly before shutting the door. He gave her one last smile before strolling back to his car, whistling.

Steven watched as the loveliest vision he'd ever laid his eyes on drove away. When he first saw her in the trunk bending over the backseat of her Acura MDX reaching for something, he couldn't help but wonder if her toned caramel-coated legs and thighs matched the rest of her. The way her little black dress hugged her bottom and hips as it rose up, stirred his manhood. He had decided to take a chance. Plus, he couldn't possibly leave a female on the side of the highway with a flat tire.

Her long, curly brown hair with subtle blond highlights flowed down her provocative bare back in an utterly sexy manner. He would've given anything to run his fingers through her soft curls, or better yet, spread them out on his pillow as he looked down at her.

He'd been pleasantly surprised when she turned around to acknowledge him. Strikingly stunning, she had a pleasant smile, high cheekbones and wore very little makeup. Her almond-shaped eyes were cinnamon in hue and when he stared into them, he felt a sense of overwhelming peace.

Steven admired all women, but Megan stirred feelings and emotions he'd never felt before in the thirty-three years of his life. Her pleasant personality and warm demeanor were a breath of fresh air.

While changing the flat tire, he couldn't get the image of Megan's short black dress and shapely legs in black heels out of his head. He had let his eyes roam all over her breathtaking body while he tried to make polite conversation. It was hard to do, considering she had the perfect hourglass figure. Her perky, rounded breasts and small waist were followed by hips that settled snuggly but tastefully in the dress she wore.

He had tried to move his eyes back up to hers so she wouldn't realize he was checking her out, but instead they'd rested on her inviting lips. Sexy, luscious lips painted in a reddish shade that he enjoyed watching move. He didn't care what she was saying, he just wanted to devour them. He felt a rise in his briefs again as he thought about the possibility of being kissed by the sexy interior decorator.

He didn't mean to step into her personal space, but he'd needed to see her supple lips up close once more.

It took everything he had in him not to drag her body close to his and kiss her senseless right there against her SUV. The way he noticed her checking him out as well, he wouldn't have been surprised if she had responded. However, he was shocked at his thought. Kissing was something he didn't do. Sex, yes. Kissing, no. It was too emotional, and he wasn't looking for an emotional relationship with anyone. Yet, kissing the beautiful Megan was all he could think about.

As he drove toward his penthouse in Midtown, it dawned on him that she didn't recognize him as the Georgia state senator Steven Monroe, son of Robert Monroe, United States senator. Coming from three generations of politicians and Harvard Law School graduates, the Monroe family were considered to be the black Kennedys because of their millions, power and influence in the political world. Because of who he was, most women usually flirted with him and did any and everything possible to garner his attention.

Steven leaned his head back on his seat and inhaled the sweet scent of the intoxicating perfume lingering in his SUV. *Damn, why on earth didn't I ask for her phone number?*

Megan searched through her console between the seats for her Sade CD with her right hand as she kept her left hand steady on the wheel. She needed to hear "Smooth Operator" one more time as thoughts of Steven filled her head. She was surprised at her thoughts but couldn't help but smile. She then glanced at herself in the rearview mirror to see how she looked when he met her. Upon finding the CD, she slid it into the CD player and waited anxiously while it loaded. She skipped the first few songs until she heard the beat of "Smooth Operator" and turned the volume up.

As she was singing the song for the second time, she saw Syd's cell number flash on the dash. She had the Bluetooth hands-free function connected to her car, which made it safer for her to talk to clients while driving. She turned off the music and pushed the cell button on her steering wheel.

"I'm almost there, Syd," Megan said as she exited the interstate. She then turned toward Atlantic Station, an outdoor mall in Midtown Atlanta that housed the swanky hotel Twelve, where the fundraiser gala was being held.

"I'm just making sure the stranger who changed your tire didn't kidnap you."

"Whatever."

"So tell me about this *kind stranger.*"

She blushed at the thought of him, and then giggled like a high school girl. "His name is Steven and that's all I know. Oh, and he looks simply amazing in a suit."

"Did you get a last name? I can do a background check."

"No, I didn't, we didn't exchange information. But I'm fine with that."

"Well...you seemed as if you were beaming so I just thought you may go out with him."

"Syd, for the last time, I'm happy being single.

My main concern is expanding my business. I'm focusing on my career right now."

Megan turned her car into the valet parking area and grabbed her purse from the backseat as the valet guy opened the door, greeted her and handed her a ticket. "I'm here, Syd. I'll see you in a few minutes."

Thirty minutes later, Megan sat at her reserved table after she gave her donation and chatted briefly with her client and mentor, Chelsea Benton, who had invited her to the gala. Megan loved to dress up and hang with her girlfriends in intimate or casual settings but big bashes weren't exactly her cup of tea. However, it was for charity, plus Chelsea had promised to introduce her to some potential clients.

She glanced over at her twin sitting beside her, who seemed to be having a great time people watching.

"Let me guess. You're watching everyone and figuring out what they're thinking just by their body language."

Sydney nodded. Her bob hair cut swished forward in the process. Their hairstyles were the only way people knew who was who. Plus their personalities were like night and day. Megan was the more whimsical, bubbly twin whereas Sydney was the serious-minded and logical one.

"Yes, but not on purpose. It's just a habit. Like right now I can tell by your pursed lips and the way your hand is resting under your chin, that you're ready to leave."

"I am, but I'll stay for a little longer. Chelsea wanted Jade and I to meet some potential clients."

"And where is your best friend?" Sydney glanced around the room.

"Right here, Tia and Tamera," a sassy voice behind them said. "Thank you for saving me a seat."

Jade Whitmore was Megan's best friend from college. Together they owned Chase and Whitmore Designs, an up-and-coming boutique decorating firm for the past six years.

Jade slid into the empty seat on the other side of Megan and placed a glass of champagne on the table. "Sorry I'm late. I had to meet with the Cannadys to pick up their last payment. Glad we're done with that project."

"Me, too," Megan agreed but her attention was diverted by the commotion at the entrance of the event. The ladies and other guests all placed their eyes on a man flanked with bodyguards and an entourage of people strolling into the gala. The man in the middle turned his back to the crowd as he stopped to shake hands and chat with a few people who approached him.

"Must be someone important," Megan shrugged and sipped her champagne as she stared at the back of the tall man clad in a black tuxedo. He turned to the side to greet a lady with a too-short dress on who in return gazed up at him as if he were the most handsome man in the world.

Megan cocked her head to the side and raised an eyebrow as a smile inched across her face and her heart and stomach began to flutter uncontrollably.

"Oh, my goodness!"

Sydney and Jade placed their attention on her, and Sydney waved her hand in front of her twin's face. "I've never seen you smile like that before. I know he's gorgeous, but stop drooling."

Megan shook her head as she tried to calm her smile and excitement down, but it was no use especially when he turned his head as if he sensed her staring at him. Their eyes locked, and a charming smile crept across his breathtaking, chiseled face. He nodded knowingly as he took a step in her direction but a couple stepped in his path for conversation. Even though he conversed with them, his eyes on hers never faltered.

Jade tapped her on the shoulder. "Megan, do you know who you're making goo-goo eyes with?"

She nodded. "Yes, that's him. The man who changed my flat tire."

"That's who changed your tire?" Sydney questioned in a surprised tone.

"Yes and apparently he *is* someone important since everyone seems to know who he is except me."

"Um…yes…" Jade started. "That's Georgia state senator Steven Monroe, self-proclaimed lifelong bachelor and one of Atlanta's most notorious playboys."

Chapter 2

"I'll call you next week about that," Steven promised, shaking his associate's hand as he tried to move away from the crowd of people that were beginning to form around him. His eyes couldn't tear away from Megan's lovely face. He was quite surprised to see her when he entered the ballroom for just some moments ago he'd taken a cold shower as he thought of her. Of course he told himself the cold shower was to cool down his temperature after changing her tire in the blazing evening sun, but he knew that was a lie.

He hadn't been in the mood to attend the fundraiser, but considering it was in the same building he lived in, all he had to do was ride the elevator down to the first floor. Plus, his best friend and campaign manager, Shawn Bennett suggested Steven at least should show his face, shake hands and give a considerable donation. But most importantly stay away from the ladies. His reputation couldn't handle any more bad press considering he had been on local blogs and news channels with a different woman nearly every week. And considering Steven's father wanted him to eventually run for the U.S. Senate seat he was retiring from at the end of the year, Steven needed to first clean up his image. While he would be a shoo-in to win the nomination because of his intellect, clean political slate and charismatic nature, the Monroe campaign team was more concerned that Steven's playboy image would cost him the opportunity to win.

So he'd made a promise to stay low-key and out of the limelight with the ladies and therefore opted not to have a date that evening. However, there was something about Megan that was drawing him to her like a magnetic force. When he entered the room earlier, he sensed the same calming peace he had when he'd initially met her. Was it her perfume in the atmosphere or her cute giggle that made him turn her way, only to find her inquisitive eyes on him? She bestowed her beautiful smile as she had when he'd changed her tire, but this one was accompanied with a look of promise that he couldn't explain. He had a feeling his smile matched hers.

Steven continued to nod and shake hands with people who approached him all the while keeping his eyes glued to Megan and her table. He briefly glanced on either side of her to make sure she didn't have a date. On her left was a woman who looked just like her, which must've been the twin sister she'd mentioned. And the other lady at the table, while drop-dead gorgeous, did nothing for him, either. There weren't any men in their presence, and he was grateful. "Hello, Megan," he said casually. "And ladies." He nodded at them but kept his eyes on Megan. "Nice to see you here. I was hoping to run into someone I know."

She chuckled with a head tilt. "Weren't you just bombarded with people *you know?* We just met an hour ago."

"Hmm...I know, yet we keep running into each other. Maybe we're supposed to be in each other's lives."

She released her signature cute giggle again, and he was glad when her friends excused themselves but not before the both of them winked at Megan. He sat in the chair across from her and dismissed his bodyguards who were actually his campaign manager and his brother, Bryce. They'd tagged along to make sure he stayed out of trouble. And he sensed their hesitancy before they strode away.

"I must say, I'm quite glad to see you. You drove away without me getting any of your information. I don't even know your last name."

"It's Chase. Megan Chase...Senator Monroe," she stated knowingly with a grin.

He threw his head back in laughter. "Does that bother you?"

"Nope. I'm forever grateful. Could you imagine me changing a tire in heels and in this dress?"

His eyes traveled over her body settling on her shapely legs and a glimpse of the side of her exquisite thighs peeking out from her dress.

No, but I can imagine you only in those heels with your legs over my shoulders. He blinked his eyes a few times and cleared the frog in his throat. At first he thought he'd spoken his private thoughts out loud.

"So that means I have your vote in the next election?"

"I don't know," she said in a teasing manner. "What makes you the perfect candidate?"

"I'm a regular down-to-earth guy who likes to help people less fortunate than myself and ultimately make a difference in my community."

"I'm sold. When does your current term end?"

"I just started my second term as a senator for Georgia so not for another two years. However, I'm considering running for a U.S. Senate seat within the next year or so, but let's keep that between us for now. It's my father's seat, and I'm sure there're a few people who would love to have it if they caught wind of my dad retiring."

"Your secret is safe with me," she said sincerely.

Steven couldn't believe he'd told her such secret information so easily. Only he, his father, brother and best friend were aware of Senator Robert Monroe's retirement plans. But for some reason he trusted the lady sitting in front of him.

"So how long have you been in the interior-design business?"

"Well unofficially since I was seven years old." She paused to laugh. "I redesigned my side of my childhood room by using watercolors and markers on the wall. I also cut up some old drapes my mother was going to toss to make throw pillows and a duvet cover. I loved it but much to my mother's dismay, she wasn't pleased with the mural on the wall. But officially when I graduated with my undergraduate degree, so six years."

"I currently live in a penthouse here at Twelve, but it was already furnished. However, I'm looking into buying a home soon and would love to hire a professional decorator."

"I'm always looking for new clients, which is one of the reasons why I'm here. Just let me know when you're ready."

She opened her evening bag and handed him a business card.

He knew it would be months before he would close on a home. He wasn't even officially looking for a house yet although he had an agent. It was just something he was considering, but he couldn't let months go by without seeing her.

"Well, do you have any appointments available this Monday? I would love to see your portfolio and talk to you about some of my ideas."

She nodded and pulled her cell phone out of her purse. "I have Monday around noon available. Is that a good time for you? If not… Friday."

He actually had an appointment on Monday at the exact same time, but he couldn't possibly wait until Friday. He didn't know if he could wait the two days until Monday. "Noon will be fine. How about we meet at a restaurant and have a business lunch?"

"That sounds good. My office is located in the Buckhead area. How about Café Love Jones? It's a jazz club, but they're open for lunch, as well. I have business meetings there quite often."

"That's a great spot. Delicious food and atmosphere."

"Glad you think so. My big brother Braxton is the owner."

"Cool. I don't know him personally, but I met him briefly at an event there a few years ago. Brother can play the hell out of a piano."

Steven then unconsciously glanced up to see Shawn tapping his watch which meant it was time to move on. He was supposed to stay focused, mixing and mingling with the crowd, not flirting with the most beautiful woman at the fund-raiser. But he remembered his promise, and reluctantly stood as the smile on Megan's soft face sank a little.

"It was nice seeing you again, Megan. I look forward to our meeting on Monday."

"Me, too." She held out her hand to shake his, but instead he raised it to his lips and kissed it tenderly. The feel of her silky, warm skin on his lips and the scent of her perfume on her wrist shook him to the core. He let his mouth linger on her hand longer than he should have, as he stared into her cinnamon eyes.

She let out a soft sigh and slowly withdrew her hand from his. He regained his composure and tried to remember where he was before he did something impulsive like pull her into his arms and kiss her until her knees buckled.

Steven cleared his throat and shoved his hands in his pockets to restrain them. "I'll see you later."

For the rest of the evening he socialized with the other guests, discussing politics all while keeping his eyes on Megan. Every now and then he'd catch her glance in his direction as Chelsea Benton escorted her and her friend around. He assumed Chelsea was introducing the women to possible clients since they were eagerly handing out business cards.

An hour later he felt a tap on his shoulder and was pleasantly surprised to look down into Megan's adorable face.

"Hey, pretty lady." He leaned over and whispered in her ear. "Having fun? I saw quite a few gentlemen trying to get to know you better."

"Um…yes, but I'm not trying to date at the present moment. However, I met some potential clients. I just wanted to say thank you again for changing my tire, and I look forward to our meeting on Monday."

"Me, too. Why are you cutting out so early?"

"I'm not really one for social events even though I should be. However, Chelsea insisted that I come."

"How do you know Chelsea Benton?"

"She's one of my mother's best friends from college. And you?"

"Her husband is golf buddies with my father, and

she did some fashion consulting for me both times I ran for the state senate."

"She's the best." Megan then let out a yawn, which caused him to yawn, as well. They both laughed, and he stepped closer toward her.

"Good night, Ms. Chase." His voice was low. Serious. He hoped the stir in his manhood stayed at bay. He wasn't in the mood for any more cold showers that evening.

If she was any other woman, he would've invited her upstairs to his place, but he knew Megan wasn't the type to say yes to that and he was glad she wasn't. Out of all the young women at the fundraiser aside from her twin and girlfriend, Megan was the only one that hadn't either batted her eyelashes and twirled her hair or slipped her phone number in the front of his pants' pocket.

"Good night, Senator Monroe."

He hesitated to leave, but just then her sister arrived to let her know the valet had pulled their cars around, and the two ladies walked away.

"Who was that?" he heard Shawn say as he approached from the side as they both stood in place staring after Megan and her sister.

"The one woman who could possibly make me settle down."

The next morning Megan awoke to the sounds of birds chirping outside the window ledge of her loft apartment and a splitting headache. Usually the echoes of birds soothed her nerves, but not this morning. She wasn't able to sleep last night. Every time she closed her eyes, she fantasized about the handsome Steven Monroe and his strong hands roaming over her figure. Or his lips moving from her hand and wandering over every inch of her body until she passed out from pure ecstasy. She'd almost swooned last night when the caress of his warm lips pressed against her skin sent her to a point of oblivion while she tried to remain composed on the outside. No man had ever stirred her like that before. But she knew getting involved with a politician was out of the question. Or any man for that matter. Right now her focus was her career and a serious relationship was out of the question.

After tossing and turning, Megan had gotten up in the middle of the night and spent a few hours online researching Steven. She'd heard of him before but because she wasn't all that interested in politics, she never paid him much attention, and she didn't read the gossip blogs. She discovered he was divorced but with no children. No mention of a dog, but it was a possibility. Men like him usually had a dog for companionship.

As Megan continued her research, she learned that Steven was a politician that believed that his constituents should be able to voice their opinions. He based his platforms on their concerns as well as his own moral and personal beliefs. As a state senator, he held monthly meetings with the citizens of his district to discuss their needs in the community. Steven had opened a children's after-school center, organized community gardens and raised funds for new roads in poverty stricken areas as well as more funding for the schools in his district. He wasn't afraid to speak his mind, which made him well liked by his constituents though frowned upon by some of his fellow politicians.

The only negative news Megan discovered was that he was dating several different women at the same time. The media labeled him as both an eligible bachelor and playboy. She found that hard to believe considering he was a perfect gentleman the night before and paid no attention to other gorgeous women who threw sexy smiles his way and dirty looks at her. However, there were plenty of pictures of him and beautiful women on the gossip blogs so apparently it was true.

Megan rose from her bed to put on a pot of coffee. Percy, her Persian cat, was staring at her from his heated cat bed on the floor. She was surprised that he wasn't in the bed with her, but sometimes Percy needed his own space. *Just like a male.* She laughed.

Megan sipped on hazelnut-flavored coffee seated at her kitchen's island and reviewed paint colors for her latest project for Chelsea. Chelsea was her role model and mentor. It was because of her that Megan had a steady flow of clients lately. She was supposed to meet Chelsea to look at fabrics in the next hour. Luckily, the store was only within ten minutes of both her loft and office. She decided since it was a lovely April day, she would walk and clear her brain.

After her shower, she threw on some jeans with

a fuchsia T-shirt and pulled her hair into a bouncy ponytail. She glanced at the clock and realized she was ahead of schedule. Grabbing her cell phone, she was surprised to see over twenty missed phone calls and text messages from her cousin Tiffani Chase, Sydney and Jade all within a span of ten minutes. The phone then rang while it was still in her hand. It was Sydney.

"What's up Syd?"

"Wow, don't you sound calm."

"Why wouldn't I be?"

"I guess you haven't seen today's paper or the local gossip blogs this morning."

"I just got up. Haven't been online yet."

"Turn on your computer and go to the Atlanta Social website.

Megan went into her living room where her tablet sat on the coffee table. She opened the website Syd mentioned and almost dropped her tablet on the hardwood floor. On the screen were pictures from the fund-raiser last night, but the main picture of the article was of her and Steven when he kissed her hand. The accompanying caption read, "Who's the senator's new lady of the week?"

"Oh, no." Megan sighed and sank onto the couch. "This can't be happening." She scrolled through some more of the event pictures, and there were four more of them laughing and having a good time.

"Girl, those aren't the only pictures of you two. I'm at the GBI office and one of the agents just brought me the social section of the newspaper.

There's another one where Steven is leaning over whispering in your ear, and you're staring at him like a lovesick puppy with your eyes half closed."

"We were just talking. I'm not dating the senator. Why would they print this?"

"Calm down, sis. This happens to him all the time. You just don't keep up. It'll all blow over I'm sure. He'll be on the same blog tomorrow with a different woman, and no one will give you a second thought."

"But this has never happened to *me* before. I don't want my reputation ruined with my clients because they think I'm dating a playboy politician. No, wait. It says 'lady of the week.' That's even worse." Megan looked at a few more local blogs she found through Google, and the same pictures with similar captions popped up.

"Try not to worry about it," Sydney said in a sincere tone. "They don't even know your name."

Megan's phone beeped with another phone call. *Perfect.*

"Our mother is calling me on the other line."

"Now you can worry. Don't answer."

"I'm not. I can only imagine what she's going to say."

"Chin up, sis. I have a meeting, but call me if you need to."

After hanging up, the phone rang again but this time from a number she didn't recognize. She decided to answer it anyway just in case it was a potential client.

"Hello?" she answered cautiously.

"Hey, Megan this is Steven."

"Oh, joy. It's the playboy politician," she said sarcastically as she walked to her bedroom that was separated from the living room with a sliding wall. She grabbed her purse and keys from the bench in front of the bed. She needed to head out soon to meet Chelsea.

"I guess you saw the blogs this morning."

"Yes, I did, and I'm not amused at all. I don't even know you! We just met yesterday."

"I'm so sorry this has happened. Trust me last night I was supposed to mix and mingle and not flirt. I'm trying to clean up my image if I'm going to run for my dad's seat, but whenever the media sees me with a woman they assume I'm seeing her...which sometimes I am."

"Maybe if you stop kissing women's hands and whispering in their ears, your photo won't get taken as much," she snapped.

He chuckled, and her breath caught in her throat. She was supposed to be mad, but how could she when his seductive voice was in her ear reminding her of the tossing and turning she did last night over him?

"You have a point, but my team sent a statement to all of the blogs and news outlets that have the pictures that we aren't dating, and that you're an interior decorator who will be working on some projects for me in the future, all of which is true."

She let out a sigh of relief. She knew it wasn't his

fault that this had happened. He was a politician from a very prestigious family so naturally he would be in the limelight. Too bad his playboy past was getting him in trouble even when the situation was innocent. While she had just met him, he seemed like a cool, down-to-earth guy. Maybe the media blew his reputation out of proportion.

"Thank you for releasing the statement. I know it's not your fault, but it did shake me up because I live a simple, drama-free life. And I like to keep it that way."

"I completely understand. I wish my life was simple at times. So, are we still on for this Monday?"

"Yes, of course. Remember, I'm not really the lady of the week, I'm the interior decorator you'll be working with." She laughed.

"I'll keep that in mind. Besides, you aren't 'lady of the week' material. More like the lady forever, and I would hate for anyone to think otherwise."

The heat in her cheeks began to rise, and she had a feeling they would be burning red if she looked in a mirror.

"Thank you. I hate to cut this conversation short, but I have a meeting in a few minutes."

"On a Saturday?"

"Normally I wouldn't schedule a meeting on a Saturday, but it's Chelsea."

"Cool. Give her my best."

After saying their goodbyes, Megan grabbed her tablet and purse and headed out the door. She felt somewhat better since Steven called.

While browsing through material in the fabric store, Sydney sent her a text that a statement had been released about her and Steven's platonic relationship and the blogs had been updated. She decided she wasn't going to worry about it. Like her sister said, it would all blow over, and some other woman would be in a picture with him tomorrow. The thought of that made her a little sad, but she knew he was the last man she should be involved with even if the very thought of him caused her to go weak.

Her main focus was expanding her business and taking it to the next level. Her and Jade were in the process of landing a guest spot on the famed show *Decorator's Dream* on the Fabulous Living Channel. They'd sent in pictures of all of their decorating jobs over the past few years and their audition video. Now they were on pins and needles waiting to hear back. Plus, much to her family and friends' dismay, Megan actually enjoyed being single at this time in her life. She shook her head to wipe the thought of dating Steven out of her mind. From now on, she would think of him as a potential client. Nothing more.

Chapter 3

"Steven, we have one more topic to discuss," Shawn Bennett said uneasily to his best friend.

Steven sat at the desk in his downtown office while Bryce and Shawn sat in the leather wingback chairs in front. They'd been discussing the latest comments about Steven from the media including gossip blogs and social media. He had begun to tune them out after a while considering it was the same conversation that'd been had over and over.

Instead, his thoughts began to wander to Megan. He couldn't seem to get her bubbly personality, cute smile, flirty eyes or whimsical voice out of his head. He didn't know which was cuter: the way she spoke or the sparkle in her eyes when she laughed. He was eager to leave for their lunch meeting just to resolve which one.

He glanced at the clock on the opposite wall and then back at the two men in front of him that he'd momentarily forgot were there. *Maybe if I pay attention to them we could speed this boring meeting up.*

"What else do we need to talk about?" he asked nonchalantly.

Bryce cleared his throat, stood up from his seat and positioned himself in front of his brother.

"Ok, big brother. It's like this. We feel that you have a wonderful platform and a good chance of winning the nomination for Dad's seat. There are constituents who will vote for you because of who you are plus they agree with your views on certain issues. You're a great senator. But because of the way you've been portrayed in the media, people may not take you seriously as a U.S. senator," Bryce said as he paced back and forth around the room. "Your escapades have caught national attention lately since there's a buzz going around about Dad retiring at the end of his term."

"Man, maybe you need to slow down some with the ladies," Shawn added. "You know...save some of the action for me and Bryce."

Steven looked at his brother and his best friend. He'd been friends with Shawn since their days at Harvard, and he always had his back. Steven knew they were both right. He wasn't trying to have a reputation as a playboy, he just happened to enjoy the company of different women. Some spent the night and some didn't. And after the last incident at the ski resort in Colorado with an alleged threesome, the media was following his every move.

"Steven, is there someone in your life you can date exclusively?" Bryce asked.

"No, not really. They were mostly one-nighters. And I don't mean one night stands, necessarily. Just one date and then I wasn't interested anymore." Steven thought over the list of women he'd been out with or slept with lately. Even though only one woman was occupying his mind at the moment.

"What about the interior decorator you were photographed with?" Shawn offered. "You two were having a grand time at the fund-raiser event. The shutterbugs couldn't get enough."

"We have a meeting at noon to discuss her possibly decorating my house... Once I find one and buy it, of course. But I doubt she would want to go out with me. She's already called me the playboy politician."

"This is exactly our point. You can easily lose the female vote if women only see you as a playboy," Bryce said.

Steven thought about what Bryce said for a moment and then gave a cocky smile.

"Or the opposite. You know, some women will vote for me because they think I'm a good-looking playboy. Have you seen these dimples? Women go crazy!" Steven said trying not to brag and more so lighten the mood of the room.

"Oh, you find this funny?" Bryce asked in an irritated tone. "The Monroe name is on the line. Our family has worked hard for generations in order to become established and to be taken seriously in the political world. Dad has groomed us for this, and you're not going to ruin my chances of becoming a district attorney one day. Plus, Jacqueline is considering going into politics, so don't ruin this for our baby sister. Shape up and get it together."

Steven nodded as he listened to his brother. He knew he was right. Fun and games were over. He was a grown man. He was a Monroe man. He knew his family was influential in politics thanks to his grandfather and father.

"What do you need me to do?"

"Cut out this playboy persona and settle down with one woman to improve your chances to win the nomination. You need to be seen in the media as a good guy and a devoted boyfriend. Ever since your divorce, you've been on this wild roller-coaster ride for the last ten years. It's time to get off."

His divorce. It should have been an annulment, but his ex-wife, Veronica, wanted the prenuptial agreement to stand so she could receive her settlement should they ever part. After only six months of marriage, Steven knew it was hopeless. Veronica had only married him because he was a Monroe. When he realized that she never loved him, he was crushed. He thought she was the one when he saw her studying in the library while both law students at Harvard. Apparently she'd done her homework and was determined to be his wife. Over the years, they remained cordial running into each at events or speaking engagements. She was now a law professor at a college in Washington, D.C., thanks to his last name that she refused to drop no matter how many millions she was offered during the divorce settlement.

Since they'd parted ways, he dated, but nothing serious ever came out of it. And once he realized they were only interested in the Monroe name, he dropped them, thus igniting his persona in the media.

"I hear you, Bryce. Which one of my past conquests should I consider?"

"Actually, Megan Chase would be the perfect candidate. You've already been photographed with her, and you two appeared quite cozy."

"Yes," Shawn said as he grabbed a folder from his briefcase. "We did a little research as always when you're photographed with a new woman. She's twenty-seven years old. According to her DMV records, she's five feet six inches and weighs 125 pounds. Her father is a principal at a local high school and her mother is a first grade teacher. They were high school sweethearts and have been married for thirty-five years. Ms. Chase has never had any arrests, and has only had one speeding ticket. She won a full scholarship to Clark Atlanta University and started her interior-decorating business out of her parent's basement along with her best friend when they graduated from college. But now they have an office in Buckhead.

"Ms. Chase's twin sister is a GBI agent and their older brother is a musician who owns a jazz club/

restaurant here in Atlanta. Her uncle on her mother's side is Dr. Francis Arrington, a world renowned heart surgeon in Memphis and all his children are doctors, as well. She likes hanging with her family and her girlfriends. Her ex-boyfriend is a doctor here in Atlanta. She helped him start his practice, but they broke up about a year and a half ago once she found out he was cheating with one of his nurses."

"Wow. Do you know her blood type, too?" Steven asked sarcastically. Shawn had done research before but never to this extent.

Shawn glanced through some papers in his folders. "Yes. She's AB."

Steven chuckled. "I was just joking."

"We aren't," Bryce stated in a firm tone. "This is serious."

"Anything else I need to know about Ms. Chase? Is she lactose intolerant? How does she like her eggs prepared?"

"Yes. She's trying to get a spot on the show *Decorator's Dream*." Shawn closed the folder and laid it on Steven's desk.

Steven then glanced down at it and shook his head in disbelief. "Well, I'm not sure if I'm totally on board with this absurd idea, but I'll give it some thought."

Megan sat nervously in the parking lot of her brother's restaurant on Peachtree Street downtown. She'd called Braxton ahead of time to tell him she was coming because she wanted to make sure her favorite booth was available because it overlooked the stage. It was the perfect spot for when jazz bands played in the evenings and occasionally during lunch.

She tapped her steering wheel nervously, trying to decide whether or not she should restart her SUV and drive home before Steven showed up. She knew it was just a business luncheon, but for some reason she felt as if they were going on a first date. Taking a deep breath, she checked her hair and makeup in the visor mirror before stepping out of the car and walking toward the front door of the restaurant. She saw her reflection in the glass doors and stopped briefly to make sure she looked presentable. She had decided to wear a pair of dress jeans with a white tee, a pink seersucker blazer and wedged sandals. Her hair was curly and swooped to one side over her shoulder. Huge gold hoop earrings and a charm bracelet completed the casual look.

She tried to tell herself that this meeting wasn't a big deal but deep down she was nervous. He made her nervous. Not because he was a politician or a millionaire. She'd dealt with people of his social status before. She was nervous because she knew somewhere inside of her, she wanted him and that scared her. She'd been on quite a few dates thanks to her girls playing matchmaker but none of the men had flustered her to this point. None of them had kept her up at night with sinful thoughts that made her cheeks turn pink like Steven had. His scent. His smile. The seductive way he gazed at her when he kissed her hand, were all imbedded in her brain.

"Megan!"

She looked up to see Steven walking down the elegant staircase of the restaurant. He, too, had dressed casually in khaki dress pants and a red golf shirt. His smile was simply charming, and she couldn't help but return it as she walked toward him. She began to get a little wobbly in the knees, and she couldn't stop smiling at the magnificent man in front of her. *Heaven help me!*

When Steven saw Megan looking up at him from the bottom of the staircase, he was captivated. He thought the dress she'd worn when he met her was sexy, but there she stood in jeans even sexier, and she wasn't even trying.

"Wow, you look great," he said, reaching out his hand to her to lead her back upstairs. "Our table is up here. I was told it's your favorite."

Once seated, the waiter took their drink and lunch order. Thirty minutes later, they were eating shrimp po' boys and fries and laughing at all of the blind dates Megan had been on lately.

"So let me get this straight," Steven said, amused, "This dude was on a date with you trying to sell you a time-share?" He laughed again, taking a sip of his tea. "Did you buy one?"

"No, I declined. Then he tried to tell me about some other get-rich-quick scheme. I have tons of stories."

"Why do your family and friends keep setting you up? You're breathtaking. I would assume men ask you out all of the time."

She lowered her head and tried to stifle a smile when he mentioned she was breathtaking. He didn't want to embarrass her. He was merely speaking the truth. She twirled a French fry around in the ketchup before looking back up and answering him.

"They do, but I always cancel at the last minute or find some reason not to go on a second date. My girlfriends say I'm just being picky so they set me up with guys that they think would be perfect for me."

"So how many dates are we going to go on before you decide to dump me, too?" he asked jokingly.

"This isn't a date. We're supposed to be discussing decorating your future home. You haven't even looked at my portfolio yet." She reached into her oversize leather tote bag and pulled out her tablet and slid it across the table to him.

"To be honest, I'm having such a great time that I forgot this was supposed to be business luncheon. My meetings are usually with old men discussing politics, investments and golf. Not with an adorable woman cracking me up with her blind-date history."

"Trust me they weren't that funny to be on, that's for sure. I've asked my friends both politely and rudely to stop."

"Why do they keep setting you up? Did something happen in a past relationship?" he asked, thinking about what Shawn read earlier.

"Ever since my last long-term relationship ended, they think I'm lonely for a man because all I do is work. But what they fail to realize is that I'm happy being single. I enjoy my freedom. I was with my ex for almost four years and my world was centered on him. I helped him start his medical practice right after I started my interior-decorating business with Jade. I began to lose sight of my dreams and ambitions that he wasn't even being supportive of in the first place. After I found out he was cheating with a nurse in his office, I dumped him and focused on me and building my business. I'm not lonely, but no one seems to understand except me."

"They sound like my brother and campaign manager. Just earlier today, they were telling me to settle down with one person. They think that would somehow improve my image and give me a better shot of winning the nomination for my father's seat."

"Well, you are a self-proclaimed playboy," she said, shrugging her shoulders and rolling her eyes away from his with a grin.

He chuckled at her sarcasm. "The media says that. Truth is, I've been married before—didn't work out. Like you, I enjoy my single life. No strings. No attachments. No hearts to break."

"I wish I could just tell my family and friends I have a boyfriend so they can stop harassing me." She threw the cloth napkin from her lap into her plate and sat back in her seat.

Steven studied her angelic face, which at the moment appeared disturbed. He knew what she was going through. But now that he'd had met Megan, he wanted to get to know her better. Even though, it seemed as if she wanted to be single and free. Heck, so did he, but he knew he needed to settle down his dating habits and clean up his image if he wanted to win the nomination. Most of the potential candidates for his father's seat were either engaged or married with families, summer homes and of course a beloved dog. He didn't even have a dog.

As he watched Megan, he saw the epitome of what he wanted in a woman. Graceful, refined, sexy without having to try, successful and independent. He was ready to learn about her other qualities, as well.

"You know Megan, you could just tell them you're dating me."

"But that would be a lie," she answered, shaking her head.

"It wouldn't have to be."

"Steven, that's ridiculous. We can't do that."

"Think about it. Your family and friends want you to date and be happy. My campaign team feels I need to stick with one person. Why not?"

"Because it wouldn't be right. It would be dishonest, and I know despite your escapades with women, you're an honest politician. You're a good man, Steven."

"Thank you, but I need someone like you and…" he paused as he thought about something else Shawn said earlier. "You need me."

She leaned over the table toward him and whispered, "I don't need to date you in name only to please my family and friends. Besides, I have a blossoming career thanks in part to having more free time to concentrate on it instead of cater to an ungrateful man."

"Really?"

"Yes, really." She sat back against her booth seat.

He leaned forward and whispered, "I can get you more clients and a chance to meet with the bigwigs of the Fabulous Living Channel. You can showcase your work on an upcoming show they're doing this summer."

She blinked her lashes several times and stared in disbelief. *"Decorator's Dream?"* she asked, leaning in toward him again with her eyes wide. Steven grabbed her hands in his when he thought he heard her heart beating faster.

"Yep, that show."

"How do you know about that show? They're only in the early-production stages."

"I know the creator."

"Justine Monroe? Jade and I sent her a copy of our portfolio and the audition video three months ago..." She stopped. She seemed to be pondering something, and Steven hoped it was a yes to his question. "Monroe...? Is she your ex-wife?"

"No. First cousin. I could put in a good word for you if..."

"If I agree to date you...in name only."

"Why do you keeping saying in name only? Am I not to get any *special* benefits?"

"You'll have the benefit of me on your arm, no more."

"So, that's a yes, Ms. Chase?"

"If I decide to do this, are you still going to see other women on the side?" Megan asked seriously.

"No, I don't intend to date anyone else. Unlike what you've read or heard through the grapevine about me, I don't have dozens of girlfriends."

"I'm sure the word *girlfriend* isn't in your vocabulary. So why me?"

"Because I need a successful, intelligent and classy woman such as yourself on my arm," he said. "Plus, you're the quintessential girl-next-door, which is the type of woman I need in order to clean up my image."

"Don't you have plenty of other female friends to ask? I read the gossip sites. There are tons of pictures with you and drop-dead gorgeous women. Supermodels, actresses, singers…someone more on your level."

"I don't want a woman like that. They get boring. They only care about fame, material things and spending my money. I want someone I can talk to. Someone to stimulate my mind. Someone to laugh with like you've made me do for the past hour. And I can save you from more horrible dates. So, yes I'd say you're the perfect candidate."

"Perfect candidate? I'm not the one running for office."

"But will you be by my side when I do?"

Chapter 4

The next morning Megan woke up earlier than normal. She wasn't a morning person, but she could no longer sleep after tossing and turning with Steven's request on her mind. He told her to think about it, and if they chose to go forward with their plans, they agreed to tell no one.

She decided to jog on her treadmill and listen to some music. She was nervous about what the future held. But at least she wouldn't have to worry about any blind dates for a while because she would be in an exclusive relationship with Senator Steven Monroe.

Her main fear was that he'd sleep with women on the side, but it wouldn't be cheating because they weren't in a real relationship. Though, he had said he wouldn't, and she believed him. Megan wondered how her ex would feel about her dating a senator. He probably wouldn't care. He definitely didn't care about her feelings when he lied and cheated on her for almost four years.

She was going to get on with her life and if that meant helping a senator clean up his image, then that's was what she was going to do. Plus, if it meant having a shot to land a guest spot on *Decorator's Dream* then it was well worth it. Satisfied with her decision, she jumped off of the treadmill, showered, dressed and headed out the door to Chase and Whitmore Designs.

When Megan arrived, Jade was speaking to the intern, Lucy, in the mostly all-white reception area that Lucy had recently remodeled for a class project. Megan, who loved antiques, was quite impressed with Lucy's mixture of modern and Louis XVI–style furniture. Light blue and lavender toss pillows laden the white chairs and couches in the client waiting area. Fresh calla lilies and orchids sat on end tables along with decorating books.

Megan smiled as she looked at her best friend. She was truly the diva of fashion and style. Her makeup was flawless which added to her large brown eyes and her auburn-colored skin. Her shoulder-length layered dark hair was curled without a strand out of place. She wore an off-white pantsuit with stilettos making her even taller than her already five-foot-seven-inch height.

"Are you forgetting our job today?" Megan inquired looking down at her khaki capris, tennis shoes and a sleeveless pink T-shirt. Her long hair was pulled back into a bun at her neck. "We're hanging wallpaper."

"I have a change of clothes in the car. Besides, that appointment isn't until this afternoon, and I have another appointment in an hour with Wade Greene, you know the sportscaster." Jade looked up from the file she was reading. "Chelsea introduced me to him at her cocktail party last month. After seeing what we did with her home, he now wants me to redo his dining and living room areas. Still, I promise to be at the Brown's to help you hang wallpaper. I just need to show him some fabric swatches for his dining room."

"And get a date?" Megan questioned her single friend.

"If I'm lucky." Jade winked and then sashayed back to her office.

"I'm going to run down to Starbucks for a caramel macchiato," Megan said, heading toward the door.

"I can go get it for you, Ms. Chase," Lucy offered. She was an eager-to-please intern. Lucy had one more semester before graduation, and Megan was contemplating hiring her full-time.

"No, I need to run a quick errand, as well. I'll be back in a few." She really didn't have to go to Starbucks considering they had a Keurig in the kitchen, but she wanted to go ahead and call Steven with her answer before she changed her mind. And she didn't want to do it in her office. She rarely closed her door when she was there because Jade and Lucy were always in and out. She didn't want them to think something was wrong, and she definitely didn't want anyone to else to know about her arrangement with Steven.

When she walked into the Starbucks, she found an empty table near the back. She figured she would order enough coffee and pastries for everyone before she left. She then nervously dialed Steven's cell phone number. She couldn't believe what she was about to do.

At exactly seven that evening, Megan's phone rang. She was sitting on the floor brushing Percy, a weekly ritual that he hated. She glanced at the caller ID and saw Steven's name. He was in a meeting earlier when she called him with her decision. They agreed to talk that evening, and he was punctually calling at the time she'd suggested.

She stood up to grab her notepad that she had earlier jotted some general questions in to ask Steven. Free from Megan's hands, Percy darted out of the bedroom to escape the brushing ritual.

"Hello?" Megan plopped down on the bed.

"Hey, it's Steven. How are you doing this evening?"

"Fine, Stevo. And how are you?"

"Stevo?" he asked taken aback.

"Well, I figured you need a pet name for me to call you. You don't like Stevo?"

"No, it reminds me of my days in high school when the nerds would call me Stevo or worse Stevster."

"I see. Well, I guess we'll think of something else. In the meantime, I have some questions that every girlfriend should know," Megan said getting her pen ready.

"Yes, I have big feet and great hands to give body massages with," he joked.

Megan felt her face getting hot at the thought of his great hands giving her a body massage with hot oil. A man with big feet could only mean one thing, at least most of the time. She smiled at the thought.

"I already have my list of questions."

"That's fine. How was your day?"

"It was good, and yours?"

"I spent most of the day reviewing a possible campaign budget with Shawn just in case I receive the nomination. I need to do some fund-raising if I'm to have a successful campaign."

"I thought all you needed was a great platform and a speech," Megan said, sounding a little naive on that subject. She was never one for keeping up with politics.

He chuckled softly before answering her.

"That's part of it, but I also have to rent the head-quarters, pay people to work there or find volunteers, buy materials, pay for advertisements, but that's not my biggest dilemma at the moment. The community center that I started and help fund is losing one of its grants, therefore losing about ten college students that would normally assist with events with the children during the summer camp."

"Can you do a fund-raiser?"

"Yes, I'm considering hosting a fund-raiser party and then writing a check to match whatever is raised. The grant funded quite a bit."

"Well, maybe I can help." Megan was always one for volunteering her services or expertise if the need arose. "I'm the assistant graduate advisor for one of the undergrad chapters for my sorority. I'll check to see if some of the girls would like to volunteer their services this summer. A lot of them are education majors so they need the experience of working with children," she said, taking notes. The undergrads were having their last meeting of the semester the following evening, and she could approach the ones that were staying in Atlanta for the summer.

"That is very thoughtful and supportive of you."

"No problem. Also, I have a few clients and friends that could possibly give a donation. And I'm sure Braxton won't mind you using the mezzanine level at his restaurant. Let me make some phone calls tomorrow and work my magic, that's if you want me to." She hoped she wasn't overstepping her bounds. Though she was only supposed to play the make-believe girlfriend, planning and organizing were her specialties.

"No, that's wonderful. Thank you," he said in amazement.

"No problem. Isn't that what girlfriends are for?" she asked jokingly.

"Yes, they are. There're some other things girlfriends are good for, as well," Steven said in a sexy tone.

"If you're going to continue talking like that, the

deal is off. Now on to my list of questions," she said getting back to the real business at hand. As much as she liked Steven, Megan knew that sex was one road she couldn't travel with him. For if she did, she'd never want to let him go.

Over the next hour, Megan learned that Steven liked to fish, and listen to jazz, classical, R&B and hip-hop. He played the guitar and gave lessons to the children during the summer camp. He was a running back during his freshman year of college but got hurt and decided not to play anymore. He never wanted to go professional, but he enjoyed football. His parents were relieved he could no longer play, especially his father who wanted him to follow in his footsteps and go into politics. He loved seafood especially shrimp, and he liked Bruce Lee movies. His pet peeve was people who complained about issues but did nothing to make a change. It was also the reason he decided to go into politics and not become a practicing attorney like Bryce. He had a brownstone in Washington, D.C., that he shared with his brother and a townhome in historic Savannah.

"Do you feel that you really know me now?" he asked in a low, deep voice that sent goose bumps down her arms. This man was driving her insane, and she didn't know how much longer she could stand having his voice in her ear.

"Overall." She put down her pen and notepad as Percy jumped into her lap. "I'm sure I'll learn more in the months to come. But I just thought of something else. When I was online looking at pictures of you, I only saw you with a bunch of females. There were only a few family pictures and some of you giving speeches during your last campaign. However, there was nothing with you and the good you do for the communities in your district such as the center and the gardens. Why is that?"

"Well one reason is that all the media and gossip blogs tend to care about is who I'm dating. Plus, I do what I do for my community because it's my passion. I'm not doing it for the publicity. I do it because I care, and I'm in the position to make a change. Everyone wasn't born wealthy like me, but it doesn't mean they can't have the same advantages. There're some articles out there though, about some of the things I've done, but unfortunately my past lifestyle outweighs the good."

"We're going to change that, Steven. It'll help with cleaning up your image. They need to see you playing the guitar with the children and getting dirty in the community garden. They need to see your philanthropy side not the philandering one. I have a reporter friend at one of the local news stations. I'll see if she can come to the fund-raiser."

He laughed. "Wow. Are you an interior decorator or an image consultant?"

"I'm the woman who believes in you and what you stand for."

"Thank you. That truly means a lot to me. Out of all of the women I've dated, including my ex-wife, you've been the only one to say that, and you're not even my real girlfriend. I don't know what I'm going to do without you when this ends. Promise me we'll always be friends."

"Of course." A lump formed in her throat. She didn't want to think about the end. Clearing her windpipe, she glanced at her notepad to see was there anything else she forgot to ask.

"I read somewhere that you don't drink alcohol. Is that true?"

"I may have an occasional glass of wine or champagne, but only when I'm in the comforts of my own home. I wouldn't want the media to snap a picture of me holding a drink. Then I'd be labeled as an alcoholic."

"Makes sense." *I guess he already has enough labels.*

"And you?"

"Occasionally a glass of wine or some girlie drink like Sex on the Beach."

"You like having sex on the beach? Me, too. I own some beachfront property if you ever want to…" Steven said in a teasing manner although she knew he meant it. She tried to ignore his comment even though a picture of them making love on the beach popped into her head.

"Steven, if we're going to do this, you have to refrain from flirting so much." *Because its making me want to jump through the phone and onto your lap.*

"I can't help it. If I can't flirt with you, who am I going to flirt with? You're my girlfriend, but I'll try to keep it to a minimum if it's making you want me."

"Want you? Who says I want you?"

"I know you have to be attracted to me to even do this and that goes both ways. I was going to ask you out anyway. Who knows? Maybe this is a way for us to be a couple and get to know each other in the process. You know, skip the courting part. Besides, you don't like dates."

She laughed sarcastically. "You know, you're funny. If you don't get the nomination, you can always go into comedy. Anyway, a little about me. I was born and raised here in Atlanta. My dad is a high school principal and my mother is a first grade teacher. My hobbies are reading suspense and romance novels, going to the movies and comedy shows. I also listen to most music genres and my favorite singer is Beyoncé. Anything else you care to know?"

She was ready to get off of the phone. She had three meetings all before noon the next day. Plus his low, sexy voice in her ear was starting to wreak havoc on her thought process, and she was beginning to wish he really was her boyfriend. And his sex-on-the-beach comment had made her rather hot in a certain area, and she needed a cold shower. *Fast.* He was quite flirtatious all of sudden, and she didn't know how she was going to make it the next few months if he was constantly flirting with her. He may just receive a special bonus after all.

"What's your favorite flower?" he asked.

"Pink roses and red tulips."

"Why tulips?" he asked curiously.

"My grandfather used to plant them in his garden when I was a little girl. When he died, they bloomed so beautiful that year. But after that they stopped coming back," Megan said getting teary eyed. "Please continue with your questions. I get emotional sometimes thinking about him."

"I completely understand. What's your favorite color?"

"Pink but I also like purple."

"You are such a girlie girl. And favorite perfume?"

"Amarige by Givenchy."

"Is that what you were wearing the day I met you?"

"Yes, it was. That's all I ever wear. Anything else? I really need to get going to type up a budget proposal for a client." She really didn't mean to get that personable with him. She'd never even told her ex the reason why she loved tulips. Perhaps because he'd never asked.

"Yes. That's all for now. Have a good evening, Megan."

"The same to you, Mr. Monroe," she answered hanging up the phone quickly.

A minute later, the phone rang again. *What now?*

"Yes?" Megan answered in an annoyed tone. She was lying on her bed still trying to get the image of sex on the beach out of her head. However, all she kept fantasizing about was lying naked with Steven on a beach towel with those strong hands of his roaming over her body and his lips placing hot kisses on her neck.

"I sometimes wish caller ID hadn't been invented. That way you wouldn't have to answer the phone with such an attitude," Steven said jokingly.

"But answering machines do exist," Megan said impatiently getting up and walking over to her sewing room. She needed to get away from her bed especially with his voice in her ear.

"You still have an answering machine?"

"No."

"I won't keep you on the phone. I just wanted to tell you thank you for helping me. I sincerely appreciate it."

"You are a good man and an honest politician despite your jaunts with women. The only thing I ask of you is that you remain honest with me," Megan said to him seriously.

"That's a promise I can keep. However, by the end of this, you're not going to want to let me go. Good night, Megan."

She sat at her sewing machine and dropped her forehead on it. His words played in her head like a broken record. *What I have I gotten myself into?*

Megan was supposed to be working on a project board for a presentation next week. However, she'd found herself unable to concentrate at home, so she'd headed to the office thinking that her thoughts of Steven wouldn't follow her there. But as she sat in her office staring at a blank board, she was so wrong.

It had been a week since Megan had agreed to be Steven's girlfriend. She hadn't seen him and a part of her was happy about that. However, she found herself missing him and that scared her. Whenever the phone rang, she hoped it was him and in some instances it was. He was out of town on business, but they spoke every day because she was planning a Jazz Wine Down Wednesday fund-raiser for the community center. She was able to reserve space in Braxton's restaurant, which was donating the food and wine. She was also able to invite people from the media. She had secured eight of the undergrads from her sorority, and six undergrads from Steven's fraternity had signed up to volunteer during the summer. Megan had negotiated that the fraternity and sorority members wouldn't be paid, but Steven would write letters of recommendation when they graduated from college, and he would attend a voter's registration drive on campus sponsored by his fraternity.

Megan hadn't told her parents she was dating Steven yet. But she figured they would know by tomorrow morning considering that night's fund-raiser event would be their first outing in public. She did tell Jade, Tiffani and Sydney that she was helping Senator Monroe plan a fund-raiser for the community center. She also casually told them she was his date for the evening. They were excited for her especially since they were invited. Jade only went to A-list events and Tiffani was glad to get out of the house and away from her four-year-old son and his recent tantrums. Ever since Tiffani's husband died of a heart attack almost a year ago, her son had been acting out. Sydney even voluntarily cancelled the date she had set up for Megan to go on the following week, much to her relief.

Megan sat at her desk contemplating her decision to date Steven. While she was indeed attracted to him, the fear of falling for him had weighed heavily on her mind since the day she accepted. Every time she thought about him, her heart thumped hard against her chest and her mind wandered to a place of lust and fantasy with him.

Lucy tapped on the ajar door interrupting Megan's amorous thoughts.

"Ms. Chase, you have a special delivery!" Lucy excitedly announced zooming into the office with her bouncy red hair and blue eyes sparkling brightly. She took Megan by the hand and pulled her out into the reception area. On Lucy's desk, were two dozen pink roses with red tulips scattered throughout in a sparkling crystal vase with a pink-and-lavender chiffon ribbon tied around it.

"Open the card. Open the card." Lucy jumped up and down like a little schoolgirl.

Megan remained speechless. Jade tapped her foot impatiently and placed her hands on her hips giving Megan a "hurry up" look.

"Girl, open the card and stop looking surprised! You know it's from the senator!" Jade demanded handing Megan the card from the bouquet.

Megan really wasn't sure if she wanted to open it in front of them. *Why is he sending me flowers in the first place? This isn't a real relationship!* But she opened the card anyway, if only to appease Lucy and Jade.

"Can't wait to see you tonight. Yours truly, Stevo." She giggled at the way he'd signed his name. *I guess he liked the nickname after all.*

She tried to act overwhelmed in front of Jade and Lucy even though she really didn't have to act at all. She was flattered.

"Oh, these are so beautiful. He remembered my favorite flowers," she said, pleasantly surprised by his gesture.

Now she realized why he asked what her favorite flower was. She was rather pleased that he had sent them and was even more elated of the added extra details of the color of the ribbons. For once, she had found a man that knew what she wanted. *Too bad he's not really my man,* she thought. Too bad her ex never thought like that. She remembered when he sent her yellow roses for her birthday after the fact because he was too busy with patients. She later discovered he was rather getting busy with his nurse at a hotel downtown.

Blushing, Megan took the arrangement to her office and placed it on her desk.

"Ms. Chase," Lucy called after her, "You have a phone call holding on line three. It's Justine Monroe from the Fabulous Living Channel."

Megan ran out of her office and collided with Jade as they immediately locked wide eyes, and then headed straight to the conference room and closed the door.

Jade sat down and stared at the phone. "Girl, this could be it! I'll pray while you answer the phone."

Megan took a deep breath before answering. She pushed the speaker button so Jade could hear, as well.

"This is Megan Chase here also with Jade Whitmore."

"Good morning, ladies. This is Justine Monroe with the Fabulous Living Channel. I have some fabulous news to share with you."

The women locked eyes again, and Jade stood up above the phone and placed her hand over her heart.

"I'm happy to say after reviewing your portfolio as well as the audition video, we would like to offer you and Ms. Whitmore the opportunity to have a segment on *Decorator's Dream.*

"Oh, Ms. Monroe, I... Thank you. We're very excited." Megan sat in the chair in front of the phone and tried to remain composed as she and Jade squeezed hands.

"Craig, my production assistant and I look forward to working with you this summer in Hilton Head. I have to go, but Craig will be in contact with you within the next few days with all of the necessary information you'll need."

"Thank you so much for the opportunity, Ms. Monroe."

After they hung up, the women gave each other huge hugs before running out to the reception area to inform Lucy.

"Now Lucy," Jade, began in a serious tone. "We'll

be gone for a couple of weeks this summer. Think you can hold down the fort while we're away?"

"Yes, Ms. Whitmore. It'll give me a chance to do some projects on my own."

While Jade and Lucy conversed, Megan thought about how quickly Justine called so soon after she spoke to Steven about the opportunity. She made a mental note to call Steven and thank him. She sighed, he had already lived up to his part of the deal, but now she had to do her part. *Why does mine seem so much harder?*

Chapter 5

The evening of the fund-raiser arrived sooner than Megan realized. She left a voice mail on her parent's home phone explaining her plans for that night so they wouldn't be in total shock if there was a picture of her and Steven in newspaper the next day. They had seen the other pictures but once they saw the statement Steven's team had released, her parents had admitted they felt better. She knew they wouldn't be home because of PTA meetings, so a voice mail was perfect. She knew sooner or later they would find out about him so she opted for the later.

Megan stood at her vanity putting the last touches of her makeup on. Steven was sending a car to pick her up, which was to arrive in thirty minutes, and she still hadn't decided on which dress she was going to wear. She'd just gotten out of the shower, but she felt herself perspiring with anxiety. She went into her bedroom and turned on the ceiling fan even though she already had the air conditioner on full blast and tossed the bathrobe on the bed. Percy just stared at her and purred.

"What am I going to wear?" she asked the cat who was now licking his paws. She walked back into the closet and looked at her evening wear and opted for a fuchsia, spaghetti strap dress with a flared, flirty skirt that stopped at her knees showcasing her smooth, freshly waxed legs.

She buckled her heels and then smiled. She was glad that Jade had convinced her to go to the spa with her after Justine Monroe's call. Megan's toes and fingernails were freshly French manicured and her hair was straight down her back with loose curls on the ends. Her hairdresser added a few strawberry blonde highlights that matched her caramel skin and brought out her cheekbones.

Looking through her antique jewelry box, she picked a simple gold necklace and big gold hoops. When she was done, she surveyed her classy and elegant outfit in the full-length mirror. She looked like a senator's girlfriend should look, she thought.

Then she decided to lose the hoops and wear diamond studs instead. She didn't want to look too flashy and draw any more attention than necessary to herself. Megan was sure the attention would be on her more so than Steven when it came to the press. That was her only worry about agreeing to date Steven. While Megan was a people person at work, she really preferred privacy in her personal life. Megan laughed at herself as she realized that her private life was about to be flipped upside down.

After she was completely dressed, Megan added a little bit more makeup and sprayed on some Amarige. She looked at the grandfather clock that once belonged to her grandmother as she walked into the kitchen. She had a few more minutes, so she decided to drink a glass of cold water to calm her nerves even though a shot of whiskey would probably work better. While she was in the kitchen, her buzzer sounded. Let the games begin, she thought as she answered her intercom.

"Yes?"

"Hello, Megan. Are you ready to go?" It was Steven. She hadn't realized he would be picking her up. She assumed he was only sending a car. At least the driver would be in the car, she thought. But that wasn't good either. She would have to start pretending before the party, and she wasn't ready for that yet.

"Yes. Just surprised to hear your voice. I was expecting a driver."

"Change of plans. I'm driving."

Great. Now it will just be us together. I think I need that shot of whiskey now.

"Okay. I'll be down in a minute," Megan answered. She ran back into her bedroom and glanced in the mirror one last time. As she walked out the room, she said to Percy, "Wish me luck!" The cat just blinked and jumped on her bed. She knew he would stay there all night.

Megan grabbed her black evening purse and a shawl and headed down to the front lobby. When she arrived she saw Steven standing alone. He was on his cell and hadn't realized she was there. He looked handsome in a dark blue suit with a light blue dress shirt and a paisley tie. Megan's heart began to beat fast again, and her lips slightly parted as her stomach churned. As she watched him, she began to remember just how important a man he really was. He was a politician, a man with power and status. He was serious-minded. He had authority and a way of taking total command of any situation. Megan was impressed and it was a solid part of what made him one sexy man. Megan smiled when she realized that like her father, Steven spoke with his hands.

Steven was in a deep conversation with Bryce. He put his hand to his head in disbelief. Another main donor for the community center decided not to offer their usual amount for the summer program because of budget cuts with their company.

"Speak with Shawn and let him…" His voice trailed off. He knew Megan was behind him. He could smell her tantalizing perfume. He slowly turned and saw her sitting on one of the Victorian-style chairs in the lobby. She gave him an encouraging smile, and he took the phone away from his ear. He was pleased at her lovely appearance and for a quick second had forgotten why he was angry. Just looking at Megan sitting there so elegantly with her legs crossed wearing four-inch heels sent his mind on a journey to speechlessness.

Bryce was still talking, but Steven hadn't heard a single word. He had more important business to tend to at the moment. He regained his composure just long enough to get off of the phone.

"I gotta go, talk to Shawn. I'll see you fellas in about twenty minutes," he rather hurriedly told Bryce and pushed the end button on his cell phone screen. He rushed over to Megan as she stood up.

Megan took a deep breath as he approached her. She was suddenly feeling nervous and nauseous about the situation she placed herself in. *How can I play make-believe girlfriend for a handsome man that I could find myself falling for? No correction. That I am falling for.*

"You look beautiful," he said and kissed her on her cheek.

"Thank you. You look nice as well," she said, thinking the games had begun. She almost backed away when he kissed her cheek, but remembered that they were in public. She would later remind him however, only kisses on the cheeks and no lips. She could only imagine how his lips would kiss other places on her body.

"Ready?" he asked, holding out his hand. She put her hand into his, and they walked out to his car. He opened the passenger side of his black Mercedes convertible for her and she slid in, and he closed the door. When Steven got into the car, she noticed the strain on his face. As he started to drive, he stared straight ahead as a Sade CD played.

"Is everything okay?" she asked him. She was concerned. She wanted tonight to be special for him. There would be possible donors there as well as the media, and he had to put on his game face.

"Another donor that donates to the summer program backed out today." He glanced in her direction and then back on the road. "You know what I think?"

"That your reputation is beginning to catch up with you?"

"Yep. Bryce said the same statement earlier."

"Remember when I told you I may have some clients who may donate to the community center? They are coming tonight with checkbooks. Let me work my magic for you," she said patting his leg. As she tried to move her hand he grabbed it and held it tight.

"Thank you for supporting me, Megan." He held on to her hand until they pulled into the parking lot at the event. Before they got out of the car, Megan told him of her kissing rule. Steven agreed unless it was absolutely necessary. Megan gave him her "I don't think so look" as Steven drove the car to the front door for valet parking.

Once inside, Steven introduced Megan to his colleagues including Bryce and Shawn who both nodded approvingly. She gave a beautiful smile and said a lot of nice-to-meet-yous and thank-yous for coming to support Steven and the community center. She was glad when Tiffani, Syd and Jade arrived. They all gathered at Megan's table while Steven spoke with his guests.

"Girl, I'm so happy for you. You two look hot together!" Tiffani said with her cute dimples displaying on her smooth, sienna face.

"Yes, girl," Jade chimed in. "So glad you finally got a man and a wealthy one at that."

"I had a feeling there was something going on between you two," Sydney said. "You were just too giddy after he changed your tire. And the way you two were looking at each other all night at the gala, I just knew you would end up together. So happy for you, sis."

"Thank you. Now, if you ladies would excuse me, ⸻ ome money. Oh, and when I re- ⸻ your checks waiting," Megan said as she bounced away.

For the next hour, Megan indeed worked her magic with her clients that she invited including Chelsea and her husband, attorney Richard Benton, as well as a few others. Real-estate investor Broderick Hollingsworth was one of Megan's top clients. She had recently redone all of his rooms in a bed and breakfast he owned in Rome, Georgia. Because he trusted her judgment, he agreed to donate a large amount and offered a free weekend for her and Steven to relax at the inn. She thanked him for the free weekend although she knew they would never use it together. She would give it to Tiffani instead who could use a weekend away, and Megan would baby sit Keith Jr.—or KJ as he was affectionately called—considering he was her godson.

While she was speaking with Sharon Diamond, a romance author, she noticed Steven looking at her with the same strained look he had earlier. Megan wasn't sure why he appeared stressed, so she quickly ended her conversation with Sharon. Besides she already had her donation. She said thank you and walked over to Steven's side.

He was deep in a conversation with a gentleman who wasn't sure if he totally agreed with Steven's views on certain issues and said he was too wet behind the ears to run for his father's seat. She was ___ ___ ___ when Steven grabbed her hand

Mr. Brown, Steven said. "Mr. Brown is one my father's colleagues."

"Nice to meet you, Mr. Brown. I'm sure you're as excited about Steven possibly running for the U.S. Senate as I am," she said warmly as she shook his hand looking him straight in the eyes. "Steven can you please be a dear and get me a bottled water. I'll stay and keep Mr. Brown company."

A few minutes later Steven returned with the bottled water as Mr. Brown and another gentleman who approached the conversation were writing checks and handing them to Megan.

"Steven, you've definitely found an angel. Where have you been hiding her? About time you settled down with *one* woman," Mr. Brown stated as he and the other older gentleman walked off to the buffet table.

"Ms. Chase, you've raised a lot of money for the community center. What have you been telling these people? You didn't make any promises I can't keep did you?" he asked teasingly.

"I told them you would give them your firstborn son if they donated." She paused to giggle. "I simply told them the truth. That you're the perfect candidate for the position and even though they might not agree with all of your political views, the children at the community center were more important than your political differences," she said, smiling up at him.

A sincere grin crossed his face. "Well, I certainly found the perfect candidate, as well. Oh, by the way, did you receive the flowers I sent earlier to your office?"

"Yes, I did. They were lovely. Thank you." She turned away. She didn't want him to see how truly happy she was about receiving the flowers. "Also, thank you for contacting Justine for me. She called today."

"She did?" he asked with a puzzled expression.

"Yes. She offered Jade and I a spot on the show this summer."

"Congratulations, except I never spoke to her."

Megan shook her head in disbelief. "Wait. What?"

"I called her and left a message, but I didn't tell her what it was about and she hasn't returned my call yet. Looks like you didn't need my help."

She smiled and then laughed. "Oh, my goodness. I'm shocked."

"Why? I saw your portfolio. You're a very talented and creative decorator. You deserve more than just a guest spot. You deserve your own show."

"Well that's the ultimate goal one day."

"Now, I know our agreement, but you aren't going to back out, are you?"

She shook her head and chuckled. "No, I want to help you clean up your image and help you win the seat." Megan stopped speaking as a reporter approached wanting to interview Steven about the community center and the rumor about him running for _____'s seat. Megan left them to scout out Braxton _____ thank in person.

She asked _____ told her that he was downstairs. Megan peeked over _____ saw her brother moving from table to table conversing with the patrons as the smooth sounds of the jazz band on the stage reverberated throughout the restaurant. She waved to get his attention, and he gave his charming smile that matched their father's. He jetted up the stairs as the group of women he had been speaking with checked him out. Megan didn't blame them. He was handsome in his dark gray suit that fit his muscular six-foot-four-inch frame. His bald head glistened under the dim lights, and Megan saw a few women fanning themselves. She shook her head and smiled as he approached and led her to an empty highboy table.

"Is everything set up how you wanted it?"

"Yes. Everything is perfect. Your staff did an awesome job. Are you playing tonight?"

"I may sit in with the band for a while but definitely on Friday and Saturday because my band is playing."

"I'm sure all of the women down there would love to hear you on the keys tonight."

"We'll see. So my baby sister is dating Senator Monroe. Have you told our parents? I can just hear Mother now."

"They don't know officially yet, but I'm sure they will by tomorrow."

He flashed a smile and Megan caught one of the waitresses looking his way blush. Her brother was indeed handsome with his perfectly trimmed mustache and goatee sitting on his chiseled, mocha face.

"Our mother will be calling you. I suggest you tell her first."

She simply nodded. Megan and her mother didn't always see eye to eye. She chatted with her brother for a few more minutes before one of the hostesses called him away.

"Hey," a deep voice said in her ear from behind her. "Having fun?" His lips skimmed the top of her ear causing her to feel faint. The emotions he made her experience in a split second were uncanny, and she needed to get out of there before she forgot they weren't really a couple and turned around to lay a juicy kiss on his inviting mouth.

She turned around slowly to face him. His handsome face no longer wore the tense expression from earlier. He looked more relaxed as he held a plate of appetizers in his hand. He dipped a shrimp into the cocktail sauce, popped the entire thing into his mouth and then ran his tongue along his bottom lip. It was such a seductive gesture that she knew she really needed to leave and quick.

"I believe the evening went well. I think we have received donations from most of the people here. I'm going to go home with Syd in a few minutes," Megan said, turning away from him to scan the room for Syd. She found her in a deep conversation with Bryce. Megan could only hope Syd wasn't telling him how she really felt about a case where Bryce had represented a man who the GBI had arrested. Syd had been certain the man was guilty although he was found not guilty. However, Bryce Monroe was one of Atlanta's top criminal attorneys and rarely lost a case.

"Oh, are you sure? The night is young, and we haven't even danced yet. Plus, if you think about it, this is our real first date since you refuse to count the lunch meeting," Steven said grabbing her hand as she turned back around to look at him. He placed his plate on the nearest table as the band began to play "Hello" by Lionel Richie.

"Well, luckily this is one of my favorite songs otherwise, I would say no," Megan said as he pulled her out onto the dance floor.

He placed her arms around his neck and his own hands around her waist.

"Are we putting on a show for the audience?" she

asked as her lips brushed against his ear by mistake. She felt him freeze for a second.

"Yes," he whispered back. They had plenty of spectators Megan noticed. *Good.* She'd made up her mind that evening that Steven would make an excellent U.S. senator. She intended to make sure that it happened, even if it meant slow dancing with him and holding his hand in public, which is something her ex never did when they were together. He didn't like public displays of affection. Even though Steven was just pretending, it still felt nice be in his warm embrace even if it was all one big lie.

The scent of his woodsy cologne whiffed into her nose. She wished it would rub off on her body so she could smell it later when she was alone in her bed. She wanted to dance with him for the rest of the evening but the song was almost over, and she hoped the band would play one more slow song so Steven would hold on to her just a little longer. She knew her brother was on the piano because she knew how he played that particular song. She tried to transfer her thoughts to him thinking that maybe he'd play one more slow song. She almost laughed at the idea but her and Sydney had their twin senses so maybe she could have it with Braxton, as well.

"Is my dancing that bad?" he whispered. "You're not smiling anymore."

She looked up at him with a smile. "Your dancing is on point."

"That's my girl," he said as he brushed the hair

over her ear that had fallen in her face. "What would you do if I kissed you right now?"

"Kiss you back and slap you later," Megan said seriously, while a heat wave rushed through her when he asked. She then found herself half wishing he would kiss her, but she knew it was all for show.

His smoldering gaze was seductive. Sexual. Dangerous.

Her breathing had become uneasy, and she suddenly became aroused, and she noticed he had, as well. She could feel his slight bulge against her pelvis area, and backed up a few inches. But he pulled her close again against his hard body. She began to wonder how it would be if they were naked and entangled in her sheets but quickly shook her head to clear her mind. Sexual tension was the last thing she wanted with Steven. He wanted to simply win the nomination, not her.

"That's a chance I'll have to take," he answered in a sexy, arrogant tone. He ran a finger alongside her cheek to her lips as they parted on command. He lowered his mouth to hers and caressed her lips with a slow, sensual kiss. A low moan escaped her throat as his tongue pushed deeper into her mouth, and she matched his seductive strokes in the same sweet rhythm.

Her hands journeyed up his neck and around to his face as he continued his passionate assault on her lips, showing no mercy. Not that she minded. In fact, she craved more than just a kiss and judging from the fervent groans he made, she could tell they were on the same page.

Megan was somewhat surprised he kissed her. She honestly didn't think he was serious, especially after she had threatened him with a slap in private. But she couldn't push him away with all of the people in the room thinking they were a couple. So of course she kissed him back. What else could she do as his pulsating tongue flicked along her bottom lip as if it belonged there? Every cell in her body was on an electrifying passionate ride that he was in control of.

He lifted his lips from hers as a protest cry escaped her mouth, and her eyes opened. Why on earth had he stopped? She could go on and on. Through the haze she was in, she could see Steven staring at her with a weird expression, and then she glanced around the room and saw all eyes on them as well as a few cheers and whistles.

"Everyone is staring," he said through a clenched smile. "Please don't slap me."

Remembering the premise of their relationship— for she had certainly forgotten for a moment—she smiled, as well. "Of course not. It's all for show."

"You think we were convincing enough? I saw a few shutterbugs, but I'm not sure. My eyes were closed, and I was too busy concentrating on your divine mouth."

"Good. You need the media to see you in a committed relationship and considering we've been in the blogs already, I'm sure tonight's pictures will have them convinced."

She knew she was convinced. Convinced she was falling for him. Hard. She tried to pull away from his embrace, but he placed a kiss on her forehead and slid his hands tenderly down her waist to her hips and finally off of her body. Megan rushed away from him and back over to where Sydney was sitting alone.

"Looks like someone is having a great time," Sydney said with a smirk.

"We were just kissing. So I saw you speaking to Bryce Monroe?" Megan said wanting to change the subject and get her mind off of the kiss.

"Yes, unfortunately. He's such an ass."

"He seems like a nice man." Megan glanced in his direction as he spoke with some of the guests. He was about the same height and build as Steven, except Bryce's hair was curlier and his complexion was more of a butterscotch shade. He had a strong jawline and a charismatic smile under a neatly trimmed mustache and goatee. He would make a great catch for someone.

"Not in the courtroom and definitely not with me." Sydney ran a hand through her bouncy bob.

"You ready to go, sissy?" Megan asked.

"I know I said I would take you home, but I just received a call from my partner. Big case and I need to head to the GBI office. I'm sure Steven can take you home. After all he did pick you up."

"But Syd…" Megan started. She didn't know if she could be alone with him again in the car especially after that crazy kiss that meant nothing to him and everything to her.

"Girl, you'll be fine. Just ask Steven now," Sydney said, nodding toward him.

Megan slowly turned around to find Steven directly behind her.

"Of course I can take you home, precious. Just give me a few minutes to say goodbye to Bryce and Shawn." He darted away before Megan could protest. Megan sat down with her lips pressed together.

"What's wrong with you? He is your man. Shouldn't he take you home?" Sydney inquired.

"Oh, sure. I just thought he needed to stay longer."

"The fund-raiser is pretty much over. Now, you know I'm the body language expert. I can tell that he is really into you and the way you almost galloped over here with that flushed face after your kiss, clearly suggests you want him, too. I thought surely you two were about to make love on the dance floor. So let him take you home and finish what he started," Sydney said.

"You sound like Jade."

"I'm just speaking the truth. Here he comes. Have a nice evening."

A few minutes later, Megan sat numbly in Steven's car fiddling with her purse. Luckily, Steven was on his cell phone talking to Shawn.

Megan stared out the window trying to concentrate on something else. Even though all she could manage to do was inhale his cologne and listen to his deep voice. She had no idea what he was saying but the angrier he became the sexier he became, and her mind kept travelling back to the kiss.

She stole glances at him wondering how long she could keep up this charade that she wasn't really attracted to him. She was becoming highly upset at the fact that he had been on the phone the entire time, which made it clear he had no interest in her. Megan shook her head angrily and then gave him an ice-cold glare. She couldn't believe she thought that kiss could've meant something to him, as well.

When they arrived at her parking garage, Steven was still on the phone in a deep conversation with Shawn. Megan reached to open her door, but Steven placed his hand on her arm and shook his head. Megan looked at him and realized his facial expression was one of annoyance but not for her.

"Shawn, I can't keep going over and over on this issue with you. You know my view and it's not going to change. So let's just drop it." Steven breathed heavily and hung up his phone without saying goodbye. Keeping his hand on her arm, he loosened his grip and then rested his head back on his seat. He turned to face Megan.

"I apologize for being on the phone and ignoring you. Trust me that wasn't my intention, baby. Shawn can be so...what's the word...?"

"Annoying?" Megan asked, feeling a little better that he wasn't trying to ignore her. Did he just say *baby?*

"Something like that. He keeps trying to change my mind about certain things. He's not in my shoes and doesn't understand the pressures politicians have to face. I'm sorry for complaining to you. I know you probably don't want to hear me babble about my political stuff."

"That's what girlfriends are for right? To listen and support their man?" Megan said, teasingly and punching him lightly on the shoulder.

Steven smiled at her comment. "I'm beginning to think perhaps that's what they're for." He chuckled and patted her hand. "I forgot to tell you thank you for tonight. You really did work your magic," he said touching her face tenderly with his hand. He moved closer to her and pulled her face close to his, resting his head on her forehead.

"Just one more little kiss?" he asked in a sexy voice that sent a tremble through her body.

"But…" Megan started.

"But what? Didn't we have a good time on our first date?"

"It wasn't a date."

"So you didn't feel anything with that kiss on the dance floor?"

"No." She couldn't tell him the truth. The last thing she wanted to do was to get caught up in a fairy tale that she knew would end sooner for him than it would for her.

He slid back to his side. "Well, let me walk you up to your loft," he said seemingly taken aback.

"I can manage by myself," she said, opening the door and stepping out of the car. He got out and pushed the remote to lock the car.

"I said I would walk with you, Ms. Chase."

"Ms. Chase? I thought we were on first name basis, Stevo," she said, giving him a sincere smile. However, he remained silent. She continued to walk ahead of him to the elevator. They remained quiet on the ride up and when they got off, he continued to follow her to her door. Megan unlocked it, but she didn't open it. She turned to face Steven and smiled at him. She stood on her tippy toes and reached up to kiss him lightly on the cheek.

"Good night, Steven. I had a lovely time on our first date."

Megan went inside and leaned her back against the door. *Boy, that was close,* she thought as Percy greeted her by rubbing around her legs.

"How did I ever get myself into this mess?" she asked herself out loud, picking up the cat and walking toward her bathroom to take a refreshing shower. Steven Monroe was making her feel things she had never felt before. She just hoped she could get through the next few months without completely falling in love with him.

Chapter 6

A week had passed since Megan had seen Steven but she'd spoken to him a few times while he was out of town. Their relationship was growing into a comfortable friendship that she pleasantly enjoyed. She was genuinely concerned about his senatorial duties, and she could tell that he loved to hear her opinions. Although politics had never sparked an interest in her before, she was up all night reading his platform, speeches and emailing him her thoughts.

The day after the fund-raiser, tons of pictures hit the internet on gossip blogs, Twitter, Instagram and Facebook. However, there was one she couldn't get out of her mind. *The kiss.* It had been snapped from so many different angles that there were at least twenty different pictures, but they all conveyed the same thing. That the senator was finally in love and had tossed aside his playboy ways for her. Of course that's what they wanted the media to think. Unfortunately when she looked at the pictures, she saw herself falling in love with a man that would never want her in that way. Sure, she figured he was attracted to her, and she sensed he wanted her but more than likely only for sex. Since it was Friday, she decided to work from home instead of going into the office. She'd brought home the duvet, toss pillows and shams she was working on for Chelsea, but Megan wasn't in the mood to work. Her thoughts were still on last Thursday night at the fund-raiser. Dancing with Steven felt nice. It had been a long time since a man made her feel special. It reminded her that she would find love again and that all men weren't like her ex.

She glanced at the clock. It was a quarter to seven. She got up and walked across the room to turn off the alarm that would sound in a few minutes. She wasn't in the mood to jog on the treadmill, so she opted to do one hundred stomach crunches on her yoga mat.

Afterward, Megan walked barefoot to the kitchen with Percy following closely behind her. He was hungry, otherwise he would still be on her bed. She took out his food and noticed the roses and tulips on her island. They still looked beautiful even after a week, and she hoped they would stay alive for just a little while longer. It had been a long time since she had flowers in her home that she hadn't bought for herself.

After giving Percy his food, Megan decided that

a cup of coffee followed by thirty minutes of yoga and meditation would help her relax. While she was rinsing out her coffee pot, her phone rang, and she already knew who it was. Her dad was the only person who would call this early in the morning. He was always at his school by six-thirty to make sure he had everything in order for the day.

Megan had been avoiding her parents. Her mother had left a very distraught voice mail yesterday about her dating Steven. But she finally decided she might as well get it over with and speak to her dad. He was more understanding. Megan didn't bother looking at the caller ID as she answered the phone.

"Hello, Daddy," Megan sighed.

"Daddy? I thought my nickname was Stevo, but I can get used to Daddy. How about Big Daddy? Big Poppa? S. Diddy, you know, like P. Diddy? No wait, it's just Diddy now." He paused, but continued when she remained silent. "Well, I was hoping to get a laugh or a smile from you this morning."

"Steven, I thought you were my father!" Megan said embarrassed. "He's the only person to ever call me this early."

"I wanted to catch you before you went to work."

"I took the day off, but I still have a project to finish and an appointment this afternoon with a potential donor for the community center." Megan walked to the kitchen table to double-check her schedule on her tablet.

"I have to go to Washington, D.C., today. I wanted to know if you could go with me."

"I didn't know I would have to travel," she said, wrinkling her brow.

"I know its short notice, but I have a black-tie charity function to attend on Saturday night that I hadn't planned on going to, but Shawn is insisting I go. Other congressmen and senators will be there with their wives and girlfriends. I thought it would look nice to have you on my arm. You can fly out on the private plane that Bryce and I share."

Private plane?

"I see. When are we returning?"

"You could come back on Sunday or Monday. But I have to stay for some meetings, so I'll return on Wednesday."

"Steven, this is such short notice. I don't have anything to wear to a fancy function in Washington, D.C.," Megan said truthfully.

"I knew you would say something like that. That's why I arranged for you to go shopping with Chelsea today at Barneys. She's already in New York City meeting with some other clients."

"But I have an appointment at two with an executive from Coke about donating to the community center."

"Shawn can go. What other excuses are you going to come up with?"

"What time are we leaving? I have to finish a project," Megan said reluctantly. She couldn't believe she agreed to go with him to Washington, D.C.

"I've arranged for the plane to take you to New York City this morning and then to D.C. once you're done shopping. I have a function to attend this evening in Atlanta so I'll meet you later on tonight. I'm sending a car to take you to the airfield around ten, so get to packing."

"I don't have Barney's money," Megan answered, thinking about what she had in her closet to wear.

"But I do." Without another word, he hung up.

Three hours later Megan was in the limo headed to a private airfield that she didn't know existed in Atlanta. Since her conversation with Steven earlier that morning, she managed to finish her project, pack and drop Percy off at Tiffani's. Megan also had the misfortune of answering the phone without looking at the caller ID while packing. When she heard her mother's voice, Megan cursed in silence and hoped the conversation wouldn't last long.

Her mother wasn't happy about her daughter flying to Washington with someone that she hadn't met yet. She told Megan about her research on Senator Monroe and that she wasn't at all thrilled with the results. Her teacher friends even told her to tell Megan to be careful.

"Megan, it's not a good idea to date him. He doesn't care for you. You just got out of a long term relationship," Mrs. Chase fussed. "You're very vulnerable right now. Men feed off of that! Men like him love that! There is no challenge for him, and he's going to just use you and then throw you away like all of the others!"

"Mother, you don't know what you're talking about. Everything is fine. I'm not trying to start a serious relationship now. We're just dating. That's all!" Megan threw her clothes into the suitcase instead of folding them. Megan and her mother never saw eye to eye, and most of their conversations usually ended because of disagreements.

"Dating? It seems as if you're flying out of town with him! I hardly call that dating! He just wants to have sex with you and then move on to some other pretty young thang!"

"Mother!"

"Megan, you're my daughter. I love you. I'm only looking out for your best interests. And dating a senator, especially one like Steven Monroe, isn't just a regular relationship, honey." Her mother paused and was silent for moment. Megan hated that. She knew that meant her mother's mind was churning for more reasons as to why she shouldn't date Steven.

"Mother..." Megan started before she continued.

"Everyone will know. You'll be on television, in the tabloids. Your life will no longer be private. This is so embarrassing!"

"Embarrassing for whom? You? Are you scared of what your teacher friends will say to you or what they've already said to you? Mother, I'm a grown woman, in case you've forgotten. I know what I'm doing. Steven is a nice guy. Now I have to go finish packing. I love you, Mom." She then hung up before her mother could bicker more.

Megan decided to call her dad on the way to the private airport. It was easier to call him at work when she knew her mother wouldn't be around to snatch the phone and voice her opinion some more. She spoke to her father briefly in between him suspending two boys for fighting.

"How did you meet him? Isn't he out of your circle? Is this Syd's doing?" Dr. Chase sounded concerned. Megan had always been daddy's little girl, and she understood that her father didn't want to see his daughter hurt again by yet another man.

"We're just trying to get to know each other. It's not that serious," Megan told her father.

"Does he play golf? I'm sure he does."

"I think so, Dad," Megan answered making a mental note to ask him.

"When do I meet him? I have some political and personal questions for him."

"Soon, Dad. I'm going to Washington with him for a function this weekend. Maybe next weekend." She had no intentions of introducing them. She doubted Steven wanted to meet her parents.

"Your mother called earlier ranting. You just be careful. You know how those politicians are, and he's a playboy."

"People change, Dad."

"Yeah, and you said that about that punk ex-boyfriend of yours. He was too arrogant and only concerned about his status and not loving and taking care of my baby girl. You know I never liked him."

"Yes, Daddy, I know. Well, I'm going to let you get back to running your school," Megan said trying to get off of the phone. Once her dad got started on a tirade, he didn't know how to stop.

"I have some teacher evaluations to do this morning, so yes I need to go."

"I'm sure they're looking forward to seeing you arrive unannounced." Megan was glad she decided not to become a teacher. She loved being her own boss and not having to worry about someone always looking over her shoulder.

When Megan boarded the private jet, she was greeted by a flight attendant. The woman held out her delicate, manicured hand to shake Megan's.

"Good morning, Ms. Chase. I'm Susan, and I'll be your flight attendant for today. Senator Monroe has informed me to take extra special care of you. Would you like a mimosa while I give you a tour?" Susan stepped aside to let Megan walk in front of her.

Megan stood in awe. The main cabin of the jet had six plush, oversize white leather chairs on top of a very beautiful gold-and-white Persian carpet. She was used to flying coach or sometimes business class, but the Monroe family jet represented accommodations seen only in illustrious magazines.

"No thank you to the mimosa, but a definite yes to the tour. This is absolutely breathtaking." She looked at Susan. "I bet you love your job!" Megan exclaimed as Susan began to show her around. In the cockpit, she made a quick introduction of Captain Simmons.

The jet was about twice the size of a motor mansion, with the same luxuries, including a mini-kitchen, wet bar, a bedroom, and a bathroom in the back of the plane.

Megan walked back to the front. She hated taking trips on a plane and preferred to be asleep during the flight. Especially the last twenty minutes because her ears would always clog up, and she wouldn't be able to hear that well for at least three hours afterward. She'd brought a bag of jellybeans and a pack of gum to snack on to prevent excessive ear clogging

She decided to sit up front in one of the reclining seats and have a glass of orange juice from the wet bar to accompany the breakfast that Susan served. Captain Simmons informed Megan that there was a thirty-minute delay because they had to wait for a clear runway at the small airport. While Megan enjoyed her breakfast of French toast, shrimp and grits, and a spinach-and-feta-cheese omelet, she was interrupted by her cell phone ringing.

"Hello?"

"Hey, I called to check on you," Steven said.

"I'm fine. I'm eating a delicious breakfast."

"Shrimp and grits?"

"Yep, and it's so good. We're taking off in a few minutes."

"I have a meeting and then a fitting for my tux to wear on Saturday. My housekeeper Greta will pick you up from the airport."

"Oh. I didn't know you had a housekeeper."

"Greta is a sweetheart. She's been with the Monroe family since I was born. She's almost like a second mom to me and my siblings. By the way, I may not be in Washington until after midnight, so don't wait up." He hesitated for moment and cleared his throat. "Megan, I need to prewarn you. Greta is expecting you to sleep in the master bedroom."

"Wait! I can't sleep in the same bed with you," she said aloud, but then remembering she wasn't alone, Megan lowered her voice. "I'm sure your brownstone has a guest room!"

"It does, but Greta also knows me, and my female guests have never slept in the guest room. Don't worry, I have a California King bed. You won't know I'm there."

"Fine! Stay on your side!"

Once Megan arrived to New York, she met Chelsea in Manhattan. Chelsea had arranged with Barneys and a few other places for Megan to try on and purchase a dress for the evening.

Chelsea spoke on her cell phone a mile a minute, speaking in her usual "I'm in control and don't you forget it" tone. She smiled and winked at Megan while they walked down 5th Avenue.

Megan walked alongside her mentor, thinking about the upcoming weekend and what her father said earlier, even though Chelsea's conversation was much more interesting. Megan had always admired Chelsea since her mother had first introduced them at a sorority meet-and-mingle tea. The two of them immediately developed a mentor and mentee bond. She admired Chelsea for her wit, sassiness and for always knowing the right thing to say in any situation. She was truly fabulous at fifty with her pixie cut hairstyle, size six frame, and stunning appearance that always turned heads.

Chelsea was currently using her wit and sassiness to appease an irate client. She talked and walked fast in her Louboutin's as if they were tennis shoes. Megan increased her pace in her flat gladiator sandals in order to keep up.

"*Chérie,* my love. The awards show is a month away. I have already spoken to someone at Versace, and they're making five one-of-a-kind evening gowns just for you to try on." Chelsea paused and rolled her eyes, which made Megan giggle silently. "No one else will have the same dress. My assistant has already spoken to a rep from Harry Winston about a diamond choker with matching earrings. Have I ever let you down?" Chelsea shook her head at Megan. "Of course not, my love. Now go finish recording that number one song and let me handle the big things," Chelsea said before her client could oppose. She pushed the off button on her phone.

"Girl, these celebrities never know what they want. That's why they hire me to tell them." Chelsea tossed her phone into her purse and placed her aviator shades in her hair as they walked into Barney's.

Megan nodded her head in agreement.

"I understand completely. I have a celebrity client right now who keeps changing her mind about what type of rug she wants in front of her fireplace. Her home is being featured in a magazine next month, and she's a nervous wreck, which is driving me crazy. However, I'm excited that one of my creations will be in *House to Home Magazine.* Now if my client will just make up her mind before the photo shoot." Normally Megan made all of the decisions, but this particular celebrity client wanted to give her two cents. Luckily, Lucy was going to handle the rug problem on Monday.

"Probably the same person," Chelsea said. "Now let's get back to why we're here. You need an evening dress for a black-tie function. There're some gowns that I want you to try on as well as some other things."

"Other things?"

"I've already called ahead and had the saleslady take out several black gowns in a size six for you to try on," Chelsea continued as Megan looked at her questionably.

"But what other things?"

"I was thinking since you're dating Senator Monroe, you may want to invest in getting a few more items. Some suits, cute sundresses for the summer. No shorts or minis. Some nice summer slacks and blouses. I know you're only twenty-six, but we're going to have to get rid of the baby doll and peasant top look you've been wearing since college. No more Gap and Old Navy, my love," Chelsea said glancing at Megan's T-shirt and bootcut jeans.

"Chelsea, I'm only here to buy a dress," Megan complained not interested in an image makeover.

"Correction, Mr. Monroe is going to buy the dress and whatever else you want. He gave me a limit and trust me it's a nice one because there isn't one. It will all be charged to his Black Card. A whole new wardrobe for the summer. We'll do the fall one when the time comes. He said that personally. I guess his bachelor days are over with!" Chelsea said looking through a rack of sundresses, pulling out several and handing them to the saleslady. Chelsea continued while the brightness in Megan's face slowly faded.

"Next week I'm going to go through your closet and tag the clothes you're not to wear while out with him just in case you get photographed. What wife of a senator do you know that dresses like you? Sweetie, you dress really cute but remember you're dating a senator now."

"I'm not married to him, Chelsea."

"Not yet, my love. Not yet. And of course I'll help you pick out your wedding gowns. You must have one for the ceremony and another for the reception. I'm sure Vera will design something special just for you. Then you'll need a whole new wardrobe as a married woman. We can store your old clothes in your guest room closet or give them to charity. I'm sure you can use the tax write-off."

"Chelsea, let's go through my closet first before we begin buying other things. I own a lot of nice suits and dresses. I have to wear jeans and sweats when I'm doing a job. I have to be comfortable if I'm on a ladder painting, moving furniture or hanging wallpaper."

"Sweetheart, I'm only following orders from Mr. Monroe. He is paying me nicely to select clothes for you. Now, my goal is to give you a new look and style of your own. We want other politicians' wives, girlfriends and even their mistresses to be jealous of you plus set out a new trend. Remember Jackie O?" Chelsea inquired placing a dozen of dresses on the chair next to Megan and going back for more.

"The rapper?" Megan asked sarcastically.

"You know exactly who I mean. First Lady Jacqueline Kennedy Onassis. Her style was graceful, elegant and classy. Everyone wanted to look like her, dress like her. People still admire her sense of style and poise. That's what I want for you. I want people to see a sophisticated young lady on the arm of Senator Monroe. Do you understand, honey?" Chelsea asked seriously.

Megan groaned as she took several dresses into the dressing room. For the next three hours she tried on more outfits than she had that entire year. She tried to suck it up and have fun, but all she could think about was sleeping next to Steven that night and hoped she wouldn't have the urge to seduce him.

Chapter 7

Megan arrived in Washington, D.C., around eight in the evening. Her ears had finally regained most of their hearing as she stepped off of the plane, chewing her fourth piece of gum. She looked around and saw an older, kind-looking lady holding a sign that read Megan Chase in bold letters. She waved at the woman, who she assumed to be Greta, and walked hurriedly over to her.

"Good evening, Ms. Chase. I'm Greta Reid, Senator Monroe's housekeeper. Your bags are being put into the car. Do you need anything before we go to the house?" Greta had a Southern accent, a grandmotherly presence and a genuine smile. Her gray hair was in fresh curls around her warm, brown face and her pleasant demeanor made Megan comfortable.

"No, and it's very nice to meet you," Megan said, shaking Greta's hand. Greta looked rather surprised when Megan took her hand.

"Now, Ms. Chase…" Greta began.

"Please, call me Megan."

"All right, Ms. Megan. Is there anything you do or don't want to eat for breakfast in the morning? I can cook just about anything from A to Z, at least that's what the Monroe family says."

"No, whatever you cook is fine with me just as long as coffee goes with it." Megan enjoyed eating a hearty breakfast when possible, and she could sense that Ms. Greta seemed like the type to cook big meals.

"Well, I haven't seen Mr. Steven for almost a month, so I'm going to fix all of his favorites," Greta said as they walked to the car.

"If you need any help, let me know."

"Ms. Megan, that's sweet of you, but you just enjoy yourself these next few days. Mr. Steven said you're a hard-working interior decorator. I'm sure you can use the break."

"Do you have any children?" Megan asked.

"I have two daughters. Both married with kids. They live in Mobile, Alabama. That's where I'm originally from. I'm usually there until Mr. Steven calls me a few days before he arrives here in Washington or in Savannah. Mr. Steven is like the son I never had as well as Mr. Bryce," Greta said as they approached the car. It was a black Lexus LS 460.

"You don't live here all the time?"

"No, Ms. Megan. I'm sort of on call for Mr. Steven or anyone else in the Monroe family. I'm retired now. I've worked for the Monroe family for many years. Changed all of the Monroe children's dirty diapers."

"Well, you're a part of the family. Do you travel with him sometimes?"

"Sometimes, but Mr. Steven is a simple guy, if you can believe that. He knows how to cook and clean for himself, even though I spent most of the day cleaning." Greta opened the back door for Megan. "He said he wanted it to be perfect for you and now I see why."

"Ms. Greta, I'm not used to having people chauffeur me around. Can I sit up front with you?"

"Of course, sugar. You know, you're different from those uppity girls I see him with in the newspapers and magazines. When he used to bring them here or to Savannah, they wouldn't even acknowledge my presence. I think he has a keeper now." Greta winked.

When they arrived at the brownstone, Greta told Megan to make herself at home. It was a beautiful, three-story building with a studio apartment on the top floor that Greta mentioned she stayed in when she was there. The masculine decorations reminded her of Steven. Sturdy, strong furniture in dark colors. Greta took her up to the second floor to the master suite. It was a large room with a sitting area with a fireplace, and two big, brown-leather, comfy-looking chairs and an oversize leather ottoman. The bed was huge with cherrywood posts. It was so high off the ground it had matching steps on both sides.

"Right around the corner is your closet. I've already put away your things for you while you toured the brownstone. What a stunning dress you're wearing tomorrow evening. I'll steam it for you before you put it on tomorrow. It got a few wrinkles from the plane ride. You know those baggage handlers just throw people's stuff around."

"Thank you so much, Ms. Greta," Megan said thinking there was a "his" closet on the other side of the master bathroom. The one that was supposed to be "hers" was empty except for her things, a few African paintings, and a stack of about a dozen books sitting on the floor.

After Megan ate a delicious Southern dinner of chicken fried steak, mashed sweet potatoes and collard greens, she retired back upstairs to the bedroom and looked through the books that were on the floor in the closet. Reading was her favorite pastime. She found a Walter Mosley novel that she hadn't read yet and quickly read through the first few chapters in one of the big comfy chairs in the sitting area. She found herself yawning an hour later and decided to get up and walk around. She went into the master bath, which was an interior decorator's dream. A beautiful antique tub with four brass legs stood in the middle. The floor and countertops were marble. There were two vanities on opposite walls. The "hers" vanity had a makeup area with a timeless antique chair. There was a shower big enough for two.

Now that Megan was on her feet, she realized how exhausted she was. She decided to take a warm shower and climb into bed. Then it hit her again that she would be sleeping in the same bed as Steven. She'd almost forgotten. But he was right about one thing—it was an enormous bed.

After a refreshing shower, she walked into the bedroom, wrapped in her towel. She remembered Greta telling her she would put her nightclothes on the bed for her. When Megan walked into the room, the sheets on the right side were pulled back, but she didn't see her pajamas on the bed. Instead, Greta had laid out the little black slip that was in the same garment bag as her evening gown.

"Ha," Megan said out loud, walking to the closet with the slip to find the pajamas. She didn't see them anywhere. She knew she packed them.

"I was on the phone arguing with my mother, packing my suitcase. I folded up the shirt..." Megan realized that the pajamas were still lying on her bed in Atlanta. *What am I going to wear to bed?* Her only other choice was her workout clothes. *They will have to do.* She slipped on a tank top and pink velour shorts. The shorts had shrunk somewhat when she last washed them, but it was better than wearing the slinky black slip. She didn't want to give Steven any ideas.

Satisfied, Megan walked back into the room, only to discover Steven asleep in one of the leather chairs by the fireplace. Time flew, she thought. It was only midnight. She had planned on being asleep when he arrived.

She stopped abruptly in the doorway and stared at him. He sat somewhat slumped down in the chair with his legs apart. His hand rested on his forehead as if he had a headache. A loosened tie hung around his neck, and the first few buttons on his shirt were undone to reveal a glimpse of his smooth chest. Megan had the urge to straddle his lap and wind her arms around his neck and run her tongue down his skin. She shook her head at the thought and began to walk toward the bed, but the hardwood floor creaked, and his eyes flew open. He smiled and sat up straight.

"You're here early," she said, feeling awkward. She didn't know if she should climb into the bed or not.

"Yep. I was able to leave the gathering earlier than planned. Have you found everything you needed?" He began to unbutton his sleeve cuffs.

"Yes, thank you. Greta is wonderful." Megan decided to sit in the other chair across from him. "These are really cozy chairs," she said, rubbing her hands on the arms of the chair to feel the texture of the leather.

"Thank you. I just bought them and had them delivered when Greta got here. I used to have an old couch sitting here. When I saw these chairs in a magazine, I knew they would look nice by the fireplace. Greta did a good job picking out the comforter on my new bed." Steven looked admiringly at the gold-and-red comforter.

"New bed?" She was rather relieved that no other woman had slept in it. *But why should that matter? It's not as if we're a couple.*

"Yes, I ordered it at the same time as the chairs. I used to have a queen sleigh bed in here, but I had it moved to an empty room down the hall. I needed a change." He walked over and ran his hand over the comforter. "I haven't even slept in it yet, and now I can't wait especially since I get to share it with a sexy lady."

"Watch yourself, Steven. You better stay on your side of the bed."

"I promise. Scout's honor. Did you enjoy your shopping spree today?" He hopped up and sat on the bed. His longs legs barely touched the hardwood floor.

"Yes, I did. Thank you. Chelsea knows what she's doing. I also picked out a really nice tie for you, as well. Maybe you can wear it on Election Day," Megan suggested. "I hung it in your closet."

"Thank you. So you just know I'm going to win the primaries and then make it to November's election?"

"Of course. I've read the information about the other potential candidates vying for your father's seat. And I'm not saying this because I know you, but I really do think you're the best candidate. The only thing that may have been holding you back was your lifestyle. But the media loves that you've settled down… Well…sort of, I suppose. So, yes, I think you have a pretty good chance of winning."

"Megan, you keep blowing my head up like this, and I'll never let you go," he said in a sexy tone that caused her breathing to pause for a second and a sensual warmth rushed over her skin.

A heated, seductive stare passed between them and for a moment, Megan wished what he said would really happen, but she couldn't dwell on that. They were simply two people helping each other obtain their career goals. The media was finally warming up to him, and she'd seen a boost of phone calls from prospective clients after the event at Braxton's restaurant. Besides, she enjoyed her freedom of being single and so did Steven. After the election, they could return to their normal lives. But would it be normal or miserable because he would no longer be a part of her life?

"Well…I'm going to go take a shower," Steven said as he strode into the bathroom and closed the door.

Megan wasn't sure what to do next. She decided to get in the bed and try to fall asleep before he returned. If she wasn't, she would pretend she was sleep. She looked around the room again before getting under the covers. Greta had indeed done a wonderful job. Now all that was needed were new curtains and a few throw rugs on the hardwood floor and the bedroom would be complete. She thought of all of this as she drifted off to sleep between the fresh Egyptian cotton sheets.

Steven let the warm water from the shower wash over his tired body. He could still smell her scent in

would say was "have a nice evening, sir" and hand him his trench coat.

"Have a great time," Greta said opening the front door. "Are you sure you don't need me to drive you?"

"No. This event may not end until late. Just get some rest. I want all of my favorites in the morning." Steven chuckled and gave Greta a kiss on her cheek. "I promise, no golfing." He grabbed Megan's hand and squeezed it gently as they walked to the car.

"You seem nervous," Steven said once they were in the car headed to the Smithsonian. He didn't want her to feel out of place this evening. He knew she wasn't used to this type of event. However, because she was such an elegant and classy lady, he knew she would be able to handle herself with the other girlfriends and wives.

"Just a little. I've been to numerous events but never a dinner fund-raiser where the plates were $500.00 each. I don't spend that much in one month on groceries!"

"Yeah, the price is quite steep, but the money raised is going to the Save the Manatee campaign in Florida. They're slowly becoming extinct." He had a soft spot for the huge animals that were being killed by ships and boats.

"Hmm, interesting. I saw recently on a documentary that the propellers on the boats are striking them, leaving scars, or even worse, causing their death. That's so sad. I'm glad to see how concerned you are about the manatees."

"I'm an animal lover."

Steven tried to stare straight ahead but his eyes kept wandering to the beauty sitting next to him. Keenan was right. She was indeed ravishing, and it took everything in him not to pull the car over and mess up her hair. However, it was clear to him that Megan wasn't interested in being anything more than friends or at least she didn't want to admit to it.

Moments later, they arrived at the Smithsonian. There were cameras flashing as they walked the red carpet, and they stopped and posed for a few pictures before going inside.

He squeezed her hand. "Don't be nervous," he reassured her as they walked into the event. "I'm by your side."

After the hostess showed them to their table, they were offered a choice of wines. They both opted for an iced tea and lemonade instead. Some other politicians and their wives or girlfriends joined their table of ten. The men mostly talked about politics, sports and the president while the women discussed fashion and what clothes they were taking on their upcoming fabulous vacations. Steven could tell that Megan was trying really hard to join the conversation, but all of the women were so superficial. Megan was down-to-earth and not concerned with such nonsense.

"So where are you two vacationing this summer, Megan?" Mrs. Douglas, the wife of U.S. Senator Richard Douglas from Nevada, asked. He was one of Steven's golfing buddies from that morning.

"Not really sure. I have a lot of work to do this

summer." Megan glanced at Steven with a "help me" look on her face.

"What do you do besides look tenderly at Senator Monroe?" Mrs. Douglas asked.

Steven smiled at Mrs. Douglas's comment. If she thought Megan was looking tenderly at him, then she must've been doing a good job of faking it.

"I have my own interior-design business in At-lanta. This summer I'm doing a show for the Fabu-lous Living Channel as well as still finding time to spend with my Steven."

"Splendid! You two have to come to our place in the Hamptons this summer." Mrs. Douglas placed her hand on her forehead. "Megan, I'm in dire need of redoing some of the guest rooms and bathrooms there. Maybe you can give me some suggestions or better yet, just do it for me." Mrs. Douglas scooted closer to Megan.

"I'll have to check my schedule, but I'm sure a few days at your summer home would be lovely, Mrs. Douglas," Megan answered sincerely. "And I'd be happy to help you with your decorating needs."

After dessert, Steven and Megan said their good-byes. He could see the relief on her face when he announced they were leaving. As they walked to the door, he heard someone call his name in a fa-miliar tone.

"Senator Monroe," a woman called after him. Ste-ven cringed before he turned around. He knew that voice in his sleep. It belonged to his ex-wife, Veron-ica. He just hoped she was on her best behavior tonight. He'd known Veronica since college, and her vindictive ways hadn't, and probably wouldn't ever change.

"Hello, Veronica," Steven said, turning slowly around. He glanced at Megan, who remained her poised self.

"Oh, Steven, it's a pleasure to see you here. I had a feeling you would be here to support the manatees this year. And who is this lovely *young* girl?"

"This is Megan Chase, my girlfriend. Megan, this is Veronica Scott, my ex-wife."

Veronica's dark eyes stayed on Steven when she addressed Megan.

"Actually, love, it's Dr. Scott-Monroe. I never dropped his last name. I love the way it sounds."

"Nice to meet you, Veronica," Megan said nodding her head instead of shaking her hand.

"Steven, we must do lunch while you're in town. I'm no longer in Fairfax. I just bought a charming brownstone in Georgetown." Veronica turned her back completely to Megan. "Kind of like the one you bought when we first got married. That seems like eons ago, does it not Steven?"

"Still at Georgetown?" Steven said, walking around Veronica to stand next to Megan and wrapping his arm around her waist, pulling her close to him.

"Oh, yes, I simply love being there. After I got my doctorate from Cornell, I applied at Georgetown and a few other colleges. But you know I love D.C. Are you still in college, my dear?" Veronica's gaze finally came to rest on Megan.

"No. I've already finished my bachelor's and master's degrees." Her voice was calm and steady. Steven was pleased. Some of the women he'd dated who had the displeasure of meeting Veronica were always tongued-tied around her.

"Megan has her own interior-design company in Atlanta. She decorates homes for celebrities and other public figures," Steven said, squeezing her even closer and then placing a sweet kiss on her forehead. She tenderly smiled back at him just as Mrs. Douglas had mentioned.

"Oh, how cute. Is that how you two met? Well, I must run. I'm here with Judge Hill, and you know he's the jealous type. Call me about lunch." Veronica strutted away.

"We'll look forward to it," Steven said, calling after her.

"Well, that went well," Megan said, withdrawing herself from his embrace but placing her hand in his as they headed out the door.

"I hope Veronica wasn't too mean. She can be a real witch sometimes."

"No, really?" Megan said sarcastically with a laugh.

"You handled yourself pretty well. Most of the women that I've dated that have met Veronica usually freeze up."

"Well, I'm not most women. Besides, I didn't feel threatened. I'm not really your girlfriend remember?"

"Oh, yeah. I almost forgot."

He hoped she would just forget, as well.

* * *

They rode in silence back to the brownstone. Overall, Megan did have a nice evening. She met some potential clients with a summer place in the Hamptons and was able to give to a charity.

Her thoughts wandered to Veronica and how exotically beautiful she was. Her waist-length natural curly hair was a jet black that brought out her dark, slanted eyes. Her skin was tanned and smooth and her makeup was flawless. She was tall and slender and could pass for a supermodel. Her diamond choker with matching earrings sparkled. Megan could tell she wasn't dolled up for the evening—that was how she always looked.

The more Megan thought about all of the women in Steven's life before her, the more she realized they were all beautiful, high maintenance women who could walk the runways during fashion week in New York or Paris. Sighing, she knew he could never fall for her.

When they arrived back to the brownstone, Megan noticed that the light in Greta's room was on. It was nearly ten o'clock. She had figured Greta would be asleep by now.

"I guess Greta waits up for you?" Megan inquired when the garage door lowered behind them.

"No, not really. She likes you and probably wants to know how your evening went."

"I like her, too," she said, getting out of the car while Steven tossed something in the trash. "She reminds me of my grandmother who passed about five years ago." Megan waited by the door that led to the keeping room.

"Greta is a wonderful person. I really don't need a housekeeper, but I like having her around." He paused. "Well, I'm off to the study to do some work. Thank you for a great evening." Steven fumbled with his keys.

"Work? Do you ever relax? Take a break?" Megan offered.

"No. Then I wouldn't be where I am today. Jeez. I sound like my dad," Steven said, still looking at the keys.

"Do you need some help finding the right key?"

"Um…no. They're just…twisted," he said, still rummaging through them. "You know, it's only around ten on a Saturday night in Washington. How about we go out dancing or something fun? I know of a really cool place. I can teach you how to go-go dance."

"Well, if you don't count a fourth-grade field trip, this is my first time in Washington, so that sounds like fun." She finally grabbed the keys from him and opened the door, which happened to be already unlocked.

"Okay, well let's change clothes and get out of here. According to you, I can use some relaxation," Steven said as they walked up the stairs to his bedroom.

"Didn't you relax playing golf? My dad says it's a very relaxing sport," she said, kicking her heels off once they were in the bedroom. They were beginning to hurt her feet. Then, remembering she wasn't at home, Megan immediately gathered the shoes and placed them neatly in the closet. She went into the bathroom and took the hairpins out of her hair. She had asked Keenan to pin her hair so that it would fall after she took the pins out. It fell perfectly with soft curls on her back. She could hear Steven talking from his closet.

"Nope. We stand around and pretend to care about the other person's golf game. We're really trying to find out each other's opinions on current issues, bills that must be passed, who's running for what and when. So you see, Megan, playing golf with the good old boys wasn't relaxing. It's all politics."

"So is this," Megan whispered to herself, looking through the clothes she brought with her. The clothes from Barney's were being shipped back to Atlanta. Luckily, Chelsea told her to keep a few of the dresses just in case they went somewhere unplanned. Megan reached back to undo her zipper when she remembered that Keenan and Greta had zipped and clasped her gown. She wasn't able to unhook the first clasp. Megan knew that it wouldn't be a good idea to call Greta because she would wonder why Steven couldn't undress his own girlfriend.

"Need some help?" Steven asked, startling her. He had changed into black dress slacks and a yellow polo shirt.

"Yes, please. If you wouldn't mind just unhooking the first clasp. I think there may be another one at the end of the zipper." Megan turned around and lifted her hair off her back.

He undid the clasp, and his hands brushed against her bare back when he lowered the zipper. Heat rushed through her as his warm hands touched her skin. She wanted nothing more than to feel his lips where his hands were. That was when Megan remembered she wasn't wearing any panties because she hadn't wanted the line to show through her dress. She turned around immediately to hide her backside, but it was too late. She heard him whisper *wow* and stepped back, as if to admire the view in front of him.

"I'll be ready in ten minutes," she said, quickly pushing him out the closet and closing the door.

"Cute tush," she heard him say through the door.

Ten minutes later they were on their way down to the garage and backing out of the driveway.

"You look lovely tonight. Is that another Chelsea suggestion?" Steven asked. The strapless purple dress was short and hitting her curvy body in the right places.

"Yes, it is. Chelsea does her job well. She's the best fashion stylist and consultant I know."

"I agree. She referred me to an excellent tailor here in D.C. When I win my father's seat, I'll definitely need one here."

Megan looked out the window. He would win the election, move to D.C. and forget all about her. She decided to change the subject.

"You have a very nice car. It's my dream car."

"Really? You want to drive it? I can have some-one drive it back to Atlanta for you. It just sits in the garage for weeks at a time."

"No. Besides, you have to drive something while you're in D.C."

"I have a few other cars that just sit in the garage. I can have the Range Rover sent to D.C. easily."

"No, my SUV is fine." Megan said. She would love to drive the Lexus, but she'd never been a gold digger, and wasn't about to start. She rarely drove her ex-boyfriend's convertible Porsche or his Mer-cedes when they were together. But every now and then, she saw his nurse happily driving the Porsche around Atlanta.

"Well, if you change your mind, let me know."

They arrived at Capital Club about fifteen min-utes later. After giving the valet the keys, Steven took Megan by the hand and they entered the dance club. They found a table in the back and ordered bottled waters. *The atmosphere is sort of young,* she thought as she looked around. It was mostly college students or fresh out-of-college-students. The floor was packed with people doing all types of dances that Megan had never seen in the clubs in Atlanta. The music blared through the speakers. Strobe lights of red and purple flashed on the dance floor. The DJ played a top forty mix.

"Isn't this place kind of young for you?" Megan screamed over the loud music. She thought they were going to a more upscale location for professionals.

"Yeah. I guess you're right. I used to come here

when I was visiting friends. I was in college at the time," Steven screamed back, looking around. "I feel sort of overdressed looking at all these young men wearing baggy jeans."

Megan was getting tired of screaming, but she didn't have a choice.

"Well, I'm still in my twenties, so I feel fine," Megan answered smiling at him.

"Yes, you certainly are fine," he said, smiling back at her with a wink.

Megan thought she heard him but wanted to be sure. "What did you say? I couldn't hear you. It's rather loud in here," she screamed.

"Nothing. I guess this place isn't for talking," he screamed back.

"Well, since we're here, let's see what you can really do, old man," Megan said, pulling him out of the chair and on to the dance floor.

"We'll see about the 'old man' comment. I'm sure I can outdance you any day of the week!" Steven said, as he jokingly started to imitate some old '70s moves, including the robot and the twist.

They danced and laughed for the next hour straight. He taught her how to go-go dance and she taught him the latest moves from Atlanta that he didn't know. Finally, the DJ played a slow song. But before Megan could turn to walk off the dance floor, Steven pulled her close to him. She didn't resist. She was too tired.

Instead, she let him hold her close. She felt as if she had drunk more than just water. Her dance high was coming down, and she relaxed in his arms. His hands slowly caressed her waist and back. His intent gaze rested on her face. He lowered his head down to hers, and she caressed his neck with her hands as her breaths became heavy. With their lips only centimeters apart, a voice in Megan's head said, *Go ahead and kiss him.* Something told Megan it wasn't make-believe anymore, well unless he was a very good actor. When she realized he was lowering his head to kiss her, she didn't turn away.

Steven kissed her softly on the lips, just enough to taste the strawberry lip gloss she had put on over her lipstick. A hint Chelsea had given if she wanted to make her lips more noticeable and luscious. She wanted him to kiss her some more, but this club wasn't the place.

"Let's get out of here," he whispered to her.

"Okay," she said barely above a whisper. As they rushed out of the club holding hands, Megan still felt the warmth of his lips on hers.

They rode in silence back to his brownstone. He continued to hold her hand, rubbing the inside of her palm with one of his fingers. She had too many thoughts in her head about what had just happened between them. She closed her eyes and rested her head back on the seat. She wasn't sure how to handle her emotions.

Once the car was settled in the garage, neither of them spoke. They still sat holding hands. Megan looked straight ahead, but he was looking directly at her. She decided to let him speak first.

"So are you going to slap me now or later?" he asked jokingly.

"Do you want me to slap you?"

"No. I really want to kiss you again," Steven said, moving toward her and running his finger along her lips. Placing his fingers under her chin, he brought her face closer to his and once again kissed her supple lips, slowly. She responded in the same manner taking her time to taste every inch of his mouth. Warm sensations coursed between her thighs as she returned his kisses with the same passion and vigor that he displayed to her. Low moans of pleasure erupted from her as he kissed her even deeper, letting his tongue penetrate the inside of her mouth.

Her hands roamed over his face while one of his hands caressed the center of her back and the other one massaged her neck. He reached in between her legs under the seat to press a button that moved her seat back as far as it would go. He then reached around her and pushed the back of the seat all the way down, his lips never leaving hers as their kissing intensified and the car windows began to slightly fog. She pulled him on top of her, and he stopped the kiss for moment, taking off his shirt and tossing it in the backseat. His lips placed hot kisses on the side of her neck as she explored her fingers along his hard, muscular back. She could feel the pulsating of his erection through his pants.

Her moaning was unrecognizable as he pulled down the top of her dress, exposing her breasts, which hard hardened and yearned for his tongue, mouth and hands to entice them. He popped one nipple into his mouth, circling his tongue around it before gently tugging it with his teeth. She let out a cry of desire as he continued licking and teasing her breasts going back and forth between the two.

"Steven…that feels so damn good. Please, please don't stop."

"Don't worry. I won't." His voice was heavy, filled with passion. "Not until you're completely satisfied."

He captured her lips once more, thrusting and winding his tongue inside of her mouth. Every fiber in her body was ablaze, and she needed whatever he had to offer to put it out. A cold shower wasn't going to do the trick. She craved him. She had desired him for so long. When she wrapped her legs around his trim waist, he stopped for a second and looked into her eyes as if searching for a sign to go ahead.

She kissed him softly at first and then licked her tongue across his bottom lip causing his breathing to stifle. He slid his hand to the hem of her dress and pulled it up to her stomach. His hand lingered on the band of her panties and then pushed them to the side. He circled her clit with his finger as erotic moans emerged from her mouth. He traced his finger down between her folds as his lips kissed the side of her neck. When he inserted a finger into her slick canal, her breathing became irregular as she thrust her hips up to meet his in and out motion. His lips left her neck trailing down her chest and stomach until he was on his knees in front of her. She shook in anticipation of what she wished would come next, and when he replaced his finger with his warm, wet tongue, she almost exploded. He raised her legs up so that her shoes were in the seat and parted her thighs as he twirled his tongue around inflicting pure ecstasy on her.

"Oh, my goodness, Steven…" she said breathlessly, clutching his shoulders.

"You're so damn wet. You're dripping. I'm the reason. Right, baby?"

"Yes…"

"Who?"

"Yes, Steven."

"That's my girl."

He continued darting in and out of her, cupping his hands under her bottom as her hips moved with the same urgency as his tongue. Her emotions and feelings for him welled up as an orgasm slammed through her body with a force that left her weak and vulnerable yet craving for more of him. The moans and cries eliciting from her were foreign and out of her character, but she didn't care. With him she felt carefree. She could let go and be herself with him and that terrified her.

He lifted up and positioned himself over her. The screech of a zipper sounded, and it wasn't hers. And the conversation she had with her mother yesterday popped into her head.

She immediately pushed him away. "No. This is a big mistake, Steven. I can't do this anymore," Megan said, squirming from under him and pushing open the car door. She pulled her dress down, and rushed into the house and up the stairs to the master bedroom. She didn't know what to do. She was ready to return home to Atlanta and back to her normal life. She had been afraid this would happen. He wanted fringe benefits, as well.

Steven sat in the car for a few minutes before going inside to face Megan. He wasn't sure what had just happened. He thought he and Megan were on the same page. The way she kissed him was like no other kiss he had ever experienced. He'd never been the kissing type. Even while married to Veronica, he seldom kissed. But when he first laid eyes on Megan, the first thought that came to mind was how bad he wanted to taste her lips. And now that he had, he wanted to kiss her juicy lips—both sets.

Sighing, he got out of the car. The last thing he wanted her to feel was hurt, because it was never his intent from the beginning.

When he walked into the bedroom, he saw her packing her suitcase. She was shaken and distraught.

"Where are you going?" he asked quietly.

"Home. I have a credit card. I can pay for my own plane ticket," she said, stuffing her things in her suitcase.

"You can't leave now," he said, taking her by the shoulders and turning her around to face him.

"Why? Because you're scared you won't win the nomination? You're scared how the public is going to look at you?" Megan jerked away, going toward the bathroom. He followed her. "I knew this was a big mistake!"

"No. I…" He stopped midsentence. Now he felt bad. He didn't want her to think he was taking advantage of her, he was very much attracted to her. He couldn't believe it. He had found the one woman who could actually change him into a one-woman man, and she didn't even want him.

"I apologize, Megan. I guess it was the music and the atmosphere. Or it could've been the fact that I was holding a very beautiful woman in my arms, who smells and tastes just like strawberries. Please don't go. Not because of how the public may perceive me, but because it's late, and we've had a long day. Just leave in the morning. We'll tell Greta you had an emergency and had to fly back home early. I'll take you to the airport myself." He hoped she would accept his apology.

"I can take a taxi," Megan said, putting her suitcase down.

"I understand if you don't want to do this anymore," he said sincerely although he had the urge to reach out and pull her close to him.

He watched as Megan sat in the leather chair, contemplating her decision.

"No, I made you a promise. You're right, it's late, and the music and atmosphere played a part, as well. New clause—no more dancing."

"It's a deal," he said, and gently shook her hand.

Chapter 8

The following Monday after her Washington, D.C., trip, Megan was back at work and glad to be doing something to keep her mind off of her fantasy life. She needed to concentrate on her own normal life for a change. She had a million things to do before she headed to Hilton Head that summer to work on the project for the Fabulous Living Channel. She also needed to get her mind off of Steven.

She sipped on a cup of coffee Lucy had made for her. It was storming that morning and no one wanted to make a Starbucks run in the rain.

It had to be the dancing, Megan thought to herself as she took another sip. It had been a while since she'd had that much fun with a man, but Steven was just the wrong man at the right time. While she enjoyed the kiss—among other things—they shared in the car, she didn't want to get her emotions involved, only to be disappointed later. She was glad she was able to leave that Sunday morning to fly back home. Steven had arranged for her to fly first-class back to Atlanta.

Megan continued sipping on her coffee as it surprisingly calmed her nerves. She asked Lucy to refill her cup before her meeting. Chelsea was stopping by to finalize plans for her daughter's bedroom, but Megan knew she really wanted the play-by-play of her Washington weekend.

Chelsea arrived promptly at ten for their meeting. She sashayed into Megan's office wearing a pink Chanel suit. Her diamond earrings and matching tennis bracelet seemed as if they would be too much for someone to wear at ten in the morning. However, it was normal for her. Chelsea believed in being ready for any type of occasion at a moment's notice. The sleeveless dress under her suit jacket could easily be a cocktail dress. Her wristlet that she always kept in her bigger purse could easily double for an evening bag.

Chelsea sat in one of the leather wingback chairs in front of Megan's glass desk and shook her head in disapproval at Megan. "What is up with that white peasant-type blouse? That should be in the bag going to the Salvation Army. I'm sure some young college girl could make use of it." Chelsea rested her Prada bag on Megan's desk.

"Good morning to you, too, sunshine. Can I get

you some coffee?" Megan asked with a hint of sarcasm in her voice.

"No. Hot water, please. I have herbal tea bags in my purse," Chelsea stated, taking one of them out and setting it on the desk.

Megan buzzed Lucy to bring a cup of hot water for Chelsea and more coffee for her. *If the next hour is going to be like this, I may need more than just coffee.*

"I love everything you did to Madison's room. I had Julie put the comforter set on this weekend, and it's simply charming. She's going to adore it when she comes home from Vanderbilt this summer. The last thing will be a nice antique chair for her writing desk."

"Julie? What happened to Amanda?" Megan wondered.

"I had to fire her. She almost ruined my hardwood floors by putting bleach in the bucket. Luckily, I caught her pouring a cap into it and was able to stop her from mopping. A good maid is so hard to find!" Chelsea exclaimed, putting her hand on her forehead.

Megan smiled and thought about how Chelsea would have fit in with the senators' wives at dinner on Saturday night. "Well, I wouldn't know anything about that. I can't afford a maid."

"But, darling, you will once you marry Steven. Now, tell me all about your trip." For the next hour Megan told Chelsea about her trip, leaving out the car incident and argument.

Later on that afternoon Tiffani and Sydney joined

Jade and Megan for lunch at the Cheesecake Factory. The rain had finally stopped and the sun was shining brightly as if it had never rained. It had been a few weeks since they'd had lunch together and Megan needed to catch up on happenings in her girls' lives. Plus, Tiffani and Jade really wanted to hear about Megan's life with the senator. And Megan knew that Sydney needed a break from profiling a new case that kept her up most of the night.

Sydney immediately grabbed the bread basket and began buttering a roll. "Ladies, I'm famished. I haven't eaten since dinner last night, which consisted of two chili dogs, three cups of coffee and two doughnuts. Maybe three doughnuts," Sydney added, as the waiter left with their food orders.

"You were at the GBI office?" Jade asked.

"Since noon yesterday," Sydney stated, squeezing a lemon into her water. "This is the first time I've left. I can't talk about the case of course, but I can tell you it's giving me a headache."

Tiffani sighed and shook her head at Syd.

"Your headache probably came from eating two chili dogs. There's no telling what kind of meat was used to make them, and you stopped eating pork years ago. You know that processed meat is just ground up left over parts from pigs, chickens, and cows all mixed into one hot dog." Tiffani was very health conscious after she found out her late husband had high cholesterol. "We really need to be more aware of what we put into our bodies. We should treat our bodies like a temple and take care of them.

Remember, this is the only body we will ever have. Can't sell it and buy another one like a house."

"You know how to spoil a good time," Jade groaned.

Megan chuckled at Jade, who was actually more of a health nut than Tiffani.

"Tiffani, I'm so glad you could make it. I know you have your hands full. Where's my godson?" Megan asked.

"He's with his grandparents," Tiffani answered. "If it wasn't for my parents, I don't know how I could've gotten through this year. They've been wonderful, and so have all of you."

Megan placed her hand on Tiffani's and squeezed it. "That's what family and friends are for. How's your father doing after that car accident a few months ago?"

"His back has been bothering him again, so Alfonso prescribed something for him and told him to take it easy the next few days." Tiffani looked at Megan apologetically as soon as she uttered her ex-boyfriend's name.

"Tiffani!" Sydney exclaimed, and then looked sympathetically at Megan.

"Oh, girl, I'm so sorry. I didn't mean to mention his name in front of you," Tiffani said with a sincere smile.

But Megan didn't care anymore. It felt good to finally be over him.

"Girl, its fine. He was your father's doctor before we started dating," Megan replied.

"Besides, she's dating a Monroe man now. Forget the doctor. Our little Megan has moved up in the world," Jade reminded everyone.

Tiffani, who still looked sympathetically at Megan chimed in. "How was the fund-raiser in Washington? I read in the newspaper that the foundation raised over $300,000 dollars to save the manatees."

"It was nice. The tiramisu was delicious. I think I may order one today with my lunch, along with an espresso," Megan said, looking at her dessert menu and trying to avoid the conversation. Even though she knew it would come up eventually. She handed them the dessert menu. She knew the only reason Tiffani liked coming to the Cheesecake Factory was for the cheesecake.

"Good idea. I'll take some to go. Dad loves it. I'll probably order him something to eat, as well. I just hope he's feeling better. I worry about him," Tiffani said.

"You know, I have had acupuncture done to help with regulating my menstrual cycle. It also helps with other ailments such as back pains," Jade explained, taking out her doctor's business card and handing it to Tiffani.

"I was reading about acupuncture in one of my alternative health books. I prefer holistic approaches as well but, well, you know men. I don't know if my dad would go for it or not. He's old-school and would probably say it's for women. Megan, do you think Steven would do acupuncture if you suggested it?" Tiffani asked.

Megan remained silent for a moment to collect her thoughts. She didn't know if he would or not. She didn't even know his favorite color or if he was left- or right-handed, so she shrugged and said, "He's a man, what do you think?"

The ladies talked some more, and then Sydney suggested that they go look at the cheesecakes on display at the front of the restaurant. Once they were at the cheesecake counter Sydney said, "We haven't spoken since you returned from your trip, sissy. Did you really have a nice time in Washington?"

"Yes and no," Megan whispered.

"Wait a minute. I know that look. You've fallen in love with Steven!"

"No! Perhaps. Yes!" she finally admitted to her sister. "We get along great. He's really a nice, down-to-earth guy. One would think because of his status and his family's wealth that he would be arrogant and cocky, but he isn't. Well sometimes, but only when he's joking about something. He's a very simple and self-efficient guy. He's so different than what's-his-face who acted like he grew up with a silver spoon in his mouth and flaunted his money like it grew on trees."

"Megan, that's all Steven knows. He grew up having money so it doesn't matter to him. Men like your ex want everyone to know they have made it. A show-off. That's why Daddy never cared for him."

"Syd, when I see him, a part of me wants to rip my clothes off and have him throw me against the wall and make me scream his name."

"Up against the wall? Megan, that doesn't sound like you."

"My point exactly, but I can't stop thinking about having sex with him in all kinds of positions. It keeps me up at night."

"Girl, you got it bad. Real bad."

"What should I do?"

"Well, the best advice I can give is to simply follow your heart. You'll know if he's the right man. It's just a gut feeling that a person has when they know that there's no one else who can make them happy." Sydney spoke in a whimsical voice, which was way outside of her character.

"Syd, is there something you need to tell me?" Megan asked smiling, as they walked back to the table.

"No." Sydney shrugged. "Just speaking in general."

The ladies enjoyed the rest of their lunch for the next hour. Tiffani promised to be home by three to relieve her parents, and Sydney had to go back to the bureau. Jade and Megan rode back to the office in Jade's convertible BMW.

"Megan, are you all right? You don't look that well. Did something you ate not agree with you?"

"My stomach is a little queasy. Just a little jet lag, more than likely," Megan answered. The truth was, she was having confusing feelings about Steven, and it was making her sick.

"When we get back to the office, just get into your car and go home. Lucy and I can handle our appointment. You look like you need some rest," Jade stated.

"Thanks. I could use some more sleep. When I got home yesterday, I finished my project boards for Hilton Head and did laundry," Megan answered. *And I was up all night thinking about my so-called love life. Mostly, fantasizing about how many ways to make love to the Steven,* she added in her mind.

"Well, just go home and get some rest. I'm sure being the girlfriend of a politician can be quite busy and exciting," Jade said, as she parked her car in the parking garage.

Megan hugged Jade and then walked to her car. She didn't need anything from her office. She had work at home to catch up on. Anything to get her mind off of Steven. Luckily, he would be in Washington, D.C., until Wednesday, and then he was going to Florida before coming back to Atlanta next week. If she was lucky, he wouldn't call unless she needed to go somewhere with him, and she wasn't sure if she would be up to going anywhere with him anytime soon.

Megan wanted time to reflect and think about the decision she'd made to date him. If she was falling for him, she didn't know how much longer she could keep up with this charade, because the truth was, she was no longer pretending.

Chapter 9

Almost a week had gone by and Megan still hadn't heard from Steven. It was Saturday afternoon, and she was preparing to leave for her godson's birthday party. She wasn't sure if she should call Steven or not. She tried staying busy by going overboard on projects for clients as well as helping her sorority with a community-service project she hadn't originally signed up for.

She hadn't thought too much about him by the end of the week, at least not during the day. But once her head hit the pillow at night, thoughts of him resided until dawn. She saw him on CNN Thursday morning while she was jogging on the treadmill. The bill he was voting on had passed, and a reporter outside of the capitol in Atlanta was interviewing him. Megan could see that he was freshly shaven and had recently gotten a haircut. His dimples were present and his teeth were white and sparkling.

She had picked up her telephone to call him, but quickly decided not to. She had nothing to say. But in a way she sort of missed talking to him. He was very easy to speak with and was usually in good spirits unlike her ex. She used to have to make him listen to her and even then she knew he wasn't really listening at all. He never wanted to know how her day was, what projects she was working on or even the simplest of concerns like how she was feeling. Steven always asked those questions, and he actually meant them.

Well, I don't have time to sit around and worry about Steven, she thought as she tried to wrap KJ's birthday gift. She hated wrapping presents and would have preferred if she could put it in a gift bag. However, KJ was turning five, and her mother told her a long time ago that children like to unwrap their presents not look in a gift bag. Megan was trying to wrap the present as neatly as possible, but then she remembered KJ was going to just rip the paper off anyway. The finished product looked somewhat decent, but she placed it in a gift bag anyway and decorated it with colorful tissue paper.

"That's better," she said to Percy holding the bag up so he could see it. The cat raised a paw at it. She knew that meant he really wanted to play with the dark blue ribbon she tied on the handles.

Megan glanced at the clock and realized if she

didn't get a move on, she would be late to her god-son's birthday party.

Thirty minutes later she was dressed in a yel-low, flowery sundress with matching yellow wedges. Chelsea had insisted this sundress would be perfect for a Saturday afternoon luncheon with the senator. Of course, a five-year-old's birthday party didn't fit into that category, but she really wanted to wear the dress. Megan pulled her thick hair back into a pony-tail. She had been so busy trying to keep her mind off of Steven that she missed her hair appointment on Thursday and had to reschedule.

"Bye, Percy," Megan said, walking to the door with the gift bag in one hand and a grocery bag with homemade potato salad in the other. Megan wasn't much of cook, but she was always praised for her potato salad.

It was Saturday, so she knew traffic would be a little hectic from Atlanta's Buckhead area to the suburbs in Stone Mountain where Tiffani lived. As Megan stepped off of the elevator, she literally ran into a familiar face with the yummy dimples that she immediately wanted to shower with kisses.

"Hello, Megan."

"Steven, what are you doing here?" she asked surprised that he was there. She had just thought about him when she was in the elevator. *Where was he when I thought about him in the shower? That's where he should've popped up.*

"Well, I was in the neighborhood and decided to stop by. No, that's not true. I just wanted to check on you." Steven raked his eyes over her body, settling them on her manicured toes.

"You could've called," Megan, suggested walking past him toward the parking garage.

"I know, but I just got back in town this morning. I've been so busy with meetings all this week. Plus, I wanted to give you some space."

"I see. Well, I have to go to my godson's birthday party. I'm running sort of late. I should be halfway there now," she said, putting her things in the trunk of her black Mustang.

"I thought you had a SUV?"

"I do. This is my weekend car. It was my first car straight out of college. An impulse buy, at least that's what my dad says. Syd has a red one just like it." Megan stood by the driver's door waiting for him to leave, even though she actually preferred to stay and talk to him.

"So Sydney has a SUV like yours, as well?"

"No. She has a motorcycle."

"Really? Bryce has one, too." He paused and looked around as if he wanted to say something else.

"I really need to go," she said even though she didn't want to.

"I guess I should've called first, but I wasn't sure if you were taking my calls after what happened last weekend."

"All is forgotten," she lied. She couldn't get it out of her head.

"I wanted to see if you wanted to hang out today. Grab some lunch or something. I remembered what you said about me needing to relax. I actually have some free time if you can believe that!" Steven said, opening the door for her.

"Really?"

"No, not really, but I am giving myself free time. I feel like I eat, sleep and dream about politics. There's always some bill I need to read over, complaints from constituents and don't get me started with the rumors in the press. Sometimes, I just want to have a normal day without distractions," Steven complained.

"Well, you can come with me to the birthday party if you want. I mean it's a kiddie party with the pony, face painting and the clown, but you can still come. Tiffani won't mind. She'll probably put you to work though," Megan offered, surprising herself.

"Cool. But I don't have a gift," he said, walking around to the passenger side of her car.

"Do you have cash on you?" she asked as she started the car.

"Why do you need some gas? I know the gas prices are getting outrageous, which is another issue we're dealing with," he said, shaking his head.

"No, this car is always on full. But Keith Jr. likes money and saves it faithfully in a tin box under his bed."

"Smart young man. It's best to start now. By the time he retires, there won't be any more Social Security, and he'll have to invest in the stock market or some annuities. But even all of that is questionable." Steven looked through his wallet. "Yeah, I have a few twenties to add to his investment portfolio." Steven took out two twenties from his old worn out wallet.

"One twenty will be fine. You can use the other one to buy a new wallet," Megan said.

"I like my old wallet. I have some new ones, but this one is special to me. It belonged to my grandfather," he said, patting it affectionately. "We were very close."

For the rest of the ride, Steven told her about his meetings at the capitol as well as the recent comments about him in the press. People liked the fact that he had settled down with one woman but most importantly, they liked Megan.

"So, how much longer am I supposed to be your girlfriend?" Megan asked wanting it to end soon so she could go back to her normal life and stop thinking she was in love with him.

"You know, I really hadn't thought about that. It's up to you. Why you have your eyes set on someone else? The ex back in the picture?"

"No. I just want to know so I can move on with my life, and I'm sure you want to get your life back to normal with the ladies," Megan said even though she didn't mean it. But she felt once they were no longer "dating" she would be over him.

"I guess we can cross that bridge when we get to that point. I hadn't thought about being without you. I still want to keep in contact with you."

"Of course. We can still stay in contact. You're a really nice guy, Steven." Megan smiled as they turned onto Tiffani's street. Her house was a beautiful two-story, cream-colored stucco in the middle of the cul de sac. There were plenty of cars already parked in the driveway. Megan hated parking on the street. She always feared someone would hit her car and drive away without leaving a note.

"You ready?" she asked once the car was parked.

"Yeah. Who's all here?" Steven asked, looking at all of the cars. "I can't believe there's almost fifteen cars for a child's birthday party."

"Jade and Syd are here. Kids from Keith's play-group, karate class and cousins," Megan answered, taking her things out of the trunk.

"Great. I love kids."

"Good. I'm in charge of face painting. You can help me with that," Megan suggested as they walked around to the backyard.

"Wow!" Megan exclaimed as she saw the scene before her. There were about two-dozen kids lined up at different stations. Keith Jr. was on a pony with his grandfather holding the reins. There were kids in the moonwalk and the older kids were in the pool. Megan saw Tiffani and Syd grilling hamburgers and Jade was fanning herself on the deck and set-ting out the paper goods. Megan was surprised that Jade had even bothered to show up. She didn't care much for a lot of little screaming children running around. Megan set her present on the gift table that was overflowing with nicely wrapped boxes and col-orful gift bags.

"Megan, Steven, great to see you two. Steven, I'm so happy you came. I didn't know you liked kids' parties," Tiffani smiled, taking the potato salad from Megan and hugging her at the same time. She then turned to Steven and gave him a big hug.

"I need a break from adults," he said, looking around at the children who were playing and running around.

"How is everything going so far?" Megan asked as they walked toward the grill.

Tiffani placed her hand on her forehead and shook her head as her curly ponytail that was sitting on top swung.

"Girl, terrible! My friend who knows how to make balloon animals was supposed to come, but he called an hour ago and said he wouldn't be able to make it. My dad has to do the pony station, which stinks by the way, and my mom is in charge of the moon-walk area. I can't have these kids getting hurt," Tiffani said in a flustered manner. Megan was used to Tiffani always remaining calm under pressure but at the present moment, she understandably couldn't control her frustrations.

"I can do the balloon animals," Steven volunteered.

"Steven, that's wonderful! The station is already set up next to the face painting," Tiffani said, pointing to the two stations by the back of the fence.

"All right, let's get started," Megan said, but she wanted to say hello to the birthday boy first.

"Godmommy!" Keith Jr. screamed as he ran to give Megan a big hug.

"Hey sweetie. Are you having fun?" she asked, picking him up and giving him a tight hug.

"Yes. Who's this man with you? Where's Dr. Alfonso? He always brings his stethoscope for me to play with. Why isn't he with you?" Keith Jr. asked as she put him down. He was no longer the little baby she used to carry around. Megan glanced at Steven who was snickering at the little boy's comment.

"This is Mr. Steven. He's a friend of mine." Megan hoped that would answer the curious child's question. "Remember, I told you that the doctor and I are no longer friends."

"Nice to meet you little fellow," Steven said, shaking the little boy's hand.

"Did you bring me a present?" Keith Jr. asked as his mother walked over to join the conversation.

"KJ, go play. That isn't a nice thing to ask," Tiffani scolded.

Steven reached into his worn wallet and pulled out the crisp twenty dollar bill and handed it to KJ. "As a matter of fact I do, young man. I heard you like to save money."

"Aww...cool," KJ exclaimed admiring the bill. "Thank you, Mr. Steven. I just got a new wallet, so this is going in there right away." He gave Steven a hug before he skipped away.

Tiffani then made an announcement on her megaphone that lunch would be served in thirty minutes. She also reminded her guests that the face painting and balloon stations were open.

For the next thirty minutes Steven made really

cool balloon animals for the children. His station was the most popular next to the pony. Megan watched him as she painted stars and hearts on the little girls' cheeks.

"So, birthday boy, what animal would you like for the great balloon master to make for you?" Steven asked KJ.

"A puppy!" KJ exclaimed jumping up and down.

"Okay, a puppy it is," Steven said as he began to make the puppy out of black and brown balloons. The children sat in awe as Steven twirled the balloons around each other. Sydney walked up behind Megan whose station was now empty.

"I'm surprised to see him here," Sydney whispered.

"Yeah. Me, too, but he stopped by my apartment as I was leaving. When I invited him, I never thought he would actually say yes. I was just being polite," Megan said as she watched Steven make the puppy for Keith Jr. The kids clapped loudly at the finished product and begged Steven to make more animals. He glanced over at Megan and smiled. She clapped her hands and smiled back.

"What was that?" Syd asked observantly.

"What was what?" Megan asked somewhat annoyed.

"The smile he just gave you and the one you gave him back. Megan you forget I'm a profiler. But most importantly, your twin sister. I know all your facial expressions because I have the same ones and usually for the same exact reasons. That smile and stare meant he loves you girl!" Sydney exclaimed.

"Syd, please stop always trying to read other people's minds. He did a good job on making the balloon puppy for KJ and that's why I'm smiling, so please let it go," Megan answered, agitated. She was never good at hiding her expressions from Syd.

"Well, I know what I saw. And I'm glad I saw it," Sydney said as Megan rolled her eyes.

Megan and Sydney walked over to the balloon station once they were done cleaning up the face-painting materials. Sydney picked up a few of the balloons that had popped.

"You did a great job with the kids and the balloons," Sydney said to Steven.

"Thank you. It was one of my duties when I was growing up. I used to entertain my younger siblings and cousins," Steven answered as he placed the unused balloons back into plastic bags.

Just then Tiffani made another announcement that lunch was ready and for the children to walk over to the round tables where Tiffani, her mother and Jade had prepared lunch.

"You know, Tiffani is so organized," Megan said as she watched her friend tell the children where she wanted them to sit. Jade walked around in her high-heeled sandals pouring fruit punch, looking completely out of place and uncomfortable.

"I hope she decides to go back to work now that KJ is going to kindergarten in the fall," Sydney said. "She never wanted to place him in day care, but I know she's running low on the insurance money now."

"Yes, I know. There are some openings at Mom's

school in the fall, and Dad wrote a recommendation letter for her, as well."

"That's good to know. Then KJ could possibly just go to work with her and save on day care."

"Yep. Just like we did when were growing up."

Sydney laughed. "And we hated every minute of it. I'm going to help Jade. She looks so uncomfortable with the children." Sydney said leaving Megan and Steven alone.

Steven leaned against the table and folded his arms across his chest. "You know I went to school with my mother, as well. I enjoyed it. Bryce and Jacqueline not so much. They stayed in trouble."

"Ha. Sounds just like Syd and Braxton. We went to elementary school with my mother and middle school with my dad. He was the assistant principal at the time."

"Jeez. I guess you couldn't wait until high school where you would be free from your parents," Steven said.

"No. My dad's brother, Tiffani's father, was the principal," Megan answered, thinking back to the times when she and Syd were in high school.

"I guess you and Syd had to be on your best behavior all the time," Steven said.

"Please! She stayed in trouble. My dad caught her smoking in the girl's bathroom in eighth grade. He suspended his own child for three days. My mother was livid at him for a week!"

"He suspended his own child? I don't want to meet him! He sounds pretty tough," Steven balked.

"Yes and no. I'm a daddy's girl whereas Syd is a mommy's girl. She said Syd was probably forced to smoke the cigarette. But the truth is she was the one teaching the other girls. Mommy was mad for weeks," Megan remembered. "Are you ready to go eat? Tiffani is serving hamburgers and chicken tenders for the children, but steaks and salmon for the adults. Syd grills the best salmon," Megan boasted about her sister as she grabbed his hand and walked toward the food area set up for the adults. They ate their lunch at the adult-only table. KJ's older cousins were put in charge of the children so the adults could take a break.

After lunch, the children were entertained again with more balloon animals, face painting and swimming. Five of the boys were spending the night, but Tiffani's father was in charge of that. Tiffani had worked hard all week to prepare for the party, and was going to relax for the rest of the evening. Megan and Steven said their goodbyes to everyone after they helped clean up.

"So did you have a nice time?" Megan asked as they were leaving the party.

"I did. Your friends are really nice," Steven said, looking through her CD case.

"You want the top down?" she asked.

"Sure, why not," Steven said, leaning back in his seat and dozing off as the sounds of Corrine Bailey Rae filled the car.

Megan looked over at him as he slept. Even in his sleep he was handsome. She kept thinking about what Syd said. Megan thought they made a nice couple as well, but she knew it was all business. She wasn't one of the fabulous glamour girls he was used to dating. Even though Chelsea had tried to give Megan a new image, she still felt like the same old down-to-earth Megan. She didn't know how she would even fit into his world.

"Wake up, sleepyhead," Megan said softly to him as they pulled into her parking garage.

Steven slowly opened his eyes and turned his head toward her. "Man, I was tired. I guess it has been a long week," Steven said as he stretched his arms and yawned.

"Yes, you were knocked out snoring over there," she teased.

"Snoring? I know I wasn't snoring."

"No, I'm just teasing. Although you were sleeping quite soundly. Perhaps you should go home and get some rest tonight instead of working," Megan suggested.

"As good as that sounds, I have some work to catch up on. I really enjoyed the party though. It was a way to leave my reality at least for a little bit. Thank you for inviting me," Steven said, getting out of the car.

"You want to come up for some coffee? I just bought some Mexican organic coffee I've been wanting to try. It will wake you right up!" Megan asked, not believing that she just asked him to come in for coffee. Men usually thought that was actually an invitation for sex.

"Yeah. That sounds great," Steven said.

When they were settled into the loft, Megan told Steven to make himself comfortable on the couch while she prepared the coffee.

"Nice place. You have it decorated beautifully. It's classy and elegant. Reminds me of you."

"Thank you. I like to come home to calm surroundings unlike all of the outrageous things my client's request. I just like to have things around me that mean something to me such as my grandmother's grandfather clock or my lamp I made out of sea shells I found on Pensacola Beach." She sat the coffee in front of him on the table and returned to the kitchen.

"It's very eclectic."

"Do you need cream or milk? Megan asked, taking both out of the refrigerator.

"Neither. I like my coffee black and just a little sugar. Anything else and the coffee loses its flavor," Steven answered, blowing the hot coffee.

"I see. Well, I like mine extra sweet with milk. I guess I will try your way eventually," she considered as she poured the milk into her coffee.

"This is delicious. I'm not really a coffee drinker. Only when I need a boost," Steven said.

"Well, I love coffee. I could drink it all day. Actually, sometimes I have, which explains why I'm up all night. Maybe I'm not a night person after all," Megan pondered.

"Yeah, maybe you just drink too much coffee," he said laughing.

"Well, it's hard to give a good thing up," she said.

"I'm beginning to believe that. So maybe you should drink decaf," Steven suggested.

"I'm supposed to. After my surgery a few years ago, I tried giving up caffeine," she said, sitting in the chair opposite him.

"What kind of surgery?"

"Nothing major. I had a benign lump in my breast. The surgeon suggested that I stop my caffeine intake. I did some research on it and a found some articles that agreed with his statement while other research stated it didn't matter. However, at that time I trusted him so of course I stopped drinking coffee with caffeine. Plus, my cousin Bria, who is an allergist, suggested I cut down on my caffeine intake. Only recently did I start again," Megan said as she glanced around the loft for a sign of Percy. She got up and looked under her bed. Sure enough Percy was laying down peeking out from under the dust ruffle.

"Do you like cats?" she asked, carrying the cat into the living area.

"I don't like or dislike them. I prefer dogs though. You can't play catch or go running with a cat, and they're too self-absorbed," he answered, rubbing the cat's head. Percy jumped down from Megan's hold and ran back into her room.

"Well, at least he let you pet him," Megan said, settling back in her chair.

"What made you get a cat?"

"It wasn't intentional. I found him as a kitten in the dumpster behind my office a few years ago. Jade and I heard this crying meow, so we got him out. Luckily, he'd managed to climb onto a bag, but he was very weak. I took him to a vet. Percy was dehydrated and very hungry, but he bounced back in a couple of weeks. I took him in only to find him a home, but grew attached, so I kept him. My ex was being a complete jerk around that time and Percy was a nice comfort."

"Megan, what happened between you and Alfonso, if you don't mind me asking you?" Steven curiously began. "I can't figure out why a man would let you go."

"Well, I don't know exactly. It's kind of hard to answer that question. I thought I was doing everything he wanted me to do. I was supportive and caring. His parents and friends loved me as well as my family and friends loved him except for my dad, that is," Megan began.

Steven walked over to the stainless steel coffeepot and helped himself to more coffee and then with a smirk on his face said, "Your dad isn't going to like anyone you bring home no matter what he does or how nice he is to you. That's how fathers are about their precious little girls, you know."

"You're going to be up all night if you have a second cup of that coffee. I told you it's very strong," Megan said, shaking her head. Men never seemed to listen, she thought.

"I'll be up late working. Now, finish telling me about Mr., I mean excuse me, Dr. Alfonso," Steven corrected sarcastically, settling on the floor beside the unlit fireplace and grabbing some oatmeal cookies Megan had placed on the coffee table.

"Well, everything was fine until right before Christmas the year before last. We started spending less time together. We were always together. Even when he was busy with his work, he would try to make time for me. He is a very popular surgeon here in Atlanta with a lot of patients. A lot of women would refer their friends because they thought he was handsome. So he had plenty of female patients, but that never bothered me. Anyway, around Christmas time we scheduled a trip to go to the Bahamas for a week and to return on Christmas Eve so we could spend Christmas with our families. Well, he had an emergency surgery to perform right before we left, and I went alone. He flew down two days later to meet me there, with a tan by the way. Now, explain to me how he got a tan in Atlanta during the winter time? The man was always bundled up! He hates being cold. Well, two days before we were scheduled to leave, he got an emergency phone call and he flew back to the States to perform yet another emergency surgery. And being little naive me, I believed him. I mean things do come up with his patients all of the time. However, when Alfonso is on vacation Dr. Bobb always covers for him if necessary, and he covers for her," Megan said and then paused.

"So, when did you finally realize that he was probably in the Bahamas the whole time with another woman?"

"Well, when I returned back to the States, of

course he was the first person I called. My car was at the airport. I called him to see if I could come straight to his house, but he didn't answer the phone. So I drove to his house anyway because, well, I did have a key. However, my key was to the front door only. When I pulled up, I remembered that Jade and I had his double doors changed out, and I didn't have the new key. I rang the doorbell and called his phone again. I could hear the phone ringing from inside of the house, but still no answer. I left a note on his door and a voice mail that I was back from the Bahamas," Megan said tired of going over this story again with someone. At least this time she wasn't crying like the time she told Tiffani and Jade.

"So what happened next?"

"Well, the next day he came over about 8:00 in the morning with breakfast and a present. He said he had been out with Curtis who is his best friend and didn't get my note until he returned home at 4:00 a.m. I later found out that Curtis and his family were in Denver, Colorado on a ski trip. He did see Curtis that night, but only to drive him to the airport."

"Interesting," Steven said, stretching out on the floor.

"Yes, very interesting considering whenever Al went out with his friends, he always called me no matter what time of night to come over or sometimes he just showed up at my door. Well, like I said, I was still being Ms. Naive, and I believed him except that his tan was much darker than it was when he left me in the Bahamas. But I didn't question him. We exchanged gifts and had breakfast. I thought surely we were going to make love afterward considering one of the gifts I gave him was a purple sheer nightgown with matching lace panties. Usually, if I gave him a gift like lingerie that meant I was definitely in the mood, but he said let's save it for later. That man had never turned down sex!"

"Megan, I don't know a man that would unless he was on his death bed and even then he would probably ask for a Lewinsky or something," Steven said sarcastically.

Megan laughed at Steven's comment as she walked to the kitchen to pour the rest of the coffee into her mug and turned off the coffeemaker.

"That coffee is going to keep you up all night, Miss Lady," Steven said, teasing her.

"Yes, I know, but that's fine. I have a lot of work to do, as well. I have some drapes to make. But let me finish telling you about Dr. Alfonso. So anyway, a few days went by before I saw him again. We were having lunch at his house, mostly leftover Christmas dinner from my parents' dinner party. I was opening the refrigerator to take out some juice when I noticed a brochure about a medical convention in Chicago on the refrigerator. I asked him about it and he casually said it was in a few months. So I said cool. Just let me know the details so I can rearrange my schedule. Whenever he attended a medical conference I always went. He never had to ask me, it was always understood that I would go because he wanted me to go with him. Well, at first he was silent and then he said that I didn't have to go because it was in March and I was always busy in March with decorating homes for the spring. I still insisted, and he said don't worry about it and quickly changed the subject. Then the doorbell rang."

"It was the girl he was seeing behind your back?" Steven asked, sitting all the way up.

"No, it was Dr. Bobb and her husband. She said they were in the neighborhood and they wanted to drop off Alfonso's gift. Well, he didn't look happy to see them at all and tried to rush them out. I gave Dr. Bobb and her husband a hug and told them to come and sit down in the living room. Alfonso had gotten a call on his cell and went to another room to take it. I asked the Bobbs about their Christmas trip and she said they didn't go anywhere for Christmas. But that they were going to Memphis for New Year's Eve to visit her husband's family and wanted to make sure that Alfonso could return the favor since she was on call for him while he was in the Bahamas. I decided not to mention that he flew to the Bahamas later because of an emergency surgery because obviously, by the way the pieces of the puzzle were fitting together, there wasn't an emergency of any kind. So I simply said we had a lovely time. They left a few minutes later to finish delivering other Christmas gifts," Megan said, taking a break from her long story.

She was trying to shorten it, but she felt that certain details were important. But she remembered a man's attention span wasn't that long, especially when Steven said, "Okay, so when did you confront the pig?"

"I'm getting to that. So later on that evening we were in his study. He was writing out some bills, and I was pretending to proofread a medical article he wrote. I decided to ask him about the medical convention again in Chicago. He said don't worry about it and that he wasn't sure if he was going to go or not anyway. I knew something wasn't right. I stood up and decided it was time for me to leave. In doing so, I straightened up the pillows on his couch. And that is when I found my evidence."

"What? What did you find? An earring that wasn't yours?" Steven questioned sitting up from his comfortable position by the fireplace.

"No, worse. A pair of red panties that weren't mine!"

"Damn! You know that girl left them there on purpose for you to find. If it was earrings he could've lied and said they were his mother's or something like that," Steven said. "Not that I would know," he added sheepishly with shrug.

"Ha. Yeah, right. Anyway, he was stunned to see them and claimed that they must be mine, but I wear a small and those panties looked a lot larger. Plus, I don't own anything red and he knows that. Anyway, he decided to tell me the truth about him and his nurse, Shelia. I had a feeling it was her. She was always trying to be overly nice to me when I stopped by the office to visit him. After an hour of arguing, I walked out thus ending our four year relationship."

"So, he didn't try to stop you or beg for your forgiveness?"

"No. He was relieved. In fact, he wanted to end our relationship anyway to be with her, and they're still together now. She lives in his home that Jade and I decorated for him before the breakup. But I've moved on. Alfonso leaving me just left the door open for the right man to come into my life," Megan answered, taking their empty mugs back into the kitchen.

"I'm so sorry to hear all of this. What a fool he is. You're a very special lady, Megan. I'm sure the right man will come along if you just let him," Steven responded, walking to the kitchen behind her.

"Yes, I know," Megan said, loading the dishwasher and trying to hide her face. She knew if he looked at her now, her facial expression would give away her true feelings for him. She was ready for him to leave so she could be alone with her thoughts.

"Do you need some help? I did drink all of your coffee and eat all of your cookies. The least I can do is clean your kitchen," Steven offered, taking one of the dish towels and wiping down the counter.

"No, Steven. It's getting late. I have bored you enough tonight."

"Are you kicking me out?"

"Yes. If you're going to be our next U.S. senator you need to go home and work on your campaign," Megan said, not really wanting him to go. Although, she felt that they were getting too close again, which was something she didn't want to do. Plus, when he mentioned eating all of her cookies, she had a different type of visual.

"You're right. I didn't realize it was almost ten," he said, walking back to the fireplace to retrieve his car keys and cell phone. Megan watched him. He was indeed the perfect man. Handsome, successful, compassionate and determined. He had all of the qualities that she wanted in a man, but she knew it was pointless to dwell on it. A relationship with him would be out of the question.

"What's wrong?" he asked, interrupting her thoughts.

Megan was startled. She hadn't realized she was staring at him so hard. She smiled and brushed it off. "Oh, nothing. I was deep in thought I guess." She turned away to hide her embarrassment.

"Hey, Meg I'm sorry if I brought up old wounds from the past. I won't mention him again," Steven said, walking toward her.

"Oh, I wasn't thinking about him," she said, walking toward the door to let Steven out. "I'm truly over him now."

"Well, I hope I had something to do with it. I mean I know this isn't a real relationship, but I hope I've brought some sunshine to your life," Steven said with his hand on the doorknob.

"You have. Good night, Mr. Monroe," Megan said smiling and opening the door for him. He lightly gave her a kiss on the forehead and left. Once the door shut, Percy ran out from under the bed and rubbed his body on Megan's legs.

"Percy, what am I doing? I have gone and fallen in love with a man I can never have," Megan said as she picked up the cat. She held Percy close as the tears started to roll down her cheeks.

Chapter 10

It was the Monday morning following KJ's birthday party. Megan, Jade and Lucy sat in their staff meeting going over the upcoming week's agenda. Lucy was finally going on her first assignment with Jade to look for vintage furniture for a client that loved antique dressers and wanted four, one for each of her bedrooms. Megan's mind was wandering during the meeting. On Sunday morning while making coffee, she had decided to try it Steven's way and drink it black with just a little sugar. She'd smiled as she realized he was right. It had in fact retained the flavor.

Megan had picked up the phone to call him but hung up before dialing. She was so used to sharing everything with her ex-boyfriends that it seemed natural to call Steven, but she'd had to remind herself that he wasn't really her boyfriend.

"Megan, are you ignoring me?" Jade asked in her usual sassy tone.

Lucy waved her hand in front of Megan's zoned-out face. "Earth to Megan. Are you there?"

"Oh, ladies, forgive me. I spaced out. What were you saying?" Megan asked remembering where she was.

"Did you want to go the furniture store with us?" Jade asked standing and grabbing her belongings from the table.

"No...I'll be at a client's home all day waiting for and arranging furniture."

"Okay, we'll be back this afternoon."

Moments later, Megan sat at her desk contemplating what she needed to do before she left. Then the phone rang. She glanced at the caller ID and saw it was Steven. She hadn't spoken to him since Saturday night. She took a deep breath and answered the phone, "Chase, Whitmore and Associates, how can I help you?" she asked in a cheery tone.

"Hey, Megan, it's Steven. How are you doing this marvelous Monday morning?"

"I'm fine, Steven. What can I do for you?"

"I just wanted to tell you that I had a nice time with you and your friends on Saturday. KJ is a good kid. I see him being an investment broker or maybe Hugh Heffner the way those little four-year-old girls were crowding around him in the moonwalk. Did you see the one that kissed him on his cheek when she was leaving? That was really cute. I like children. They say and do the darnedest things. Do you want children?" he inquired.

"One day. I have to find the right man first," Megan answered. Even though she felt as if she had found the right man, she knew that soon after he received the nomination, their relationship would be over, and she would be alone again.

"I also wanted to tell you that I'm going out of town tomorrow on the campaign trail this week to help out a friend in another state. Anyway, I'll be back on Saturday morning. If you need anything, just leave a voice mail or text on my cell."

"Will do."

"I was hoping to see you tonight. How about I bring some Thai food over, and we watch movies together, unless you'd rather be alone."

Megan didn't want to be alone, and she was looking forward to seeing him considering he would be gone for the rest of the week. She took a deep breath and said, "That would be nice. Thai food and you, of course, are more than welcome to come over this evening."

"Great. I'll see you later."

The rest of the day passed by slowly as Megan remodeled a dining room and a living room for a client. She was looking forward to Steven coming over that evening, and she could barely concentrate on her job. Once home, Megan changed into a pair of jeans, but then decided to slip on a polo shirtdress and pulled her hair back into a loose ponytail. She vacuumed her hardwood, cleaned the kitchen and hung up all of her clothes that were scattered on the bed. Megan kept glancing at the clock. He'd texted her earlier and said he would be over around seven.

Megan sat on the couch and watched her grandfather clock slowly tick by. A little after the hour, her intercom buzzer sounded.

"Yes?"

"Delivery for Megan Chase," Steven said trying to disguise his voice. A few minutes later he was standing in her living room carrying two big bags of Thai food.

"Wow! Did you bring enough for the whole building?" Megan teased as she took the bags from him and placed them on the island in the kitchen.

"Well, I wasn't sure what you liked so I bought different things we can sample. There's a bottle of wine in that bag. I'll put it in the freezer for a few minutes to chill."

"Great!" Megan exclaimed as placed the takeout boxes on the table and then grabbed plates and wineglasses.

"So, do you have any good DVDs? I see you have about two hundred of them over there."

"Yes, but you've probably seen them all," Megan said crossing the room to read off the titles.

"Baby, I rarely go to the movies. I don't have time. Besides, I prefer to watch movies at home. Do you have any nongirlie movies?"

"Yes. But I don't have any scary movies unless you count Scary Movie one, two and three as scary.

I have a lot of comedies." Megan scanned through her collection.

"Let me see what you have. Comedy movies are my favorite next to suspense and drama. *Crimson Tide* is my all-time favorite," Steven said kneeling down on the floor beside her.

"Well, I don't have that, but how about *Kiss the Girls* with Morgan Freeman? It's a suspense movie. I read the book before the movie came out. I couldn't put it down! However, I was picturing Denzel Washington as Alex Cross not Morgan Freeman. Do you want to watch it?" Megan asked, holding up the DVD.

"You know," Steven said, moving closer to her, "I was just thinking about that."

"Cool. I'll put it in," she said, still looking through her collection of movies trying to ignore the fact that he was so close to her that she could feel his breath on her neck.

"I wasn't referring to the movie," Steven replied. Tossing the DVD case on the floor, he kissed Megan passionately on the lips. Megan responded willingly as he laid her down on the floor next to the DVD stand. Steven kissed her hungrily while reaching his right hand under her dress to feel her thighs. His other hand fiddled with her ponytail. He tossed the scrunchy across the floor and dug his hands into her hair.

Passion surged through her as he kissed her, sinking his tongue deeper into her mouth as muffled moans caught inside her throat. His kisses were like the fairy-tale kisses she had always imagined, but never experienced. Passionate. Erotic. Sensual. When his lips left hers she let out a loud cry as he kissed her on her ears and then her neck. His hand trailed down her body and then back underneath her dress, kneading her thighs. When his hands began to pull down her panties, all her senses rushed back into her head, and she pushed him off of her.

"Wait we can't do this," Megan interrupted before jumping up and running to the bathroom with Steven closely running after. She closed the bathroom door before he could come in. She splashed some water on her face as Steven opened the unlocked door.

"Damn it, Megan! Stop running away from me. From us."

"Steven, this is all wrong. You don't want a real relationship with me. This is just pretend until after the election," Megan cried.

"What? You honestly think that? You mean to tell me you didn't feel anything a minute ago? Or even when we were in Washington? Or, hell, when we first met? I'm tired of pretending. I want a real relationship with you, I want to be with you, Megan Chase," he said standing behind her looking at their reflection in the mirror. He placed his hands on her shoulders, but didn't turn her around. "Don't we look good together? We make the perfect team. I knew we would the minute I laid eyes on you," he whispered into her ear, his lips lightly brushing it. She flinched as his lips touched her. Megan looked at their reflection in the mirror.

"Steven..." She turned around to face him with happy tears filling her eyes.

"I think, my lady, we've done enough talking for one night," he said as his lips came crushing down on hers.

Steven lifted her up in his arms and carried her to the bed laying her down gently on the comforter. He placed his body on top of hers, kissing her gently on the lips, trying to savor every inch of her delicious mouth.

Steven had never felt so intense and passionate about a woman before. He knew this was the woman who he wanted to see as he closed his eyes every night and couldn't wait to wake up to the next morning.

"Can I help you out of your dress?" he asked, sitting up to take off his shirt to bare his smooth rippled chest and abdomen. Megan smiled as she ran her fingers and then lips over his chest twirling her tongue around one of his nipples. While she continued to arouse him further, he quickly lifted the dress off of her, throwing it across the room with his shirt.

"Damn, baby. You're so beautiful," he complimented as he raked his eyes over her fuchsia lace bra and panties. He licked his lips as he pulled her toward him to feel her hot bare skin under him.

Once she was nude, he lifted her off of the bed and guided her against a nearby wall.

"I had a fantasy about you pushing me against

this very wall," she said, unbuckling his belt. "And having your way with me."

A cocky half grin crossed his mouth. "Oh, really?"

She nodded, displaying a sexy, lazy grin, and kissed him lightly on the lips as she removed his belt and unbuttoned his slacks.

"Well...I am..." He paused as he returned the kiss and licked her lips. "Here to make all your fantasies come true, precious."

He turned her away from him and placed her hands on the wall causing her to let out fervent moans of pleasure. "Part your legs."

He began slowly gliding his tongue from the base of her neck down her back until he was at her center. Megan moaned loudly as his tongue licked and drank her womanly juices. He squeezed her butt and then slapped it, sinking a finger into her as she squirmed and pleaded with him.

"Oh, Steven, please don't stop," she yelled out, pressing her head on the wall as he continued to tantalize her insides with his tongue and fingers. His answer to her was putting his fingers in as deeply as possible, causing the first of many orgasms that night.

Her legs, and her balance, became undone as he lowered her to the floor and held her in his arms as he massaged her clit. Her cries of passion and desire shattered across the room. He kissed her damp forehead and rubbed her hair until she came down from her high.

"Do you have protection?" she whispered.

"Be patient, my love, we have all night."

"Can't we just skip the foreplay? I've waited so long to have you, Steven," she begged, putting her hand on his very erect penis and massaging it through his pants.

"My insatiable, little Megan," he whispered with his lips hovering over hers. "You want it right now?"

"Yes," she cried out.

"Right here up against the wall like in your fantasy?"

"Wherever you intend to."

"Oh, I intend to make love to you in every possible position tonight, in every possible place in this loft. If we run out of rooms, we may have to go to my place."

"I think I have some condoms somewhere."

"Are they Magnums?"

"Um...no."

"Then that won't work." He took her hand and placed it directly on his penis that was now fully erect and ready thanks to her pleading. "Don't worry, my love. I came prepared."

"Go get it."

He stood them up, placing her back on the wall. He obeyed, taking a few packs of condoms out of his back pants pocket and held them up much to her delight. He wasn't used to a woman barking orders at him. Smirking, he stared at her exquisite body leaning on the wall and stepped toward her, pulling his pants and boxer shorts down at the same time and stepping out of them. "Let's get one thing straight.

I'm in charge and in control," he said placing a condom over his firm rod.

She gulped with wide eyes as she glanced down and then back up at him with a wicked grin on her face.

"Oh, really?" she asked sarcastically.

"Yes, really," he said as he picked her up by her buttocks as if she were light as a feather and slid her up the wall. She wrapped her legs tightly around his waist, and he immediately entered her, wasting no time with his strong thrusts causing her to scream out his name in ecstasy. He pounded her harder and harder while she dug her nails deeper into his shoulders. He knew he would have scars later on but he didn't care. The warmness and wetness of her made him sink further into her spirit and mind. She was causing him to feel things he'd never felt before, and he wanted to make sure that all of him was in tune with her. The more she cried out his name, the more he gave it all to her.

Megan wrapped her legs and arms tighter around him as he carried her from the wall and placed her on the bed. She stared up at him with loving eyes as he filled her even deeper. They rocked back and forth concentrating on each other intently. He moved her legs around his neck and held her hands to the bed, as he went all the way in and then all the way out. Her hips met his strokes at the same cadence.

As they screamed out together, he felt all of the emotions bottled up in his heart rush out of him. He grabbed hold of her tightly as he panted her name and a few curse words over and over in the crook of her neck. As his breathing slowed down, he lifted his head and kissed her lightly on the lips.

He was satisfied yet ready for round two with her. The room was quiet except for the soft sound of the ceiling fan above. Neither of them spoke and there wasn't any need. Their lovemaking had spoken louder than any words they could have uttered to each other.

An hour later, they were still intertwined together lying on top of the comforter. Megan tried to wrestle away from his hold to grab the blanket at the end of the bed. Steven pulled her closer into his body so that her back was completely pressed against his muscular chest.

"Where are you going?"

"To grab the blanket."

"I'm not keeping you warm enough?"

"You are. I just feel weird lying naked on top of the comforter."

"I want to see and feel your sexy little body next to me," he said and then kissed the base of her neck. She let out a soft sigh at his touch and technique. She could feel the hardness of him urgently bearing against her bottom and then the tear of a condom wrapper.

"I need to be inside of you again, Megan," he heavily urged in her ear causing her to feel a shooting sensation as he dived into her once again. He turned her over on her stomach as he continued long strokes, in and out, making her dig her fingers in the mattress. Each time it was more intense causing her to release shuddering orgasms one after the other.

After the fifth orgasm, Megan was so out of it, she barely knew where she was. All she knew was that the man she loved was making her feel so damn good.

He pulled her up so she was on her knees. He placed his hands on her round bottom to guide her.

"Am I making you feel good, baby?"

"Oh, yes. The best," she truthfully said.

As he came inside of her, she swore she heard a roar of a lion escape him.

Megan fell limp on the bed as he rolled off of her. She could still feel him pulsating through her as she laid on her back staring up at the ceiling trying to catch her breath from their escapade. She could tell by the aching in her legs, she may be sore the next day, but it was well worth it.

He lay next to her on his back with his head turned toward her.

"Do you smoke?" she asked.

"Um…no? Why, do you smoke?"

"No, but if I was to start, this would be the perfect time to," she said laughing.

"I agree," he said, pulling her close to him.

Chapter 11

Megan was floating on cloud nine. She had heard of the expression and was now experiencing it. She'd never been happier in a relationship. Steven was kind, thoughtful and honest. He sent flowers, texts on her cell phone and voice mails when he was away from her. He was still busy, but he always found time for her. Megan was also happy because her dad finally liked someone she brought home. Steven and her dad had already played golf at the golf course in her parent's subdivision, and they were planning a weekend trip to see Tiger Woods play.

One evening, Megan was looking over some swatches at her office. She didn't like to work late at night but she had to prepare for the beach house she was decorating that would be featured on the

Fabulous Living Channel. Jade and Lucy had already left and Steven was in meetings all day. They were supposed to have dinner, but at around 4:00 p.m. he'd called and cancelled. He said that he had a lot of work to catch up on and would be at his office all night. She decided to stay late and catch up on work as well since she would be at a client's home for the rest of the week. After work, she decided she would stop by his office and surprise him with dinner. She knew he wouldn't mind since she'd done it a few times before, much to his enjoyment.

She called one of her favorite places to dine and ordered two dinners to go. She wanted to spend as much time with Steven as she could before she left for Hilton Head in a few days.

Megan parked her SUV next to Steven's Range Rover. She noticed another car in the parking lot that didn't look familiar. She hoped he wasn't in a meeting. It was nine at night. Her goal was to convince him to eat and then follow her back to her place for a little romantic time. She walked around to the front of the building. *The door is unlocked so he must be in a meeting,* she thought. She walked into the empty "showroom," as Shawn called it. Ten cubicles were in the middle of the room. On the walls were the copy machine, faxes, water cooler and the worktables. In the back were Steven's and Shawn's offices, a conference room and break room with a bathroom. Steven would usually hold any meetings in the conference room. So she decided to wait in his office.

As she walked back to his office, she noticed the

door was ajar and the light was on. Megan went to the door and stuck her head in. She saw Veronica sitting in Steven's chair and Steven sitting on the desk facing Veronica with his back to the door. Veronica saw Megan peeking in and smiled sweetly at Steven rubbing her hand on his knee.

"I enjoyed catching up over dinner tonight," Veronica said loudly enough for Megan to hear and rubbing her hand back and forth. "We must do this again real soon."

Megan entered the office.

"Oh, hello dear," Veronica said sweetly to Megan. Steven turned around quickly and stood up. He looked surprised and guilty.

"Hello, Veronica. I didn't know you were in town," Megan stated still remaining poised.

"Yes, Veronica came into town this morning. She's speaking at Atlanta Memorial College for a Women's Day program tomorrow," Steven answered calmly.

"I must run now. I need to read over my speech again." Veronica stood, displaying a very short red dress that was clinging to her figure like a glove. "Thank you for a lovely time tonight. Call me and let me know if you can escort me to the banquet on Saturday. You know I only prefer to have a handsome man on my arm, and Judge Hill is unavailable. But you and I always look good together at black-tie affairs," Veronica said kissing Steven on the cheek. She then turned her tall frame toward Megan.

"Bye, Maggy, It was nice to see you again," Veronica said. She then grabbed her purse off of Steven's desk and sashayed out of the office smiling.

Megan waited until she heard Veronica open and close the front door

"I thought you were here working late?" Megan asked in a composed tone.

"I am. I intend to be here until midnight, if not later. Shawn will be back at ten. We have some things to go over. Is there something wrong?" Steven said sitting down in his chair and looking over some papers on his desk, avoiding eye contact.

Megan felt the anger rising in her, but she decided to remain poised and listen to his side of the story of what she'd just walked in on.

"You cancelled our dinner plans this evening," Megan said. She walked over to where he was sitting and stood over him with her right hand on her hip. "And then had the audacity to have dinner with your ex."

"Megan. I didn't just have dinner with her. The president of Atlanta Memorial College was there as well to persuade me to speak at the Woman's Day ceremony tomorrow," Steven said as he stood up and placed his hands on her waist.

Megan stepped back. She was too upset for him to touch her. She didn't want to lose trust in him, but if he was beginning to act like Alfonso, then she was in the wrong relationship once again.

"Really? Are you speaking at the program?" she inquired.

"Yes. I told her I would attend the opening session in the morning."

"You and Veronica looked really cozy when I came in. Are you also escorting her to the banquet on Saturday?"

"No. What's with all of the questions tonight?"

"You lied to me, Steven."

"I didn't lie to you. She called after I cancelled our dinner plans. It was all business. Veronica means nothing to me." Steven grabbed her hands.

"And I guess I don't either if you can't tell me the truth." Megan stormed out of his office and into the showroom.

"Megan, I don't have time for the jealous girlfriend act. I'm in a very serious time in my life right now," Steven said following after her.

"You know what? I don't have time for the ex-wife act right now either. Steven, I heard the way she was speaking to you!"

"She only did that because you were here. This evening at dinner, she barely spoke to me. She was on her cell phone most of the time. Trust me the only man she is after right now is Judge Hill. He's trying to make it to the Supreme Court one day. You've seen the stories on the news about that. Veronica is all about gaining prestige. I know you realized that when you met her in Washington."

"What if someone got a picture of you at dinner tonight with her? It could be all over Twitter and Facebook by now."

"The dinner was at the president's home. There

was definitely no one there to snap any pictures. It was just an innocent dinner. Trust me, there is nothing going on between Veronica and I."

A thought popped into her mind. "Why was Veronica even here at your office if you had dinner at the president's home?"

"We rode together, and she came inside to use my computer for a work-related issue. That's all."

Megan knew he was telling the truth, but she was still uncomfortable with his ex-wife being in his life, especially one as beautiful and vindictive as Veronica. Megan walked over to Steven and put her head on his chest.

"Our first fight," she said staring up at him. He bent down and kissed her tenderly on the lips.

"Well, I guess we need to do some making up," he said walking her back to his office.

"Here?" she asked surprisingly. "Shawn will be here in about thirty minutes." She said looking around.

"Just real quick," he said, kissing her on the neck.

"Okay. But you're never real quick," she said as he carried her back to his office and laid her down on the couch for their make-up session.

"So are you going to hang out with me and Shawn tonight? I know you have some work in your car. You can use the conference room," Steven suggested once they were done and sitting on the couch in his office.

"No, baby. Just come over when you're finished. You have a key. Besides, I'll still be up working on some sketches for the *Decorator's Dream* project. We can make up again when you come over," Megan said, grabbing her to-go bag off the table. She hadn't eaten since lunch.

"It's a deal. I promise," he said.

Steven didn't come over until two in the morning, but they were both too exhausted to make love again. Instead, they cuddled while Percy watched from his bed. Steven also suggested a possible minivacation when she returned from Hilton Head.

Before Steven left that morning, he reassured her he wasn't going to take Veronica to the banquet.

The rest of his week was full with visiting different colleges in the state to discuss his plans for the continuation of the Hope Scholarship. In addition to some other educational programs beneficial to college students.

According to a pole in the Atlanta Newspaper, Steven was in the lead by 75% as a favorite to run for the U.S. Senate now that his father had officially put the rumors to rest that he was indeed retiring at the end of the year.

Steven decided he would announce his plans to run for the U.S. Senate seat soon, as the primary deadline was approaching. He was happier however, that he no longer had to pretend with Megan. They were an official couple. There was a picture of them in the paper with a caption that read, "Has the senator finally settled down or is this just a publicity stunt?" The article went on to comment on his progress and compared his views with other potential candidates.

After Steven returned from speaking at Atlanta Memorial College, he looked over the itinerary Shawn had left for him for the rest of day. He was supposed to have lunch with his father and Bryce and spend dinner and the rest of the evening with Megan. She was leaving the next morning for Hilton Head, and he wanted to spend as much time with her as possible before she left for a week, possibly longer.

As he sat at his desk, Steven thought about lunch with his dad and brother and knew it wouldn't be pleasant. His father was in town to discuss the upcoming election. Steven checked his watch. It was almost one, and he knew if he didn't leave his office now, he would be late for his lunch meeting at the French Peasant.

Arriving twenty minutes late, Steven saw his father and brother sitting in a booth at the back of the restaurant under a skylight. Mr. Monroe always made sure he was given the best table in any restaurant. The art on the walls was intricately wood-carved flowers. Megan had told him that she had designed a client's dining room to replicate the restaurant. The young couple had their wedding reception there and wanted the same atmosphere in their home. Steven suggested the French Peasant to his father because he knew his dad enjoyed intriguing artwork and would appreciate his son being considerate of him. His father stood up to shake his hand, but Bryce stirred his ice tea with his straw and smirked at Steven.

"Son, you're late. That's not a good trait for a pol-

itician. They're watching you all of the time, even
when you don't realize it. Don't forget you're a very
important man. Have been since the day you were
born," Mr. Monroe stated, shaking his hand. Steven sat down and glanced at Bryce who was still
smirking. Steven wondered who "they" were while
he looked at the menu.

"So, Dad, how's Washington?" Steven asked, hoping to sway the conversation off of him. He really
wanted to enjoy a relaxing lunch with his father and
brother, although he could sense from Bryce's facial
expressions that their father had a lot to say.

"My son's political career is at stake. Let's order.
We have a lot to discuss."

Steven glanced at Bryce who continued reading
the menu, probably glad the heat wasn't on him for
a change.

For the next hour, Mr. Monroe drilled and debated
Steven on every issue that would come up during
the election. When they were done with lunch and
his mock debate, Mr. Monroe sat back in his chair
looking proudly at his son.

"You're definitely a Monroe man. You both are.
We never let anything stand in our way of getting
exactly what we want." He leaned over the table toward his sons and whispered. "If you keep doing
what you're doing now, you'll be president one day.
Your brother could be the attorney general and, of
course, you'll find something for your sister and your
old man?"

"Of course, Dad. You're the reason I'm where I

am today," Steven complimented. As much as he hated to admit it, he knew he was just like his father. Ambitious, hardworking and determined not to let anyone get in the way of his destiny.

"So now tell me about this Megan Chase. Do we know her family? I haven't had a chance to do an investigation on her yet because you usually recycle your women quite quickly. But I see she's lasted for a few months now, and the media loves her. Is she part of the Chase family that we met a few years ago at Martha's Vineyard?" Mr. Monroe said during dessert.

"She isn't part of the Chase family we met at the vineyard," Steven said as he added way too much sugar to his coffee. His father was making him slightly nervous with his concern for his relationship with Megan.

"I'm glad you've finally settled down with one girl. I was hoping Shawn and Bryce would talk some sense into you. I know you hadn't planned on remarrying again, but remember it's up to you and Bryce to carry on the Monroe name, with more boys of course. Our family legacy and heritage has been around for generations and it must continue. Could this girl possibly be the one to help make that happen for you?" Mr. Monroe asked, concerned.

"Dad, I hope so. She's perfect in every way, sort of like Mom. She's supportive, independent and doesn't care about playing games."

"Just checking, son. But you mentioned to me that she had her own business. There's nothing wrong

with a career woman, but the wife of a U.S. senator needs to be supportive of you. Her main obligation should be you and your family. I'm not trying
to sound like a male chauvinist. Your mother taught
school, but it wasn't as demanding as having her own
business. We don't need any more problems in this
family. You already had one divorce, and you know
I did everything possible to keep that quiet. And I
can't believe that one is flaunting the Monroe name
like she's still part of this family," Mr. Monroe said
slamming his fist down on the table causing the fork
on his dessert plate to fall to the floor.

"We understand, Dad, but I promise you I know
what I'm doing with Megan. She's a wonderful person," Steven said taking the bill from the middle of
the table.

"It's not Megan I'm worried about," Mr. Monroe
said, looking at his cell phone screen and then turning it around to show Steven.

Chapter 12

Megan exhaled as she finished packing the last-minute items that Chelsea suggested, or rather demanded, that she pack. Chelsea had finally left and Megan was exhausted. She'd spent that entire afternoon trying on different outfits. Chelsea had put together a list of clothes for Megan and Jade to wear on the show and had even faxed it to the producers.

Megan took a long refreshing shower, dressed and waited impatiently for Steven to arrive. She had planned a romantic evening for them. The candles were lit in every area of the loft and she had champagne chilling in the freezer. Her Thai take-out order was on the way. Everything was perfect including her new black lace panty-and-bra set under her short black dress she wore the night she met Steven. He told her she looked stunning that night and wanted to see her in the dress again. Megan wanted to make sure he had something to hold him over until her return from Hilton Head.

Megan placed her suitcases by the door so she would be ready in the morning. Steven was taking her to the airport at five in the morning and afterward dropping Percy off at Tiffani's home.

After the Thai food was delivered, she glanced at the clock. Steven would be there soon, and she was ready to eat. She decided she would nibble on an egg roll but her cell phone ringing interrupted her trek to the kitchen.

"What's up Syd?"

"Hey, Megan," she said uneasily. "You're calm."

Megan's heart stopped. The last time Sydney said that, there was a picture of her and Steven all over internet. "More pictures of me and Steven?"

"Steven, yes. You, no. I just emailed you the link."

Megan grabbed her tablet and clicked on the link, her heart stopping again. "I'll call you back."

She paced back and forth with her tablet in her hand in disbelief. In front of her were pictures of Steven from that morning at the Women's Day Program. One of which was with him and Veronica. There were actually several with him and Veronica posing with the students or guests at the event. However, the one that had both Megan and the media in a frenzy was captioned "Is the senator getting cozy with his ex-wife again?" In the picture, Veronica and Steven were walking and holding hands as she stared back at him with a loving smile on her face. Steven was smiling at her, as well.

The article went on to suggest that while the senator was more than likely running for his father's soon to be empty U.S. Senate seat, were he and his ex-wife making amends and getting back together?

At the sound of the doorbell, Megan's anger propelled even higher because she knew who was on the other side of the door. And he was about to feel her wrath.

"Percy, you may want to hide under the bed, sweetie. Mommy's pissed," she said as she stormed toward the door armed with her tablet. Percy followed orders and darted under the bed.

She swung the door open, and the handsome smile Steven wore faded into a questionable stare.

"What the heck is this?" She shoved the tablet in his hand.

He came in and closed the door, tossing his overnight bag on the floor.

"Humph." Megan glanced down at the bag. "You might as well pick that up because you only have two minutes to explain."

"Megan, there's nothing to explain," he stated calmly. "You knew I was speaking this morning at Atlanta Memorial College. You knew Veronica would be there."

"Yes, but what I didn't know was that there was still something going on between you two. I can't believe I actually believed you last night when there she was rubbing on you and flirting with you in front of me. Now there's a picture of you two holding hands and staring all lovey-dovey at each other." She snatched her tablet out of his hand and pointed to the evidence.

"Baby, I know the picture looks suspect, but we weren't really holding hands. She was pulling me along because I arrived late, and I was going on in five minutes. She was rushing me through the crowd and showing me where to go."

"And the lovey-dovey smiles?"

"We were laughing at the crowd of girls whistling and screaming, 'We love you Senator Monroe' and some other choice words about how fine and handsome I am. The event was recorded and it clearly shows just what I told you. You're more than welcome to watch it. It was on the local news station earlier. I have nothing to hide from you."

"You think I'm stupid?"

"No. I think you're making a big deal out of nothing. You remember the first pictures that circled the net with us? How I was leaning over and whispering in your ear and you were supposedly staring at me all mesmerized according to the media. When actually I was screaming in your ear because the music was loud, and you were staring up at me to listen better."

Megan sighed and sat on the couch. She closed her eyes and rested her head on the pillow. She didn't know what to believe anymore. She loved Steven, but she was beginning to grow tired of life in the spotlight especially now with this Veronica thing. Even though it was probably innocent, the media didn't perceive it that way. He had come full circle and cleaned up his reputation during the past few months thanks to her but also thanks to his determination.

His scent whiffed in her nose, and she sensed he was kneeling in front of her. She opened her eyes as tears fell from them, and he reached up and wiped them just as more silent ones began to fall.

"I'm not him, Megan. I would never cheat on you or disrespect you. I love you way too much to do that."

He gathered her in his arms and moved to the couch, positioning her on his lap. She laid her head on his chest as he gently rubbed her hair.

"I love you, too, Steven, and I do believe and trust you. I just don't trust Veronica."

"Megan, Veronica isn't interested in me at all. Believe me, she wants Judge Hill. She only invited me to the event at the last minute because she's a friend of the president at Atlanta Memorial College, and she wanted to make a good impression. It was all for show for her. That's it."

"Well, when I walked in yesterday she was all over you…"

"Before you walked in, she wasn't. She always does that whenever she meets whoever I'm dating. She likes to intimidate people."

"Well, she doesn't intimidate me."

"That's my girl," he said planting delicate kisses on her neck and ears. He ran his hand down her side. "I see you're wearing my favorite dress tonight."

"I wanted tonight to be special since I'm leaving in the morning."

"And it will still be special, I promise." He kissed her lightly on the lips. "I smell Thai food."

"Yes, it was delivered right before you arrived." She tried to scoot out of his embrace, but he pulled her closer.

"How about dessert first," he suggested as his sexy, dark gaze rested on her face, and he pulled the hem of her dress up to her thighs.

"That sounds wonderful…" She was interrupted by Steven's cell phone ringing.

"Sorry, babe, I told Shawn to only call if it was absolutely necessary. I'll put it on speaker so I can continue my tongue journey on your body."

"Shawn, what's going on?" Steven asked as he still held on to Megan and ran his finger alongside her face.

"Man, we have a major problem. A reporter just called asking if you were in a relationship with Megan only to clean up your image. I told him of course not, and you two were very much in love."

"Okay, that's true. So what's the problem?" Steven asked as Megan listened intently.

"He also stated he had a reliable source that could state otherwise. This reliable source claims she overheard Megan getting upset on the phone about having to sleep in the same bed as you in D.C."

Megan sat up when she realized who it was. "Susan. She must've heard me say that on the plane. Oh, no! Steven, I'm so sorry."

"That's bull! Why is Susan doing this to me?" Steven said as Megan slid off of his lap with wide eyes. He got up and walked away from her and into the kitchen with the phone still on speaker in his hand.

"Well, apparently her and Bryce were having an affair, but he broke it off with her recently and then fired her yesterday."

"I had no idea about them, but why punish me?"

"Bryce said she's trying to extort money from him. When he refused to give her what she asked for, she threatened to tell the media about what she overheard Megan say that day on the flight. I told the reporter none of that was true and hung up the phone. But you know women. Some of them never forgive or forget. They hold grudges for a long time. Man, try to have a nice evening with Megan. I just wanted you to know so you wouldn't hear it or read about it first from another source. I'll release a statement as soon as it comes out in the news."

Steven pounded his fist on the island in the kitchen. He knew he shouldn't be worried, but he was announcing his candidacy for the U.S. Senate seat in a few days. He shook his head. Megan rubbed his back to console him.

"Baby, don't worry about this. Like Shawn said, she's a female with a grudge who just wants money. We know the truth and that's what matters. Your constituents are more interested in what you can do for them not who you're dating," Megan said, trying to comfort him.

"I guess you know I don't handle stress well."

"I know you don't. However, you have people around you that care about you and have your best interests in mind, especially me. Shawn said he would take care of it, right?"

"Baby, I don't know what I would do without your love and support. I love you so much," Steven said looking into her eyes.

"I love you, too," Megan responded smiling up at him as he picked her up and carried her to the bedroom.

He placed her down on the floor, and she slowly unzipped the side zipper of her dress, letting it fall off of her feet. His eyes raked over her body and then he pulled her to him. His fingers slid down her back, unhooking her bra on the way to her bottom where he pulled her panties down over her heels.

"Leave them on," he whispered in Megan's ear.

"With pleasure, Senator Monroe."

He kissed her softly, twirling his tongue around hers in an unhurried, loving caress. Picking her up again, he carried her to the bed, their lips still on each other. Once on top of her, his kisses became more intense. He kissed her deeply with all of the passion he had in him to prove to her that he needed only her. He hated the thought of ever losing her over something that wasn't true.

"I love you, Megan. You hear me. You're the only woman I've ever loved." He kissed her forehead, the tip of her nose and her lips, which formed a huge smile.

"I love you, too, Steven and would love to show you as soon as you take off your clothes."

He slid off the bed and starting unbuckling his pants. "You're right. Why am I fully clothed, and you're lying there with your sexy self wearing nothing but heels and perfume?"

She giggled. "Hurry up."

He rejoined her, laying his body on top of hers once more and claiming her lips in a seductive kiss.

Megan could feel his erection in between her legs. She wanted to wiggle her hips so he could slip in, but she also wanted to savor tonight since she was leaving in the morning. Instead, she kissed him ferociously on the lips while his hands roamed her smooth body.

She took in his kisses and touches hungrily. She felt the urgency in him as she forced her tongue deeper into his mouth to mingle with his. She wanted him to know that she was all his. Being in his loving arms again made her feel safe and secure.

Megan let out soft moans while he kissed her neck and shoulders before trailing down to her breasts that ached for his caress. When he finally reached her stomach, Megan knew where he was going next. She arched back and let him kiss her inner thighs and then the sweet spot in between that had missed his savory tongue. Megan moaned his name over and over again as his tongue licked her most sensitive spot. Once she climaxed, Steven looked up into her heat-filled eyes and knew she was ready for him to take her.

Steven reached in her nightstand and put on his protection. He grabbed her close to him and flipped them over so she was on top. He guided her down inch by inch until he was buried all the way inside. She breathed out and began to slowly move up and down as his hands clasped her butt and pulled her all the way down on him. Her cries of passion became louder as their rhythm increased with each stroke.

Waves of pleasure crashed through her body as her orgasm erupted, shaking her to the core. He flipped her over as they were still joined together and began to give slow, tantalizing thrusts that caused more sensations to flow through every cell of her body. She wasn't sure how much more she could take as she held on to his shoulders as each thrust from him summoned an erotic moan from her. She began to meet his thrusts pulling him deeper into her heart and soul. Their eyes never strayed from each other's faces as the glow of the candles settled on them. They climaxed together moments later, still kissing and staring at each other intently. He kissed her eyes that were lightly misted with tears.

She giggled. "That tickles."

"You're ticklish everywhere. You even laugh sometimes when I'm kissing your other set of lovely lips."

"Only when you have a five o'clock shadow."

He kissed the tip of her nose. "You're adorable, you know that?"

"And hungry. You wore me out." She slid from

under him, and he repositioned them so that she could place her head on his chest.

"Hmm…whenever we have Thai food we always have dessert first."

"Then we should have Thai food more often. Um…Steven?"

"Yes, babe?"

"Can I take my heels off now?"

He laughed out loud and patted her butt. "Of course, babe, and then let's go eat. You know, I'm really going to miss you."

She kicked her shoes off and kissed his cheek. "I'm going to miss you, too."

He captured her lips and flipped her over on her back.

Chapter 13

"Girl, I am so glad we have a day of rest," Megan said as she and Jade lay out by the pool of the beach house that they were staying in on Hilton Head while decorating the home next door. It was Sunday morning, and the ladies were finally able to relax. They had spent three long days going over the renovations with the crew. On Monday, they were to shop for furniture while the crew finished putting in the new kitchen cabinets and granite counter tops that Megan and Jade had chosen.

Megan was glad for the busy work, though. She hated to admit it, but she needed a break away from her life in Atlanta. With the Veronica situation and then Susan trying to expose Megan's relationship with Steven, she needed a breather. She felt better after Shawn released a statement stating that while Megan did tell Steven she didn't want to sleep in the same bed with him, it was because they'd just began dating and she would feel uncomfortable sleeping next to him so early in the relationship. The media seemed to believe it and some of the reports stated that Megan had moral values and other young ladies should follow suit.

Megan was disappointed when she couldn't be by Steven's side on Friday as he officially announced he was running for the U.S. Senate seat. She was able to speak with him briefly afterward before having to meet with the producers of the show about the progress thus far.

"What do you feel like doing today?" Megan asked.

"Sip on mimosas and eat lobster tails," Jade answered as her and Megan toasted their champagne glasses. "But seriously, let's go have lunch at the restaurant that is catering the food for the show. Those shrimp and grits…"

"…were to die for."

Thirty minutes later, they were dressed in sundresses and headed toward the front door.

"What's all that noise?" Megan asked, grabbing her purse from the foyer table and putting on her shades. She handed Jade her purse and shades, as well.

"I don't know. Is the crew working on the house? I thought we were all off today." Jade shrugged as they walked toward the front door.

Megan opened it and was immediately bombarded with cameras flashing, microphones and tape recorders in her face. All the people were speaking at once saying her name, Steven's name and Veronica's name, but she couldn't understand what they were asking. Jade stood in front of her and shielded her away from the reporters, pushing them back with her hands.

"Stand back," Jade yelled. "Ms. Chase isn't answering any of your questions. Now leave. You're trespassing on private property."

"But we just want to know how she feels about this," a reporter said, handing Jade an Atlanta Newspaper along with a few loose photos.

Jade glanced down at them and then back at the reporters. "She has no comment, and I suggest you leave before I call the police or I take my mace or something else out of my purse," Jade said, unzipping her purse on her arm as the reporters stepped back. She turned around, pushed Megan back into the house, and slammed the door and locked it.

"Oh, my goodness!" Megan screamed. "This is ridiculous. Why are they here asking about those pictures taken at the Women's Day Program? It wasn't that big of a deal." Megan plopped on the couch and raised her knees up to her chin. "If they watch the video, they'll clearly see they weren't holding hands. She was pulling him."

Jade glanced back at the newspaper and then the photos in her hand. She sat next to her best friend and spoke softly. "Megan, this is today's newspaper, and the pictures are from last night." She sighed as she handed Megan the paper.

Megan looked at the picture, and her heart immediately sank. In the picture, Steven and Veronica's arms were wrapped around one another as they spoke to another couple at the banquet that Steven had said he wasn't taking Veronica to.

"That lying bastard!" Megan threw the paper across the room.

"You took the words right out of my mouth."

"He said he wasn't taking her to the banquet. When I spoke to him last night, he said Shawn suggested that he go because he'd just announced his candidacy for the Senate ticket. He said Bryce was picking him up." Megan paced back and forth with tears running down her face. "I'm just so tired of this. Is this what my life has become? Now I have reporters hounding me down out of town looking for a statement!"

"Girl, I'm so sorry. Maybe…he…" Jade comforted, handing Megan a tissue and sitting her back on the couch.

Megan shook her head and dried her eyes but more tears came rushing down. "No…this is too much. Apparently, something is still going on with them. The first time…I let it slide, but this is different. He said he wasn't taking her. Heck, he wasn't even going and now that I'm out of town, he decided to take her!"

Megan's phone began to ring from inside of her purse. She knew it was Steven because of the ringtone.

Megan answered it as calm as possible. "What?"

"Baby, it's not what you think, I promise."

"You sound like a broken record, and I'm going to turn it off right now." Megan pressed the end button on the screen and then turned off her cell phone. She handed Jade the photos from the couch and the newspaper off the floor. "Can you burn these? But I guess it doesn't matter. They're all over the internet."

"Of course. Anything else? A glass a wine? A shoulder to cry on?"

"Both," Megan stammered as the tears began to fall uncontrollably.

Steven rang the doorbell at the beach house and then banged on the door. He'd been calling Megan and even Jade but neither would answer their cell phones. He found out from his cousin Justine exactly where Megan was staying and flew out on his private plane to see her face-to-face.

He rang the doorbell again, and Jade opened the door with a scowl and her hands on her hips.

"What?" she asked with an attitude.

"I need to see Megan."

"Humph. Not today you won't. Now back up so the door won't hit you when I slam it."

Steven was already frustrated, and he didn't need Megan's best friend to instigate.

"I just want to speak to Megan," he said calmly.

"She doesn't want to see you ever again. Now I suggest you…"

"It's okay," Megan said walking into the foyer

and standing next Jade. "I know I told you make him go away, but I need to tell him exactly how I feel."

Jade stepped back and let Steven inside. "Okay, I'll be in the kitchen if you need me." She cut her eyes at Steven before walking out of the room.

Megan walked to the living room and Steven followed her. He hated the situation they were in, but he planned on making it right. He wanted nothing more than to pull her into his arms and comfort her. He hated that her eyes were red and her tear-stained face was swollen from crying. He hated that she'd been crying over something that wasn't even true.

She stood by the window that overlooked the ocean with her back to him. She breathed in deeply before turning around with a glare of anger and a fed-up expression in her eyes. But when she spoke her voice was calm and steady.

"Steven, I've had some time to think this afternoon about our relationship. How we met, how we started to date and why we dated in the first place. I knew you were a playboy. I knew about your ex-wife and your past escapades, but I still fell in love with you despite the mixed reservations that I had. But I can't do this anymore."

Tears started to well in her eyes, and she turned away. He then grabbed her and pulled her toward him to face him.

"What are you saying?" He screamed out, surprised at the hatred in her eyes.

"This is a life I don't want. I'm tired of the reporters, your past women, the time away from you.

I want my life back the way it was. I went to work, I came home, worked on projects, went to lunch, on shopping sprees, the spa with my girlfriends and lousy blind dates. Today just made me realize even more that this is not the lifestyle I want to be a part of."

"Megan, I completely understand, but what you think happened didn't. I wasn't with Veronica last night at the banquet."

"Did you not see the paper today?" she asked, the calm in her voice was now replaced with anger.

"I mean, we weren't at the banquet together. She was there with Judge Hill."

"Humph, well you two looked real close with your arms wrapped around each other laughing and having a great time with some other couple, and I looked at the all of the pictures. I never saw Judge Hill."

"Those were her parents. I was just making polite conversation with them, that's all. Judge Hill arrived late so that's probably why there aren't any pictures of him. I've done nothing wrong except be in the right place at the wrong time."

"Steven, even if what you say is true, I simply can't do this anymore." She turned away from him, facing the window once more.

A lump formed in his throat, and he couldn't breathe. He hesitated to ask his next question in fear of already knowing her answer.

"You don't want to be with me?" he quietly asked standing behind her with his hands positioned to touch her shoulders to turn her to him once more.

But the hurt he was beginning to feel prevented him from stepping closer to her. He'd seen the resentment in her cold stare and heard it even more in her tone.

Steven didn't wait for a verbal answer. Her silence said it all.

Chapter 14

Megan sat on her couch wrapped in her favorite pink throw blanket looking over design boards and paint swatches for a new project. A new builder to the metro Atlanta area was starting five new subdivisions and wanted Megan and Jade to decorate ten model homes. He'd seen their work on *Decorator's Dream* three months prior and knew their style would be perfect for his floor plans.

Lucy was done with her internship and was now officially a member of their decorating staff. Her first assignment was to decorate two of the ten homes for the project with Megan overseeing. Business was better than ever since their official debut on the Fabulous Living Channel. Plus, the fact that Megan was the ex-girlfriend of a famous senator added to the high demand for their business. They were in the process of hiring another decorator as well as looking for a bigger office. Jade and Megan also thought it was time to hire a full-time secretary instead of using an intern to do office work. After many interviews, they settled on a young woman named Corrine, who was the only candidate not starstruck by Megan and Jade.

Megan had thought about Steven during the past few months. It was kind of hard not to, considering wherever she went there were billboards, campaign posters and bumper stickers endorsing his run for the U.S. Senate. She was glad that he'd won the primary and she had watched some of his speeches and debates. He'd called her repeatedly and sent flowers upon her return from Hilton Head, but Megan didn't want to be bothered. At one point, she considered hearing him out and perhaps giving him another chance but changed her mind when saw him hugged up with a model at some event. Apparently, he'd moved on and was back to his previous lifestyle.

When Election Day arrived in November and he'd won the seat, she'd wanted to call him and congratulate him but didn't. However, she was pleasantly surprised that he'd worn the tie she gave to him and couldn't hold back a smile when he looked into the camera, ran his hand down the tie, and winked.

The sound of the doorbell interrupted Megan's thoughts of the type of hardwood floors to select for her next project. She wasn't expecting anyone and the only way to get into her building was by calling her through the intercom system or punching in the code that only a few people knew. At least the reporters wouldn't be at her front door even though some had been waiting for her recently outside of the parking garage and at work to ask questions about her break-up with Steven and his recent win.

Peeking out of the peephole, she was surprised by who was standing on the other side of the door. She reluctantly opened the door halfway as Percy darted into the bedroom.

"How did you get into the building? I changed the code."

Steven cocked his head to the side with an arrogant grin. "I have my resources. May I come in? I promise not to stay long."

Megan inhaled and stepped aside to let him in. She closed the door but didn't take her hand off of the handle. Her heartbeat sped up, and she hoped he couldn't hear it. He looked handsome and refreshed in a burgundy sweater with black slacks perfect for the coolness of Atlanta in November. He smelled divine, and his presence reminded her how much she missed him.

"What can I do for you?" She was amazed at how calm and steady her voice was but she couldn't let it show that she was a nervous wreck inside.

He pulled an envelope out of his pocket and handed it to her. "I'm having my victory party at your brother's restaurant tomorrow evening around eight. I would love for you to come. I know it's last minute. I hadn't planned on having one, but my father insisted so my mother planned it this week."

She glanced at the envelope but didn't open it. She remained silent as he continued.

"I know things didn't end well between us, but you were there for me when I needed you and winning the election kind of sucked when I didn't have the woman I love by my side to celebrate."

"Yes, I saw that you won. Congrats. I guess in the end we both got what we wanted. You're now a U.S. senator, or will be officially once you're sworn in at the beginning of the year. And I have a slew of new clients because I dated you." She turned the handle on the door. "Anything else? I have a lot of work to get back to," she lied. She really needed him to hurry up and leave before she found herself wrapped in his warm embrace. She wasn't sure how much longer she could remain composed.

"I sincerely hope you'll be able to make it to the party. It's just an intimate affair with close family and friends…and it would be nice to see your beautiful face among the crowd. Despite everything, I was always faithful to you, Megan. I love you very much and miss the hell out of you. I know my life isn't the simple, normal, drama-free life that you're used to. I honestly hope one day you'll forgive me for what you think I did. If we never get back together, just know you're the love of my life, and I'll love you until I take my last breath."

He closed the gap between them, and Megan found herself against the door. She wanted to move.

Needed to move. But her feet were glued to the floor and his intoxicating scent and his inviting mouth, prevented her from doing so. He lowered his head and kissed her gently on the lips as an exhaling moan escaped her mouth. Her tongue joined in the seductive dance he bestowed on her. He yanked off the pink blanket she was wrapped in and he placed her hands around his neck as his hands found their way around her waist meshing her body into his. He kissed her fervently as if he couldn't get enough and as if it he was hungry and only she could satisfy his appetite. And then he stopped, and she let out a moan, wondering why on earth he halted their passion.

"I want you to think about everything I said especially the kiss we just shared that told me everything I needed to know."

He kissed her lightly on the forehead and left without another word, closing the door behind him.

Megan somehow made it back to the couch on wobbly legs as tears burned her eyes. She could still feel the warmth of Steven's mouth on hers and smell his woodsy cologne on her clothes. She dropped to the couch, grabbed her cell phone and told Sydney everything that had just happened.

"So, are you going to the party? I can pick you up on the way."

"I don't know and…wait a minute. On the way? Were you invited?"

"Um…" Sydney paused. "Yes, I was invited, but I wasn't sure if I was actually going to go."

"You and Braxton are traitors. Not only is it at his restaurant, you're the one that gave Steven the new access code, aren't you?"

"Yes, but I did it because you've been moping around for the last three months, burying yourself in work. When you broke up with what's-his-name, you didn't mope and while you buried yourself in your work, you didn't become a hermit. Bryce said Steven's been moody and didn't even care if he won the election or not. He didn't even want a celebration party."

Megan replayed her sister's words in her head. "Bryce said? I thought you couldn't stand Bryce. Called him an ass if I remember correctly."

"He is an ass, but I ran into him at the federal building, and he told me how much Steven missed you and that he hated how things ended. I never believed anything was going on with him and Veronica. Besides, she's engaged to Judge Hill now."

"Sydney, it's not that easy. I..."

"Do you still love him? That's the question you need to ask yourself. Can you go on with your life without him in it?"

The next evening, Megan sat on her couch changing channels and flipping through a home magazine. She finally settled on the evening news to see what the weather would be like next week since one of her projects included an outdoor living and dining area.

Megan waited for the weather segment to come on by putting the television on mute. She continued perusing through the magazine placing stickies on the items she liked. Percy jumped on the couch causing the remote to fall to the floor and the volume went back up. She heard a very familiar deep voice on the television. It belonged to Senator Steven Monroe. He was touring an after-school program with the news anchor. He looked debonair in one of the tailored suits that Chelsea had most likely suggested for him. He was also wearing the tie that Megan had given him again. The news anchor even commented on the tie stating that it looked like the one he wore on Election Day. With a sincere smile, Steven replied, "This tie is very special to me because of who it's from, and I'll cherish it always."

His statement reminded her of the first time she saw his worn wallet that had belonged to his grandfather, and Steven carried it all the time. She flipped the television off, kissed Percy on the head and ran to her closet taking the rollers out of her hair and throwing her nightgown off in the process.

Less than an hour later, she pulled up to Café Love Jones. She took a deep breath and walked inside of the restaurant. An unfamiliar hostess approached her. Megan knew the entire staff at her brother's restaurant.

"Excuse me miss? Are you here for dinner or the private party on the mezzanine?"

Megan glanced at the staircase that was roped off and had a huge bodyguard standing next to it. One of Steven's campaign posters was on an easel.

"The private party for Steven Monroe."

"May I see your invitation please?" the young hostess said with her hand held out.

"Oh...I don't have it but..."

"Then you can't get in."

Megan had to stop herself from laughing. "I'm the owner's sister."

"Sweetie, three ladies just left here saying the same exact thing. I get it. Senator Monroe is once again Atlanta's most eligible bachelor, but it's a private party for family and friends only. So unless you have an invitation, you aren't getting in."

"Look, I can go anywhere I want to in this restaurant and right now I need to get upstairs. So I suggest you tell big bad wolf over there to move so I can get by." Megan was not about to let anything or anyone stand in the way of her mission.

"What's going on?" Braxton asked coming from the hallway that led to another private room and looking at Megan and then at the hostess.

"Mr. Chase, this woman is trying to get into Senator Monroe's private party. She's the tenth person I've had to turn away. She lied and said she was your sister."

"She *is* my sister Megan, who was definitely invited to the party." Braxton turned toward the bodyguard. "Rick, please let my sister upstairs."

Rick removed the velvet rope, and Megan gave her big brother a kiss on the cheek before running up the stairs in her four-inch heels.

When she made it to the top, she scanned the room for Steven. She spotted him talking to Bryce at the bar. Steven's back was to her. She glanced around the room and saw Syd, Jade and Tiffani all wearing wide smiles and motioning for her to keep walking. Sydney even mouthed, "Go get your man."

Megan took a deep breath and made her way across the room. Bryce, who was leaning on the bar, saw her first but didn't make eye contact. Instead he kept listening and nodding his head. As she moved closer, Steven stopped talking and chuckled.

"Amarige?" he asked.

She smiled. "Yes, it's the only perfume I wear."

Bryce patted Steven on the back, gave Megan an encouraging smile and left. She moved to where Bryce had stood and stared up at Steven.

"You came."

Megan ran her hand down his familiar tie. "Of course, where else would I be? It's your big night."

"Would you like to dance?" He held out his hand.

She placed her hand in his as he walked her out to the empty dance floor. "I'd love to but didn't we agree not to dance together again because of where it always seems to lead?"

He nodded his head and glided his hands around her waist as he drew her toward him. "Hmm...well, if I remember correctly, we had our very first dance in this same spot followed by a very sensual kiss."

He lowered his head and kissed her gently on the lips. She heard cheers and claps from their family and friends. They both stopped kissing and laughed. But then his facial expression turned serious.

"I've missed you, Megan. I can't spend another

second without you. I've been miserable these past few months."

"Me, too, Steven. I'm sorry I ever doubted you."

He kissed her forehead and lowered to one knee as tears welled in her eyes. The room became silent except for a few "oohs and aahs" from the women.

He took both of her hands and placed them over his heart as she began to tremble with anticipation. "Megan Rochelle Chase, will you please do me the honor of being my wife?"

"Oh, Steven. Yes! Yes, I'll marry you."

He stood and captured her in his arms twirling her around in the air as their friends and family ran out to the dance floor to hug and congratulate them.

Later on that evening after a few rounds of love making, they cuddled in front of her fireplace facing each other. Steven ran his hands through her unruly curls and kissed her softly on the lips.

"I've never been happier in my life than I am right now, babe," Steven said in between tender kisses. "I knew when I met you that you would change my life forever."

"And I knew when I met you, that you would be my perfect candidate for love."

Epilogue

One year later

"**W**hat?" Megan asked sarcastically as she sat on the bed in her hotel suite at the Four Seasons Hotel flipping the channels on the television.

Jade, trying not to wrinkle her lavender dress, sat carefully on the bed next to Megan.

"You're getting married in less than an hour, and you're trying to watch TV?"

"Jade, relax," Megan patted her best friend's hand with a smile.

"Relax? My best friend is getting married, and I'm supposed to relax? Tiffani, Sydney! Are you going to help me out?"

Sydney came over, also in a lavender dress, and

sat next to Megan who was still wearing her slip. Her princess wedding gown hung on the door.

"Jade, leave Megan alone even though I'm surprised at her coolness. Tiffani, I remember you were a nervous wreck on your wedding day," Sydney reminded. Tiffani nodded her head as she finished her makeup.

"Yes, I remember my wedding day. I was a nervous wreck because of the rain."

Megan then got up and walked toward her wedding gown.

"Ladies, help me with the gown please. My dad will be in here soon. And for your information, I'm not nervous because I'm marrying the man of my dreams. I've waited a whole year to marry him, and the day has finally arrived. You know so many good things have happened this year and getting married on New Year's Eve makes it all the better," Megan said as Sydney buttoned up her wedding gown. Jade nodded her head in agreement.

"I agree girl. I'm still in shock that we have our own television show now on the Fabulous Living Channel! The first season was awesome!" Jade exclaimed.

"Yeah, it was cool traveling to different cities with you in a motor mansion looking for the best decorated homes and planning my wedding all at the same time."

"Well, season two of *The Best Decorated Homes* starts filming in a few months so don't go get pregnant anytime soon!"

"You're so silly. I do want children, but I want to enjoy my husband first. That sounds so unreal to say. *My husband!* Ladies! I'm getting married!"

Five hours later, Megan and Steven sat at their table at Café Love Jones, kissing each other softly. Braxton was having his annual New Year's Eve party and the newlyweds and their friends went over to the restaurant after the reception.

Megan had never been more ecstatic than she was at that very moment. She had won the heart of the man she'd dreamed of since she was a little girl. Being with him made her realize that she'd never even been in love until she met Steven Monroe almost a year and half ago thanks to her SUV's flat tire.

Megan glanced around the room, and her eyes landed on Sydney and Bryce in a heated debate as usual.

"All our siblings seem to do is get into heated discussions about the law," Megan said, nodding her head in their direction.

Steven turned to glance at them and then back at Megan with a snicker. "Yes, they clearly don't get along, but we're all family now. Speaking of family, we haven't discussed when we want to plan for ours."

"How about we spend the next few years practicing, starting tonight?"

"Perfect. I was thinking the exact same thoughts."

* * * * *

THE BOYFRIEND
ARRANGEMENT

ANDREA LAURENCE

One

"You have got to be kidding me!"

Sebastian West scanned his proximity card for the third time and yet the front door of BioTech—the biomedical technology company he co-founded—refused to open. Seeing his employees moving around inside, he pounded his fist on the glass, but all of them ignored him.

"I own this company!" he shouted as his secretary walked by without making eye contact. "Don't make me fire you, Virginia."

At that, she came to a stop and circled back to the door.

"Finally," he sighed.

But she didn't open the door as he'd expected. Instead she just shook her head. "I'm under strict orders from Dr. Solomon not to open the door for you, sir."

"Oh, come on," he groaned.

She couldn't be moved. "You'll have to take it up with him, sir." Then she turned on her heel and disappeared.

"Finn!" he shouted at the top of his lungs, pounding on the glass with angry fists. "Let me in, you son of a bitch."

A moment later Sebastian's former college roommate and business partner, Finn Solomon, appeared at the door with a frown on his face. "You're supposed to be on vacation," he said through the glass.

"That's what the doctor said, yeah, but since when do I take vacations? Or listen to doctors?" The answer was never. He certainly never listened to Finn. And as for vacation, he hadn't taken one in the decade since they'd started this company. You couldn't be off lying on a beach and also breaking barriers in medical technology. The two were incompatible.

"That's the whole point, Sebastian. Do you not recall that you had a heart attack two days ago? You're not supposed to be in the office for a minimum of two weeks."

"A mild heart attack. They didn't keep me in the hospital for more than a few hours. And they're not even sure I really had one. I'm taking the stupid pills they gave me, what more do you want?"

"I want you to go home. I'm not letting you in. I've had your badge deactivated. I've also sent out a memo that anyone who lets you in the building will be terminated."

So much for piggybacking through the door behind someone else. He did have a laptop, though, if he could get Virginia to bring it out to him. That wouldn't technically be breaking the rules if he worked from home, right?

"I've also had your email and remote access accounts temporarily suspended, so you can't even work from home." Finn was always remarkably good at reading his mind. He'd been able to do it since they were in college. It was great for working together. Not so great for this scenario. "You are on mandatory medical leave, Sebastian, and as a doctor, I'm sorry, but I'm going to enforce it. I can handle things for two weeks, but I can't run this company with you dead. So get some R and R. Take a trip. Get a massage. Get a hand job. I really don't care. But I don't want to see you here."

Sebastian was at a loss. He and Finn had started this company after school, pouring their hearts and souls into technology that could make people's lives better. He was the MIT engineer and Finn was the doctor, a winning team that had developed advanced technologies like prosthetic hands and electric wheelchairs controlled by a patient's brain waves. That seemed a noble enough cause to dedicate his life to. But apparently a decade of trading sleep and vegetables for caffeine and sugar had caught up with him.

Of course he didn't want to die; he was only thirty-eight. But he was close to a breakthrough on a robotic exoskeleton that could make paraplegics like his brother walk again.

"What about the new prototype for the exo-legs?"

Finn just crossed his huge forearms over his chest. "Those people have gone a long time without walking. They can wait two more weeks while you recover. If you keel over at your desk one afternoon, they'll never get it. As it is, I'm having a defibrillator installed on the wall outside your office."

Sebastian sighed, knowing he'd lost this fight. Finn was just as stubborn as he was. Normally that was a good match—they never knew when to take no for an answer. But that wouldn't benefit him in this situation. He knew the doctor's orders, yet he'd never once imagined that Finn would enforce them this strictly. He'd just thought he'd work ten-hour days instead of the usual eighteen.

"Can I at least come in and—?"

"*No*," Finn interrupted. "Go home. Go shopping. Just go away." With a smug expression Finn waved at him through the glass and then turned his back on his business partner.

Sebastian stood there for a moment, thinking maybe Finn would come back and tell him he was just kidding. When it was clear that Finn was deadly serious, he wandered back to the elevator and returned to the lobby of the building. He stepped out onto the busy Manhattan sidewalk with no real clue as to where he was going to go. He'd planned to take it easy for a few days and head back to work today. Now he had two full weeks of nothingness ahead of him.

He had the resources to do almost anything on earth that he wanted. Fly to Paris on a private jet. Take a luxury cruise through the Caribbean. Sing karaoke in Tokyo. He just didn't want to do any of those things.

Money was an alien thing to Sebastian. Unlike Finn, he'd never had it growing up. His parents had worked hard but as blue collar laborers they'd just never seemed to get ahead. And after his brother Kenny's ATV accident, they'd gone from poor to near destitute under the weight of the medical bills.

Scholarships and loans had gotten Sebastian through college, after which he'd focused on building his company with Finn. The company eventually brought money—lots of it—but he'd been really too busy to notice. Or to spend any. He'd never dreamed of traveling or owning expensive sports cars. Honestly, he was bad at being rich. He probably didn't even have twenty bucks in his wallet.

Stopping at a street corner, he pulled his wallet out of his back pocket and noticed the leather had nearly disintegrated over the years. He'd probably had this one since grad school. Maybe he should consider getting a new one. He had nothing better to do at the moment.

Up ahead, he spied Neiman Marcus. Surely they sold wallets. He made his way across the street and over to the department store. Sebastian stopped long enough to hold the door for a group of attractive women exiting with enough bags to put a kid through a semester or two of college. They looked vaguely familiar, especially the last one with the dark hair and steely blue eyes.

Her gaze flicked over him for a moment and he felt it like a punch to his gut. His pulse pounded in his throat as he tried to unsuccessfully swallow the lump that had formed there. He didn't know why he would have such a visceral reaction to the woman. He wanted to say something but he couldn't place the woman and decided to keep his mouth shut. Half a second later she looked away, breaking the connection, and continued on down the street with her friends.

Sebastian watched them for a moment with a touch

of regret, then forced himself into the store. He made a beeline for the men's department and quickly selected a wallet. He wasn't particularly choosy with that sort of thing. He just wanted black leather and a slim profile with enough room for a couple cards and some cash. Easy.

As he found a register open for checkout, he noticed a strikingly attractive brunette ahead of him. Sebastian realized she was one of the women he'd just seen leave the store a few minutes before. The one with the blue-gray eyes. He wished he remembered who she was so he could say something to her. They'd probably met at one event or another around town—Finn forced him to go to the occasional party or charity gala—he couldn't be sure, though. Most of his brain was allocated to robotics and engineering.

Not all of it, though. He was red-blooded male enough to notice her tall, lean figure, long, chestnut hair, big blue eyes and bloodred lips. It was impossible not to notice how flawlessly she was put together. She smelled like the meadow behind his childhood home after a warm summer rain. Deep down inside him something clenched tightly at the thought.

What was it about her? He told himself it was probably nothing to do with her, exactly. The doctor had told him to refrain from strenuous physical activity—*Yes, that includes sexual relations, Mr. West*—for at least a week. It had been a while since he'd indulged with a lady, but maybe since it was forbidden, his mind was focusing on what it couldn't have.

Why was he so terrible at remembering names?

As Sebastian got closer to the counter, he realized the woman was returning everything in her bag. That was odd. If the register was correct, she'd just purchased and immediately returned about fifteen hundred dollars' worth of clothes. He watched as she slipped out of her leather coat and shoved it into the empty department store bag, covering it with the packing tissue so you couldn't see inside.

His chronic boredom was temporarily interrupted as she piqued his curiosity with her actions. "Excuse m—" he started to say.

She turned suddenly and slammed right into his chest, forcing him to reach out and catch her in his arms before she stumbled backward on her sky-high heels and fell to the ground. He pulled her tight against him, molding her breasts to his chest until she righted herself. He found he really didn't want to let go when the time came. He was suddenly drunk on her scent and the feel of her soft curves pressing into his hard angles. How long had it been since he'd been this close to a woman? One he wasn't fitting a prosthetic to? He had no clue.

But eventually he did let go.

The woman took an unsteady step back, pulling herself together with a crimson flush blooming across her cheeks. "I am so sorry about that," she said. "I'm always in such a hurry that I don't pay attention to where I'm going."

There was a faint light of recognition in her blue-gray eyes as she looked up at him, so he knew he was right about meeting her somewhere before. "No, don't apologize," he said with a wry smile. "That's the most exciting thing to happen to me all week."

Her brow furrowed in disbelief.

Perhaps, he mused, he didn't look as boring as he was.

"Are you okay?" she asked.

He laughed off her concern. She was tall for a woman, especially in those stilettos, but he didn't really think she could inflict damage to him. "I'm fine. I'm just glad I was able to catch you."

She smirked and looked down self-consciously. "I suppose it could've been worse."

"You actually look really familiar to me, but I'm horrible with names. I'm Sebastian West," he said, offering her his hand in greeting.

She accepted it tentatively. The touch of her smooth skin gliding along his sent an unexpected spark through his nervous system. He was usually focused on work, and other pursuits, like sexual gratification and dating in general, typically took the back burner. But with one simple touch, physical desire was moved to the forefront.

Unlike their brief collision, this touch lingered skin-to-skin, letting him enjoy the flickers of electricity across his palm. The connection between them was palpable. So much so that when she pulled her hand away, she rubbed it gently on her burgundy sweater as if to dull the sensation.

"You do look familiar," she agreed. "I'm Harper Drake. We must've met around town. Perhaps you know my brother Oliver? Orion Computers?"

That sounded familiar enough. "He's probably pals with my friend Finn Solomon. Finn knows everyone."

Harper narrowed her eyes for a moment, looking thoughtful. "That name sounds familiar, too. Wait…

are you involved in some kind of medical supply business?"

Sebastian's brows rose in surprise. That wasn't exactly how he'd categorize what he did, but the fact that she remembered that much stunned him. And, to be honest, it pleased him just a little bit.

"You could say that." He grinned.

Harper beamed. She was pleased to finally place this guy in her mind. When she'd caught a glimpse of him earlier, he'd grabbed her attention. He'd looked so familiar when he'd held the door for her that she was certain she'd known him from somewhere. Unfortunately, Violet being so hell-bent on running up the street to pick up Aidan's wedding present had meant she couldn't stop.

Once she'd split from her best friends, Lucy Drake, Violet Niarchos and Emma Flynn, she'd stealthily circled back to Neiman Marcus to return everything she'd just bought. She couldn't have that weighing down her credit card for long. She hadn't expected to run into the familiar man again. Certainly not literally.

Real smooth, Harper.

"Okay, well then, I think it must've been one of the hospital benefits this past winter."

He nodded. "I do think I went to one of those. Finn tries to get me out every now and then."

Sebastian West didn't have a face she could forget, even if she lost context. He had a strong jaw, a nearly jet-black goatee, eyes just as dark, and a crooked smile that stirred something inside her. No, she'd remember him for sure. If she had a type, he'd be it.

It was a shame he wasn't one of the rich CEO guys

her brother associated with all the time. She didn't mean to be shallow, but meeting a guy with his act together financially would certainly benefit her current situation. It would also make her feel a little better about how things would be handled once it all changed on her birthday.

The last seven years had been one long, hard lesson learned for Harper. One in the value of money the spoiled little rich girl she'd once been had never really experienced before. She would be the first to admit that her father had basically given her everything she'd wanted. After her mother died, he'd spoiled her. And continued to spoil her until he'd no longer had the resources.

Harper had never imagined that the well would run dry. When it had, she'd made a lot of necessary adjustments in her life. At least secretly. It was embarrassing enough that she'd blown all the money she'd inherited when she'd turned eighteen—especially since she was an accountant—she didn't need anyone else knowing about what she'd done.

After falling from the top of the world to her current spot near the bottom, she'd earned a whole new appreciation for money and for the people who were good at managing it. And soon, when she had money again, she intended to be very careful about how she handled it. That included triple-checking every guy she dated. Not that she intended to date Sebastian…

"Well, I'm glad we bumped into each other today," Sebastian said with a sly grin.

Harper chuckled. As her gaze broke away from Sebastian's for a moment, she saw Quentin—her ex, of all people—walking toward them. Grabbing Sebastian's arm, she turned them both toward a display of men's shoes, hoping maybe Quentin hadn't seen her. "I'm sorry," she muttered under her breath. "I'm trying to—"

"Harper?"

Damn it.

Harper turned to face the ex-boyfriend she'd done her best to avoid for the last two years. She stepped away from Sebastian, leaning in to give her ex a polite but stiff hug. "Hello, Quentin," she said in a flat, disinterested tone she knew he wouldn't pick up on. He never did.

"How have you been?"

Lonely. Anxiety-riddled. "I'm great. Never better. How about you?"

"Amazing. I actually just got engaged."

Engaged? Quentin was engaged. The one who didn't want to commit. If Harper hadn't already been feeling crappy about being the last single friend in her social circle, this moment would've been the straw that broke the camel's back. She pasted a fake smile on her face and nodded. "That's great. I'm happy for you."

Quentin didn't notice her lack of sincerity. "Thank you. Her name is Josie. She's amazing. I can't wait for you to meet her. I think you two would really get along."

Harper had to bite her tongue to keep from asking why his ex would have any interest in hanging out with his fiancée. "I'm sure we would."

"So, Harper…" Quentin said as he leaned in to her. His arrogant smile made her shoulders tense and the scent of his stinky, expensive cologne brought to mind nights with him she wished she could forget. "Will I be seeing you at Violet's wedding? It's the event of the year, I hear. I can't believe she's flying all the guests to Dublin for it. And renting out a castle! It's wild. Maybe I should've dated her instead of you." He chuckled and she curled her hands into fists at her sides.

"I am going," she said with a bright smile she hoped didn't betray her anxiety over the upcoming trip. "I'm one of her bridesmaids."

"Are you going alone?" Quentin cocked his head in a sympathetically curious way that made her hackles rise.

Why would he assume she was going alone? They'd been apart for two years. He'd moved on. Surely she could've found someone to replace him by now. She hadn't, but she could've. "No. I'm not going alone. I'm bringing my boyfriend."

The minute the words passed her lips she regretted them. Why had she said that? Why? He mentions a fiancée and she loses her damn mind. She didn't have a boyfriend. She hadn't even committed to a houseplant. How was she supposed to produce a boyfriend in a couple days before the trip?

Quentin's eyes narrowed in disbelief. "Oh, really? I hadn't heard you were dating anyone lately."

Harper was surprised that he'd been paying attention. "I've learned to keep my private life private," she snapped. After their messy, public breakup, it had been another lesson hard learned. She hadn't even considered dating for six months after they'd ended due to the trauma of the whole thing.

"Well, who's the lucky guy? Do I know him? I look forward to meeting him at the wedding."

A name. She needed a name. Harper's mind went

completely blank. Looking around the department store, her gaze fell on Sebastian as he perused a nearby display of dress loafers.

"You can meet him now. Sebastian, honey, could you come over here for a minute? I'd like you to meet someone."

Sebastian arched his brow inquisitively at Harper as she mouthed the word "please" silently to him. He wandered over to where she was standing. "Yes, *dear*?"

"Sebastian, this is my ex, Quentin Stuart. I've mentioned him, haven't I? Anyway, I was just telling him about the two of us going to Ireland for Violet and Aidan's wedding."

Quentin stuck out his hand to Sebastian. "Nice to meet you, Sebastian…?"

"West. Sebastian West." He shook Quentin's hand and quickly pulled his away.

"Sebastian West as in BioTech?"

"Actually, yes."

Harper didn't recognize the name of the company, but then again she didn't know much about Sebastian because they weren't really dating. She remembered a brief discussion at a party about him working in medical supplies and how he didn't get out very much. She'd figured he'd sold wheelchairs and hospital beds or something. Maybe she'd been wrong. Quentin wasn't the type to waste brain power on remembering things that didn't impress him.

"Wow, Harper. Quite the catch you've got in this one." An uncomfortable expression flickered across his face and quickly disappeared. "Well, I've got to run. I was on my way to meet Josie and I'm already late. I'll see you two lovebirds on the plane to Dublin. I look forward to speaking with you some more, Sebastian."

Harper watched Quentin walk out of the store. Once he was gone, her face dropped into her hands. She just knew she was bright red with embarrassment. "I am so sorry," she muttered through her fingers.

Sebastian surprised her by laughing. "Want to tell me what that was all about?"

She peeked through her hands at him. "Um... Quentin is my ex. It was a messy breakup, but we still hang in the same social circles from time to time. When he asked about my date for the wedding we have coming up, I panicked. I told him you were my boyfriend. It's a long story. I shouldn't have dragged you into that, but he put me on the spot and you were standing right there." She gestured toward the display and shook her head. "I'm an ass."

"I doubt that," Sebastian said, a twinkle of laughter still in his dark brown eyes.

"No, I am. I've made the whole thing ten times worse because now I'm going to show up at the wedding without you and he's going to know I lied. And I just know he's going to show up with his beautiful, new fiancée and I'm going to feel even more like crap than I already do."

Harper knew she should've just owned that she was single. How bad would that have been? To just state proudly that she'd been dating and not interested in settling down or settling on the wrong guy. She was almost thirty, but that was hardly the end of the world. In fact, *her* thirtieth birthday couldn't come soon enough. It brought a twenty-eight-million-dollar payout with it that she was desperate to get her hands on.

"Don't worry about what he thinks," Sebastian said. "He seems like a schmuck."

"I'm no good at the boyfriend thing. I have questionable taste in men," Harper admitted. "It's probably better that I just make up boyfriends instead of finding another real one."

Sebastian nodded awkwardly. "I'm glad to help. Well, I hope the wedding goes well for you."

"Thanks." She watched him leave. But with every step he took, the more panicked she became. She had no easy way of contacting this guy once he walked out the door. She didn't want to let him get away quite yet for reasons she wasn't ready to think about. "Sebastian?" she nearly shouted before he got out of earshot.

He stopped and turned back to her. "Yes?"

"How would you like to go on an all-expenses-paid trip to Ireland?"

Two

Sebastian didn't know what to say. He'd never had a woman offer him a vacation, much less a woman he hardly knew. Actually he didn't have women offer him much of anything. It was impossible when he never left the lab. The only woman he was ever around on a daily basis was his assistant, Virginia, who was in her late fifties and married.

"Um, run that by me again?"

Harper closed the gap between them with an apologetic smile on her face and a sultry sway of her hips. So many of her features were almost masculine in a way, with piercing eyes, sharp cheekbones and an aquiline nose, but there was nothing masculine about her. Her dark brows were arched delicately over eyes that were like the stormy seas off Maine where he was born.

He imagined a similar maelstrom was stirring inside

her to make an offer like that to a complete stranger. Surely she could find a romantic interest if she wanted one. But he was willing to say yes to almost anything she offered when she looked at him that way.

"My friends are getting married in Ireland next weekend. They're flying everyone there, plus putting all the guests up in a castle that's been converted into a hotel. It wouldn't cost you anything to go but some leave from work. I'm not sure what your boss is like, since this is short notice, but I was hoping you would be interested."

"In going to Ireland?"

She nodded. "With me. As my boyfriend. I just introduced you to Quentin as my boyfriend and said you were going, so he's going to expect you to be there."

His brow furrowed. Her boyfriend. For a week. In Ireland. What could go wrong? Absolutely everything. Pretending to be her lover could be complicated. But what could go right? His gaze raked over her tall, lean figure with appreciation. Everything could go very right, too.

Wait—*crap*—he wasn't supposed to be "active." Just his damn luck. "Just to be clear—are you wanting or expecting you and me to…um…"

"No!" Harper was quick to answer with wide eyes. "I mean, not for real. We'd have to pretend to be a couple around everyone else—kiss, be affectionate, you know. But when we're alone, I promise it's strictly hands off. I'm not that hard up. I just can't go to this thing alone. Not after seeing Quentin and finding out he's engaged. I just can't."

Sebastian blinked his eyes a few times and tried to mask some of his disappointment. He wasn't sure if he could stand being around her, touching her in public and then just flipping the switch when they were alone. The doctor wanted him to, but he wasn't the best at following doctor's orders.

This day had done well to throw him off his game. First, getting locked out at work with mandatory vacation and now this. A beautiful woman wanted him to travel with her to Ireland for free and pretend to be her lover. That just wasn't business as usual for him. He wasn't entirely sure what to say to her. It seemed foolish to say yes and downright stupid to say no.

"I'll pay you two thousand dollars to go. It's all the money I have in my savings account," Harper added, sweetening the pot as she seemed to sense his hesitation.

She was serious. Her insecurity struck him as odd considering how confident and put together she seemed. He wasn't sure why this was so important to her. There must be more to the situation with her ex than she was telling. "Aren't your friends going to wonder where I came from? You've never spoken about me before and suddenly I'm your wedding date?"

Harper waved away his concern. "I'll take care of that. My friends have been so wrapped up in their own lives lately they'd probably not notice if I did have a boyfriend. They certainly haven't mentioned that I don't have one."

"And why is that?" Sebastian couldn't stop himself from asking. But if he was going to pretend to be her boyfriend, he needed to know if there was something about her that repelled men. From where he was standing, he didn't see a thing wrong with her. She was beautiful, well-spoken, poised and polished. Aside from the slight hint of desperation in her voice, she seemed like quite the catch. There had to be something wrong with her.

She shrugged and sort of fidgeted before responding, showing the first sign of vulnerability, which he was glad to see. "Like I said, I don't have the best taste in men. Things haven't worked out with anyone I've been attracted to since Quentin and I broke up."

"You can't find a decent man to go to dinner with you, but you trust me enough to travel across the ocean with you, share a bedroom and make out in front of your friends?" There was a flaw in her logic here. "I could be crazy. Or a criminal. Or married. I could attack you in your sleep or steal your jewelry. The possibilities are endless."

Harper scoffed at his trepidations. "Honestly, I take that risk on every date I go on in this town. Have you seen the guys on Tinder lately? No…you probably haven't." She chuckled. "I know you have a job, you smell nice, you're handsome and you went along with my lie just now, so you're easygoing. You're already a head and shoulders over every date I've had in the last six months. If you don't want to go, or can't, just say so. But don't turn it down because you're concerned about my blatant disregard for my own welfare or poor sense of judgment. My friends are already well aware of that flaw in my character."

"No, I can go. As of this morning my schedule is amazingly wide open for the next two weeks." That was an understatement. But was this what he should spend his time doing? He didn't exactly have a more tempting offer.

"Do you find me physically repulsive?"

Sebastian swallowed hard. "Not at all. To the contrary, you're the most beautiful woman I've laid eyes on in a very long time."

Harper's eyes widened a touch at his answer, but she quickly recovered with a sly smile curling her lips. It must have boosted her confidence because she moved a step closer to him, closing the gap until they were nearly touching. "Do you think you'd have trouble pretending to be my lover? Or have a problem kissing me?"

Every muscle in Sebastian's body tightened as she spoke. The warmth of her body and the scent of her so close caused an instant physical reaction that would answer any of her questions if she bothered to notice. He balled his hands into fists at his sides to keep from reaching for her. He'd craved the sensation of touching her again since the moment he'd let her go after the collision.

He shook his head stiffly. "No. I think I can manage that."

Harper's gaze never left his. "Okay, great. Are you opposed to a free trip to Europe? You have a passport, right?"

"I have a passport, yes." It had no stamps in it, but he had one. Finn did most of the travel around the world, schmoozing on behalf of their company. Sebastian kept his nose in his paperwork and schematics, but Finn had made him get a passport anyway.

"Okay. Then I see no reason why you shouldn't say yes."

Neither did he. Why was he making this so hard?

It really was a simple thing. He had no reason not to go. All he had to do was walk around Ireland with this stunning woman on his arm. He had no intention of taking her money, but a trip would be a nice distraction without any work on his plate for the next few weeks. What else was he going to do? Finn was right that he could help more people healthy than dead, but taking a break was hard for him. Being a couple thousand miles from his work would make it easier.

"When do you leave for the wedding?"

"Monday afternoon."

"It's Friday morning. Three days? Are you serious? Won't your friend think it odd that you're suddenly adding a guest to her wedding on such short notice?"

"Not really. I RSVP'd for two. I just needed to find my plus one."

"You're cutting it awfully close. Desperate?"

"I prefer to think of it as optimistic."

"Three days…" he repeated. Something about this whole situation struck him as insane, but there was a fine line between insanity and genius.

"So does your silent resignation mean you're at least considering coming with me?" Harper grinned wide, her whole expression lighting up with excitement.

It was hard for him to turn her down when she looked at him like that. He wanted her to keep looking at him that way for as long as possible. "Well, yes, I am. I'm just not sure I'll make a very good boyfriend, fake or otherwise. I'm kinda out of practice."

"I'm not worried about that." Harper leaned into him and wrapped her arms around his neck in an unexpectedly intimate way. His whole body stiffened as she pressed against him. "You know what they say."

Sebastian took a deep breath and tried to wish away the sudden rush of desire that coursed through his veins as she stood close. It seemed wrong to react like this to a woman he'd just met, despite how easily she was able to coax it out of him. "What's th-that?" He stuttered in his response, something he hadn't done since elementary school. She had managed to get under his skin so quickly.

"Practice makes perfect."

He nodded. "I've heard that."

Harper frowned, lowered her arms and looked down to where his hands were tensely curled at his sides. She took them in her own and moved each one to rest at the curve of her hips. "Relax, Sebastian. I'm not going to bite. We've got to be a lot more comfortable touching each other if we're going to convince anyone we're really together."

He splayed his fingers across her denim-clad hips and pressed the tips into the ample flesh there. With her so close, he wanted to lean down and kiss her. Her full, pouting lips and wide, innocent eyes seemed to plead for it. Indulging seemed like the natural thing to do. She felt good against him. Perhaps too good for the middle of Neiman Marcus. There was definitely not going to be a problem faking attraction with Harper. The problem would be pretending that the attraction wasn't real when no one was watching.

"I'll go," he blurted out, almost surprising himself.

Harper stiffened in his arms, looking up at him with a smile that was hesitant to believe him. "Are you serious?"

Sebastian nodded. "Yes, I'm serious. I'll go to Ireland with you as your fake boyfriend."

With a squeal of excitement, Harper hugged him tight. Before he could prepare himself, she pressed her mouth to his. He was certain it was supposed to be a quick, thank-you peck, but once their lips touched, there was no pulling away.

Sebastian wasn't imagining the palpable sexual energy between them. The way Harper curved against his body and opened her mouth to him was proof of that. He wanted to take it further, to see how powerful their connection really was, but this was neither the time nor the place, so he pulled away while he still could.

Harper lingered close, a rosy flush highlighting her cheeks. "Listen, I've got to go. Would you care to walk me to my apartment? I don't live far."

"I can't." He wanted to—quite badly—but he got the feeling it was an invitation better declined at the moment if they were going to spend the next week together. Things could get weird before they even left.

Harper pulled away just enough to let a chill of air rush in where the heat of her body had been. "Why not?"

He picked up the wallet he'd set down on a display when he'd spoken with Quentin. "I still have to buy this."

A light of amusement lit her eyes. "You're so literal. I can wait while you check out."

It would be so easy to say yes. He took a deep breath and thought up another valid reason. "I also have some things to take care of if I'm going with you on Monday."

Harper pouted for a moment before she nodded and covered her disappointment with a smile. "Okay. Well, I'm going out with my girlfriends tomorrow, but how about we get together on Sunday night? We can get to know each other a little better before we get on the plane."

"At your apartment?"

"A bar is probably a better idea. Being you're a stranger and all, right?"

He breathed a sigh of relief. He could avoid temptation in a bar. Once they got to Ireland, he wasn't so sure. "That sounds good."

"Give me your phone."

Sebastian handed over his cell phone and Harper put her information into his contacts.

"Text me so I have your information, too. We'll get together Sunday."

With a smile and a wave, Harper handed over his phone and disappeared from the store. Sebastian watched her walk away and, with every step she took, was more and more convinced that he was making a big mistake.

"I know that we're leaving Monday and I should probably be packing or getting ready, but I really needed one last girls' night before we go." Violet eased back into the sofa cushions with a large glass of wine in her hand. "Why didn't any of you tell me how stressful weddings could be?"

"Well, Oliver and I eloped, so it wasn't stressful at all," Lucy said. "Besides, in the end it's just a party. Now, nine-month-old twins…that's stressful."

Harper chuckled at her new sister-in-law's observation. The twins—Alice and Christian—were little darlings, but the minute they started walking, she got the feeling they would be tiny tornadoes of destruction. Especially Alice. She was a little spitfire, like her namesake, their great-great-aunt Alice.

"No one said you had to fly all your friends and family halfway around the world to get married," Harper pointed out, taking a sip of her wine. "You could've had a ridiculously expensive and over-the-top affair here in Manhattan like Emma did."

Emma came into the room with a frown pulling down the corners of her flawlessly painted rose lips. "My wedding was not over the top. It was small and tasteful."

Harper arched an eyebrow and laughed. "You may have only had thirty people there, but I'd hardly classify it as small and tasteful."

"I had a beautiful reception."

"You had an ice vodka luge," Harper challenged.

Emma twisted her lips and sighed. "That was Jonah's thing. He insisted." She settled beside Violet on the couch. "And it would've been ten times bigger if my mother'd had her way. You saw what she did with my baby shower. But seriously, don't stress too badly about the wedding, Vi. It's in Ireland. In a castle! It will be beautiful, I promise."

"It will," Lucy chimed in. "You've got an amazing wedding planner who has it under control. The best in the city. All you need to do is show up and marry the love of your life. That's easy."

Violet smiled. "You're right. Aidan has told me the same thing a dozen times. I just can't stop stressing out about every little detail. In a week from today I'll be Mrs. Aidan Murphy! Have I forgotten something?"

"If you have, it doesn't really matter. As long as both of you show up, say I do and sign your license with a qualified officiant, you'll be married at the end of the day. Everything else is just details," Emma said.

Violet nodded. "You're right. I know you're right. I just need to say it until I believe it. What about you guys? Are you packed and ready to leave yet?"

The women around the coffee table nodded. "Everything is ready. Just a few more things to throw in the luggage before we go. We're leaving the twins with Oliver's dad," Lucy said. "That's the biggest stressor for me. I haven't been away from them since they were born, but there's no way I'm flying overseas with twins at that age.

"Knox is older than the twins, so I'm hoping he does okay on the flight. It will be his first," Violet explained. "I couldn't leave him behind, though. It seems wrong to marry his father without having him there."

"Of course. I'm sure he'll do great. Georgette is staying with my parents, but they'll have her nanny with them, so I'm not worried." Emma turned to Harper. "What about you? Are you ready to go? At least you don't have men and kids to wrangle before the trip. I almost forget what it's like to just have to worry about myself."

"Yep," Harper said. She took a deep breath and prepared herself to tell the story she'd come up with after talking to Sebastian. Her intention was to tell them as little as possible, but she knew she had to fill the girls in on her new beau before the trip. They were the only ones who would really care. If she sold the story to them, everyone else would take it at face value.

Including Quentin. Hopefully. If he didn't buy it, there was no point in continuing the ruse. This whole ridiculous scheme was designed with the sole purpose of making him believe she had someone in her life. That she wasn't pathetically single and still pining for him. Because she was anything but pining. She was glad to have Quentin out of her life. He was just too egomaniacal to see her single status as anything other than a reflection of her wishing they were still together.

Selling it to her friends wouldn't be so easy, though.

"I've got the dress, the passport and…uh…the boyfriend all ready to go." She said the words quickly and then waited for the inevitable response.

Emma, Violet and Lucy all paused as anticipated and turned to look at her. The questions came too fast and furiously for her to respond to any of them.

"What?"

"Your boyfriend?"

"Am I missing something, here?"

Harper winced and nodded when they finally quieted down. "Yeah, um, his name is Sebastian." She got up to refill her wine and stall the conversation a moment. She was going to need some alcohol to get through this conversation. When she came back into the room from the kitchen, the girls were sitting frozen in place with expectant looks on their faces. "He's the guy I've been seeing for a few months."

"Months?" Violet wailed. "You've been seeing a guy for *months* and didn't think to mention it to us?"

"You guys have all been busy with your own lives. Babies, weddings…" Harper explained. "And, to be honest, I didn't want to jinx it. It wasn't that serious at first and I got tired of mentioning guys to you all and then we didn't get past the third date. Things were going well, so I wasn't ready to talk about him yet. Just in case."

"And now you're ready to talk? 'Cause you're sure as hell going to give us every detail," Lucy sassed.

Harper shrugged. Not really, but the time had come to spill some information if she was going to pull this off. "I guess I have to if I want to bring him on the trip."

"I noticed you RSVP'd for two, but you left off the guest's name," Violet said. "I was wondering what that meant."

"Yeah, I was hopeful that things would work out for him to come," Harper continued to lie, noting that after pretending she had money for a decade, pretending to have a boyfriend wasn't as hard as she'd thought it would be. "But if it fell apart between us, I thought I might bring a friend. Or no one. But things are great and so Sebastian is coming. I'll give you his information to add to the travel manifest."

"I'm eager to meet him," Emma said. "And intrigued. You haven't really had much luck dating since you and Quentin broke up. Where did you two meet? He's not one of your Tinder finds, is he?"

"Oh, no. Those were a mess. I actually met Sebastian at one of the hospital fund-raisers this winter. The one raising money for the orthopedics center, I think." That, at least, wasn't a lie. They had met there. They just hadn't started dating. "He works with medical equipment. He can tell you more about all that. Anyway, we hit it off and he asked me to dinner. Things have just sort of progressed from there."

"Wait," Violet said, sitting at attention on the sofa. "We were all at that fund-raiser. Do we know him? Sebastian who?"

"Sebastian West." Harper was suddenly nervous that maybe they did know him. She and Sebastian hadn't gotten together to talk yet, so she ran the risk of getting caught not knowing something obvious about him if any of the girls knew who he was. Quentin had recognized his name and company, so it was a possibility.

Thankfully none of them perked up at hearing his full name. "I doubt any of you know him. He spends more time working than socializing. He's super smart. I'm excited for you all to meet him." She grinned wide and hoped she was selling her story.

"We're all excited," Violet echoed as her eyes narrowed at Harper in suspicion. "I can't wait for Monday."

Harper took a large sip of her wine and nodded with feigned enthusiasm. "Me neither."

Three

Sunday evening Sebastian arrived at the bar a full fifteen minutes before he was supposed to meet Harper. He wasn't particularly anxious about their meeting, but he couldn't stand just sitting around his apartment any longer. He'd sat there for the last two days trying to fill the hours. Without work, he found he had far too many minutes on his hands.

He'd spent as long as he could packing and preparing for the trip. He'd taken his clothes and his tuxedo to the cleaner. He'd carefully collected his toiletries and underthings, but that had taken only a few hours out of his newfound free time.

Sebastian had tried reading a book. He'd watched some television. Both had bored him after a short while. By Sunday afternoon he'd had nothing to do but pace around his apartment and wish away the hours. He wasn't sure how he'd get through the next two weeks if he hadn't met Harper and had this trip to Ireland fall into his lap. He might just go insane. How was that supposed to improve his health? Mentally weak but physically strong? What good was that?

When his watch showed it was almost time to meet Harper, he'd rushed out the door. He'd taken a table in a quiet corner, ordered himself a gin and tonic with lime—ignoring doctor's orders—and awaited her arrival with his notebook open to read over some notes. He carried it almost everywhere he went, writing down ideas and schematics when they popped into his head. He'd learned the hard way that he could lose the spark of inspiration if he didn't immediately capture it.

This way he was still waiting, but at least he was out of the house and potentially doing something productive in the meantime. Thankfully, Harper showed up a few minutes later. She was looking attractive and fashionable once again with layered lace tops and a long sweater over skinny jeans. Today her dark hair was pulled up into a bun, highlighting the line of her neck and her dangly earrings.

Sebastian was once again struck by the fact that this woman should be able to find a boyfriend easily. He didn't understand why he was even there pretending to be one. Then again, the same thing could probably be said of him. Life was complicated sometimes.

"Thanks for coming. And thanks for doing all of this," she said as she settled into her chair across from him.

"No problem. Would you like a drink?"

"Just water for me," she said with a polite smile. It surprised him. A glass of wine or a martini seemed far more her speed. He didn't question it, however, and waved down the bartender for her water.

"Are you packed and ready to go?" she asked.

"Mostly. What about you?"

"The same. I feel like I'm not ready, although I can't imagine what I haven't packed yet."

"Don't forget the slinky lingerie," Sebastian said. The sudden image of Harper wearing some kind of silk-and-lace chemise came to his mind and made him immediately regret his words. He didn't need that vision haunting him over their next week together.

"What?" Harper's eyes were suddenly wide with concern.

"It was a joke," Sebastian soothed. And that's what he'd intended it to be, even if a part of him wouldn't mind if she threw a nice piece or two in there.

"Oh," she said, visibly relaxing. Apparently the idea of being his girlfriend for real was not nearly as appealing to her as it was in his own mind. "Yeah, no, I'm packing the ugliest pajamas I've got."

"Flannel footie pajamas with a zip front?" he asked.

"Yep. I'll be dressed as a giant pug dog."

Interesting. "Trapdoor for convenience?"

"No, just a front zipper, but they do have a tail and a hood with puppy ears and a nose I can pull up."

"Excellent. Since pugs aren't my thing, I'm sure the sight of you in that dog outfit will squelch any misplaced attraction that might arise between us."

"Perhaps I should buy you one, too. I saw one that was basically a poop emoji costume."

"Not Spider-Man or Deadpool? You went straight for the poop emoji?"

"Yeah, sorry."

They both laughed for a few moments and the tension dissipated between them. Sebastian was relieved. He didn't want either of them to be uncomfortable. It would make the week ten times longer than it would be already.

"So tell me everything I should know about you," Harper began. "I'm your girlfriend, after all, so I need to know all the important things."

Sebastian tried not to wince at the thought of talking about himself. He hated doing that. He tried to think of what he would share with someone if he were really dating them, but he found he didn't know the answer to that, either. "I'm from Maine. A small coastal town called Rockport, specifically. I went to MIT. Technically, I'm a mechanical engineer, but I've branched out quite a bit after college."

"I thought you worked for a medical supply company."

Sebastian frowned. That was probably his fault. He liked to keep the details of his work vague. "Not exactly. BioTech is a medical research and development company. My partner Finn and I develop new medical technology."

"Your partner? You mean you don't just work there?"

"Eh, no. We started the company together out of college. I own it."

Harper frowned, wrinkles creasing her forehead. "Are you serious? I offered you every penny I had in savings to go on this trip and you're the CEO of a company? You probably make more in an afternoon than I do in a paycheck."

Sebastian held up his finger in protest. "You offered

me the money. I never said I would actually take it. And I'm not going to, of course."

"So you're rich. Why didn't you say something? Like when Quentin asked about your company?"

At that, Sebastian shrugged. "I'm not the kind to flaunt it. Finn is the face of the company. I'm the mad scientist behind the scenes. I'm happy with the anonymity. I've seen how being well-known and wealthy has complicated his love life and I'm not interested in that."

"In a love life?" Harper asked with an arched brow.

"In a *complicated* love life. Or, hell, maybe a regular one. I work too much for any type of relationship to succeed."

"But you're going to drop everything and go with me on a trip to Ireland on short notice?"

Sebastian sat back in his chair and sighed. It would be easy to tell her that he'd had a heart attack and was on mandatory vacation, but he didn't want to. He didn't like people knowing his business, especially when it changed how they perceived him. Whether it was knowing he was rich, or sick, or used to be poor… it didn't matter. He liked private things to stay private. "When you're the boss, you can do what you want," he responded instead.

She shook her head. "I can't believe you didn't say anything until just now. What if I hadn't asked? Would you have waited until someone recognized you on the plane and I looked like a fool for not knowing my boyfriend is a millionaire?"

"Of course not! I would've told you. And you're one to point fingers, Harper. You're keeping plenty of secrets yourself."

She straightened in her chair and narrowed her gaze at him. "What is that supposed to mean?"

"I saw you walk out of Neiman Marcus with your friends. Then you ditched them and came back ten minutes later to return everything you'd bought. What is that about? It's not buyer's remorse, I'm pretty certain."

Harper's lips twisted in thought as she considered her answer. "I'm trying to save money."

Sebastian looked at her with a pointed expression on his face. There was more to it than just frugality, of that he was sure. He'd done his research since they'd met. Her family owned Orion Computers. She lived in a really nice apartment on the Upper East Side. But she only had two grand in her savings account? That didn't add up in his mind.

His silence prompted her to keep talking. "I'm having a bit of a cash flow shortage. I'm embarrassed about it, so I haven't told anyone, even my friends and family. Until I get things straightened out, I'm trying to be smart about my money, but I have to keep up appearances."

"Like blowing a fortune on designer clothes and then immediately returning them?"

"Yes."

"Don't they notice you never wear them after you buy them?"

She shook her head. "You need a map to get through my closet. Things disappear in there, never to resurface."

Sebastian nodded thoughtfully. "Sounds like a complicated charade to keep up. Pretending to have a boyfriend should be a piece of cake."

"Well, thankfully it's a short-term thing. I should be

back on my feet soon and then no one needs to know I lied about it. And as for you and me…well, I'm sure we will have a sad, but not unexpected, breakup not long after we get back from the trip. Not so soon as to be suspicious, but we can't wait too long or people might start inviting us to things as a couple here in town."

"Sounds tragic. I'm already sad."

Harper looked at him with a smile. "I'm enjoying your sarcastic sense of humor. We might actually be able to pull this off."

"I think so, too. Of course, over time I think you're going to become too clingy for me and we're going to want different things from our relationship."

She groaned. "Ugh. You sound like Quentin. Don't do that or we'll have to just break up now."

Sebastian laughed. "So since we're going to be around that guy, should I know what happened between you two?"

Harper winced at the thought. "That is a story that would require something stronger than water to talk about."

"A cocktail then? My treat," Sebastian added. He waved over the bartender. It wasn't until then that it occurred to him she might be drinking water out of necessity, not desire.

"That's sweet of you. A Cosmo, please."

Once the man returned with the dark pink beverage, Harper took a sip and sighed. "We were together for three years and we've been broken up for two. We met at a party and we really seemed to hit it off. Things went well between us, but I noticed that it didn't seem to be going anywhere. We'd stalled out at the point where most people take the next step."

"He didn't want anything serious?"

"I thought we were already serious, but I suppose that was my mistake. I was thinking we were on track to get engaged, moving in together...do all the things that other couples around me were doing. But he was always working. Or said he was. He's an attorney and kept insisting he had to put in the long hours if he was going to make partner. I thought it was because he wanted to build a solid future for us, but the truth was that he was perfectly content where we were."

"He was seeing other women."

"Bingo. While I was officially his girlfriend in the public eye, I found out there were three of us he was keeping on the hook. He used long hours at work as his excuse to run around town with different women, and I didn't even question it. I don't know if he couldn't decide and thought that he'd eventually know which one he wanted, or if he just liked keeping that many balls up in the air at once. But eventually I found out about the others and broke it off. When I confronted him, all he said was that he just wasn't ready for a commitment."

Sebastian frowned. "He told you the other day that he's engaged now, didn't he?"

Harper's posture deflated slightly in her chair and he found he hated that. He wanted to punch Quentin in the face for taking such a beautiful, confident woman and leaving her broken.

"Yes," she said softly. "He's bringing her on the trip. You see why I can't go alone? I just can't face him and his fiancée in the state I am in. I'm almost thirty. I'm happy with my life on most days, but I have to admit that I'm not at all where I expected to be at this point.

I'm sure everyone else looks at me and thinks I'm the sad, single one in the group."

Sebastian understood. He knew what it was like to be judged by people. While Harper had worked hard to keep up appearances, he'd simply buried his head in his research and tried to block out the rest of the world. It had served him pretty well. Eventually, though, he'd known his avoidance mechanisms would fall apart. His had fallen apart when he'd hit the floor in cardiac arrest. Hers might all come crashing down when her delicately structured pyramid of falsehoods took a hit. He hoped he wouldn't be the reason it fell.

"I will strive to be the imaginary boyfriend you've always dreamed of having someday."

"You go up first," Sebastian said as they stood on the tarmac together. "I prefer to sit in the aisle seat if you don't mind."

Harper nodded and climbed the steps ahead of him to board the private plane. The minute she stepped on and turned the corner, she realized the Boeing Business Jet that Violet's father, Loukas Niarchos, had chartered for the flight wasn't going to be like any plane she'd been on before. Instead of a first-class cabin, she found herself walking through a lounge with a bar, seating areas with couches and swivel chairs, flat-panel televisions and a variety of tables. To the left there was a doorway leading to an executive office where she could see Loukas already chatting on the phone, his laptop open.

A flight attendant greeted them with a smile and directed them through the lounge into the next room to the right. There they found what could be either a conference room or a dining table that sat twenty for a meal. Each chair was plush camel-colored leather with a seat belt if it was necessary. Harper got the feeling the kind of people who chartered flights on this plane wouldn't tolerate turbulence.

"This is like being on Air Force One," Sebastian muttered into her ear as they walked through a narrow hallway past a fully appointed bedroom suite, two full-size bathrooms with showers, and a galley kitchen currently manned by two more smiling flight attendants. "Is this how you're used to traveling?"

Harper shook her head. "No. I'm used to boring old first class unless I'm traveling with family on the Orion corporate jet. That's nice, but it only seats eight. And there's no bedroom. Or office. Or cocktail lounge. My family is normal rich, not filthy rich."

Sebastian chuckled and nudged her forward. "Good. I don't think I could handle a filthy-rich girlfriend. I'm glad this is a first for us both."

At that point, the plane finally opened up into a traditional seating area. Appointed like a large, first-class cabin, there were six seats in each row. They were in sets of two, divided by two wide aisles. Each seat had its own television screen, blanket, pillow, and controls that allowed its occupant to lay fully flat for sleeping on the overnight flight. A flute of champagne and a chocolate-covered strawberry stenciled with the letters *V&A* in edible gold awaited each guest at their seat as well as a handwritten card in calligraphy with each person's name.

Violet was certainly out to throw a memorable wedding, if nothing else.

They'd been assigned row thirteen of sixteen, seats

A and B, so she made her way down the right aisle through the crowd of familiar faces. They were nearly the last to board, so the area was bustling with activity as guests settled in. Quentin hadn't been kidding when he'd said this wedding was the event of the year. People salivated over the idea of receiving a coveted invitation, but the guest list had been kept down to less than a hundred by virtue of the plane and the wedding venue.

Even then, Harper still knew almost everyone on the plane. A few friends and family of Violet's fiancé, Aidan, were unfamiliar to her, but there were far more of Violet's circle than anyone. She smiled and waved politely as she pressed on, even when she saw Quentin in the back row on the far left. He was sitting beside an attractive brunette who seemed a little young for him, but Harper was trying not to let her bitterness color her opinion.

"Here we go," she said as she stopped at their row. Emma and Jonah were seated across the aisle from them in the center section, and Harper could see Emma was already heavily appraising Sebastian from her seat. She tried not to focus on that, instead stowing her bag and her coat in the overhead bin to clear the aisle for others to board.

"Introductions!" Emma said before Harper could even slide into the row to sit.

She pasted on a bright smile and turned their way. "Sebastian, these are my good friends Jonah and Emma Flynn. I work for Jonah's gaming software company, FlynnSoft. You guys, this is my boyfriend, Sebastian West."

Jonah stuck out his hand and the two men exchanged a firm handshake. "Good to meet you both," Sebastian said. "Harper has told me how much she enjoys her job at FlynnSoft. I'm sure that reflects well on you, Jonah."

She tried not to look impressed and instead turned toward her seat. It wasn't until that moment that she noticed a small, white envelope on the window seat. She picked the envelope up and settled in so Sebastian could take his place at her side. She looked around, wondering who might've put it on her seat, but no one seemed to be looking or paying any attention to her. There weren't envelopes like this one on the other seats. Just one for her, with her name written on the front in nondescript block letters.

While Sebastian put his bag in the overhead bin, Harper opened the envelope and pulled out the single page inside. It was handwritten, and relatively short, but it delivered a huge impact.

I know your little secret. If you don't want everyone to find out the truth and risk your big inheritance, you'll do exactly what I say. Once we arrive in Ireland, you'll go to the bank and withdraw a hundred thousand dollars. Then you'll leave it in an envelope at the front desk of the hotel for "B. Mayler" by dinnertime tomorrow. Miss the deadline and I'm going to make a big problem for you, Harper.

She read the words a dozen times, trying to make sense of it all, but there was no way to make sense of what she was seeing. Her heart was pounding in her ears, deafening her to anything but the sound of her internal panic. The fantastic plane and everyone on it faded into the background.

This was blackmail. She was being blackmailed.

How was that even possible?

Harper had been so careful about her secret. Aside from sharing some of it with Sebastian yesterday, no one, not her closest friends or family, knew the truth. Not even her brother or father knew about her financial difficulties. She'd kept it quiet for over eight years, working hard to make ends meet until the next payment came and she didn't have to fake it any longer. Sebastian had been the first to question her curious behavior, and it hadn't seemed to hurt to share a little information with him considering her birthday was right around the corner.

But someone had found out her secret, and that was a big problem.

Her grandfather on her mother's side of the family had set up a thirty-million-dollar trust fund for both her and her brother when they were born. It included a two-million-dollar payment on their eighteenth birthdays followed by a twenty-eight-million-dollar payment on their thirtieth birthdays. Harper's thirtieth was only a few weeks away now. She could see the light at the end of the tunnel. She should be coasting to the finish line, but her foolish youthful behavior had put everything at risk.

After her father ran into financial troubles with his gold-digging second wife, her grandfather had added a new provision to the grandchildren's trusts—if it was discovered that they had been financially irresponsible with their first payments, there would be no second payment. Ever-responsible Oliver had had no problem managing his money and had made his own fortune many times over. He hardly needed the second payment by the time his thirtieth birthday came around. But not Harper. By the time the provision was added, her frivolous lifestyle had already helped her blow through most of the first two million.

When she found out about the addendum, she'd realized she had to keep her situation a secret. Her grandfather couldn't find out or she'd risk the money she desperately needed. That second payment would put an end to her charade. She wouldn't have to eat ramen noodles for weeks to pay her massive building fee at the beginning of the year. She wouldn't have to return everything she bought and scour the thrift stores for designer finds to keep up her facade of a spoiled heiress. Harper wouldn't blow this new money—she wasn't a naive child any longer—but it would be nice not to have to pretend she had more than two grand in her savings account.

Thankfully that two thousand dollars she'd earmarked for Sebastian could stay put. It was all she had aside from her FlynnSoft 401K with its stiff withdrawal penalties. Where was she going to come up with a hundred thousand dollars by tomorrow? In a month, easy. But now…it was an impossible task.

"Are you okay?"

Harper quickly folded the letter closed and shoved it back into the envelope. She looked over at Sebastian, who had settled into his seat and buckled up. "I'm fine," she said. "Just reading over something."

"You look like the plane is about to crash," he noted. "You're white as a sheet. Since they haven't even closed the cabin door yet, I was concerned."

"Flying isn't my favorite thing," she lied, and slipped the note into her purse. "Even on a fancy jet like this.

My doctor gave me some pills and I hope to wake up in Ireland before I know it."

"Sleep? And miss a minute of this luxurious travel?" Sebastian picked up his crystal champagne flute. "Shall we toast before you slip into a drug-induced coma?"

Harper picked up her drink and fought to keep her hand from trembling with nerves. "What should we drink to?"

"To a safe, fun and *romantic* trip," he suggested with a knowing smile.

"I'll drink to that." She gently clinked her glass to his and downed the entire flute in one nervous gulp. Sebastian arched a curious eyebrow at her, but she ignored him. She needed some alcohol, stat, before that note sent her into hysterics.

Turning away from him, she fastened her seat belt, sat back and closed her eyes.

"You'll be fine," he soothed. "You're surrounded by friends and family. I'm here to hold your hand through the whole flight if you need me to. You don't have a thing to worry about."

Normally he would be right, and if her nerves were over flying, it might be helpful. But she couldn't feel safe and relax knowing that one of the people on this plane—one of her very own friends and family—was her blackmailer.

This was going to be a long trip.

Four

"What a great room!"

Harper followed Sebastian into their room at the hotel, grateful to finally be there. The flight itself had been uneventful once they'd taken off. She'd taken the pills with another glass of champagne—probably not the best idea—and woken when the wheels touched down in Dublin. Even if she'd had the money to pay her blackmailer, she hadn't had the chance to stop at a bank and get it. Two chartered luxury buses had picked them up at the airport and transported everyone on the nearly three-hour drive through the Irish countryside to their final destination of Markree Castle. The castle and its sprawling grounds had been renovated into a hotel and the entire location had been rented to house their group and host the wedding and reception.

Sebastian had looked out the window on the bus,

contentedly taking in the lush green landscape as it went by, but Harper hadn't been able to enjoy it. Every person who'd passed by her was run through a mental checklist of potential guilt or innocence. She supposed that was the most unnerving part of it all. This wasn't just some random internet criminal who'd dug up some dirt and tried to make a dime off her. It was someone she knew. Someone she trusted. She couldn't quite wrap her head around that.

Like she didn't already have enough to worry about on this trip. She eyeballed Sebastian as he sat on the bed and gave it a test bounce. It wasn't a large bed—a double perhaps—which would mean close quarters at night. Harper hadn't thought much about that when she'd concocted this plan. A lot of hotels in Europe had twin beds and that was what she'd expected. Just her luck that they'd end up with a room obviously appointed for lovers. Lovers who wanted to be close all the time.

She'd have to thank Violet for hooking her up, she thought drily.

The room was small but well done. There were towels twisted into swans in the bathroom, rose-scented bubble bath on the edge of the claw-foot tub, candles, lace curtains, red foil-wrapped heart chocolates on their pillows, a velvet love seat by the fireplace… Were this any other trip with any other man, Harper would be thrilled with the romantic vibe. It might help set the mood for their romantic ruse, but at the moment, pretending to have a boyfriend seemed pretty unimportant. Now she wished her only problem was being single.

As it was, it felt like the universe was just screwing with her.

"What's wrong with you?"

Harper turned toward Sebastian with a frown. "What do you mean?"

He watched her, stroking his dark goatee with thought. "I mean, you've been acting funny since we got on the plane to come here. I thought it was nerves, but it's been hours since we landed and you seem as distant as ever. We're in Ireland. Everyone thinks we're an adorable couple. You should be happy. What's going on?"

It was just her luck that her fake boyfriend would be so in tune with her emotions. Quentin wouldn't have noticed, but he was rarely concerned with anything but himself. She opened her mouth to tell him that she was fine, but his movement stopped her.

Getting up from the bed, he crossed the room and stood directly in front of her. He was close enough to reach out and touch. It took everything she had not to fall into his arms and let his strong embrace protect her from the outside world. But that felt a little too forward for their current situation.

Instead he stood close, without touching, looking deeply into her eyes. "And don't tell me it's nothing," he added. "My mother carried the weight of the world on her shoulders but would always insist that everything was fine. It was something then and it's something now. I know it when I see it."

Harper wanted to tell him. She needed to tell someone. Maybe he would know what to do, because she sure as hell didn't know how to handle this situation. She'd never been blackmailed before. Pulling away from him, she grabbed her purse off the entryway table and withdrew the small envelope from inside it. She handed it to Sebastian without a single word of explanation.

Sebastian's gaze flickered quickly over the note. By the time he was finished, his mouth had fallen into a deep frown of displeasure. Combined with his dark hair and eyes, something about his usual easygoing demeanor seemed to shift to almost wicked. Like she'd angered Bruce Banner. She almost expected his eyes to glow red with fury when he looked up at her. Instead she found them unexpectedly soft with concern. He was irate, but not with her.

"Where did this come from?" he asked, holding the note up.

"It was on my seat when we got on the plane. That's all I know." Harper wrapped her sweater tighter around her, as though it would help. She wished she had something more to go on, but she didn't. It was on generic white stationery and written with a block print text that anyone could do. There was nothing to give any kind of hint about who had left it there.

"Why didn't you say something to me?" he asked.

"When? When we were trapped on a plane for eight hours with eighty other people—one of whom was probably the blackmailer? They were likely watching me, waiting for my reaction to finding their little love note. So I didn't give them the satisfaction of panicking. I took my pills and went to sleep like it was nothing. But it's not nothing. I'm worried sick about this whole thing. Thankfully you're the only one to notice."

Sebastian looked over the note again before handing it back to her. His mouth tightened with irritation, highlighting the sharp, square lines of his jaw and the dark goatee that framed it. "So you suspect it's one of the wedding guests? Not the flight crew?"

Harper shrugged and tore her gaze from the tempting curve of his bottom lip. She wanted more than anything to focus on that. To lose herself in Sebastian's kiss and forget about the mess she was in. She got the feeling he wouldn't mind indulging her with a little distraction. But this wasn't the time. Blackmail was serious business.

"I'd never seen any of the crew before. We were one of the last couples to board, so almost any of the guests could've put it on my seat. As you've read, I'm supposed to leave the money at the front desk, so it has to be someone that's still here in Sligo with us. I'm sure the flight crew is back in Dublin."

She sank onto the bed, clutching the note in her hand. Where she hadn't allowed herself to really react on the flight, now, in the privacy of their hotel suite, she felt herself starting to emotionally unravel. "What am I going to do, Sebastian?" she asked with eyes squeezed tightly shut to trap the tears. She hated to cry.

She felt the bed sag beside her and Sebastian's comforting warmth against her side. "The way I see it, you've got three options. One, you pay the blackmail. That will keep your secret under wraps, but you're giving the blackmailer the upper hand. I don't know what you're being blackmailed for, but at any time they could demand more money to stay quiet. You'll never really be free of the blackmailer's hold on your life. But that's a risk that might be worth taking. Only you can answer that question."

She knew paying the blackmailer wasn't the best

choice, but it was the one she'd take if given the chance. Unfortunately that wasn't an option for her. "I couldn't pay it even if I wanted to. I told you before that I was in a tight spot financially. It's possible that given some time I could go to a bank and get a loan with my apartment for collateral. But they want it tonight. By dinnertime. That's just impossible, especially considering we're in the middle of a remote estate in the Irish countryside. Even in Dublin, I couldn't have pulled it off."

"Okay," Sebastian said after listening to her logic. "The second option would be to call the police. Blackmail is illegal. They could take prints off the card, perhaps leave a dummy package at the desk for the culprit to pick up and then arrest them. You'll run the risk of the secret being exposed in the process, but they'll get their punishment."

Harper shook her head. She didn't want cops involved. Not in this situation. It would be bad enough for her to lose her inheritance and for everyone to find out what she'd done. She didn't need her story being in the newspapers, too.

"What's option three?" she asked.

"Option three is to expose the secret yourself and take their power away."

She could do that, but it would be a twenty-eight-million-dollar decision. Just the thought made her stomach start to ache with dread. She was stuck between a rock and a hard place. "I… I can't. It will ruin everything I've worked so hard to achieve."

Harper felt Sebastian's arm wrap around her shoulders. She couldn't resist leaning into him and resting her head against his chest. It was soothing to listen to the beating of his heart and enjoy the warmth of his embrace. It had been a long time since she'd had someone in her life to hold her like this. To listen to her when she had worries on her mind. She knew she had been lonely, but she didn't realize how deeply she'd felt it until this moment.

"Harper," Sebastian said after a long silence with her in his arms. "I have to ask this. Whether or not you answer is up to you, but it's hard for me to help you when I don't know. What could you have done to be blackmailed for?"

She knew the question would come eventually. Harper dreaded having to explain her youthful stupidity to anyone, but for some reason it was worse to tell Sebastian. He was successful, like her brother. He never would've made the mistakes she'd made. But she needed to tell someone. To have one person on this trip she could trust. He was the only one she could eliminate as a suspect since he couldn't possibly have left the note on her seat.

Harper sighed heavily and buried her face into his chest to avoid speaking for a little while longer. She pressed her nose to his collar and breathed in the spicy scent of his cologne and his skin. It was easy to stay there and pretend that everything would be okay for a little while longer.

"I'm a spoiled little rich girl," she said at last.

"Tell me something I don't know," Sebastian responded unexpectedly.

Harper sat up sharply and frowned at him.

"I'm kidding," he said. "Please continue. I'm just trying to keep things light."

Harper slumped over and sighed. "My brother and I originally had trust funds set up for thirty million dollars each. When my mother died, my grandfather decided that, without her guidance, it might be better to break it into two payments. A small, two-million-dollar payment when we turned eighteen, followed by the rest when we turned thirty."

"Makes sense. An eighteen-year-old is more likely to blow all the money and have nothing to show for it."

"Exactly. And, basically, that's what I did. My father had given me everything I could ever want. When I went off to college, I continued to live that way, just on my own money for a change. When I started to run low, my father pitched in. But then he ran into his own financial problems and I was on my own."

"I don't hear anything that's blackmail worthy. Did you spend all the money on drugs or something?"

"Of course not! I spent it on shoes. Clothes. Trips. Makeup. Designer handbags. Expensive meals. Nonsense, really, but what I'd always been used to. And, no, nothing was criminal. Embarrassing, but not criminal. I went to Yale for a finance degree and yet I was a fool with my own money. No…the problem came after my father got a divorce. My grandfather was worried that our dad had set a bad example and added an additional requirement to the trust to keep us in line—if we blew the first payment, we wouldn't get the second."

"Does he know what you did?" Sebastian asked.

"No. Most of the money was long gone before he even added the stipulation, but I'd transferred the funds into my private accounts so no one had any insight into my finances. But someone has found out. And if I can't magically come up with a hundred grand, it's going to cost me a cool twenty-eight million instead."

* * *

Sebastian's blood was boiling. He was pretty sure his doctor wouldn't be too pleased that his relaxing vacation time had been overshadowed by drama of the worst kind. He could hear his pulse pounding in his ears as he marched down the stone hallway of the castle.

Harper was still in their room, spinning in circles and attempting to unpack her luggage. He'd stepped out to give her some privacy and to get a little air. The truth was that he didn't want her to know how angry he was over her whole situation. After her confession, she might mistakenly think he was angry with her and he was anything but.

Instead he was feeling remarkably protective of Harper. It was almost as though she really was his girlfriend. With her curled up in his arms, it was hard for him to remember this was all a sham. It certainly felt real. Maybe too real for the first day of the charade.

Before he'd left the room, he'd promised to keep her secret, with one caveat. If he found out who her blackmailer was before she did, he couldn't promise her that he wouldn't cause some trouble for the jerk. She might not know that Sebastian had grown up on the wrong side of the tracks, but he had and, at a moment's notice, the scrappy kid who'd used his fists to defend himself could come out. Whomever was putting Harper through this hell deserved a black eye. Or two.

Even as Sebastian headed down the staircase to the main lobby, he could feel his hands curl into tight fists. He was strung tight, clutching his notebook under his arm and ready to fight at the slightest provocation. He hadn't been sure where he was going when he'd left the room, but he found himself loitering around the front desk. Perhaps the culprit would be there, waiting on a payment to be dropped off.

He was in no mindset to work, so he set aside his notebook, grabbed a copy of the local paper and settled into a large wingback chair by the fireplace. Despite being early summer, it was Ireland and that still meant cool weather, especially given they were near the northwest coast. The fire offered a comfortable, draft-free place to sit in the stone behemoth of a building.

Sebastian glanced over the words in the paper, but he was focused more on the comings and goings. There were few at this hour of the afternoon. It was likely that many had fallen prey to jet lag and were napping in their rooms before the welcome dinner. Most of the people he saw in the lobby were wearing the uniforms of the hotel staff.

After about thirty minutes, out of the corner of his eye, he noticed someone approach the front desk. He turned his attention fully to the man standing there, realizing almost immediately that it was one of the few people on the trip he actually knew—Harper's ex, Quentin.

That made sense. Harper had mentioned that she'd been short on cash basically since college and she'd only dated Quentin a few years ago. If they'd been at all serious, there had to have been signs of her difficulties. Sebastian had noticed it in minutes. Quentin, of all people, should have been able to tell if Harper was broke. If not, maybe she'd confided in him and forgotten about it. And perhaps he might also know that her financial luck was about to change. It made sense. But would he be bold enough to try to get a piece of it?

Quentin stood nervously waiting at the counter for the desk clerk to return and, after a brief exchange Sebastian couldn't hear, turned and headed back toward the elevators empty-handed. He glanced around the lobby as he walked, an almost agitated expression lining his face. And then his gaze met with Sebastian's pointed glare.

He knew he could turn away. Try to appear more subtle in his appraisal. But at the moment, Sebastian didn't care if the bastard knew he was watching him. Let him know they were on to his sick game. Let him check the desk twenty times tonight. He was going to be disappointed. No matter what Harper wanted to do, she was right about one thing. There wasn't going to be any way to pull a hundred grand out of thin air in a foreign country.

It might even be a tricky thing for Sebastian to do and he had ten times that much cash in his checking account at any given time. Banks simply didn't like handing over that much money. There were too many checks and balances, wire transfers, international calls and such before they parted with it. Perhaps if they were in Monte Carlo where people parted with larger amounts in the casinos on a regular basis, but rural Ireland? Not likely. If Quentin was behind this blackmail plot, his timing was crappy.

Quentin quickly broke their connection with an anxious biting of his lip and turned his back to wait for the elevator. Within a few seconds it opened and he disappeared without looking back in Sebastian's direction.

Sebastian was so engrossed in watching his mark that he didn't notice someone approaching his chair.

"May I join you?"

He turned and recognized Harper's older brother standing there. Oliver and his wife, Lucy, had been introduced briefly to him on the bus, but they really hadn't had time to talk aside from some basic pleasantries. Sebastian expected that he had questions for the new boyfriend. Any brother worth his salt would when his little sister was involved, even if she was a grown woman. "Please, have a seat. I'm just trying to stay awake until dinnertime, so I could use some company."

Oliver chuckled and settled into the other wingback chair. He had a cut-crystal lowball glass in his hand filled with some ice and a dark amber liquor. "I know how that is. International travel messes with your internal clock. I'm hoping to eat a huge dinner, have a couple drinks and pass out at a reasonable hour. Whatever that is. I'm not sure if Harper told you, but Lucy and I have nine-month-old twins. Our sleep schedules haven't been reasonable in quite some time."

"I can imagine. I wouldn't be surprised if the two of you did nothing but sleep when a wedding event wasn't taking place." Sebastian hadn't noticed any children on the flight but Violet and Aidan's toddler, so he presumed they were all back in New York with their nannies and their grandparents. Sounded like the perfect getaway to relax, nap and have some alone time together.

And yet he was downstairs with Sebastian instead.

"Lucy is actually napping right now. I told her not to because it would screw up her sleep, but she told me to mind my own business and go downstairs." Oliver chuckled and sipped at his drink. "They're a sassy group of women, my sister included. I never thought

I'd be roped into all of it, and yet here I am. Do you know what you're getting yourself into, Sebastian?"

He smiled. He was pretty sure he was in over his head when he'd agreed to go on this trip and she'd kissed him in the department store. "If I didn't, I'm getting a good feel for it on this trip," he said. "It's been quite the experience so far and it's only the first day here. Being the odd man out allows me to sort of observe from the fringes, which is fine by me. To be honest, I don't spend a lot of time with people. Certainly not like this. My business partner, Finn Solomon, is the outward face of our company. I spend most of my time sketching out plans or tinkering with my latest ideas in the lab at work."

"I used to be that way. When I inherited Orion from my father, the company was a mess. Apple was king and PCs weren't cool anymore. Especially those old tower dinosaurs everyone had at work or in their closets. I sacrificed a lot of my personal life sitting with my engineers, trying to brainstorm new computer products that would make us competitive again. Now, of course, we're back on our feet and I'm able to shift my focus to other more important things, like Lucy and the twins. Say, have you been married before?"

Let the prying begin. Nice segue. "I haven't. I suppose I've been more focused on building our company, so I've never married or had any children."

Oliver nodded thoughtfully. "You know, all of Harper's friends have recently settled down and had children. After Violet and Aidan get married this weekend, Harper will be the only single one left."

"She's mentioned that."

"I suppose she feels some pressure to follow suit."

Sebastian narrowed his gaze at Oliver. "You're asking if Harper is barking up the wrong tree with me since I'm a thirty-eight-year-old workaholic bachelor?"

Oliver simply shrugged and sipped his drink. "Is she?"

"I suppose I'm getting to the age where I need to take the idea of a family more seriously, but until Harper, it hadn't really crossed my mind. I'm not opposed to it, no, but it simply hasn't been in the cards for me yet."

Her brother listened thoughtfully and nodded. "I was the same way until Lucy blew through my life like a hurricane. I didn't think I was ready for marriage or children, either, but she changed everything. It was like my eyes were suddenly opened and all I could see was her and our future together. Is it like that with you and my sister?"

That was something Sebastian didn't think he could lie about. It was easy to pretend to date and to be attracted to Harper because he was attracted to her. But to love her? To envision their future together? That was different and he had no doubt her brother could spot it if he fibbed. "It's only been a few months, but I think we're definitely getting to a more serious place. I care for your sister," he said.

And he did. He didn't want to see her get hurt, be it by him or Quentin or whomever that sleazy blackmailer was. That meant he cared a little, even for a woman he hardly knew. It was hard not to when he'd been drawn into her world and her problems so quickly. If Lucy was a hurricane, perhaps Harper was a tornado, plucking him from a wheat field and sucking him up into the swirling drama of her life.

"Listen, I don't want to do that stereotypical brother thing where I threaten you not to hurt my sister and wave around my shotgun. It's kind of cliché and not that effective, if Quentin is any evidence of that. I also don't own a shotgun. But I will say that you're the first man my sister has seriously dated in quite a while. I'm happy for you both, but I'm also nervous. She's kept this relationship quiet and the fact that she's suddenly announcing it to the world means she's feeling more comfortable with her feelings for you, whatever they may be. My sister is all sarcasm and sass on the outside, but all that is there as a barrier to protect the fact that she's really a marshmallow on the inside. She gets hurt easily."

Sebastian listened carefully. Even though he knew this relationship wasn't real, he took her brother's words to heart. He'd already been a witness to Harper's softer side—the side that was nervous about what other people thought of her and the part that was tied in knots over her secrets being exposed. She definitely had a soft underbelly. To be honest, seeing that part of her had endeared her to him more than he realized. She wasn't just the snarky single friend living the footloose and fancy-free life in Manhattan. She was more than that. Much more. And it made Sebastian curious to unearth more of her hidden layers.

Oliver glanced down at his watch and sighed before finishing off his drink. "Well, I'm glad we could have this little chat. I'd better head upstairs and wake Lucy so she has time to freshen up before dinner. I'll see you and Harper there in a little while."

"We'll see you later," Sebastian said with a wave. He watched Oliver disappear from the lobby and glanced back over at the hotel front desk. He hadn't been watching it for at least fifteen or twenty minutes. Anyone looking for the package of blackmail money could've come and gone and he'd missed it while chatting with Oliver.

Frustrated, he folded up the newspaper and decided to follow Oliver's suit. It was almost time for the welcome dinner in the great hall and he could use some time to change. With a sigh, he picked up his notebook and headed for the staircase to find Harper to report on what he'd seen, carefully leaving out her brother's little chat.

As far as he was concerned, Quentin should be at the top of the suspect list and he was going to keep an eye on him.

Five

Since everyone was tired, the welcome dinner was short and, for that, Harper was relieved. Aidan and Violet said a few words, thanked everyone for coming, and every couple was given a gift bag. Inside were some useful essentials: a schedule of activities, a map of the property and some authentic Irish chocolates.

Harper had difficulty focusing on any of the food or conversation. Her eyes kept running over each guest, wondering which one was expecting to be a hundred grand richer before bedtime. No one was watching her, no one was acting odd, and yet she could feel someone's eyes on her. Her gaze flicked over to Quentin. He seemed a little out of sorts tonight. He fidgeted with his food and didn't engage anyone, even his fiancée, in conversation.

After Sebastian had mentioned seeing her ex go by

the front desk, it had confirmed her suspicions that he might be behind this. He was the only one who made sense. He knew a little about her situation, or he had back when they dated. The question was whether or not he needed money badly enough to use it against her. She didn't know. A hundred grand wasn't a lot in the scheme of things. All she knew was that she hated being in the same room with him. She wanted to escape upstairs as soon as she could.

At the same time, as they got up to leave the great hall, Harper realized she was also dreading going back to the suite with Sebastian. When he'd returned to the room before dinner, she had thankfully already dressed for the evening. She'd been in the process of curling her hair in the bathroom as he'd entered their room. He'd gone about changing his clothes, paying no attention to the fact that Harper was in the next room with the door wide open.

She'd tried not to stare in the mirror at him as he'd walked around in his navy boxer briefs, laying out his outfit. She'd told herself that it was surprise, not desire, that had caused her to study his mostly naked body so closely. She'd expected the mad scientist to be soft through the middle from long hours at the lab and less-than-ideal eating habits, but he wasn't. His body was long and lean with hard muscles that twitched beneath tanned skin that extended far below his collar line.

How did he get a body like that working in his lab for long stretches of time?

"Ye-ouch!" she'd hollered, pulling her attention back to the blazing-hot curling iron where it belonged. She'd sucked at her burned finger and focused on finishing her hair, even when he'd come into the bathroom still in his underwear. He'd bent over the sink to splash water on his face and beard, then combed his hair back and was done. Men had it so easy.

"Could you put on a robe or something?" she'd finally asked. Despite her best intentions to ignore him when they were alone, she was sure to burn off a chunk of hair if he kept walking around mostly naked.

Sebastian had seemed startled and mildly insulted by the request at first, but had quickly retrieved one of the resort robes and covered up.

She'd thanked him and the tension between them eased. They'd finished dressing, gone down to the great hall and sat together throughout the meal, engaging in polite conversation with those around them. They'd smiled, leaned into each other, shared bites of food and were as lovey-dovey as they could stand to be until they were finally released for some welcome rest.

Now that she'd had an eyeful of what he was hiding under his suits, Harper wasn't sure how well she would sleep tonight. Not lying a mere inch or two from Sebastian for hours on end.

They bypassed the elevator and walked slowly and silently up the staircase together to their suite. About halfway up, Harper felt the brush of Sebastian's fingers against her own. She looked down and put her hand in his when she realized he was intentionally reaching for her. He was right. They should be holding hands. She couldn't let any awkwardness that happened behind closed doors impact the show they were putting on for everyone else.

If only touching him didn't unnerve her the way it did. His hand was large and warm, enveloping hers in a way that made heat radiate up her arm. By the time they reached their room, her blood was humming through her veins and she felt as if the silk pussy bow that tied at the collar of the Fendi blouse she'd chosen was about to choke her. She also felt flush in the otherwise cool castle. That could only be Sebastian's doing.

He let go of her hand long enough to open the door and let her step in ahead of him. He followed behind, pulling the door shut and fastening the privacy latch.

Harper wasn't the only one who was oddly overheated. As she untied the bow at her neck, she watched Sebastian slip quickly out of his suitcoat and tug his tie loose. She found her eyes drawn to the hollow of his throat as he unfastened his collar and continued down the line of buttons until a touch of dark chest hair was exposed.

Suddenly the thought of pressing a kiss against that part of his neck appeared in her mind. The warm scent of his skin, the stubble brushing her cheeks, the rhythmic thump of his pulse against her lips... An unwelcome tingle of desire surged through her whole body, making her belly clench and her breasts ache with longing in the confines of her bra.

When her nervous gaze met his, she found a questioning look in his eyes and a room that was abruptly very quiet. "What?" she asked before turning away to focus on kicking out of her pointy-toed heels.

Sebastian just shrugged and sat in a chair to pull off his shoes. "You were staring at me, that's all. I was waiting for you to say something. Did I get some shepherd's pie on my shirt?" He looked down at the pristine gray shirt.

She wished he was a mess. Maybe then she could ignore the building attraction between them. Instead, he'd been the perfect companion so far. Perfect aside from being too attractive, too nice and too supportive. A soft, pasty midsection would really help her control her libido right now, but she knew that what was under that shirt was anything but. "No. I just…got lost in my thoughts, I guess."

It was then that, with them both in states of partial dress, they found themselves at an impasse. Harper didn't know what to do next. She certainly wasn't about to tell him what was on her mind. If she stood there any longer, he'd continue to undress like before. She supposed she could gather up her pajamas and take them into the bathroom to change like this was a sleepover with a group of shy ten-year-old girls. Perhaps that would give him time to change privately, as well.

She turned to where her luggage was sitting open and started riffling through it. Thankfully she'd thought to pack pajamas that were less than intriguing. She had passed on the dog onesie—it was too bulky— but had chosen something just as unappealing. There was a piece of nice lingerie for show, but the rest was purely practical in nature. They were flannel, for the potentially cold Irish nights, and long-sleeved, to keep any glimpses of exposed skin to a minimum.

"Here," he said.

Harper turned her attention to Sebastian in time to see him deliberately taking off the rest of his clothes. "Um, what are you doing?" she asked, clutching her pajamas to her breasts for dear life as she realized what was happening.

"I'm getting this out of the way." He shrugged off his dress shirt and stepped out of the suit pants that had pooled at his feet. "We can't spend this whole week tiptoeing around each other and if you keep burning fingers on your curling iron while you sneak peeks at me, people are going to start asking questions. We're sharing a room. Sharing a bed. It doesn't matter what does or doesn't happen in the bed—we need to be more comfortable around each other. You said so yourself when we first agreed to this whole thing." Standing in nothing but those same navy boxer briefs, Sebastian held out his arms. "Take a good look. Get it out of your system. It's just the standard equipment."

Harper watched with confusion and curiosity as he displayed himself to her. His equipment was anything but standard. Her gaze flickered from his defined biceps to the chest hair across his pecs to the trail that ran down his stomach to the gray waistband of his briefs. She was tempted to glance lower, but he turned, giving her a look at his muscular back and curved rear end, as well.

"Well?" he asked with his back to her.

"Why are you so tanned?" she blurted out to her own embarrassment.

He turned around to face her with a smile. "You're staring at my ass but your only question is why I'm tanned?" He shrugged, unfazed by her question. "Okay, well, my apartment building has a rooftop pool. I swim a lot. It's one of my stress relievers. It's not enough, apparently, but it's what I do. I'm not big on going to the gym. It's boring."

"What do you mean it's not enough?"

Sebastian's lips twisted for a moment in thought and he shook his head. "Nothing. There's not enough stress relievers in the world when you're in my line of work, that's all." He looked down at his chest and back at her. "Seen enough?"

Harper nodded nervously.

Sebastian mirrored her nod and sought out a pair of lounging pants from his bag. He tugged them on and looked at her with a wry grin. "Now when you talk to your girlfriends about getting me out of my pants, you don't have to lie."

Harper smiled, still fiercely holding her pajamas as though they were a protective armor. It felt silly after that to hide in the bathroom to change, but was she brave enough to do it out here?

"Your turn."

Her gaze met his. "What?" she said with obvious panic in her voice. Did he honestly expect her to parade around mostly naked because he had?

He held up his hands to deflect the blowback. "I'm just kidding Harper. Relax."

Harper held in a nervous twitter of laughter at his joke. "Oh."

"It's nothing I haven't seen before, anyway," he added. "I'm sure it's nice and all, but I'm not about to hurt myself while I stare at you."

Harper didn't know if she should be relieved or offended. He'd told her before that she was beautiful, but at the moment he seemed as though he couldn't care less about catching a glimpse of her naked body. Maybe he was using reverse psychology on her, she couldn't be sure, but she had the sudden urge to take off her clothes and prove him wrong.

Against her better judgment, she went with the surge of bravery and decided to put him to the test. "That's good to know," she said. She set her pajamas on the edge of the bed and pulled her blouse up over her head. She paid no attention to Sebastian as she straightened the straps of her cream-satin bra and unzipped her pencil skirt. She let it pool to her ankles, bending slowly to pick it up off the floor and to give him all the time he might need to see her cream thong and firm ass. She'd spent a lot of hours in the gym working on that butt and he damn well better be impressed by it.

She wanted to turn and look at him. For some reason, she wanted to see naked desire and need in his eyes. She knew it was there—she could practically feel his gaze on her body. But she didn't dare look at him. She wasn't sure what she would do if she found what she was looking for. Would she act on it? Ignore it? As it was, they would both spend tonight aching for something they couldn't have.

Harper decided not to turn in Sebastian's direction. It was enough to know that he hadn't moved from his spot since she'd started undressing. She forced herself to step into the plaid pajama pants. She unbuttoned the flannel top and readied it to put on before reaching back to unfasten her bra. Before she could slip it from her shoulders, she caught a blur of movement from the corner of her eye and a moment later the bathroom door shut hard. The shower came on not long after that.

So much for being comfortable around each other and getting it out of their system, she thought. Harper continued to put on her pajamas with a grin.

It was only the first day and she could already tell this was going to be a miserably boring trip.

It was not at all what she had envisioned when they'd been invited to the glamorous overseas wedding of

Violet Niarchos and Aidan Murphy. Yes, sure, they'd flown on a snazzy chartered plane and were sleeping in a private Irish castle, but watching the Queen of England snore into her teacup would be more exciting than hanging around this rotting pile of bricks with a bunch of blowhard billionaires.

She'd heard the wedding coordinator talking to her assistant on the plane about the week's itinerary. It sounded like one boring event after another with no end in sight. The week promised "highlights" like a round of golf for the gentlemen, a tea party for the ladies and shopping excursions into the sleepy village by the sea.

Couldn't they have at least stayed in Dublin for a night? Every person who walked past her in the hallway was worth a bloody fortune and yet hadn't the slightest clue how to have any fun with their money.

If not for the little blackmail scheme she was running, the whole trip would be a waste of her time. So far, even that had proven fruitless as far as money went, but it had been something to do. Watching Harper squirm under the pressure of blackmail was nice, but it wasn't what she really wanted.

That spoiled little princess needed to shut up and pay up. She could afford it. It was one tiny fraction of the fortune she was set to inherit from her dear old grandfather. Harper hadn't worked for or earned that money. It was to be dropped in her lap just because she'd been born into a family that handed down multi-million-dollar trust funds just as easily as other people passed hazel eyes and freckles down to their children.

She might not have all the money now, but she would have it soon. In the meantime, Harper could easily get her hands on it. She could borrow it from one of her rich friends, her brother…even her new boyfriend was loaded. Basically anyone on that flight could hand over the cash without blinking. Harper just needed the right motivation to ask.

Harper didn't deserve twenty-eight million dollars. She didn't even deserve the twenty-seven million, nine hundred thousand that would be left after she paid the blackmail.

She deserved it. She needed it.

And she was going to get it before the week was up.

That was the longest night of Sebastian's life.

As it was, he'd stayed in the bathroom far longer than was necessary. After he'd showered and tried to take the edge off, he'd meticulously brushed and flossed his teeth, rinsed with mouthwash, washed his face…anything and everything he could do to kill time and wipe the image of Harper's near naked body from his mind.

She might as well have been naked. That tantalizing little thong left almost nothing to the imagination and with the creamy color that nearly matched her skin, the rest of it just blended away. He'd tried to play it cool. Act like the mature adult he thought he was when they'd started this little game. He'd gritted his teeth, tried to think of the most un-arousing things he could, and even closed his eyes for a moment or two. But he hadn't been able to keep his gaze away for long. When she'd moved to take her bra off, though, he'd known he'd had to go.

It was that or… No. That hadn't been an option.

Theirs was a fake relationship. Despite all the hand-holding, embraces and canoodling they did in public, it was all fake. They weren't in love. They hardly knew one another. When he'd signed up for this, he'd thought it wouldn't be that hard to pretend to be Harper's lover. Now he wanted it for real so badly he could hardly draw in the scent of her perfume without gaining an erection.

By the time he'd come out of the bathroom, almost all the lights were out and Harper had been in bed. She'd been lying on her side with her back to him, so he'd been able to get into bed, turn off the nearby lamp and go to sleep without having to face her again.

At least that had been the idea. Instead he'd spent most of the night tossing and turning. He'd felt anxious. Squirmy. Filled with nervous energy that he couldn't shake. He should have been exhausted after staying up all day to adjust to the time change, but it hadn't mattered. All Sebastian's body cared about was the warm, soft female lying mere inches from him.

He remembered seeing the light of dawn through the curtains right around the time he was finally able to doze off. The next thing he heard was the shower running. When Harper emerged from the bathroom—fully dressed, thank goodness—she sat in the chair and rifled through the welcome bag they'd received the night before.

"What's on the agenda today?" he muttered into his pillow with a gravelly, sleepy voice.

"Today they've chartered a bus into the nearby town of Sligo if anyone wants to go shop or sightsee. It leaves at ten, after breakfast is done."

"And when is breakfast?"

"About fifteen minutes from now."

Reluctantly, Sebastian pushed himself up and swung

his legs out of bed. "I'll be ready in ten," he grumbled as he stumbled into the shower and turned on the water.

He quickly washed his hair and body, cleaned up his goatee, and was ready to go in ten minutes, as he'd predicted. He was wearing a more casual outfit for a day in town, so the jeans and polo shirt had come together quickly. Harper was dressed more casually, as well. When she stood to leave, he couldn't help but notice her skinny jeans were like a second skin. They clung to the delicious curve of her ass and thighs, bringing back flashes from the night before that were not breakfast appropriate.

"Is something wrong?" she asked.

If he didn't want to embarrass himself, yes.

"No," he said and reached for a windbreaker in the closet. "I was just considering a jacket." He folded it over his arm and carried it in front of him as they headed downstairs to eat.

"Miss Drake?" a voice called out as they reached the lobby and headed toward the great hall.

They both stopped, turning their attention to the front desk where a clerk was looking their way. The woman had an envelope in her hand that looked eerily familiar.

Sebastian's empty stomach started to ache with the feeling of dread. It was a similar envelope to the one Harper had received on the plane. He wasn't sure why that surprised him. She hadn't met last night's blackmail request, so another note had arrived. He hadn't been in the lobby to see who had left it there. When he'd mentioned seeing Quentin loitering around the desk the night before, Harper hadn't seemed surprised, which had just reinforced his idea that he was the suspect to watch.

"I have a message here for you, ma'am," the clerk added in a thick Irish accent.

Harper knew what it was, too. They walked together to the front desk and she took the envelope from the woman's hand. It had her name written on it in the same nondescript block text. "Thank you," she said.

"Did you happen to be working when they left the note? To see who left it?" Sebastian asked.

"No, sir. I just started my shift. The previous clerk said it had been left at the desk early this morning while she was setting up the coffee station. She didn't see who left it, either. Is there a problem?"

"No," Sebastian said with a reassuring smile. "Thanks so much." He turned back to Harper, who was looking at the envelope with a face almost as white as the parchment. "Let's take that back upstairs," he suggested. "Breakfast can wait."

She nodded blankly and let him lead her out of the lobby. He glanced around, looking for someone loitering curiously in the area, but it was mostly empty. A couple he didn't recognize was looking at magazines in the corner, but there was no one else there. They were all likely in the great room gathering for their first authentic Irish breakfast.

Back in the room, he escorted Harper over to the love seat and sat beside her.

"You know, with everything else going on last night, I almost forgot I was missing the deadline. This morning, the thought hadn't even crossed my mind. How could I forget about something like that? And then I saw the envelope in her hand and I remembered what a mess I was still in. Now I don't want to open it," she said.

"Why not?"

"Because…it's not going to be good. He's going to be angry because I didn't pay the blackmail money. There's one of two things in this note—a second chance to pay or notification that my secret is as good as public knowledge by now. I could walk into the dining hall and everyone could know the truth about me."

"You won't know which it is until you open it."

With a sigh, she ran her finger under the lip of the envelope and ripped it open. She pulled out another small card, identical to the first, with the same block-style text inside. Harper held it up to read aloud.

"It seems your payment got lost in the mail, Harper. Yesterday was a tiring day of travel, so I'm going to be kind and give you another opportunity to give me what I want. This time, to make it easier, make it one hundred thousand euros in an envelope at the front desk by noon tomorrow. Don't disappoint me again.'"

Harper's hand dropped into her lap with dismay. "Great, now the price has gone up. When I looked at the exchange rate yesterday, it was in the euro's favor. He's now asking for something in the neighborhood of a hundred and twenty thousand dollars in the name of 'convenience.' I mean, why not?" She giggled, bringing her hand to her mouth just in time to stifle a sob. "I couldn't pay the hundred grand, so two days later, naturally, I should be able to pay that and more."

Sebastian wrapped his arm around Harper's shoulders and pulled her tight against him. She gave in to the embrace, burying her face in his chest and holding on to him. He hated seeing her upset. He wasn't a very physical person by nature, but if he got his hands on her blackmailer, he wasn't sure what he would do. At the moment he wanted to choke the guy until tears ran down his cheeks like Harper's did.

"What am I going to do?" She sniffled against his polo shirt. "He's not going to go away. I don't have the money. I don't know what to do, Sebastian."

He sighed and stroked her hair as he tried to come up with an answer. He wasn't sure there was a way out of this that wouldn't be painful somehow. "Do you trust any of your friends enough? Lucy or Emma maybe? Your brother perhaps?"

"Trust them enough for what?"

"Enough to ask them to help you with this. To give you the money. Just a loan until you get to your birthday and can pay them back."

Harper pulled away and shook her head. She wiped the tears from her cheeks, leaving black smudges of mascara that he wanted to reach out and brush away.

"I can't do that. I just can't."

"You don't think they'd give it to you?"

"No, they would. Each and every one of them would in a heartbeat," Harper explained. "That's why I can't ask. I'm not going to abuse their friendship like that. Besides, they'd want to know what it was for. They'd worry that I was in some kind of trouble."

"Aren't you?" he asked.

"Yes, but not trouble I want any of them to know about. This whole thing is so embarrassing. Really, even if I wasn't at risk of losing my inheritance, I wouldn't want anyone to know about the financial trouble I'm in. I'm an accountant. It just looks so awful."

Sebastian gently stroked her back, considering his options in this situation. Initially he hadn't been in favor of paying the blackmail, but this wasn't going to go away. This person was going to get the money or ruin Harper's life in the process. "What about the bank?" he asked.

She looked up at him, confusion creasing her brow. "What do you mean?"

"What about seeing if the local bank would lend you the money? When we go into town today, we can stop at a bank and see what options you have."

"Not many," she said. "Without collateral, getting that much money would be nearly impossible. If by some chance they did agree to loan me the money, it would be at an outrageous interest rate."

"Not necessarily," Sebastian said thoughtfully. "What if I cosigned?"

Harper sat back against the arm of the love seat and looked at him with an expression he couldn't quite read. "Are you serious?"

He shrugged. "Yeah."

"That's really sweet of you to offer, Sebastian, but I can't ask you to do that. It wouldn't be right."

"Why? I have no intention of paying a dime of the money back. It's all on you. And if you don't pay it when your inheritance comes through, I'll see to it that there are unpleasant consequences for you, if it makes you feel better about it."

She blinked a few times as though she were trying to process his offer. "You'd really do that for me?"

"Of course," he said. "You're my girlfriend. Don't

you think the blackmailer would think it suspicious if you couldn't come up with the money somehow and yet your boyfriend is a millionaire?"

Sebastian wasn't sure what the reaction would be, but he certainly wasn't expecting her to throw herself into his arms. Before he knew what was happening, Harper's lips were pressed to his once again. Just like at Neiman Marcus, she was enthusiastically thanking him with her mouth. Unlike at Neiman Marcus, this time there wasn't a crowd of onlookers to keep the kiss PG-rated.

If he was honest with himself, he'd been wanting this kiss since that one had ended. Not one of the quick pecks she gave him when they were out in public, but a real kiss. One where he could taste the cool mint-toothpaste flavor on her tongue and let his hands roam until they discovered that under today's long-sleeved T-shirt she was wearing a lace bra.

The kiss intensified as his palms cupped her through her shirt. Harper moaned softly against his mouth and moved closer to him on the love seat. It would be so easy to pull her into his lap, whip the shirt off her head and bury his face between the creamy breasts he'd only glimpsed the night before. But he wouldn't. Not now.

As much as he didn't want to, Sebastian forced himself to pull away. This wasn't the time or place for this to happen. If he and Harper ever transitioned from a fake relationship to a real one, he didn't want it to be because she was emotionally compromised or felt indebted to him.

He rested his forehead against hers as he took a cleansing breath and chuckled to himself.

"What's the laugh for?" she asked.

"I was just thinking that I would've offered to co-sign yesterday if I'd known I'd get that kiss in return."

Harper grimaced and shook her head with mock dismay. "Let's get back downstairs. We don't want to miss the bus to Sligo."

Six

"Wipe that anxious look off your face."

Harper clutched her purse to her chest and frowned at Sebastian. "I can't help it," she argued. "I don't like walking around with this much cash."

"You're not walking through downtown Manhattan. You're riding a bus with friends through the Irish countryside. We'll be back at the castle in a few minutes. No one on the bus is going to mug you, I'm pretty sure."

She could only sigh and shake her head, diverting her attention out the window to the passing scenery. Ireland was a beautiful country with rolling, emerald hillsides, misty valleys and wild, gray seas. She wished she was able to enjoy it. Harper had always wanted to go to Ireland but never managed to make the trip before. But now that she was here, all she could think about was the twenty-five thousand euros in her Birkin purse and the bastard she was about to give it to.

"Maybe B. Mayler is on the bus. Ever think of that? Maybe he followed us into town."

Sebastian turned to look over his shoulder at the people on the bus. "I doubt it. Besides, he wouldn't need to steal it from you. You're about to give it to him outright."

He was probably right. She hadn't seen Quentin on the bus or in town. She half expected to see him sitting in the lobby when they arrived, waiting with baited breath for her to leave the package at the front desk, especially after Sebastian had seen him at the desk the night before. She hated to tell Quentin that he was going to be disappointed.

Twenty-five thousand euros. Not a hundred thousand. That was all the bank would give her even with Sebastian's signature on the loan. If they'd had more time…if she'd had better credit, more collateral…if Harper'd had ties to Ireland… Their reasons for limiting the amount of the loan had gone on and on. She supposed she should be happy to have gotten this much. She was a quarter of the way there. Maybe it would keep the blackmailer happy until she could get more.

Looking into her purse for the twentieth time, Harper checked to make sure the bundle of bills was still there. It was in a white envelope, labeled as directed, and included a note that explained this was all she could get until she returned to the United States. She intended to leave the package at the front desk as they went in. Then, maybe, she would be able to take a deep breath for the first time since she'd spied that envelope on her plane seat.

Or perhaps not.

As they pulled up the curved gravel driveway of Markree Castle, she closed her bag to make sure the envelope wouldn't fall out. Sebastian stayed close by her side as they exited the bus and walked into the hotel.

Despite their situation, it was nice to have him be there for her. He hadn't signed up for any of this drama when he'd agreed to come on the trip as her boyfriend. He'd been promised a free vacation and instead he'd been roped into a blackmail plot. And yet he hadn't complained. He'd been her sounding board, her shoulder to cry on and, at the moment, her personal bodyguard. Harper didn't know how to thank him for everything he'd done so far. If she'd come on this trip alone, she wasn't sure what she would've done.

They stopped at the desk long enough for her to hand over the package with instructions for the desk clerk. She slipped it into a blank mail slot on the back wall and went to answer the phone as though it was nothing to her. Harper supposed it was. Just something left for a guest. Who would imagine it was filled with thousands of euros in cash?

"Let's go upstairs," Sebastian suggested. "We need to get away from the desk so he can come pick it up."

Harper didn't argue. She just took his arm and let him lead her away. It felt good to cling to him, to have the strong support of his body against her own. It meant so much to have him there for her. It had been a long time since she'd had that in her life. When so much of her day-to-day existence was a lie, it was almost impossible to let people in. Even her best girlfriends, the people who knew her better than anyone, didn't know the whole truth about her.

As they stepped inside their room and he closed the door behind them, she realized how lonely she had been. Even when she had been with Quentin, something had been missing. She was holding part of herself back from everyone, never letting anyone completely in.

But Sebastian knew all her secrets. And he was still there with her. At least for now.

Harper didn't expect him to stay around after the end of the trip. He had a life to return to and so did she. But they had the here and now together and, for her, that was enough. She just needed to feel like she wasn't going through this by herself. She wasn't lonely when he was around. She didn't have to pretend to be someone she wasn't. It was such a relief to be able to let her guard down and just relax into who she really was for the first time in forever.

She turned to look at Sebastian. His large, dark eyes were watching her from across the room the way they always did. He constantly seemed to be in silent study of the world around him. Of her. Perhaps it was the engineer in him, taking things apart and putting them back together in his mind. Figuring out how things worked. What made them tick. What made her tick. The idea of him instinctively knowing just how to push her buttons was enough to make her need to slip out of her suddenly too warm jacket.

He was one of the most intense men she'd ever encountered. And now, in this moment, she wanted to lose herself in that intensity.

"Sebastian."

It was all she said, yet she knew her tone conveyed so much more to him than just his name. He bit thoughtfully at his full bottom lip as his gaze narrowed at her. At last, he started moving toward her at an un-hurried pace. Their gazes never broke away from one another as he came nearer. And even when he was close enough to reach out and pull Harper into his arms, he didn't touch her. He just studied her, taking in every inch from her dark ponytail to the cobblestone-scuffed deck shoes she'd worn into town.

This was her move to make. Their relationship was set up with parameters she'd defined. If they were going to cross a line, she had to be the one to do it. And that was fine by her.

Her lips met his before she could lose her nerve. Their kiss this morning had been proof that there was more between them than just some arrangement. Excitement and gratitude had overridden her good sense then, but the kiss had been about anything but saying thank you. The current running beneath the surface was one of mutual attraction, undeniable chemistry... they had just been holding back out of respect for the agreement they'd made. This relationship was supposed to be all for show, right?

But all that went out the window when he looked at her the way he did. Touched her the way he did.

"Make me forget about all of this," she said in a des-perate whisper against the rough stubble of his cheek.

Sebastian didn't hesitate to give her what she'd asked for. Within seconds her shirt was over her head. His hungry mouth traveled down her chin and throat to bury in the valley between her breasts. He nipped at her delicate skin with his teeth even as he unclasped her bra and cast it to the floor.

The sensations were so overwhelming, all Harper

could do was close her eyes and try to take it all in. His hands moved quickly to cover her exposed breasts. She groaned as her tight, sensitive nipples grazed his rough palms. His fingertips pressed into her flesh, squeezing and kneading her breasts.

The moment he drew one tight bud into his mouth, Harper's head fell back and she cried out to the ceiling. His silky, hot tongue bathed her skin, sucking hard and then biting gently with his teeth until she gasped. She gripped his head, trying to pull him closer as she buried her fingers in the dark waves of his hair. She couldn't get close enough.

Then he pulled away.

Sebastian stood fully upright for a moment, his hands encircling her waist. He held her steady there as his dark eyes studied her face. He seemed to take in every detail, from the curve of her lips to the scar across her brow where she'd fallen out of a bunk bed as a child.

Harper suddenly felt self-conscious as she stood there, topless and exposed to his scrutiny. What would he see if he looked that closely? She wanted to turn off the lights, to cover up, pull away before he found something he didn't like about her body.

Then he shook his head and said, "Beautiful," under his breath and she tried to put those worries aside to be the beautiful woman on the inside that he saw on the outside.

With his firm grip on her, he pulled her across the wooden floor to their four-poster bed. He pushed her back until she was sitting on the edge. Harper eased back just as he moved forward, planting his left knee and fist into the soft mattress beside her. Hovering over her, he used his right hand to trace faint circles across her stomach.

It both tickled and turned her on at the same time. She tried hard not to squirm under his touch, but her body couldn't stay still. She ached to move closer and pull away all at once. Then he moved down and brushed his fingers over the button of her jeans. With a quick snap, they were undone and he pulled the zipper down to the base. He probed under the fabric, tracing over the lace that protected her center.

Harper gasped as he grazed her most sensitive spot once, twice, then a third time, more forcefully, making her back arch up off the bed.

Sebastian's gaze fixed on her. Ever the engineer, he studied her expressions and her every reaction to his touch. With a satisfied smirk, he eased back and hooked his fingers beneath her jeans. He slid them over her hips and down her legs, throwing them to the floor.

His hands replaced the denim, sliding back up her legs and gliding over every inch of her skin. His mouth followed in their wake, leaving searing kisses along the insides of her ankles, calves, knees and inner thighs. When he reached her panties, Harper expected him to pull them off like he had with her jeans. Instead he grasped the side with his fist and tugged hard until the pieces came off in his hand. He threw the torn strips of fabric away.

"That's much better." With nothing else in his way, he pressed her thighs further apart and leaned in to lap his tongue over the newly exposed flesh.

The sensation was like a lightning bolt through her core.

"You're buying me new panties," she gasped.

"Those were twenty-five dollars and I can't afford to replace them."

"Fine," Sebastian said. "I'll buy. You three pairs. For every one. I destroy." With each pause in his speech, his tongue flicked over her again.

"Are you planning to rip them all?"

"It depends." He spread her legs wider and moved his mouth more furiously over Harper until she was once again squirming beneath him.

"Depends on what?" Harper gasped and gripped the blankets beneath her in tight fists.

"On whether or not they get in my way."

Harper made a mental note to keep her nicer panties in her luggage. That was her last coherent thought.

At that moment Sebastian slid two fingers inside her. He thrust them deep, positioning the heel of his hand to grind against her clit. His whole hand started moving and she began to unravel. The combination was like nothing she'd ever felt before. She found herself yelling out, gasping and crying, even long before her release. The sensations were almost overpowering.

Her orgasm came fast and furiously. She wasn't prepared for how hard the pulsating waves would pound her body. She shuddered and rocked against his hand, shouting with the power of her release until it had nearly zapped all her strength. It took all she had to reach down and grab his hand, pulling it away from her. She couldn't take any more. Not quite yet, at least.

Harper closed her eyes and collapsed against the mattress. Her skin was pink and flushed, the butterflies still fluttering inside her. She swallowed hard, noting her raw throat as she gasped for breath. She wasn't entirely sure what she'd expected from Sebastian, but it hadn't been that. She'd never experienced an orgasm like that in her life. It was intense. Overwhelming. Amazing. And as soon as she recovered, she wanted to do it again.

Sebastian's weight shifted on the bed and she heard him walk into the bathroom. She opened her eyes when she heard him come back in. He had gotten rid of his clothes and replaced them with his pajama pants.

Bending down, he scooped her into his arms and placed her properly onto the bed. He crawled in beside her and tugged the blankets over them both.

Harper was surprised. She didn't think they were finished. She was great, of course, but she thought for sure that he would want some for himself. Maybe he didn't have protection with him. She'd have to be sure to correct that before they got together again.

Instead, he rolled onto his side and wrapped his arms around her, pulling her into the warm nook of his body. It was unexpected, but perhaps exactly what she needed.

"What are you thinking about?" he asked.

"Not a damn thing," Harper said. She could barely string together a coherent sentence at this point.

"Good. Mission accomplished," he said.

"You know what I've noticed?"

Sebastian clung to consciousness long enough to make a thoughtful sound in response to Harper's question. "Mmm?"

"I've realized that I really don't know anything about you, but you know everything about me."

The question was enough to jerk him from the comfortable nap he'd almost settled into. Apparently the post-coital bliss he'd induced in her was short-lived and her mind was spinning again. With his eyes wide open now, he sighed. "That's not true. We met up before the trip and talked about each other for the cover story."

Harper snuggled against his chest and let her fingers twirl through his dark chest hair. "Yes. We talked about a few things, but you were pretty light on details. You know all my deepest, darkest secrets and all I know is that you went to MIT."

"There's not much more about me to tell," he said. It was a lie, but the one he preferred people to believe. "I had a very boring, uneventful life before I went to college and met Finn. Then we started a business, invented some stuff and got rich in the process. My life is still boring, I just have more money. Unlike you, there's no secret dramas, no trust fund stipulations, no blackmail plots. You're not missing out on much with me, I promise."

Now it was Harper's turn to make a thoughtful sound. Eventually she stilled and her breathing became soft and even against his chest. Of course, she had riled him up and fallen asleep, leaving him lying in bed with a brain no longer interested in sleep.

Part of him felt bad about lying to Harper mere minutes after giving her an orgasm. She had been brutally honest with him about her life, but that was out of necessity, not out of a willingness to share her past with him. He'd been sucked into her blackmail plot or he was certain she wouldn't have told him, just like she hadn't told anyone else. He was just there. And he was okay with that. She just shouldn't expect him to reciprocate.

It wasn't because he had huge skeletons in his own

closet. His uncle Joe had gotten a DUI for driving his riding lawnmower to the gas station drunk to get more beer. That was the closest his family had come to brushes with the law. No scandals. No secrets. They were just the one thing that he couldn't be once he'd found himself dropped into the world of Manhattan society against his will—poor.

Harper had been angry with him initially for not telling her that he was rich. It was her presumption that he wasn't—he hadn't said anything either way. He typically didn't. Sebastian wasn't the kind to present himself like the usual power-hungry Manhattan CEO, so most people wouldn't think he was, much less believe him if he insisted otherwise. Finn was the suave one: well-dressed, well-spoken, well-traveled. He reeked of money and prestige. No one ever questioned that he was the president of BioTech.

Sebastian flew under the radar and he liked it that way. He didn't like the way people changed around him when they found out he was rich. All of a sudden people acted like he was more important and things he said were more interesting. He'd go from being mostly ignored to receiving invitations to play racquetball at the club. He didn't play racquetball and had no intention of starting. It was all perception. His wealth shaped how people saw him.

And the same would be true if his rich friends found out he'd come from a dirt-poor background.

At the moment he was sleeping under the same roof as some of the most powerful business owners and billionaires in Manhattan. When he'd been introduced as one of them, they'd welcomed him with open arms. He was good enough for Harper, he owned his own company…he must be good people. But would they respond differently if they knew he was fifteen years removed from what they considered to be poor white trash? That his parents would be living in the same trailer he'd grown up in if he hadn't bought them a house with his first million?

Harper had money troubles of her own, but even at her poorest, she had more money than his family'd had growing up. He'd had to bust his ass to earn scholarships and get through college to build a career and wealth of his own. None of it had been given to him by his daddy or grandpa or anyone else.

While he'd been sympathetic to her plight when she'd told him about blowing her first two-million inheritance, a part of him had winced internally at the thought of it. Finn had some family money that helped them get started, but it was nowhere near enough. What could Sebastian have done if someone had handed him two million to get BioTech off the ground? They could've gotten a decent facility up and running instead of working out of a garage the first year. They could've gotten their first major product into production years earlier.

And she'd blown it on purses and shoes.

Harper had obviously grown up a lot in the years since she'd made those mistakes. She'd not only managed to support herself, but do a good enough job at it that no one questioned that she wasn't still rich. But with that big balloon payment looming in her future, he had to wonder if she would be back to her old habits.

It would take longer to blow through twenty-eight million, but she could still do it. Then what? There would be no third payment to bail her out again unless some rich relative died.

Or she married well. To a rich CEO perhaps?

Sebastian sighed and looked down at Harper as she slept peacefully on his chest. He didn't want to think that way about her. She hadn't seemed at all like the typical Manhattan gold digger. But she certainly had seemed a lot more interested in him once she'd realized he was rich and not just some wheelchair salesman. Yes, he could easily revive the glamorous lifestyle she had once lived. Since things between them had accelerated so quickly, a part of him worried about her motivations.

She'd been completely in love with that creep Quentin only two years ago. A guy who might very well be blackmailing her right now. She herself had said she didn't have the greatest taste in men, and choosing Quentin certainly seemed like a style over substance choice in his opinion.

That said, she genuinely seemed attracted to Sebastian. She hadn't asked anything of him, even though they both knew he could pay off that blackmail and put an end to it all. If it would ever end. She'd barely agreed to let him cosign the loan. And yet part of him was still concerned about what Harper was after.

He didn't mind getting physically closer to her. He was happy to. Holding her warm, soft body in his arms was one of the best things to happen to him in a long time. He actually wished he could've taken this afternoon further, but he knew putting the brakes on when he had was the right choice for now. He'd felt his heart racing uncomfortably in his chest as she'd come and had decided he needed to stop there. He'd promised to help her forget her problems and he'd done that.

The doctor had told him he would know if he was feeling well enough to indulge. It had been almost a week since his attack, so hopefully that would be soon. But that was about as far as he was willing to go with Harper. At least for now. There were too many unknowns, too many balls in the air for him to let this fake relationship develop past much more than a simple vacation fling.

Once they were back in New York, he would return to his lab, she would inherit her fortune and they'd likely go their separate ways. He didn't have time for a relationship and she wouldn't need his help any longer. Things would fall apart. So planning for the worst, Sebastian intended to keep his distance.

Seven

This was too easy, really.

Although she was hardly a criminal mastermind—she'd never committed a crime in her life before this trip—this wasn't proving that difficult. All she'd had to do was tell the woman at the desk that she needed a new room key. The overly trusting employee had made a new one for her without question or identification and handed it over. After all, they were all friends and family here for a wedding. Certainly a trustworthy crowd…

Then all she had to do was wait. Today's itinerary included a trip to a few tourist destinations of interest, including a local abbey and a ruin of another old castle. She'd feigned a migraine and stayed at the hotel while everyone else loaded into the buses to go.

Once she was certain they were good and truly gone, she made her way to Harper's room. The door opened right up, revealing the relatively tidy space. She took her time looking around at the antique furniture and heavy velvet drapes. The room was much nicer than the one she was staying in, but she wasn't one of the bride's best friends like Harper was.

After the courier she'd hired picked up the package at the front desk and brought it to her in the castle's east gardens, she'd been certain her plan was a success. Then she saw the note inside and counted only a quarter of what she'd been expecting. It was a lot of money to be sure, but not enough.

Harper seemed to think that she was the one in control of this situation. That she could just not pay, for whatever reasons she could come up with, and everything would be okay. That was not the case. That meant taking her threat up a notch.

She'd only intended to leave a note in the room. She'd wanted to invade Harper's space and unnerve her by showing what she could do if she wanted to. But once she was there, she realized she had an opportunity to make this a more lucrative visit and create a huge impact at the same time. She opened the largest piece of luggage and dug around inside. Most of the clothes were hanging in the closet, so all that was left in the bag were some intimates and a Louis Vuitton jewelry roll tied up with a leather cord. Bingo.

She unrolled the bundle, looking over the neatly organized pieces of jewelry in the different pockets. A few looked like nice costume jewelry, but in one pouch she pulled out a pair of diamond stud earrings that were at least one carat each. She slipped them into her purse, following with a necklace with a fat, pear-shaped sapphire pendant. Last, she pocketed a diamond-and-ruby tennis bracelet and an aquamarine-and-diamond cocktail ring. All nice, but somehow she'd expected more from Harper. Maybe she'd left her pricier pieces at home this trip.

In the other piece of luggage, Sebastian's she assumed, she found a fancy pair of gold-and-emerald cufflinks in a velvet box and an old pocket watch. She wasn't a jeweler, but she knew enough to estimate that she'd made up for a good chunk of the money Harper had shorted her. It was a start, at least. She'd have a jeweler back in the States appraise her haul later.

Harper seemed to think there was no way she could come up with the money, but she just wasn't putting her mind to it. Just flipping through the clothes in the closet, she spied a couple designer pieces that would fetch a pretty penny on Poshmark. The Hermès Birkin purse she was carrying the other day would, too. There was a waiting list to get one of those bags. Even the case she kept her jewelry in was worth at least a couple hundred dollars.

Harper had a lot of expensive things. There wasn't a single designer piece in her own closet, but then again, she wasn't pretending to be rich. Having these things was all part of Harper's ruse. Of course, if she could get her hands on stuff this nice just to fake out her friends and family, she could get the money, too.

Part of her wanted to blow the top off Harper's whole lie just to expose how shallow she was. What a horrible thing it was to be poor! She was just trying to make it by until that next big payment from grand-dad, then everything would be okay again. In their lifetimes, most people would never see the amount of money she'd already blown, never mind what she was set to inherit later.

There were worse things than being poor in this world. Perhaps being shallow? Being a liar? Maybe even a thief? She laughed at that thought. She didn't look at this as theft. She was just an instrument of karma in this scenario. If she got a tiny piece of the pie in the process, that was just a bonus.

She turned around and looked at the tidy, elegant room. Housekeeping had already come for the morning and left chocolates on the pillows. It hadn't been a part of her original plan, but she decided on the spot that it could use a little redecorating. Just to make the place look lived in, of course.

When she was out of breath and the room looked like it had been hit by a tornado, she took the white envelope out of her pocket and left it on the nightstand.

She had officially turned up the heat on Miss Drake.

They'd spent a long afternoon touring the Irish countryside and Sebastian had enjoyed it. It was a quiet, peaceful country to just sit and soak in the atmosphere. A good choice for a vacation location and he was sure his doctor would approve. Outside Dublin, most of the towns were small and laid back. No honking taxis and aggressive panhandlers. Just old historic sites and friendly people, all with stories to tell.

Despite the peaceful scenery, having Harper in the seat beside him on the bus had the opposite effect. The nearness of her kept his pulse fairly high. Every now and then he would get a whiff of her perfume. She would lean in to him to say something, touch his knee and playfully kiss him. At this point, the lines of their relationship were so blurry, he didn't know if she was really kissing *him* or if it was all for show. Though if people were suspicious of their relationship, it was a little too late to care. The wedding was tomorrow. They would be back in the US before long.

So did she mean it?

Sebastian tried not to overthink it. Instead he turned back to his notebook and worked on a sketch he'd started at the abbey. It seemed an odd place to get inspiration for medical equipment, but there had been a statue in the museum that was wearing some kind of armor. The shape of how it fit to the knight's leg had got him to thinking about prosthetic and robotic legs in a whole new way. That was all it had taken for him to lose all interest in old churches and to turn his focus back to work.

"You're not even listening," he heard Harper say.

Snapping out of the zone, Sebastian looked up. "What?"

"You're a million miles away. Did you hear a word I said?"

He shook his head sheepishly. "I didn't. I was focused on my work."

"I thought so. What is that?"

He sighed and looked at the rough sketch. It would take a lot of refinement for the doodle to become a cutting-edge piece of equipment, but it was a start. "One day, it may be BioTech's latest design for a robotic prosthetic. This one is for the leg."

She looked at the sketch thoughtfully. "Is that the kind of thing you usually work on?"

He shrugged. "It varies. Our very first product, the one that put us up with the big boys, was a prosthetic arm. Looking back at it now, it seems like such a crude design, but it changed everything for patients at the time. Lately we've been using 3D printing to develop custom fits for patients. Insurance wouldn't pay for something like that, so most people couldn't afford a customized fit until now. That's made a huge difference in comfort for people who've lost limbs."

"Do you work a lot with soldiers?"

"Yes. We also work with accident victims or people born with various birth defects. That's only part of what we do there. My latest project is for paraplegics. If I can get a successful prototype finished—one that can be produced affordably enough—it could change the lives of thousands of people that are wheelchair bound. This sketch is part of that."

There was a long silence and when Sebastian turned to look at Harper, he realized she was staring at him, not his sketches. "What?" he asked.

She smiled and reached out to brush a chunk of dark hair from his eyes. "I've never seen you like this."

"Like how?" He looked down to take inventory of himself self-consciously.

"I've never experienced your passion for your work. I guess I thought you were just another guy making a buck on medical research, but you really seem to care about what you're doing. Your work is amazing."

"Thank you," he responded awkwardly.

It always made him uncomfortable when people gushed at him about his research. He didn't do it for the feel-good factor. He did it for people like his brother who faced a lifetime lived with physical limitations. If he could finish the exo-legs, it meant he would have accomplished his biggest dream. Seeing his older brother walk again would mean he'd finally succeeded. The money, the success, the praise…it was all nice, but that wasn't what he wanted. He wanted to see the look on his mother's face when she saw her oldest son walk across the room unassisted. To him, that was worth sacrificing most of his life. Unfortunately he'd pushed too far and almost sacrificed all of it.

"So what inspired you to go into this line of work?" she asked.

He'd been waiting for that question. That was a slippery slope in conversation and Sebastian wasn't ready to go there. Not with reporters and not with Harper. He had a prepared answer for those times, however. He'd done several interviews and never wanted to bring his brother or his past into the discussion. It wasn't because he was embarrassed to talk about his brother's accident or his family situation. It was more that he wanted to maintain their privacy as well as his own. He didn't need the headline claiming he was a "rags to riches" success driven by his poor brother's tragic accident. That simplified the story far too much.

"I was always interested in robotics and engineering," he began his practiced story. "When I met up with Finn, he was in medical school and we got the idea to combine our specialties and start a company together after graduation. It was easy to develop a passion for the work when you see how it can impact people's lives."

"I imagine it is. I'm a corporate accountant for Jonah's company. There's no passion there, but I'm good with numbers so I got a finance degree. We're a video game company, though. It's hardly important work."

"It's important work to the people that love to play those games. Every job is critical in a different way. Finn says I'm a workaholic, but when you're doing something that can change someone's life, how do you justify walking away from your desk for a moment? Especially for something as trivial as a vacation?"

"I guess it's about balance. You don't want to burn out. But look—here you are on a vacation. Sounds like that's a big step for you."

Sebastian chuckled to himself. She had no idea. "It is. I haven't been out of my labs this long since we started the company ten years ago."

"So how were you able to do it now?"

He tensed in his seat. What was he going to say? A doctor-enforced break? Not the answer he wanted to give. He was supposed to be a successful guy. He didn't want to show weakness to Harper or any of the other people on this trip. Like a pack of wild animals, they could easily turn on the weakest member. He didn't want to give any of them the ammunition to come for him. Not his background, not his health, not his fake/real relationship with Harper. If he let out too much about himself, he might be the next one blackmailed.

"You gave me no choice," he said with a laugh. "A beautiful woman walks up to me in a department store, asks me out and offers me a free trip to Ireland. How can any red-blooded man pass that up?"

Looking up, Sebastian noticed they had reached the hotel. He was relieved to end the conversation there. "Looks like we're back."

Everyone gathered their things and shuffled back

into the hotel. The arrival couldn't have been better timed. He was more than happy to stop talking about himself. All he wanted to do now was to go upstairs, take a hot shower and get ready for dinner. Tonight they were hosting some kind of authentic Irish dinner show at the castle with traditional music and dance. It sounded interesting enough.

"I'm ready to take off these shoes," Harper said as she slipped her key card into the door. She took two steps and stopped short, sending him slamming into her back.

"What's wrong?"

Harper pushed open the door and revealed the mess that had once been their hotel room. Their things were scattered everywhere. Furniture was overturned. It was awful.

"Don't touch anything," he said. "We've been robbed."

"Don't touch anything?" Harper asked. "What are we going to do? Call the police?"

"That was my thought."

Harper walked into the room and picked up a familiar white envelope sitting on the nightstand. "Think again. If we call the cops, the blackmailer will expose me for sure."

With a sigh, Sebastian slammed the door shut and walked in to survey the mess. "So what does it say? I take it he wasn't pleased by the partial payment."

"It says that he's taken a few things to make up for the missing money. That was just a punishment, though. He still expects a hundred and twenty thousand dollars before the wedding reception ends." She looked up with despair in her eyes. "What about the twenty-five thousand euros he's already got? It's like it didn't even count. That or he's just jacking up the fee every time we miss a deadline." She dropped her face into her hands. "This is never going to end."

Sebastian walked over and sat beside her on the mattress. "It will end. He can't string this along forever. You're going to turn thirty and once you inherit, there's nothing to hold over your head. Or he exposes you and there's no money to be had. But it will end." He wrapped his arm around her shoulders. It wasn't the best pep talk he'd ever given, but it was something.

He didn't know what else to say as they sat and looked at their destroyed hotel suite. It must have taken quite a bit of time to do it, but given they'd been gone for hours, the blackmailer had had all the time in the world.

"Did you bring anything valuable?" he asked.

"Just a few things. Mainly pieces I was going to wear to the wedding." Harper got up and sought out her overturned suitcase. "My jewelry roll is gone. Oh, wait…" She spied it in the corner and picked it up. She poked through a couple pockets and shook her head. "He got all the good stuff. That sapphire necklace belonged to my mother," she said, tears shimmering in her eyes.

Sebastian cursed and stood to go to her. "We can call the cops. We don't have to mention the blackmail. You'll need the report for your insurance claims."

"What insurance?" she chuckled sadly. "You're talking like I have the money to insure all this stuff. I don't. It's gone. It's all just gone. Probably forty thousand dollars' worth of jewelry, easy. Did you bring anything?"

Sebastian hadn't really thought about his things. He hadn't previously been a target of the blackmailer, but he supposed if they wanted money, they'd get it from anywhere. "Not much," he said. Looking around, he found the box with his cufflinks for his tuxedo. It was empty. Figures. The only other item he had with him was his grandfather's pocket watch, but it wasn't worth anything. He carried it for sentimental value.

He dug around in his stuff, flinging pillows out of the way, but found that it, too, was gone. He turned a chair right-side up and sat with a disgusted huff.

"What did he get?" Harper looked at him with wide eyes of concern.

"My great-grandfather's pocket watch," he said. "He was a train conductor. It's not worth a dime to anyone but me. I can't believe the bastard took it."

Harper groaned. "Oh, no. I'll replace anything you lost once I get my money," she offered. "I know I can't replace your grandfather's watch exactly, but I'll do whatever I can. I'm so sorry to have dragged you into this whole mess."

"It's not your fault," Sebastian said. "But we've got to find a way to put an end to it all. Maybe I just need to give you the money."

"Sebastian, no," she said, crouching at his knee. She looked up at him with a dismayed expression. "I can't ask you to do that. You've already done too much."

He shook his head. "I don't want to pay him. He doesn't deserve the damn money, but it might be the only answer we have. But if we do pay him," he said with angrily gritted teeth, "I want all our stuff back."

* * *

"So what do we know about this Josie?" Lucy asked in a hushed voice over a delicate china plate of tea sandwiches.

They were at Violet's bridal tea, a ladies-only event. All the men, Sebastian included, had gone to play a round of golf, followed by some day drinking that would likely run until the rehearsal dinner. This was one of Harper's first real opportunities to sit with her friends without Sebastian or the other guys since they'd arrived in Ireland.

Violet was at another table near the front, being adored by all the ladies in attendance, leaving Harper, Lucy and Emma to sit in the back corner and gossip as they often did. They all shrugged in response to Lucy's question, Harper included. She didn't know, or really care much about Quentin's new fiancée. She had bigger, more pressing worries, but she was interested in why the others were so concerned.

"I hadn't met her before the trip, but I had heard about her through the grapevine. To hear it told," Emma said as she gripped her teacup, "the engagement was quite the surprise to everyone. Given his current situation, I think a lot of people felt that Quentin might have chosen a woman with a fatter bank account and better connections. As far as I know, Josie is a broke nobody. She's a secretary for a financial firm or something. Not exactly what I was expecting. Of course, all that could've happened after he proposed and then he was stuck with her."

Harper perked up in her seat at Emma's story. "Given his current situation? Stuck? What do you mean by 'all that'?"

Emma and Lucy shared knowing glances before turning back to Harper. "We hadn't said anything because bringing up Quentin in conversations always seemed to put you in a bad mood."

"Yes, well, talking about someone's ex is hardly a way to perk up their day. Unless it's bad news. Is it bad news?"

Lucy nodded. Her dark eyes lit with excitement. "Apparently he was cut off by his dear old dad."

Harper sat back in her seat, her jaw agape. That certainly was news. Quentin was an attorney, but he was a long way from being the successful hot shot he pretended to be. Most of his money had come from his family. When they were dating, she recalled him getting a ten-thousand-dollar-a-week allowance from his father. He'd been twenty-eight at the time, giving Harper a run for her money when it came to being spoiled.

"He's the low man on the totem pole at his law firm," Harper said. "Without his allowance, he would be in big trouble. He couldn't afford his apartment, his car...he certainly couldn't afford the giant engagement ring I've seen her sporting, either."

"Exactly," Emma said.

"Do we know why he got cut off?" Harper asked.

Lucy shook her head. "I haven't heard anything specific, but you know he had to have done something his dad really wasn't happy about to get cut off."

"So why would someone in his position propose to a woman that won't be any help with that situation? There are plenty of rich, single women in Manhattan that he could've chosen instead. He could've even come crawling back to you," Emma said.

"Not likely," Harper said. Quentin knew Harper didn't have any money or he might've tried. She couldn't tell the others that, though.

"What's so special about her?"

"I don't know. He loves her, maybe?" Harper replied with a sarcastic tone.

"Love? Quentin? Come on, now." Emma snorted. "If he was capable of that, he would've married you years ago. Maybe she's from an important family or one of his clients' children. No, my bet is that his father disapproves of the engagement and cut him off when he found out Quentin proposed. Unless she's got more to offer than meets the eye, I think he's searching for his relationship escape hatch. Once this wedding is over, he's going to drop her like a rock to get back in daddy's good graces. You just watch."

"Why would he propose to a woman his father didn't like?" Lucy asked. "Could she be pregnant?"

The three turned to where Josie was seated sipping tea. Her dress was fairly tight, showing no signs of a baby belly. "I doubt it," Harper said.

"I wonder if he just wanted to be engaged to someone at the wedding to make Harper jealous and it ended up backfiring on him."

Harper turned to Emma and frowned. "That's silly. Who would make up a fake relationship just to make someone else jealous?" The irony of the words were not lost on her.

"Maybe not jealous. Maybe he just didn't want to come here and face you on his own."

"He hasn't even spoken to me the whole trip. I doubt he's given me much thought at all."

"Well, you may be right, but I think it gives him the

perfect motive to pick a random girl to be his fiancée for a few weeks."

Harper lifted her teacup and sipped thoughtfully. Being cut off by daddy also gave her the one piece of the puzzle she'd been missing—the perfect motive for Quentin to blackmail her.

Eight

Sebastian was exhausted from a day golfing with the others but keen to get back to Harper to tell her everything he'd overheard during the trip. Between eighteen holes and half a dozen beers, mouths had loosened among the gentlemen. In addition to getting to know them all better, he'd picked up some stock tips, improved his swing and gotten some more dirt on her ex, Quentin.

As the bus pulled up in front of the castle, he spied Harper walking out toward the east gardens. When they unloaded, he trotted off after her, catching up just as she reached the intricate hedges that outlined the borders. She sat on a stone bench that overlooked the formal pattern of flowerbeds in bright summer colors that contrasted with the lush green of the grass.

"Harper!"

She turned and looked over her shoulder at him. She was wearing a pretty, pale pink, eyelet sundress with a matching sweater. "Hey there, Arnold Palmer. How did the golf go?"

He strolled the rest of the way toward her to catch his breath. He needed to do more running, apparently. "Awful," he said as he dropped down beside her on the bench. "I couldn't tell them I'd never played before, so I had to fake it and claim I was rusty from working too much."

"You've never played golf? What kind of CEO are you?"

Sebastian chuckled. "The kind that doesn't take clients out to schmooze on the greens. That's Finn's job. I work. But I have played golf. Just not this kind. I'm used to the windmills and the alligators that swallow your ball if you putt it into the wrong hole."

"Miniature golf. You've played Putt-Putt. Yeah, I'd say that's a little different."

"I'll tell you, though. Once I got the ball near the hole, I was an excellent putter. Just took me five swings over par to get that close."

Harper winced and laughed. "Wow. Lose any money?"

He shook his head. "I'm not that stupid. There was no way I was betting on my game. I did offer Quentin a wager, though. I bet him a thousand dollars that he'd shank his next ball into a sand trap."

She arched her brow curiously. "And?"

Sebastian reached into his pocket and pulled out a roll of hundred dollar bills. "I think I jinxed him. He basically shot it straight into the sand dunes and couldn't get out. Completely rattled the guy. I didn't feel guilty about it, though. If he's your blackmailer, then this thousand may have come from the money you paid him yesterday. If that's true, then I'm glad to steal some back." He handed the cash over to Harper.

"What is this for?" she asked, looking at the bills uncurling in the palm of her hand.

"For whatever." He shrugged. "It's not my money, so you can light cigars with it for all I care. Pay it to the blackmailer. Pay it on the loan. Get a really expensive manicure. Save it for a rainy day. Whatever you want. Just spend it knowing that I took it from Quentin. That should make it all the sweeter."

Harper closed her fist around the money and nodded. "It will," she said before slipping it into the little wallet pocket of her cell phone case. "Anything else interesting come up this afternoon?"

"Lots of man talk. Mostly bluster without substance. It got a little heated about the Yankees once alcohol got involved. The groom's face turned as red as his hair when someone said something about the Mets being a better team. I was smart enough to stay out of that. I don't know enough about sports to comment intelligently."

"Really? You didn't play sports in school?"

Sebastian frowned. "No. That wasn't my thing," he said. He supposed it might've interested him if he'd had the time. Maybe the swim team. But the fees to participate in school sports had been too high and all his free time had been taken up by working to help support his family. He hadn't had the typical frivolous youth, but Harper didn't know that. "I did learn something interesting about Quentin, though."

Harper turned toward him on the stone bench. "Me, too. But you go first."

"Okay. While we were talking, someone mentioned that Quentin was in some legal hot water. Apparently he'd tried to flip some real estate and used shoddy contractors to save money. The people that bought the place took him to court and the judge sided with them, awarding them a settlement to correct some of the repairs. Guess for how much?"

"A hundred thousand dollars?"

"Bingo."

"That is interesting. It certainly gives him a reason to come after me for exactly that much money. Especially after what I learned about him at the tea party."

"What's that?"

"His father cut him off, financially. We're not sure if it's because he disapproves of the fiancée, or maybe because of his legal troubles, but he isn't getting any more money from his father. I can tell you that's huge. He's probably hurting for cash right now. Even that thousand-dollar loss to you today likely stings."

Sebastian only shrugged. "He should've turned down the bet, then. He's too cocky to think he will lose."

"That is Quentin for you. Looking back, I know I dodged a bullet with that one."

"I'm sure you did. For all your dating angst, I hear you're quite the catch. All the gentlemen I spoke to think rather highly of you," Sebastian added with a smile.

Harper blushed with embarrassment and pushed a stray strand of dark hair behind her ear in an endearing way. He liked the way she was wearing it today. It was down in loose waves, almost like wild morning-after hair. It made him think about how it had cascaded across the pillows the other afternoon as he'd pleasured her. When he'd touched it, it had felt like silk between his fingertips. He wanted to touch it again.

"Do they now?" Harper said. "What did they say?"

"Well, they all congratulated me for winning you over. They said you were an amazing woman and that I would be a fool to let you slip through my fingertips."

Sebastian knew their words to be true before the men had confirmed it. Harper, however, seemed dumbfounded by the whole conversation.

"Really?"

"Yes, really."

"Even Quentin?"

Sebastian nodded. "Even Quentin. I don't know if it's all part of his game or not, but he said there were times when he knew he'd made the wrong choice letting you go."

Harper gasped. "I can't believe it."

"I don't know why. You're smart, beautiful, funny, sweet…"

"Quit buttering me up."

"You tend to lie a lot, though," he added with a smile. "Of course, they don't know that. They did mention that you have expensive tastes and might be costly to keep, but that you were worth it."

Harper laughed aloud at the final observation. "That sounds more like I was expecting to hear. How funny. Who knew golf with the boys could be so enlightening?"

It certainly had been for him. He'd already been dreading the end of the trip and their run as a couple, but his chat with the other men had made him wonder if maybe he shouldn't push harder for something more with Harper. Something beyond the physical. He'd been worried about letting himself get too close, but perhaps in time it might be possible. If he let himself do it. If he could take a step back from his work and allow life to take its place. Balance had never been his strength. He was balls-to-the-wall, all or nothing. Here, a relationship was easy because work wasn't interfering. Back home, the relationship would interfere with his work.

And that was only if Harper was open to the possibility. Now that he'd filled her head with compliments about how great a catch she was, he might not be what she wanted. He was a great stand-in for a boyfriend in a pinch, but would she want him once they were back in the States again? Maybe only if her grandfather cut her off.

"I guess the men's golf game is just as big a gossip cesspool as the ladies' tea," Harper said with a smile. "Did my brother say anything embarrassing?"

"Not much. He'd already said his peace to me a few days ago. The first day we arrived, actually."

Harper's eyes got big as she stiffened on the bench. She put her hand on him, squeezing his forearm. "What? No. What did he say?"

Sebastian chuckled. "Nothing too embarrassing, just basic big-brother stuff. I think he was just worried about you. He wanted to make sure my intentions were honest. He gave me a little insight into you, too."

"Like what?"

"Like, I'm not telling you," Sebastian retorted.

"So unfair. You've got all the insight into me and

you're this puzzle box I can't get into." With a sigh, Harper pushed up from the bench.

"Where are you going?"

"Back inside to get ready for the rehearsal. I'm a bridesmaid, you know."

Sebastian stood with her. Before she could get away, he wrapped her in his arms and pulled her close to him. "I forgot to say how nice you look today."

Harper smiled. "Thank you. You don't need to lay it on so thick, though. I don't think anyone is watching us out here together."

She seemed to think that every word, every caring gesture, was part of the game when it wasn't. How was he supposed to know if anything she said or did with him was genuine? That orgasm was genuine enough, but everything else? He couldn't be sure. Perhaps the idea of something real between them was a bridge too far.

But for now, he was going to go with it.

"I don't really care," he said, dipping his head and capturing her lips in a kiss.

As rehearsed, Harper marched down the rose-petal-strewn aisle in her lavender bridesmaid gown clutching a bundle of purple-and-cream roses with dark purple freesia and ranunculus in her hands. She was the last of the bridesmaids, with the rest of the wedding party already waiting up front with the minister.

Today, the Markree Castle gallery was acting as the chapel where the wedding was taking place. The long hall was lined with wooden paneling and pale blue-green walls. As she made her way down the long stretch of chairs that lined the aisle, she looked up to the pitched wood-beam ceiling and the intricate stained-glass windows that adorned the far end of the chapel, taking in their beauty.

Turning to the left, she lined up with Emma and Lucy to await the arrival of Violet in her wedding finery. She glanced over at the groomsmen across the aisle. They all looked handsome in their black tuxedos and lavender ties. Even little Knox had a matching tux. Aidan had managed to comb his wild red hair into submission for the special occasion. He was practically beaming with his eyes laser-focused on the back of the hall for the arrival of his bride.

The musical crescendo started and all the guests stood. The doors opened and Violet stepped through on the arm of her father. Even knowing what the dress looked like on Violet, Harper still felt the magnificence steal her breath as everything came together so beautifully.

The Pnina Tornai gown from Kleinfeld's was a beautiful but relatively plain gown from the front, allowing Violet's beauty to shine. It was a strapless, white ball gown with a crystal belt and corset top that molded to her perfectly. Her neck was as long and graceful as a swan's with her hair up and a simple diamond-and-pearl choker at her throat. In her hands, she carried a magnificent hand-crafted brooch bouquet made of silk rosettes in different shades of purple and covered in Swarovski crystal pins in two dozen different styles. Dripping from the teardrop-shaped bouquet were strings of pearls and strands of crystals.

But that was just the beginning. Harper heard the gasps of the guests as Violet passed and the back of the dress was revealed. That was where the beauty of the gown shone. From the waist down, the dress was a waterfall of large, silk roses that cascaded to the floor several feet behind her. The moment Violet had put on the dress at the bridal salon, they'd all known it was the one. Few other dresses could stand up to the grand venue like this one could.

As she looked out, Harper spotted Sebastian in the crowd. He'd chosen to sit on Aidan's side since he had fewer guests attending.

He was looking incredibly dapper in his tuxedo. He claimed he hardly ever wore it, but it fit perfectly and suited him well. The only thing missing were his cufflinks that had been stolen. She had gone that afternoon to Oliver's room and borrowed a pair, claiming Sebastian had forgotten to pack his own.

Unlike everyone else in the church, whose eyes were on Violet, Sebastian's eyes were on Harper. When he realized she had turned his way, he smiled and gave her a wink before looking over to Violet with the others as she stepped up to stand beside Aidan.

Harper handed her bouquet off to Lucy so she could straighten Violet's train and veil. Once they were perfect for pictures, she took the very heavily jeweled bouquet so Violet could hold Aidan's hands during the ceremony.

Once the service began, Harper looked down at the beautiful arrangement in her hands and the reality of the moment finally hit her. She was the last of her single friends. Practically, she'd known that. Violet and Aidan had been engaged for a while as they'd planned the event, so it's not like it had snuck up on her. But until that moment, she hadn't allowed herself to really grasp what it meant.

She was on the verge of thirty, hardly an old maid, but seeing the last of her friends pair off made a wave of sadness wash over her. Why hadn't she found someone like they had? She should be happily engaged and ready to start her life with someone, and yet here she was, basically bribing a man just to pretend to be her boyfriend at the wedding.

Her gaze drifted back to Sebastian. He was sitting in the chair, listening attentively to the service. She was so thankful he was there with her for this. Yes, it was because she had asked him to be, but she wondered what would've happened between them if things had gone differently. If he had asked her to dinner instead of her asking him on this trip...if there had been no wedding and they'd decided to go for drinks after they'd met at the store...would they have become real lovers instead of ones just for show?

In that moment she wished they were in a real relationship. Not just because she didn't want to be alone, but because she found she really cared for Sebastian. He was smart, handsome, thoughtful and kind. He was there for her when she needed someone. There was a part of her that was extremely susceptible to being treated the way he treated her. That part of her wanted to fall head over heels for him.

The other part didn't know where they stood.

Yes, they had crossed the line of their fake relationship that afternoon in their room, but their ruse had muddied the water. Was their attraction real or did they just think they were into one another because they spent all day flirting and pretending to be a couple? She was pretty certain that her draw to Sebastian was authentic. The moment she'd laid eyes on him outside

Neiman Marcus, she'd been attracted to his dark eyes and strong jaw. She'd wanted to know more about him instantly.

Honestly, after spending a week together, Harper found that she still wanted to know more about him. Mainly because he wasn't opening up to her the way she'd hoped. In all their conversations there had been plenty of chances for him to tell her about his childhood or where he'd grown up. His time in college. Anything outside of work. But that was really all he spoke about. His work was his life.

She knew Sebastian was passionate about his job, but she couldn't help but feel that there was more to him that he wasn't sharing. Intentionally. That worried her. Not because he was keeping potentially damaging secrets that would run her off, but because he didn't think he could open up to her.

If he didn't think he could share with her, what would happen once they returned to New York and didn't have a wedding packed full of events to get through? Would he call her? Would he want to kiss her again? Or would he return to his lab and disappear into his tools and toys the way he had before the trip?

She didn't know the answer. And that uncertainty scared her. Perhaps because no matter what the answer was, she knew it was already too late for her. Those dark eyes and that crooked smile had already captured her heart.

Maybe it wasn't being the last single friend that was troubling her today. Being single hadn't really ever bothered her before. Maybe it was knowing that, yes, she wanted a romantic moment like this for herself, but that she wanted it *with Sebastian*. She wanted him to be the man to whom she recited her vows to love, honor and cherish. She was upset because she knew deep down that she would never have this moment with him.

The loud sound of applause jerked Harper out of her thoughts. She turned to the altar in time to realize that the wedding ceremony had ended. Aidan and Violet were sharing their first kiss as husband and wife.

"Ladies and gentlemen, may I present for the very first time, Mr. and Mrs. Aidan Murphy!"

Violet turned to Harper to get her bouquet and face the crowd of wedding guests. Harper moved behind the bride to straighten her dress and veil one last time before Aidan scooped up Knox in his arms and they marched down the aisle as a family. Once they departed, she took her bouquet from Lucy.

Lucy followed the bouquet with a tissue she'd tucked away in her bra. "Here," she said, despite fighting tears of her own. "Don't mess up your makeup before the photos."

It wasn't until that moment that Harper realized she was crying. But it wasn't because of the beautiful service—it was because she knew she was right about her future with Sebastian. She dabbed her eyes, took a deep breath and pasted a smile on her face for the cameras.

No matter what, she still had a wedding reception to get through.

The new Mr. and Mrs. Aidan Murphy walked down the aisle together, holding their adorable toddler. Both of them were beaming with happiness and it took everything she had to not scowl at them as they went by. She put a fake smile on her face and clutched her program as the rest of the wedding party followed in their wake.

First was tech heiress Emma and her rebellious, gaming CEO husband, Jonah. The two of them were so beautiful together that she already hated their daughter. She was still a baby, but she would no doubt grow up to be a Victoria's Secret Angel or something. Behind them was the formerly poor but incredibly lucky Lucy, who'd managed to inherit half a billion dollars from her boss, then married her boss's nephew, Oliver, with his computer empire. She wished she'd had that kind of luck, but she'd learned she had to take control of her own destiny.

Last down the aisle was Harper on the arm of a groomsman that must be a friend of Aidan's because she didn't know him. She'd only studied the people with enough money to matter on this trip. This guy didn't matter. None of these people really did. Once she got her money, she was pretty sure she'd never see the likes of most of them again. That is, unless she uncovered another scandalous tidbit to make some more money off of them.

The guests at the wedding stood and started filing out of the gallery toward the dining hall for the cocktail reception. After thirty minutes of that overly romantic ceremony, she needed a drink. Maybe two. Or four by the time dinner rolled around. This was going to be a long night.

They were headed back to the States soon and she could feel time was running short. Time in Ireland. Time with all of these people. Time to execute her plan and make off with the money she needed.

The blackmail payment was supposed to be at the

front desk before the reception ended, but she wasn't holding her breath. Every other deadline had passed with disappointment. Why would this one be any different?

She wanted her money. She didn't want to have to pull the trigger and expose Harper. That wouldn't do either of them any good. No, Harper was being obstinate, insisting she couldn't pay when they were surrounded by people who could just write a check for that amount if they wanted to. Harper only had to ask. But she wouldn't.

Harper was going to ruin things for her. So that meant that she had no choice but to ruin things for Harper.

Nine

Sebastian spun Harper on the dance floor and then pulled her tightly against him. Dinner had been excellent, but he couldn't wait to take Harper out for a spin. He wasn't much of a dancer, but it was the only socially acceptable way he knew of to hold her body against his in public.

"You really look beautiful tonight, Harper. Have I said that yet?"

"No," she said with a smile, "but thank you. You should know, though, that I'm just a bridesmaid, so I can only be pretty. At a wedding, only the bride can be beautiful. It's the rules."

He leaned in to her and the scent of her floral perfume tickled at his nose, putting his nerves on high alert. It made him want to pull her closer. Or better yet, to tug her off the dance floor and head upstairs to their hotel room. His medical restrictions on sexual activity should be over now. He'd take it slow just in case, but he needed to indulge in Harper at least once before all of this came to an end.

Sebastian pressed his lips to the outer shell of her ear. "Well, don't tell Violet, but I think you're the most stunning woman here tonight. I don't care who the bride is. You take my breath away even when you're wearing that ugly purple dress she picked for all of you."

When he pulled away, he could see Harper blush before she glanced down to look at her dress with a critical eye. "You don't like my dress? I like it. I mean, I like it for a bridesmaid's dress. I wouldn't wear it to the Met Gala or anything, but it's pretty enough."

He didn't know what one would wear to the Met Gala, but he was pretty sure this pale purple frock with flowers on the shoulder wasn't it. "To be honest, I think you would look much prettier without it."

Her brow arched in suspicion. "I think you just want me to be naked."

Sebastian shrugged. "If you want to look your best, my vote is for naked."

"Just like a man," she groaned. "No respect for the power of fashion."

That was true. For all his money, Sebastian didn't know one designer from the next, nor did he care. He'd be just as happy buying all his clothes at Target, if Finn would let him. He was more about function than style most days. He couldn't even tell you the name of the designer he was wearing right now. It was someone important. Finn had made sure of that. But without slipping out of his jacket to look at the name sewn inside, he had no clue.

What he did know was that the tuxedo was getting hot. Or maybe it was dancing so close to Harper that was overheating him. Looking around, he spied a door that opened onto a courtyard.

"You want to get some air? It's getting a little warm in here."

Harper glanced around the room for a moment and nodded. "Sure. I think we still have a little time before they cut the cake."

Sebastian took her hand and led her off the dance floor. They made their way around a few tables before they reached the door that opened up to the courtyard. Out there, half a dozen small bistro tables and chairs had been set up. Each table was decorated with a floral arrangement and a flickering pillar candle protected from the breeze with a tall hurricane glass. At the moment, no one was outside, giving them some privacy.

He stepped over to the stone wall that separated the patio from the gardens beyond. It was a clear, cool night with a sky full of stars. He couldn't imagine this many stars existed if he lived in Manhattan his whole life. He'd only seen this many on nights in Maine as a kid. Even so, it hardly held a candle to the beauty of the woman standing beside him.

He hadn't just been flattering her earlier, it was the truth. It would be so easy in a moment like this—with candlelight highlighting the soft curves of her face and stars reflecting in her eyes—to let his guard down and fall for Harper once and for all. The music and the moonlight seemed to be conspiring against him tonight, wearing down his defenses. This week was supposed to be relaxing and yet he'd spent the entire trip fighting with himself.

He hadn't expected any of this when he'd agreed to come to Ireland. Yes, he'd thought he would spend a few days holding hands with and kissing a beautiful woman overseas. He'd never imagined that he would be tempted to take their fake relationship seriously and open up to her. That he might look forward to returning to New York and spending time with her instead of rushing back into his lab at the first opportunity.

If he had, he might not have taken the trip. His work was at such a critical point. Could he risk taking time away to build something serious with Harper? He wasn't sure.

"Ahh, this feels good," Harper said. "Normally it would be cold, but it got so hot in the ballroom."

"Maybe it's all the champagne," Sebastian offered.

"Or maybe it's the pressure," she said with a sigh.

"Pressure? What kind of pressure?"

Harper leaned her elbows against the patio wall to look out at the garden. "The reception will be over soon and my time is running out. That means the blackmailer is going to realize he isn't going to get any more money out of me. He won't have any choice but to expose my secret. I wonder how long he'll wait. Will he reveal the truth tonight? Wait until the morning and ruin my flight home? Maybe wait until we're back in New York and have something printed in the paper so everyone, not just the wedding guests, finds out? I wish I knew how it would happen so I could brace myself for it."

Sebastian had been enjoying the romantic evening with Harper and pondering a future with her, and all the while her mind was on her troubles instead of her company. Perhaps he'd better put those thoughts aside before he regretted them. "And here I thought you might be enjoying the wedding reception."

She shook her head sadly and straightened up. "I wish I could. This was supposed to be a great trip and a special wedding for one of my best friends. Instead it's been nothing but a waking nightmare where everyone has Irish accents. I really just want to get on the plane and go home so I can get started dealing with the fallout."

Sebastian took her hand in his. She felt so small and delicate in his grip when she was speaking in such a defeated tone. "You're going to be okay, you know."

"What do you mean?"

"I mean that no matter what happens, you're a strong, independent woman. You've made the best of your situation before and you'll continue to make the best of it, regardless of what the blackmailer does. He might feel like he's in control of your fate, but he's really not. How you handle your situation is entirely up to you."

Harper studied his face for a moment and nodded. "You're right. And I think I'm going to start handling the situation right now." She turned away from him to head back into the reception.

Sebastian reached out and grasped her wrist before she could get away. "Wait. What are you going to do?"

She took a deep breath and straightened her spine. "I'm going to confront Quentin and put an end to this."

"Quentin? May I speak with you privately for a moment?"

He hesitated, looking at his fiancée before whispering into her ear and nodding to Harper.

Harper hadn't had any discussions with Jessie or Josie or Jamie—whatever her name was. She wasn't interested in chatting with her ex-boyfriend's new fiancée. It was hard enough to look at the glittering diamond rock on her ring finger and not think about the bare finger on her own hand. The only difference lately was that when she imagined a man down on one knee proposing, there was only one face that came to mind.

And it sure wasn't Quentin's.

He finally disentangled himself from his fiancée and followed Harper out into the hallway. "What's this all about, Harper? Josie doesn't really like me talking to you, to be honest. The sooner I'm back in the reception, the better off I'll be."

Harper couldn't care less about Quentin's fiancée and her jealous streak. "This won't take long. All I want to say is that I can't give you any more money, Quentin."

She'd hoped that her blunt confrontation would catch him off guard and he might give something away. Instead he stopped short and narrowed his gaze at her. "What are you talking about, Harper?"

She crossed her arms over her chest. "Oh, cut it out. I'm tired of playing these games, *B. Mayler.* I've given you all the money I can get my hands on right now. You've stolen jewelry from my room and that will have to suffice until—"

"Wait," Quentin said, holding up his hands. "I haven't stolen anything from your room. I don't even know where your room is in this place. And what money? Seriously, Harper, I have no idea what you're talking about."

Her ex's tone gave her pause. It was a sincerely confused voice and it matched the expression on his face. "You're being sued, right? And your dad cut you off, didn't he?"

A ruddy blush of embarrassment came to his cheeks. "How did you hear about all that?"

"It's a small world. But I know it's true, so don't pretend you don't need the money."

"Sure, I could use some money. I wouldn't have dropped fifty grand on Josie's ring if I knew my dad was going to cut me loose a few weeks later. He doesn't like Josie, but I'm sure he and I will work that out. And the lawsuit is no big deal. My attorneys are handling it. But I don't know what my problems have to do with you."

"You're going to stand there and tell me that you're not the one that's blackmailing me?"

"What? No, I'm not." His eyes widened in concern and he leaned closer to speak in a softer voice. "Someone is blackmailing you?"

The concern in his voice might as well have been a punch to the gut. Harper didn't know what to say or do, but the truth was plain as day when she looked into his clueless face: Quentin was not her blackmailer.

So who the hell was?

"You know what? Just forget I said anything," Harper said. "Go back inside before Josie gets upset."

Quentin hesitated for a moment and then nodded, silently returning to the reception hall.

Harper was relieved to see him go without a fight, but the relief was short-lived.

From the very first blackmail message, she'd been fairly certain that Quentin had been behind it. He was the only one with the slightest inkling of her financial difficulties. When they'd dated and she'd finally opened up about her problems, he'd actually coached her on some financial planning. They'd even used the same financial advisor. But no one else, until she'd told Sebastian, had known.

Maybe she was fooling herself. Maybe everyone saw through her ruse and was too kind to say anything. They just let her carry on as though no one was the wiser. If that was the case, then anyone could be the blackmailer.

Harper stood at the entrance to the reception hall and watched everyone enjoying themselves inside. Violet and Aidan were cutting the cake while a crowd gathered around them. Flashes from cameras and the *awws* of bystanders drew everyone to the corner where the towering confection was on display. A few people were sitting at their tables, chatting and sipping their flutes of champagne.

Some people she knew better than others, but who was capable of blackmailing her? Of ransacking her room and stealing both her and Sebastian's things? She didn't even know where to begin looking for a new suspect.

"Miss Drake?"

Harper turned her attention to the waiter who had come up beside her. He had previously been carrying a silver tray of champagne flutes, but now his tray held nothing but the miserably familiar white envelope.

"I have a message for you," he said. "It was left at the front desk."

Of course it was. "Thank you," she said with a sigh and accepted the letter. She supposed she should open it and see what the latest threat entailed. The money was due by the end of the reception. There was only an hour or so left in that and she was pretty sure that both of them knew she wasn't paying it. So what was the point?

She slipped the envelope into the front of her bra to read later. Maybe. What did it matter in the end? She wouldn't have the money. Unless the blackmailer was bluffing the whole time, her news was going to come out sooner or later.

When she'd first told Sebastian about the note she'd received on the plane, he'd told her that one of her courses of action would be to expose the truth before anyone else could. To take the power back from the blackmailer. At the time, the idea had been out of the question. She would be throwing everything out the window if she did that. Now she wondered if that hadn't been the best policy all along. Perhaps if she spoke to her grandfather and explained her situation, he would understand. Or not. Perhaps he would cut her off and that twenty-eight million would vanish into thin air.

So what?

It seemed like a ridiculous thought to have. It was a life-changing amount of money. She'd been scraping by for years waiting for the day that money would arrive. But now that she stood there, she realized that things hadn't been so terrible. She had managed just fine. She had a good job at FlynnSoft that paid well and offered amazing benefits like a gym, a no-cost cafeteria and coffee shop, and insurance for minimum premiums and co-pays. Her beautiful, large apartment was paid for. The fees and insurance were high, but she paid them every year without fail.

No, she didn't have all the latest fashions. Her high-end pieces were either relics from her previous spending days or lucky thrift store finds. She had learned over the years how to get by without keeping up with the Joneses. If she told the truth about her situation to her friends and family, the pressure to shop and spend money with them would likely go away. No one had ever treated Lucy any differently when she'd been the poor one in the group. After she'd inherited half a billion dollars and married Harper's rich brother, she was still the same old Lucy.

Perhaps she could be the same old Harper. Just a little less flashy. She'd spent the last eight years just trying to get to her thirtieth birthday when perhaps she needed to be happy that she had made it all this time on her own. If she wasn't pretending to be something she wasn't, she could make changes to make her life easier. Maybe she could sell her flashy apartment for something more reasonable, then pocket the profit into savings. She could sell some of her designer clothes that she never wore anymore.

The realization that she didn't need her grandfather's money was a profound one for her. Suddenly it was as though a great weight had been lifted from her shoulders. She didn't know who her blackmailer was, but she was about to stick it to them. The one thing they couldn't have counted on was the spoiled heiress Harper Drake having the nerve to go it on her own.

Straightening her spine, Harper marched into the reception hall with a feeling of purpose. Cake was being distributed and the happy couple was sharing a piece at their table near the front. The band was playing a soft instrumental piece and the dance floor was empty for the moment. This was her chance.

She snatched a flute of champagne from a passing server and climbed the steps of the stage. Several people had made toasts to the couple from this perch earlier. Violet had only had bridesmaids since she said she couldn't choose a maid of honor from her three best friends. Harper could easily be the next one from the wedding party to make a toast to the happy couple.

The stage band saw her approach and eased out of the song they were playing so she could offer her good wishes to the bride and groom. She nodded and waved to them, taking the microphone from the stand and walking to the edge of the platform.

"Hello, everyone. I'm Harper Drake and I've known Violet for many years. Our families knew each other growing up, but we really got close when Violet and I went to Yale together and joined the same sorority. Pi Beta Phi sisters forever!"

The crowd laughed and applauded. "It's true. There, I made best friends for life. Not just Violet, but also Emma and Lucy, who is now my sister-in-law. Over the last few years, I've seen each of these beautiful, smart, wonderful women find love and happiness. I could not be happier for all of you. And tonight, I want to raise a toast to Violet and Aidan. May your lives together always be as magical as the fairy-tale wedding where it started."

She raised her glass and the room applauded and joined her in the toast. Harper didn't leave the stage, however. She waited for the applause to die down and continued. "Tonight, in this room, are some of the most important people in my life. So I wanted you all to hear the brief announcement that I'd like to make. No—I'm not engaged or pregnant, so let's just get that out of the way," she said with a smile. "I actually want you all to know that I've been lying to you.

"Every day for the last eight years or so, I have gotten out of bed and lived a lie. I have carried on with my life as though nothing has ever changed, but the truth is that I am broke. Flat broke. It seems silly in retrospect to lie about something like that, but my pride got in the way. No accountant wants to be seen as a poor money manager and that's what I was. I was spoiled rotten and when the well ran dry, I didn't know what to do."

Harper sipped her champagne and took a moment. Her eyes stayed focused on the tapestry on the back wall. She feared that making eye contact with someone might make her start to cry and she didn't want to do that right now.

"You're probably wondering why I'm up here telling you this. It's because someone found out about my lie—someone in this very room—and they've been using it to blackmail me. You see, if my grandfather found out I wasted all my money, I would lose the rest of my inheritance. So they've harassed me throughout this entire trip. They've taken thousands from me I couldn't afford to give, ransacked my hotel suite and stolen family pieces that can never be replaced. They've demanded money that I can't pay. And I won't ever pay it because my inheritance is basically out the window at this point.

"So I'm up here tonight to tell all of you the truth and to apologize for misleading you. And also to tell my blackmailer, whomever he or she is, that they can kiss my ass. Thank you."

She put the microphone back in the stand and made her way off of the stage as quickly as possible. She had done what she'd had to do, but she wasn't sure if she was ready to face the backlash yet. The room was unnervingly quiet, but eventually the band started to play again.

"Harper!"

She heard someone shout her name, but she didn't stop. She couldn't stop. She just wanted to get out of the ballroom as quickly as she could.

Harper made it out of the party and down the hall-way before she felt a warm hand clamp down on her wrist. She stopped, spinning on her heel to find Se-bastian standing behind her.

"Let me go, please," she said. "I just want to go back to our room."

He looked at her with his big, dark eyes and nod-ded. "That's fine. But you're not going without me."

Ten

Alone in their suite, they took their time getting undressed. There was no sense of urgency pressing them on. Tonight, she knew, they were going to savor the moment. It was their last night together and an emotionally heightened one after everything that had just happened downstairs.

"Unzip me please," she asked, presenting her back to Sebastian and lifting her hair.

He had already slipped out of his jacket and tie. He approached her, gently taking the zipper and sliding it slowly down her back. Harper could feel his fingertips grazing along her spine as he traveled down to the curve of her lower back. His touch sent a shiver through her whole body. She closed her eyes to savor the sensation of his warm breath against her skin.

His large, firm hands cupped her shoulders, pushing the one floral strap down her arm. With little effort, her dress slipped to her waist and then pooled at her feet in a puddle of lavender chiffon.

She heard his sharp intake of breath and realized he had discovered her lavender lace boy shorts. She had strategically chosen them for several reasons. First, was how they would wear beneath the dress. Second was that the cut highlighted the curve of her butt nicely. And last, they were replaceable when Sebastian tore them.

She felt his fingers grip the clasp of her strapless bra and then it fell to the floor with the rest of her clothes.

"Looks like you dropped something," he said.

Harper glanced down at the floor and realized that the note from the blackmailer she'd tucked into her bra had fallen out. She bent to pick it up and held it thoughtfully in her hand. "Another love note," she said.

Without hesitation she walked across the room to the fireplace and tossed it inside. The flames immediately started to blacken and curl the corners, then the whole thing was engulfed in the orange blaze. Although she hadn't intended it to be a symbolic gesture, it felt like one now. Consequences be damned, she was done with her blackmailer.

"Now, enough of that interrupting my trip." Harper turned back to Sebastian and approached him. She started unbuttoning his dress shirt, feeling immediately calmer and content as her hands ran over the chest hair hidden beneath it. "I don't want to think about anything but you and me right now."

She pushed his shirt over his broad shoulders and then wrapped her arms around his neck. Her lips sought his out tentatively. When they met, she molded against him, pressing her breasts into the hard wall of his chest to get as close to him as she could. "Make love to me tonight," she whispered against his mouth. "I want you. All of you."

Sebastian kissed her tenderly and then pulled away. There was a hesitation in him she didn't understand, but she shoved her doubts away when he said, "Whatever you want, darling."

His words made her smile. She hooked her fingers into the loops of his pants and tugged him over to the bed. Harper sat on the edge, bringing his waist to her eye level. There, she unfastened his belt, unbuttoned and unzipped his tuxedo pants, and slipped them down with his briefs.

She reached out for him then. He was hard and ready for her without even touching. She wrapped her fingers around his soft skin and stroked gently until she heard him groan. She moved faster, leaning in to flick her tongue across the tip.

"Harper!" Sebastian nearly shouted, grasping her wrist to still the movement. "Wait a minute," he said. "Before we… I don't have anything."

Harper leaned over to the nightstand and pulled a small box of condoms out of the drawer. "I picked these up when we were in town one day."

After their last encounter, she'd wondered if not having protection had put the brakes on things and she hadn't wanted to run into that problem again.

The breath rushed out of his lungs all at once. "Oh, thank you," he groaned. With that worry off his mind, Sebastian seemed to become more engaged. He pressed Harper back against the pillows and covered her body with his.

She loved the feel of his weight holding her down, the scent of his cologne and skin teasing her nose, and the heat of him warming her chilled body. His lips and hands were all over her, leaving no inch of skin unloved as he moved lower and lower down her body.

His fingers brushed over the lace barrier between them. To her surprise, he eased them from her hips and tossed them to the side. "I like those," he said when he caught her surprised expression. "If I ruin them, you can't wear them again."

Harper laughed, but the sound was trapped in her throat when his fingers dipped between her thighs and stroked her center. Instead it came out a strangled cry as he knowingly teased the right spot. When his finger slipped inside her, Harper's inner muscles clamped down and both of them groaned aloud.

"I wanted to take my time with this," he said, shaking his head.

She reached for the condoms and handed him the box. "We can take our time later. I want you right now. I'm ready."

"So am I." He didn't hesitate to tear open the box and grab one of the foil packets from inside. Within seconds Sebastian had the latex rolled down his length and in place.

Harper shifted her legs to cradle him between her thighs and slid her hips lower.

He leaned forward, bracing himself on his elbows.

Harper lifted her knees to wrap them around his hips, but he stopped, leaning down to kiss her instead. "Thank you," he whispered.

"For what?"

"For this week. I know I was supposed to be helping you, but I needed this time away almost as much as I need you. So thank you for that." Sebastian kissed her again and this time he pressed his hips forward and entered her, ending any further conversation.

Harper gasped against his lips as Sebastian filled her. She gripped his face in her hands and kissed him hard even as he eased back and surged forward into her again. She was surprised by the stirring of pleasure deep inside her. It wasn't something she expected based on past experience, but there was something about the way he moved. A tilt of his hips, maybe, that made every stroke more amazing than the last in a way she couldn't even describe. It was just like Sebastian to have mastered the mechanics of sex.

It was so intense, she had no choice but to close her eyes and hold on. She clung to his bare back and lifted her hips to meet his every advance. Her cries grew louder and louder as her release built inside her and she couldn't hold back any longer. She shouted his name as the dam broke and the rush of pleasure surged through her.

He thrust harder then. Previously his movements had been controlled and measured in a way that was distinctly Sebastian. He seemed to be taking his time and yet ensuring every stroke made the maximum impact. As her orgasm started to fade, she realized the calculated Sebastian was giving way to a man on the edge.

He thrust hard, again and again, until he finally stiffened and groaned in her ear. He held perfectly still for a moment, his eyes squeezed tightly shut. Then he collapsed beside her on the mattress, his breath ragged with strain.

Harper curled up against his side, resting her head on his chest to listen to his heartbeat, which was faster than she expected. They lay together like that until both his breathing and his pulse had slowed to normal. At that point, he seemed to relax. He wrapped his arm around her and placed a kiss against her forehead.

"Everything okay?" she asked, lifting her head to look up at him.

"Yes, we're good," he said. "Great, actually."

Harper chuckled and lay back. "I'm glad. I've been fantasizing about this moment all week."

"Really?" Sebastian laughed. "I'm sorry to make you hold out so long. I figured you had other things on your mind. Speaking of which, you were really amazing tonight."

"Well, thank you. I aim to please."

Sebastian swatted her bottom playfully. "That's not what I meant. I was talking about the reception. It took a lot of guts to get up there and take control of your situation. I was really proud of you."

"Oh," she said in a sheepish tone.

"What prompted it? You went to talk to Quentin and the next thing I know, you're on stage."

"I spoke with him, but it was apparent that he wasn't involved. That scared me. I had no idea who I could be dealing with and I decided it wasn't worth hiding any longer. You had been right from the beginning—exposing myself was the only way to take back my power. But I don't want to talk about that anymore. It's taken up this whole trip and I want to put it behind me. Tonight I'd rather talk about you for a change."

She felt Sebastian stiffen in her arms at the mention of talking about him. "Please," she added. "Tell me something I don't know about you. Like why you decided to go into medical technology. What inspired you? And I don't mean whatever practiced answer you put together for the company web site. The truth. What happened?"

He'd spoken about combining his engineering skills with Finn's medical expertise before and it seemed a winning combination, but there was still more to it. She could tell. No one dedicated themselves to their work like that without a reason. A personal reason.

Sebastian sat thoughtfully for a moment. The silence was long enough for her to worry he might not answer. But then he began.

"I was a shy, nerdy sort of kid. I liked to tinker. My older brother, Kenny, was more outdoorsy. He was always riding his bike or skateboarding. He stayed active."

Harper felt anxiety start to tighten her shoulders. She should've anticipated that this conversation wouldn't be a cheerful one. With his type of work, inspiration likely came from some kind of tragedy. She wanted to kick herself and yet, in the moment, was so grateful he was sharing, she would happily listen to any story he told.

"His best friend in high school ended up getting a four-wheeler for his birthday one year. My brother had graduated from high school at that point and he and a couple friends had gone camping somewhere to ride the ATV and hang out for the weekend. I don't know the details of what happened, but Kenny ended up rolling the four-wheeler. He was wearing a helmet, thankfully, but the ATV landed on top of him and crushed his lower spine. They were so deep in the woods, they couldn't land a helicopter out there to get him, so they had to carry him out on a gurney until they could reach an ambulance, which drove him to a place where the helicopter could pick him up."

Harper grasped his hand in the dark as he spoke, squeezing it tightly.

"The accident severed his spinal cord. He was eighteen and doomed to be a paraplegic for the rest of his life. I saw the toll his accident took on him and on my family. It was my hope that doing the work I do, someday I could develop something that would help him. One of the projects I've worked on for years has been a mechanical exoskeleton that would allow Kenny to walk again."

"That sounds amazing."

"It does. But so far, it's been the one thing that has eluded me. I have the technology together. I have a prototype that works in the lab. But my goal is to create something anyone can afford. Not just for rich people or ones with good insurance. That is going to take more time. That's why I work so much. For Kenny. And all the other Kennys in the world."

Harper had asked the question and now she knew the answer. In that moment she almost wished she hadn't. Now she knew just how important his work was to him. It was personal. It was his first love. Unlike Quentin, who used his work as a cover for affairs, Sebastian was truly a workaholic. It made her wonder if that meant there would never be any room in his life for anything—or anyone—else.

It was then that she realized that she was fighting a losing battle with him. No matter what happened between them, she could never fully have Sebastian in her life. She would be better served by keeping her feelings to herself and moving on once they arrived home.

There was someone out there for Harper. Someone who would love her, treat her well and let her be the most important thing in his life. Unfortunately that man just wasn't Sebastian West.

"Ladies and gentleman, welcome to New York. The current time is nine thirty in the evening."

Sebastian perked up in his seat after the wheels hit the ground and the pilot announced the long flight was finally over. He wished he'd been able to sleep on the way back and have it go as quickly as flying over, but that wasn't the way it worked.

Instead he'd spent most of the flight watching the television in the lounge with several other wedding guests. Harper had been…quiet…since they'd left Ireland. He wasn't sure what was wrong. Things had to be looking up. The blackmailer was out of business, they didn't have to pretend to be dating any longer, they were back home…life could return to normal.

Even Sebastian was relieved to know he only had a few days left on his leave before he could get back into the office. He might not burst through the door like usual, but he had a lot of exciting sketches in his notebook and he was ready to get to work on the prototypes as soon as possible.

Perhaps Harper wasn't interested in things returning to normal. Going home meant facing the consequences of her actions with her grandfather. Even Sebastian had to admit that he wasn't quite ready for their fake relationship to come to an end. But she hadn't voiced any interest in continuing. Perhaps he had read too much into their physical connection.

They were two of the last people off the plane. Most everyone had their drivers picking them up in black, luxury sedans, so the parking lot of the small airport emptied quickly. By the time they collected their bags and went out to where they'd parked, Sebastian found it was just the two of them.

"So now what?" he asked, setting down his luggage beside his car. Although he rarely drove it in the city, he had a blue BMW that he traveled back and forth to Maine in from time to time.

Harper set her bag down and sighed. "I've got an Uber coming to get me."

"That's not what I meant," he said. "I meant with us."

She crossed her arms over her chest in a defensive posture she'd never taken with him before. "I don't know. The week is over. Thank you very much for being my boyfriend on the trip. You were very…thorough."

"Thorough?" He couldn't keep the irritation from his voice. "Is that what you call it?"

"What else would you call it, Sebastian?"

There was a tone in her voice that he couldn't pinpoint. He wasn't sure if she was daring him to admit that it was more than just for show or not. Did she want him to profess his undying love and beg her to be his girlfriend for real? Or did she just want him to lay out his feelings so she could stomp on them? The way she'd pulled away from him today made him unsure.

"I sure as hell wouldn't—"

"Your time is up, Miss Drake," a woman's voice interrupted him.

Both Harper and Sebastian turned their attention to the shadowy figure standing in the dark, empty parking lot outside the airport.

The person took a few steps closer into the beam of an overhead light and Sebastian could finally make out who was standing there.

He didn't know her name, but he recognized the woman as Quentin's fiancée. And more importantly, she was aiming a gun at Harper.

Without thinking, he took a step forward and put his arm out to shield Harper. "What the hell are you doing pointing a gun at people?" he asked.

"Josie?" Harper asked from over his shoulder. "What's going on?"

"Surprised?" The woman smiled but it came out more like a smirk. "I bet you didn't suspect little old me for a second, did you? Of course not. You haven't given me a second thought this whole trip. I wasn't important or rich like the rest of you. I was just the disposable arm candy."

That was true. Sebastian had hardly paid any attention to the younger woman who'd always seemed glued to Quentin's side. To be fair, he hadn't really known many of the people on the trip, but Josie had been a silent, ignorable presence. Harper hadn't even known the woman and she knew everybody.

If that was true, how had Josie managed to get hold of such personal, private information about Harper?

"You're the one blackmailing me?"

"Guilty," Josie said without moving the gun a centimeter. It was still fixed on Harper, even if it had to go through Sebastian to get there.

"I don't understand," Harper said, pushing his arm out of the way. "How did you find out about my trust conditions? Did Quentin tell you?"

Josie shook her head. "All Quentin provided me was access to you. The rest I got on my own. If you'd bothered to speak to me this trip, you might've discovered that I work for your financial management firm. I know everything about you, Harper, including the provisions of your trust. I just knew a spoiled diva like you would've blown it. It only took a little digging to find out what I needed to know. Honestly, it was too easy."

"Why would you do this to me, Josie? I've never done anything to you."

"Aww, it wasn't personal, Harper. It's just about the money. It could've just as easily been any one of you."

"It was personal to me. Ransacking our room? Taking my late mother's necklace, his grandfather's watch—that was personal. I've spent the last week tied in knots because of you. And for what? Just some money?"

"You say that just like a rich person. You've gotten good at fooling everyone. Yes, I just did it for some money. That's enough for most people, although I have to admit I haven't gotten much cash out of the deal. I've spent this whole trip trying to get my point across with you, but nothing seems to be working. I've threatened you, stalked you, raised the price, promised to expose you, and here I stand with mere pennies of what you owe me."

"I don't owe you anything. Nobody owes you a

damn thing. Everything you've gotten was taken by force."

"And everything you've gotten was given to you on a silver platter. All you have to do is give me the money and I'll be on my way."

"You of all people know that I won't have any money until after my birthday. How can I pay you what I don't have?"

Sebastian wished he could think of something to do. Like some smooth kung-fu move to kick the gun out of Josie's hand and then wrestle her to the ground. But he was an engineer. At best, he could outthink her. If he could get his heart to stop pounding so loudly so he could focus.

"Like you couldn't get it if you needed it with all your rich and powerful friends. Violet spent more money on the rehearsal dinner alone than I was asking for. To tell the truth, I feel like I've been accommodating. I doubt there are many other blackmailers out there that would've given you as many chances as I have, Harper. But I'm done being nice. I need the money and I need it now."

"Why would I pay you another cent?" Harper asked. "It's all over, Josie. It's been over since the wedding. Everyone knows my secret. You can't blackmail me with it anymore."

She nodded. "That's true. That's why I brought along the gun. This isn't so much a blackmailing anymore as an armed robbery. I want my money."

"Why do you need money from me? You're marrying Quentin. His family has plenty of money. A hundred thousand is nothing to them."

"And I'm nothing to Quentin," Josie replied with

narrowed eyes. "It turns out he was just using me to make you jealous. He proposed and brought me on this trip just because he knew it would bother you. He never expected daddy to cut him off in the process. Now that the trip is over and he sees you're in love with someone else, he's dropped me like a rock and gone crawling back for forgiveness. So the money is more important than ever, actually."

Sebastian watched the heated discussion continue to volley between the two women. He curled his hands into fists at his sides as frustration and anger built inside him, but he felt an unpleasant tingling sensation running down his left arm. It forced him to shake out his hand in the hope it would go away.

It didn't.

The women continued to talk, but he found he couldn't focus on their words any longer. He felt the panic start to rise in him. Yes, Josie was holding a gun on them, but this was a different kind of panic. A familiar one. He was getting dizzy as he tried to focus on the two small figures standing in front of him. He reached out for Harper to steady himself before he stumbled.

"Sebastian!" Harper said in a startled voice. "What's wrong? Are you okay?" she asked.

He wanted to answer her but he couldn't. His chest was suddenly so tight he could barely breathe, much less speak. As the vise tightened harder on his rib cage, he realized that this wasn't just some random panic attack. This was another heart attack—a stronger one than last time.

The doctors had warned him to take it easy. And he'd tried. He'd done as best he was able and yet here he was—looking into the eyes of the woman he loved and wondering if it was for the last time. Was it done? Had he lost his chance to say all the things to Harper he'd been too afraid to voice? Could he say enough in time?

"I love…" He gasped and hunched over, unable to finish. His hand slipped from her shoulder and he heard her scream as his knees buckled beneath him.

Blackness enveloped Sebastian and he was unconscious before he hit the hard pavement.

Eleven

"Harper?"

Harper sat up from a dead sleep, making the best she could out of the recliner in Sebastian's hospital room. Still groggy, she wiped an unfortunate bit of drool from her chin and looked around. That's when she realized that Sebastian was awake.

She leaped from the chair to stand at his bedside. "You're up," she said with a smile.

"I guess. I feel like I've been hit by a truck." He brought his hand up to his face, dragging all his IV tubes along with it. "What happened? Where am I?"

Harper was surprised but relieved that he didn't remember the last few days. It had been a roller coaster of tests, bloodwork, scans and, finally, a stint placed in one of the arteries to his heart. He'd been out of it most of the time. Harper had just sat by his bedside waiting for the next bit of news from the nurses and doctors caring for him.

"You had a heart attack at the airport," Harper explained. "You've been in the hospital for a couple of days."

Sebastian frowned as he looked around, taking inventory of his body. "Why does my wrist hurt?"

"That's how they went in to put a stint in your chest."

He put his hand against his chest and shook his head. "Wow."

Harper sat on the edge of the bed. She'd been filled with a mix of emotions over the last few days that she'd never expected—and never wanted to experience again. First was the fear of being shot by a vengeful and bitter Josie. She'd never anticipated being confronted with a weapon like that and had hardly known how to respond. When Sebastian collapsed, Harper had reacted and rushed to his side, forgetting all about Josie. She wasn't sure how long her blackmailer had stood there with the gun, but eventually Harper looked up and Josie was gone. Apparently she hadn't wanted to hang around for the fire department and ambulance to arrive.

Since then, she'd hardly given that situation any thought. The fear of suddenly losing Sebastian before she could tell him how she felt had taken its place in her mind. All the way to the hospital, she'd sat in the back of the ambulance, racked with guilt at thinking she'd put him in a dangerous situation that had almost killed him. Then days of anxiety waiting for the results of all his tests.

Finally, and most recently, she was angry.

That was the most surprising emotion, but the one

she couldn't shake. The night before, the doctor who had been treating Sebastian had come in with another man he introduced as Sebastian's cardiologist. They'd spoken to her about his ongoing condition like it was something she was aware of. They'd discussed how this was more serious than his previous attack. Two weeks away from the office wouldn't be enough this time.

As they'd continued, it became harder for her to keep a neutral expression on her face. Harper hadn't wanted them to know she had no idea what they were talking about. But the more they'd talked, the more things about Sebastian had started to fall into place.

Like why the workaholic could drop everything and take a trip to Ireland. He wasn't *allowed* to work. Not after his last heart attack had driven him to the floor of his lab less than two weeks ago.

Two weeks ago he'd had a heart attack and he hadn't said anything about it. He'd acted like nothing happened and got on a plane with her to Ireland. The truth of it made her mind spin. What if something had happened in Ireland? That castle had been out in the middle of nowhere, literally hours from Dublin. How long would it have taken to get him to a hospital with a state-of-the-art cardiac care unit?

If he had told her, at least she could've known to watch for the signs. Or when he'd collapsed, she would have known what it was and been able to tell the 9-1-1 operator and the EMTs he had a heart condition. As it was, she'd just sat helplessly, crying and saying, "He just collapsed," over and over in despair and confusion.

Talking to his business partner hadn't made her feel any better. Finn was listed as his emergency contact and medical power of attorney, so he'd been called into the hospital the minute they'd arrived. He was the one who had authorized the tests and cleared it with the hospital for Harper to stay even when she wasn't family. She was indebted to Finn for that alone, much less the information he'd shared with her while he was there.

"The doctors said you're going to be okay. But you've got to take it easy. You'll probably be discharged tomorrow. Finn has set up a nurse to stay with you at your apartment."

"I don't need a nurse," he argued.

"Finn says, and I agree, that you lost your ability to make decisions in this arena when you had that second attack. You're not going into work. You're getting a nurse to make sure you're taking all the medications and eating well. You're supposed to register for a cardiac rehabilitation program to help you rebuild your stamina and design an exercise regime to keep this from happening again. You have to do it all, to the letter, or you're going to have another attack. You might not bounce back the next time."

Sebastian opened his mouth to argue with her and then stopped himself. "Okay. You're right."

Harper had practiced what she'd wanted to say to him a few times in her mind. She wasn't sure it would come out right, but she had to try anyway. "It's been a long couple of days in this hospital, Sebastian."

"I bet. Weren't you wearing that outfit on the flight home?"

Harper looked down, but she knew he was right. She hadn't gone home. She had ventured down to the gift shop for a toothbrush and some other toiletries to get her through, but other than that, she hadn't left his side. Their suitcases and everything in them had been left behind at the airport where they'd run into Josie. In the ambulance, she'd called Jonah and he'd gone back to pick up their things for them. He and Emma had offered to bring her whatever she'd needed, but she hadn't wanted to be a bigger imposition than she'd already been.

"It's been even more stressful for me because it came out of the blue. Young, healthy thirty-eight-year-old men do not just drop to the ground with a heart attack, Sebastian."

She watched as his jaw tightened. "I didn't think it was important."

"Important?" she cried. "You didn't think it was important to tell me that you were recovering from a heart attack? That you were supposed to be recuperating? I didn't need to know that because *it wasn't important*? We had sex, Sebastian. That could've killed you."

Sebastian sighed. "I didn't want you to treat me like I was fragile. I'm not fragile. The sex didn't kill me. Not even close. And if that woman hadn't tried to kill us, I probably wouldn't even be here right now."

"That's not what the doctor said. He said that you were supposed to schedule a heart catheterization while you were off from work to check for arterial blockages. Not only did you not schedule it, you left the country instead. You could've died, Sebastian. Right there at my feet. And I wouldn't have had the slightest clue as to what was happening to you or why because you didn't tell me."

"I thought I had it handled. I didn't want to worry you when you had your own problems to deal with."

"If it were only that, I might buy it. But it's more

than just your heart condition, Sebastian. Yes, you kept something so important a secret from me, but you haven't opened up to me about anything else, either."

"I told you about my brother."

She nodded. "Only as it pertained to your work and your inspiration. You never share anything about your past, your feelings. You just won't let me in."

That was the crux of it: how could he possibly care about her—really, truly care about her—if he was shutting her out like this?

It was then she realized that maybe this was a problem of her own making. This wasn't supposed to be a real relationship, despite how far they'd gone off the rails. They weren't supposed to confide in each other, get physical and fall in love. She was the one who'd broken the rules and fallen for him. She'd poured her heart and soul out to him and gotten nothing in return. So this was really a mess she'd made. She couldn't be mad at him for sticking to their agreement. He didn't love her. And she had to be okay with that.

But she didn't need to stay around and witness the evidence of her foolishness any longer. If she stayed, she would say something she would regret and she didn't want to agitate him any more than she already had when he was in this fragile state.

"Where are you going?" he asked as she stood and scooped her purse up from the floor.

"I'm going home."

"Why?"

Harper stopped and looked at him one last time. "Because the wedding is over," she said. "Thanks for pretending to be my date this week. I couldn't have gotten through it all without you."

He sat up in the bed and reached for her. "Wait. Are you coming back?"

She moved toward the door, finally shaking her head. "Why would I? Now I know you're going to be okay. You're in good hands. Goodbye, Sebastian." She slipped out the door before he could respond.

Dashing down the hallway, she rushed into the nearest elevator to keep from changing her mind.

"Mr. West, you have a visitor," Ingrid called from the living room.

Sebastian had heard the phone ring a few minutes earlier and assumed it was the front desk. They were the only ones who called the house line. That meant he either had a delivery coming up or a visitor. He'd already received some flowers from his parents and a plant from work, so he'd figured there might be a guest coming upstairs. He had gotten out of bed, put on some real clothes and straightened his disheveled appearance in anticipation of company.

Looking in the mirror was rough. His goatee was getting long and the rest of his beard was starting to fill in with coarse, almost black hair since he hadn't shaved since in Ireland. He needed a haircut, too, as the dark waves were getting wild and fighting his comb to stay standing straight. His eyes were bloodshot and he was bruised and scabby from the elbows down from the hospital using him as a human pin cushion.

It really was a lost cause. A brush through his hair and a swig of mouthwash was the best he could do on short notice. He wanted to look somewhat put together just in case it was Harper.

He'd had a couple visitors since he'd gotten home

from the hospital—his family had even driven down from Maine to see him—but the only person he really wanted to see was Harper. So far, she had eluded him.

He made his way down the hallway to where his home health aide, Ingrid, was waiting on him. She smiled and gestured to the couch where someone was sitting. It was Finn.

Damn.

"Don't get too excited to see me," Finn said in a dry tone. "I wouldn't want to put too much strain on your heart."

Sebastian made his way over to his recliner next to the couch and settled into it.

Ingrid brought them both bottles of sparkling water and then disappeared into the kitchen to give them some privacy.

"Sorry," Sebastian said. "I was hoping you were someone else."

"Harper, perhaps?"

"Yes." There was no sense in trying to deny it.

"Has she been by to see you since you left the hospital?"

"No." It had been several long, lonely days without her smiling face and sassy attitude.

Finn frowned at his partner. "That seems odd. Are you sure that she's okay? She wouldn't leave your side for a moment at the hospital."

Sebastian didn't remember most of his time at the hospital, but knowing she'd been there, so dedicated to making sure he was okay, made him feel better. He'd never had someone like that in his life before. And yet he'd managed to ruin it the moment he'd woken up. "Yes, well, once she determined I was okay, she left and said she wasn't coming back. I was just being optimistic that she'd changed her mind."

"What did you do?" Finn said in his usual accusing voice.

Sebastian shrugged it off. "I suppose I deserve that," he admitted. When things went wrong around the office, it was typically Sebastian's doing. He'd overload the breaker and cause a building-wide blackout. He'd set off the smoke alarm with his latest project and sent everyone marching out to the street while the fire department searched the building. Honestly, there were times where he wondered why Finn wanted to be his business partner. Or even his friend. But sometimes you had to overload the breaker to achieve greatness.

"She was sick with grief when I saw her at the hospital the first time. That woman loves you and cares about you very much. If she isn't here with you this very moment, you screwed up pretty badly."

"Okay, yeah, I screwed up," he said. "I didn't tell her about…well, anything. Including my heart condition. She said I was shutting her out. I guess I was."

"Why would you do that? She's by all accounts an amazing woman. I know her family, too. You don't drive a woman like that away when she loves you, Seb."

"I don't know why I did it. I guess it's just all I know how to do. I'm not a relationship guy. I'm an engineer. A pioneer in medical technology. I don't know how to be that and a man in a serious relationship. Is it even possible to be both at the same time?"

Finn chuckled and shook his head. "You'd better figure it out or you're going to be a lonely old man. I can't have you coming to my house for the holidays every year for the rest of your life. Eventually you're going to become our creepy uncle Sebastian."

"You're the one that invited me to your family Thanksgiving," Sebastian pointed out in a bitter tone.

"Of course I did. Otherwise you would've been at the office working. Or sitting at home eating who knows what with a plastic fork. If you're going to shake up your life, you've got to make a lot of changes."

Sebastian was used to his fair share of lectures from Finn—it was one of the side effects of working with a doctor—but for the first time in his life, he was actually listening to what his partner had to say. "Okay, fine. Fix me, Yoda. I'm a ball of clay in your hands. Turn me into a pastier, hairier but more charming version of you."

Finn ran his palm over his shaved head and twisted his lips in irritation. Fortunately he was used to Sebastian after years of working together. They were very different, but they complemented each other well. Sebastian's inventions wouldn't have been nearly as successful without Finn there to guide and market them. And Finn probably would've settled into some nice, boring dermatology practice on the Upper East Side if he hadn't had Sebastian pushing him to do more important things with his life.

"You've got to take better care of yourself, for one thing."

Sebastian couldn't help rolling his eyes. "Thank you, Dr. Obvious. But not all of us can be hunky Shemar Moore look-alikes with chiseled abs and muscular thighs like tree trunks."

"You think looking this good is easy?" Finn quipped. "It takes a lot of work. I'm at the gym five days a week. While you're getting junk food delivered to the office, I'm drinking protein smoothies or bringing in grilled chicken breast and kale salad for lunch. Life is a series of choices. You've just got to make better ones."

"You sound like my nutritionist," Sebastian grumbled. He'd already met with her and had his first cardiac rehab appointment. Basically he'd just walked on a treadmill while they'd done an EKG and monitored his blood pressure. It would get harder from there. As for the nutritionist, she'd decided to sign him up for a meal delivery service while he was recuperating. There was going to be a lot of lean protein and vegetables he couldn't recognize in his future.

Finn crossed his muscular arms over his chest. "I might know what I'm talking about, Sebastian. I *am* a doctor, you know."

"I know. And listen…" Sebastian leaned forward and rested his elbows on his knees. "For all my blustering, I am taking this all to heart. I know this is serious and I'm changing. I want to change. At this rate, I won't live long enough to be your kids' crazy uncle Sebastian, and I know that. I've always had this drive in me and succeeding was more important than anything else, including my own health. But you were right."

Finn held up his hands to halt the discussion. "Wait. Repeat that please. I want to cherish it."

Sebastian smirked at his partner. "You were right, Finn! Anyway, I'm trying to be serious for a moment here. My work is important, but I'm not helping anyone if I'm too sick to continue. I can't sacrifice my life, my health or my relationships to make my inventions a reality. There's more to life, and I realize that now. I realized it the instant I hit the ground."

He shook his head, thinking back to that night as he'd stared down the barrel of Josie's gun and felt his chest tighten like a rubber band was wrapped around him. "It was the scariest moment of my life. As I went down, I looked at Harper and realized what was happening and how serious it could be. My life could've been ending. In those few seconds, all I could think of was that I'd never told Harper that I loved her. I was going to die and she was never going to know. I tried, but then I passed out."

Finn listened silently, a pained expression on his face. "That sounds horrible. Why didn't you tell her the first chance you got at the hospital? It might've changed everything for the two of you."

"I don't know. I've kicked myself over how that whole thing played out. I was so disoriented at first and before I could get my bearings, she was laying into me about keeping secrets. I instantly went on the defensive and then she was gone. But she was right, I wasn't telling her things. I have so much I need to share with her. But I need to start with how much I love her. That's the most important part."

"Wow," Finn said. "It's true. You've really fallen hard. I can see it in your face when you talk about her. I wasn't sure I'd ever see the day you looked up from your notebook and noticed someone other than a client. And to fall in love... If you can fix this, you might beat me to the altar. Maybe I can be your kids' crazy uncle Finn."

"Shut up," Sebastian groaned. "You've got women

lining up outside your apartment. If you could just pick one to keep, you'd be married in no time."

Finn laughed. "Probably so. If you're serious about wanting to marry Harper, maybe I'll catch the garter at your reception. You never know what can happen then."

Sebastian's expression instantly sobered. "I am serious about marrying her. I'm serious about all of this. I want to get my health in order so I can go to her and feel confident that I'm not selling her damaged goods. Then I want to tell her how I feel and, hopefully, she feels the same way. If she does, I'm going to propose right there on the spot. Time is too precious to waste. I don't want to give her the chance to slip away from me again."

"If you're really planning to propose, I know a good diamond guy. I could give him a call and have him bring some pieces here to the apartment."

That was a relief. Sebastian didn't even know where to start when it came to that. He couldn't name the four Cs if his life depended on it. "Set it up. I've still got to talk to her father and ask permission, but I want to move forward on everything. I want it all in place when the time comes."

"Sure thing." Finn picked up his phone and typed in a few things. "I'll have him text you."

"Perfect. It feels like everything is falling into place. I just have one more little thing to do first."

"What's that?" Finn asked.

"I have to figure out where Harper lives."

Twelve

"Come in."

Harper took a deep breath and turned the knob that led to her grandfather's study. She had been fearing—dreading—this moment since she was twenty-two years old. Now here she was, a woman of almost thirty years, and she felt as nervous as ever.

It was easy to be brave in Ireland when she'd been thousands of miles away from the consequences of her poor choices. With Josie having disappeared and the blackmail behind her, Harper knew she had to face her grandfather and the reality she'd avoided all this time. She had to tell him she was broke. Odds were that he'd probably already heard the news by now, but she'd wanted to tell him in person as soon as she had the chance.

"Afternoon, Grandpa."

The elderly man looked up from his desk and smiled at the sight of his only granddaughter.

"Harper! What a surprise! You're looking lovely, as always. For a moment I thought it was your mother standing there. You certainly have come to look so much like her as you've gotten older."

Harper gave him a hug, ignoring the tears in his eyes as they both thought about the woman who'd been taken from them too soon. As she sat, Harper realized that she was older now than her mother had been when she died. It was hard to believe. Life could be so unfair sometimes. It made Harper feel foolish for wasting all her emotional energy on such silly things when her mother had been facing her own death and leaving her children behind at the same age.

"To what do I owe this visit?" his asked. "I didn't expect to see you before your birthday. The big one is coming, isn't it?"

Harper smiled and nodded. "Yes, I'll be thirty."

"I suppose you'll have a big party to celebrate with your friends. Blow some of that inheritance on expensive champagne?"

She winced and shook her head. Considering everything that had happened over the last week, she hadn't planned anything. Turning thirty was depressing enough. Add that she was now going to be single and broke going into her thirties and she couldn't gather up much reason to celebrate. "Not exactly. That's why I came by to see you today. I needed to talk to you about my trust fund."

"Can't wait until the end of the week for the money?" he asked with curious gray eyes. "I suppose I could loan you a few dollars until then."

"No, Grandpa," she said, reaching out to stop him from pulling out his wallet. "I'm not here to borrow money. I'm actually here because I needed to tell you something."

His brows went up in surprise and he eased back into his leather chair. "Okay. What is it, Pumpkin?"

She took a deep breath, trying to figure out how she was going to tell him the truth. Pumpkin had screwed up. She'd thought that losing out on the money would be the hardest part, but she was wrong. Telling her grandfather what she'd done was far worse. The sun had risen and set on Harper as a child as far as he was concerned. He would be so disappointed.

"I'm broke, Grandpa."

He narrowed his gaze at her, visibly trying to piece together what she meant by that. "Broke, you say?"

"Yes. I've been keeping it a secret all these years because I was embarrassed and I didn't want to lose the rest of my trust fund. But I'm coming clean. I blew all the money when I was in college and I've been faking it ever since."

"So all these years...you never once asked for money. Your father didn't have any. How did you get by?"

Harper shrugged. "Like everyone else. I worked hard. I saved every dime I could instead of blowing it like I would've in the past."

"But no one knew the truth? Not even your brother?"

"No, I didn't tell anyone. Not Oliver, not Daddy. I didn't want anyone to know, especially you."

"If that's the case, why are you telling me this now, Pumpkin?"

Now it was her turn to frown. "Because I should be

honest. You added the provision that said if I misman-
aged the first payment, I wouldn't get the second. And
I blew it. I wanted—no, needed—to tell you the truth,
so you can have your financial manager do something
else with the money. I've forfeited my share."

Her grandfather reached for the candy bowl on the
edge of his desk. He grabbed a soft caramel and handed
a second one to her. For as long as she could remember,
he'd always had caramels in his study. He unwrapped
the candy and chewed it thoughtfully. Harper could
only hold on to hers. She was waiting for his response.
The rebuke. The disappointment. For him to announce
that he was donating her inheritance to a charity.

But he didn't. He just chewed his caramel and
watched her. Finally he said, "Something else is wrong.
What is it?"

"You mean aside from throwing away twenty-eight-
million dollars?"

He nodded. "That's just money. Something else is
bothering you. Something more important."

Sebastian. Could that be what he saw? "I've just
had a rough week, Grandpa. Nothing has been going
my way, be it my love life or anything else. Someone
tried to blackmail me and they stole Mama's sapphire
necklace when I didn't pay them in time. The guy I
love lied to me and I don't know what to do. Really,
losing the money is just the latest thing to come up.
I'm not having a big birthday celebration. I don't feel
much like celebrating."

"Tell me about this man. You said he lied to you."

She nodded. "He kept me in the dark about so many
things in his life. I worry that he can't open up to me.
Why would he keep things from me?"

"Why would you keep your friends and family in the dark about your own situation, Harper? I imagine you'll find the answers to your questions about your gentleman in your own motivations."

"I was embarrassed. I didn't want anyone to know I could be so stupid. They might treat me differently." As she said the words aloud, she realized her grandfather was probably right about Sebastian and his secrets. Would she have treated him differently if she'd known he was physically fragile? Perhaps. Was he embarrassed that he'd let his drive get in the way of his health? Probably.

Since they'd started out as a week-long fake romance, there'd been no reason for him to tell her those things. Honestly, if she hadn't been blackmailed, she wouldn't have confessed her own truths to Sebastian. Why would she expect him to do the same?

They had a lot to learn about each other. A week wasn't nearly enough time to peel back all the layers and expose the secrets shared with only the most intimate of partners. She'd overreacted out of fear, she knew that now. Seeing Sebastian lying on the ground surrounded by EMTs...the sirens, the wires, the shouting... It had been all so unexpected, so scary. Josie and the gun hadn't been important anymore. All that had mattered was Sebastian.

She'd almost lost him in the moment and she hadn't understood why. Then she'd turned her back on him and walked away—losing him for certain—just for doing the same thing she'd done her whole life.

She was a fool.

"Harper, why do you think I added that provision to your trust?"

She turned back to her grandfather and shook her head. "To scare me straight? I was a spoiled little diva. I'm sure you didn't want me to make the same mistakes as Daddy did."

"That's a little harsh," he said. "You just didn't know what it was like to go without. You didn't grow up poor, like I did, so you didn't have the appreciation for it. That wasn't your fault. But you have it now, don't you?"

Harper chuckled bitterly. "Most certainly. I kick myself every day for wasting what I had. I think about what I could've done differently. If I'd been smart or industrious like Oliver…"

"You don't have to be like your brother. He's one of a kind, and so are you. Let me ask a different question. If you were to have a second chance and someone handed you that two-million dollars over again, what would you do?"

She didn't even have an answer at first. "That's hard to say, Grandpa. I'd probably go wild and pre-pay my co-op fees and utilities for the next year. Stick the rest in the bank for a rainy day."

Her grandfather's old, weathered lips curled into a smile. "Okay then." He reached across his desk for his cell phone.

Harper was confused by his response. "Okay what?" she asked.

"Okay, it's time to call my estate manager and discuss releasing the rest of your trust fund."

"What do you mean, *release it*?"

He reached out and patted her hand. "Happy birthday, Harper. I'm satisfied that you've grown into the mature, responsible woman I've always known you could be. And as such, you're about to be twenty-eight-million dollars richer. Now go find this man you're in love with and plan a proper birthday celebration."

Sebastian walked into the lobby of Harper's building as though he were approaching the X on a treasure map. Finding where she lived hadn't been an easy task. To ask for it from her friends was to admit he'd never been to her home before—an incredibly suspicious fact considering they were dating. But without any other options, he'd had to confess the truth about their fake relationship to Emma when he'd hunted her down at FlynnSoft. But it was only when he'd told her that he was hopelessly in love with Harper, for real, that she'd given him the address for Harper's building.

He was in the process of signing in at the front desk when he heard a voice from over his shoulder.

"She's not home."

Sebastian paused and turned to find Harper standing behind him with a full bag of groceries in her arms.

"That's a shame," he said. "I really wanted to talk to her about something important."

Her blue-gray eyes searched his face for a moment. "Something important, huh? Well, maybe I'll let you up and you can wait for her. I'm sure she'll be interested in hearing what you have to say for yourself."

Ouch. Okay. "I'd really appreciate it."

Harper smiled and headed toward the elevator with him in her wake.

Sebastian hadn't been sure what kind of reception he would receive after the way they'd parted at the hospital. So far, it had been pretty neutral, but he was going up to her apartment. She could've just turned him away. That was something.

Running into his arms and kissing him would've been another option, but he may not deserve that. He had a lot of apologizing to do before hugs and kisses would be on the agenda. Her semi-frosty reception proved that much.

When they stepped into her apartment, Sebastian got his first real dose of what Harper's life was like. It was a nicer place than he had—a remnant of her old life—decorated with some familiar and inexpensive IKEA pieces. As she set her groceries in the kitchen, he noticed a nice bottle of champagne and a couple pouches of ramen noodles. He supposed she had learned balance over the years.

Sebastian hovered awkwardly at the entrance of the kitchen as she put away her groceries. He was waiting for the invitation to talk, but she hadn't given him one yet. He wanted to sit and look her in the eye, not try to apologize while she was distracted with chores.

Finally she folded the paper sack and looked at him. "Do you want a drink? I want a drink."

"I'm not really supposed to," he admitted. He really wanted one—it would ease the tension—but he was working on a new healthy lifestyle. Day drinking two weeks into the plan would doom him to failure. "Some water would be great, though."

She eyed him for a moment before she nodded and pulled two bottles of water out of the fridge. She handed him one and pointed to the wall. "Let's head into the living room. People always congregate in the kitchen and I hate that."

Sebastian backed out of her way and followed her lead into the open and airy living room. She had comfy couches, a few nice pieces of art he recognized and a decent-size, flat-screen television on a shelf. There was a wall of books on one side of the room and a wall of windows on the other. From where he was, he could spy a glimpse of green—Central Park—a few blocks away.

"Have a seat," she said as she settled onto the couch.

He opted for the oversize chair just to her right, facing her. Their knees almost touched as they sat, but he kept his joints to himself for the moment, no matter how badly he wanted to touch her. "Thanks for talking to me, Harper."

She shrugged and opened her water. "The last time I saw you, you were on death's door. I was hoping to hear you were doing better."

"I am," he said proudly. "I've been going to cardiac rehab three times a week and they've started me on a new lifestyle program that will make me more mindful of what I eat and how much rest I get. It's made a huge difference already."

Harper listened to him talk but nothing more than a casual interest lit her eyes. "I'm glad to hear that."

"Me, too. Going forward, I know I can't let my work overtake my life. I want more than a career and a string of patents under my belt. I want a life, too. A wife. Maybe a family."

That got her attention. She sat more upright in her seat, her brows knitting together in thought. "That's a big change for a workaholic bachelor. What's going to keep you from losing yourself in your work again and this time ignoring your new family instead of just your health?"

She didn't think he could change. "I'm not going to ignore you, Harper. I couldn't possibly."

"I didn't mean me," she said. "I just meant in general. Old habits die hard. Like keeping secrets. Trust me, I know."

"I'm sorry I lied to you. It wasn't that I didn't trust you with the different aspects of my past. I was just… embarrassed. You understand that, don't you?"

"Of course. But I told you everything, Sebastian. You told me almost nothing."

"If you hadn't been blackmailed by Josie, would you still have told me? Or was it only out of necessity?"

The self-righteous expression on her face softened a little. Her gaze dropped to the cap of her water bottle as she fidgeted with it. "And then I find myself clutching your unconscious body in the middle of a parking lot, screaming. When the ambulance arrives, I can't tell them your medical information. I can't say if you have a history of cardiac problems. I know literally nothing. You could've died and there was nothing I could do to help."

"I shouldn't have put you in that position. I never dreamed it would happen again or I would've said something."

Harper nodded. "I understand we started off with the whole fake relationship thing, but that's over. The wedding trip is over and now this is real life, Sebastian. Real feelings. We're not playing a game any longer. I need to know the truth."

"About what?"

"About *everything*. I want to know everything you've been keeping from me before I can consider continuing this relationship."

"Right now? You just want me to lay out my whole life story right now?" He had an engagement ring burning a hole in his pocket. He was desperate to hear her say yes and move forward, but Harper wasn't having it.

She sat back against the couch cushions, making herself visibly more comfortable. "Do you have somewhere you need to be, Sebastian? Work, perhaps? It's a Saturday, but who knows with you."

"No," he insisted. "There's nowhere I need to be but right here, right now. I'll tell you whatever you want to know if it will make you feel more comfortable in loving me. Because I love you, Harper. I've never let myself love a woman before. I'm not sure I'm going to do things right, but I can't help how I feel. I'll do anything you want me to if it means you'll tell me that you love me, as well."

Harper's jaw dropped at the first mention of the word "love" and stayed there until he was done speaking. "Well, why don't you start from the beginning? You've never said much about your family or where you grew up. Just about your brother's accident."

Sebastian nodded and sat back in his seat, ready to tell her whatever she wanted to know.

"I grew up poor," he said. "And so we're clear, not the kind of poor you've been. I mean dirt poor. Oldest-trailer-in-the-trailer-park poor. I never owned a new pair of shoes until I went to college and bought them myself. Until then, every bit of clothing I'd ever had was my brother's hand-me-down. My parents did everything they could to get ahead in life, but there was always something on the next horizon ready to knock them back down.

"When my brother and I were old enough, we worked to help make ends meet. Kenny worked at the burger place near our high school. I liked to tinker and helped my dad with fixing the car and such, so I ended up working at a shop that fixed old lawnmowers and small engines. If I could, I'd mow people's lawns after I fixed their mowers, too, for extra cash. Every penny went to my parents. For a while, we were doing okay. My dad got a promotion, my brother graduated from high school and started working full time. Then he had his accident."

Harper was watching him speak so intently, he wondered if she was even breathing. He shook his head and sighed. "We had insurance, but Kenny fell off the plan when he graduated. He didn't have any at work yet, either. There was a little coverage from the owner of the ATV, but it wasn't nearly enough. He spent my entire senior year in hospitals and rehabilitation centers. The bills were crippling. My mom had to quit her job to stay home and take care of him, making it worse."

"How awful," she whispered.

"I was determined to do more than just rebuild lawnmowers my whole life. I wanted to make something of myself so I could help my parents and my brother. That's what drove me. I worked as much as I could after his accident, and the only money I ever kept for myself was enough money to apply to MIT and take my entrance exams."

"How are they now?" Harper asked.

Sebastian finally found a reason to smile.

"They're great. With my first million, I bought my parents a real house in Portland that was near the doctors and specialists Kenny sees regularly. It's nice, but not too big for them to maintain, and it's fully wheelchair friendly so my brother can get around. I bought them an accessible van and I send them money every month to help take care of things. My dad continues to work out of pride, but he should be retiring in a few years."

Harper smiled and reached out to put a hand on his knee. "I'm glad to hear it."

"We've all come a long way. It took a lot of hard work to get there. I don't regret it or the toll it took on my health to get there. I just know I need to do better going forward."

"I can understand why you did what you did. To start with nothing and build a company like yours is amazing. I bet you look at someone like me, who squandered a fortune, and resent the hell out of it."

Sebastian shook his head. "I don't. Everyone comes from a different place, but that makes them who they are. You made your mistakes and you grew from them. You owned them. I'm not sure I'd be strong enough to stand up and do what you did at the wedding. Even with the money I've made, giving up almost thirty-million dollars is heartbreaking."

"Well, actually, it turns out that I didn't."

He frowned at her. "What do you mean?"

"I spoke with my grandfather. I came clean about the whole thing. He decided I'd learned my lesson and gave me the money anyway. That's why I bought the champagne. Today is my birthday. My grandpa wanted me to throw a big party but I wasn't ready for all that after what happened in Ireland. I thought I might have a little celebration by myself. Would you like to join me?"

Sebastian smiled. "I would." He wouldn't have more than a sip since he was trying to be good, but he would certainly toast to her birthday.

They got up and went to the kitchen where she

poured two champagne flutes. Back in the living room, they sat, this time both of them on the couch together.

"Happy birthday, Harper," he said, raising his flute. "I'm glad I was able to be here today to celebrate with you. I wasn't sure if I would have the chance to tell you that. Or any of the other things I said to you today. Thank you for giving me the chance."

Harper smiled and clinked her glass against his. "Thank you. This isn't how I imagined my birthday, but it couldn't have been better, really. I've learned a lot about myself the past few weeks. Without Josie trying to blackmail me, I might not have realized that I could get by on my own. Or that I didn't need money and fancy cars to define me. I also wouldn't have realized how important you are to me, too."

Sebastian's heart stuttered in his chest and this time it had nothing to do with his clogged arteries. He set his untouched drink on the coffee table. "I'm sorry I didn't know it was your birthday today. I would've brought you a present." He reached into his pocket. "Instead, all I have is this."

Her gaze locked on the blue box and her jaw dropped once again. "What…" Her voice trailed off.

"I told you before that I love you, Harper. And that I'm ready to find some balance in my life. But what I left out was that I want to find that balance with you. Just you. Life is too short to hesitate, and I can't risk losing you again."

Sebastian slid off the couch onto one knee and opened the box to display the emerald-cut halo ring inside. "I promise that I won't keep secrets from you anymore. I promise I will never make my work seem more important than you or our family. You are the most important person in my life, Harper. I never knew I could love someone the way that I love you. Please do me the honor of being my wife, Harper Drake."

He looked at her in time to see her eyes flood with tears. "Yes," she whispered with a smile that spread from ear to ear.

Sebastian slipped the ring onto her finger and squeezed her hand in his. They stood and she leaped into his arms. He pulled her tight against him and kissed his fiancée for the very first time.

This was the start of their future together. A future he almost didn't have, but that he would cherish with Harper for as long as he could.

Epilogue

"Merry Christmas, everyone!"

Harper heard the commotion at the door and rushed out of the kitchen to see who had arrived. She was excited to host her first Christmas with her family and Sebastian's family all together.

Sebastian was hugging his mother as she came through the door. His father was right behind her with arms full of presents. And in the back was Kenny. *Standing.*

With the help of Sebastian's exoskeleton prototype, his brother moved in a slow but steady pace through the doorway with a wide grin on his face. He looked almost as happy as Sebastian himself.

Nothing could match his excitement. This was the culmination of his dream. The best Christmas gift he could ever give his family. She knew watching Kenny walk across the room and sit by the fireplace unaided was the greatest present Sebastian could ever receive.

It was his sketches from Ireland that made the difference. He didn't realize it at the time, but once he returned to his lab, Sebastian had a breakthrough. She could tell it pained him to come home at a reasonable hour each night when his mind wanted him to keep pushing, but his goal had still been achieved in the end.

The two families were introduced and everyone gathered with drinks and appetizers in the living room. Harper was just about to return to the kitchen for more eggnog when Sebastian caught her eye.

He reached under the tree for a gift and gestured for Harper to follow him down the hallway to their bedroom. "I wanted to give you this now," Sebastian said once they were alone.

"Now? It's only Christmas Eve."

"Please open it."

Harper sighed and accepted the beautifully wrapped present from her fiancé. He'd already given her such a beautiful engagement ring, she felt guilty accepting a present from him. She opened the golden foil lid and found a collection of sparkling items wrapped in tissue paper.

A sapphire necklace. A ruby tennis bracelet. Diamond earrings. An aquamarine cocktail ring. Emerald cufflinks. An old pocket watch.

It couldn't be.

Harper's eyes grew wide as she looked down at the gift and back up at Sebastian. "This is my mother's jewelry. And your things, too. Josie stole all of this. How on earth did you get it back?"

Sebastian grinned even wider than he had when

his brother had successfully walked through the front door of their apartment. "Well, it turns out that our little blackmailer went after someone else to make some cash. Instead of paying, they went straight to the police. All these items were found in her apartment when she was arrested. The cops contacted me last week because the jewelry matched the description in the police report we filed."

She picked up the pocket watch and looked at it in wonder. Harper had thought she might never be able to replace this special piece for Sebastian. "They said they couldn't find Josie."

"Apparently that wasn't her real name. But after she tried to blackmail Quentin—"

"My ex, Quentin?" she interrupted in surprise.

"Yep. When he got the threatening letter, he remembered what happened to you and led the cops straight to her door. Turns out her name is Amanda Webber. I hope she looks good in orange."

Harper smiled and handed Sebastian his great-grandfather's watch. "Merry Christmas, my love."

"Merry Christmas, Harper."

* * * * *

MILLS & BOON MODERN IS
HAVING A MAKEOVER!

The same great stories you love,
a stylish new look!

Look out for our brand new look
COMING JUNE 2024

MILLS & BOON

 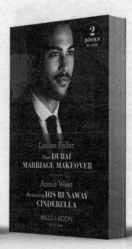 

MILLS & BOON

THE HEART OF ROMANCE

A ROMANCE FOR EVERY READER

MODERN
Prepare to be swept off your feet by sophisticated, sexy and seductive heroes, in some of the world's most glamourous and romantic locations, where power and passion collide.

HISTORICAL
Escape with historical heroes from time gone by. Whether your passion is for wicked Regency Rakes, muscled Vikings or rugged Highlanders, awaken the romance of the past.

MEDICAL
Set your pulse racing with dedicated, delectable doctors in the high-pressure world of medicine, where emotions run high and passion, comfort and love are the best medicine.

True Love
Celebrate true love with tender stories of heartfelt romance, from the rush of falling in love to the joy a new baby can bring, and a focus on the emotional heart of a relationship.

HEROES
The excitement of a gripping thriller, with intense romance at its heart. Resourceful, true-to-life women and strong, fearless men face danger and desire - a killer combination!

From showing up to glowing up, these characters are on the path to leading their best lives and finding romance along the way – with plenty of sizzling spice!

To see which titles are coming soon, please visit

millsandboon.co.uk/nextmonth

LET'S TALK

Romance

For exclusive extracts, competitions
and special offers, find us online:

f MillsandBoon

X @MillsandBoon

⊙ @MillsandBoonUK

♪ @MillsandBoonUK

Get in touch on 01413 063 232

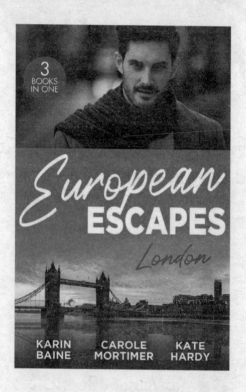